NEVIL SHUTE

Most Secret

NEVIL SHUTE

Most Secret

Original Illustrations by Terence Greer

Distributed by
HERON BOOKS

Published by arrangement with
William Heinemann Ltd., London

Published in Canada by arrangement with
William Morrow & Co. Inc.

© *Illustrations, Edito-Service S.A., Geneva*

3613

A burnt child dreads the fire.

Proverb.

1

SO much happened in the two years that I spent at the Admiralty, I had a finger in so many pies, that I have found it difficult to say exactly when it was that this thing began. From my engagement diary it seems to have been about the middle of July in 1941, and I should say that it began with a telephone call from McNeil.

I reached out for the receiver. I remember that it was a very hot day and I was flooded out with work. There was dust all over my desk because I had the window open, and outside the bricklayers were repairing what the *Luftwaffe* had done to us. I said irritably: "Six nine two."

"Is that Commander Martin?"

"Speaking," I said shortly.

"This is Brigadier McNeil. I am speaking from one hundred and sixty-four Pall Mall."

"Oh yes, sir?" I replied. The address meant nothing to me, and I wondered sourly why the Army could not say in short time who they were and what they wanted.

"Captain Oliver gave me your name. We've been talking about an operation this morning. I think perhaps I'd better come along and see you."

"Very good, sir. When would you like to come?"

"About three o'clock this afternoon? Is that convenient to you?"

"That's quite all right for me. I'll expect you then."

He came to me in the afternoon. He was a man of forty-five or fifty, a typical soldier, very smartly dressed. His belt, his buttons, and the stars and crowns upon his shoulders were beautifully polished; his uniform sat on him without a crease, and the red staff tabs blazed out immaculate from the lapels of his tunic. He had short, greyish hair and china-blue eyes. He looked pleasant enough, determined, absolutely straight, and—I thought at first—rather stupid. You felt to look at him that he would be wonderful upon a horse.

I got up as the messenger showed him in. "Good afternoon," I said. "Will you sit down?"

I

He laid his hat and gloves upon the corner of my desk, and dropped his gas-mask on a chair. He said: "I understand that Admiral Thomson is away?"

"He's away a good deal, sir," I replied. "We deal with routine matters from this office in his absence. Anything that's beyond us goes down to V.A.C.O. by the courier."

He sat down on the chair beside the desk, and I went back to mine. "V.A.C.O.?" he said.

"Vice-Admiral for Channel Operations. Admiral Thomson."

"Oh, I see," he said. "That's his proper title, is it? Just wait a minute, and I'll write that down." He slipped a pencil and a notebook from his pocket; I watched him as he wrote, slightly amused.

He put them away again, and turned to me. "Well now," he said. "Let's start at the beginning. You know the office that I come from?"

I shook my head. "I'm afraid I don't, sir. One hundred and sixty-four Pall Mall, did you say?"

"That's right. Well . . ." He paused for a moment, considering his words. "We do various things from that office," he said at last. "We come directly under the War Cabinet." He hesitated again. "One of our jobs is to do what we can to keep up the morale of the French."

I nodded, and waited for him to go on.

"That's Cabinet policy, of course," he said. "We mustn't let them lose faith in a British victory. They never have lost faith, taking it by and large. Even in the worst days they believed that we would win. It's our job to keep their faith in us alive."

I passed him a cigarette. "I suppose our wireless broadcasts help in that," I said. "Do they—the average Frenchman—does he listen to them much?"

"Oh, everybody listens," he said. "The B.B.C. is doing a good job, for all that you read in the newspapers. But that's not my concern. You'd never keep their heart up upon broadcast talks and news alone. But something concrete, any little bit of activity or sabotage that can be contrived—that puts new life in them. Just any little thing to show them that the Germans aren't having things all their own way. These daylight sweeps that the R.A.F. are doing over France help us enormously."

I knew now what was coming, more or less. "This activity and sabotage," I said quietly. "You mean, you send people over to the other side?"

"Sometimes," he said shortly.

He blew a long cloud of smoke, and seemed to consider for a minute. "What I came over to see you people about was this," he said. "One of our young men produced a scheme the other day—a proposal that we thought rather well of. But what he proposed was so much a naval operation that I put it up to Captain Oliver. He sent me over here to see your admiral."

I took a cigarette myself from the packet on my desk and lit it. "This is all a bit outside my line," I said. "Anything like this would have to go to the V.A.C.O."

"Yes, I expected that."

I was curious, of course; anybody would have been. I said: "If you care to tell me about it I can probably tell you straight away if it conflicts with anything that we are doing. Or if you'd rather, sir, I'll put in a call to Admiral Thomson right away and make an appointment for you to go down and see him."

"He won't be in London very soon?"

"Not before Thursday of next week," I said. "I could fix up for you to see him then."

He shook his head. "I'd better not wait so long." He thought for a moment, and then said: "I think I'd better have your view on it. It has to do with the fishing fleet based on Douarnenez."

I wrinkled my forehead; few naval officers know much about the coast of Brittany, for all that it is only just across the way. "Douarnanez?" I said. "That's the place just by the Saints, isn't it?"

"That's right," he said. "It's on the west coast, twenty or thirty miles south of Brest. There's a long bay running inland just north of the Ile de Sein, and Douarnenez lies at the head of that bay. It's time we did something for Douarnenez. They've been having the hell of a time."

"Why is that?"

He knocked the ash off his cigarette. "Well," he said, "they're a very independent sort of people round about those parts, and they don't like the Germans. And they don't like being conquered, either. You know, the Bretons never really think of themselves as French. They have their own language and their own customs, just like the Welsh in this country. There's always been a Separatist movement among their intellectuals, never very serious—Brittany for the Bretons, and all that sort of thing. And now the Bretons don't regard themselves as having been defeated. They say that the rest of France ratted on them, and let them down."

"About right, too," I said.

He shrugged his shoulders. "Well, anyway, that's the way they look at it. In Douarnenez they were pretty uppish with the Germans just at first, and there were a lot of executions."

"Uppish?"

"Throwing excrement at German officers, and demonstrations of that sort. The *Boche* won't stand for that; he shot thirty of them in one day, in public, up against the market-place. That only made things worse, of course. I don't know how many have been executed in all—possibly a hundred, maybe more. It's difficult to get the figures. It's not a very big place, about fifteen thousand inhabitants, I think. Now they've gone sullen and all bloody-minded, and the Gestapo are working on them."

"That doesn't sound so good," I said.

"It's not. That's why I want to do something for them. Put on a bit of a show."

I glanced at the solid, well-dressed officer before me with a new respect. It was impossible not to like him, not to appreciate his manner. He was absolutely candid, absolutely direct. He sat there looking at me like a great St. Bernard dog.

I asked: "What sort of show have you got in mind, sir?"

He said: "Well, there are several of the German *Raumboote* based upon the port. We want to do something against one of those."

I thought for a minute very hard. "The *Raumboote* is rather like our own M.L., isn't it? I've not had a great deal to do with them myself."

"Much the same sort of thing," he said. "They use them for the fishery patrol."

"And you want to do something against one of those?" I reflected for a moment. "That's because they are based upon the port, and because everybody knows about them?"

He nodded. "That's exactly it."

Instinctively I recoiled from the idea. "I see that you want to create a diversion, sir," I said slowly. "But tell me, why must it be a naval diversion? What I mean is this. Anything done upon the sea tends to develop into a big show, because you have to cover your stake. A ship—any sort of ship—takes a long time to make and costs a lot of money. You may plan to fight your *Raumboote* with one ship, but before long you'll find it necessary to send other ships in support of your one ship.

4

And before you know what's happening your little show has turned into a considerable operation."

I paused. "I don't know much about these matters," I said diffidently. "But I should have thought a land diversion would have served as well. A bomb laid up against an oil-tank, for example. There you only risk one man and one bomb."

"It wouldn't have the same effect," he said. "As a matter of fact, an oil-tank is very difficult. It has been done, but the chance of getting away without detection is very small. A bridge is easier, and high-tension cables are very simple, of course. You can hurt them quite a lot by blowing up the pylons, and they can't put a guard on every pylon in the country. But none of those would influence Douarnenez very much."

"No?"

He shook his head. "Their minds are turned entirely to the sea. I thought the same as you at first, but you must understand the sort of town it is. The whole life of the place is centred round the harbour and the fishing fleet. It's just like Brixham must have been thirty years ago."

I nodded without speaking.

"It's got the strongest fishing fleet in France," he said. "But I suppose you know all about that."

"I'm ashamed to say I don't," I said. "I know it's quite a big fleet. How many vessels sail out of Douarnenez?"

He pulled out his notebook again. "I can give you that." He fumbled for a little, and found the page. "On March 1st there were a hundred and forty-seven sardine-boats, Diesel-engined wooden vessels sixty to seventy feet long. There were thirty-six sailing tunnymen, ketch-rigged, about a hundred and ten feet long. And there were seven sailing crabbers, about a hundred and thirty feet. A hundred and ninety vessels all told, excluding small boats."

"That's a very strong fleet," I said. "What do all those ships do now?"

"They still go out fishing."

"Are those the fishing-boats that the destroyers see when they make their sweeps? Between Ushant and Belle Isle?"

He nodded. "Those are probably the ones they see. The tunnymen go down to the Bay of Biscay; the sardine-boats don't usually go south of the Ile de Sein. It's the sardine fleet that concerns us now."

I stared at him. "Wait a minute," I said slowly. "I thought I knew something about this. Didn't two or three of them come

5

into Falmouth in June of last year? Loaded with refugees? Or am I thinking of some other boats?"

"No, that's right," he said. "There are several of them in Falmouth harbour now."

"Big, beamy boats, with a high sheer and one mast laid down in a tabernacle? Go everywhere with their engine?"

He nodded. "If you ever saw their nets you'd know them again. Very fine-mesh nets, dyed blue."

The suggestion crystallised the image in my mind; blue gossamer nets hung up to the one mast and drying in the sunlight, very foreign-looking in Falmouth harbour. "Of course I know those boats," I said. "I saw them there this spring."

I stubbed out the butt of my cigarette and glanced at him. "What is the exact proposal, sir?"

He fixed his candid, china-blue eyes on me. "My young men want to cut out one of the *Raumboote* and destroy it."

"I see," I said thoughtfully. We sat in silence for a minute. "How do they propose to do that?"

He said: "Let me give you the whole thing. I told you that there were a hundred and forty-seven sardine-boats sailing from Douarnenez. That's quite true, but for one reason or another not more than about sixty are at sea on any one night. They go out after midday, according to the tide, and go to their grounds —thirty to sixty miles away perhaps, anywhere between Ushant and the Saints. That depends on where the fish are."

He paused, and then went on: "There are five *Raumboote* based on Douarnenez at the moment. Two of those are always at sea with the sardine fleet—sometimes three. The fleet stays out all night and usually for a second night. Then that fleet comes back to harbour, and a fresh lot go out next day."

I said: "What do the *Raumboote* do? What are they there for?"

"To stop the Bretons making a run for England."

"I thought there was a German in each boat?"

He shook his head. "Not in every boat. There's usually a German reservist petty officer, an old *Bootsmannsmaat* or someone of that sort, in every other boat or every third boat. But there aren't enough of them to go round. The Germans depend a good deal on the fact that the wives and families of the crews are left on shore. If any boat is manned by Bretons without many home ties of that sort, then that boat gets one of the old German petty officers allotted to it."

"I see that," I said. "All the same, I should have thought it would have been a fairly simple matter for them to slip away by night."

He shook his head. "It's not quite as easy as it might appear. They have to have a working light for handling their nets. The boats with Germans in them have an orange shade over this light; that tells the *Raumboote* where the Germans are. The *Raumboote* cruise around on the sea side of the fleet all night, counting the lights all the time. If any boat tried to get away she'd be spotted by her light. If she put out her light, it's probable that one of the Germans in the other boats would see, and light a flare to call the attention of the *Raumboote*."

I lit another cigarette and sat for a moment, staring out of my window at the bricklayers working in the dusty, sun-drenched court.

"How is the *Raumboot* armed?" I said at last.

He consulted his notebook again. "Let me get this right." He turned the pages. "One flak gun on the forecastle. Two machine-guns just aft of the bridge. One light flak—an Oerlikon or something of that sort—mounted right at the stern."

"And searchlights, of course?"

"There are searchlights on each side, mounted on the wings of the bridge."

I stared at him curiously. "Did all this information come to you from the other side?"

He said seriously: "Well, it doesn't just come. We have to send over and get it."

"Quite so," I said.

There was a little pause.

"You say that one of your young men brought forward this proposal," I remarked. "That was for dealing with a *Raumboot*?"

"That's right," he said.

"How does he intend to make the first contact with it? Would you require us to supply White Ensign ships to carry out the operation?"

He said: "Oh no. That wasn't what we had in mind at all. What he proposes can be carried out with the resources that we have available. But as it is essentially a naval operation, we felt that you must know about it and pronounce upon it."

"I understand," I said. "What is it that he wants to do?"

"The *Raumboote* control their sardine-boats by coming up alongside and shouting at them through a megaphone," he said. "That's how they manage them. So long as they stick to the

7

fishing-grounds arranged beforehand the *Raumboote* just cruise round and leave the boats to themselves. But if one strays away, the *Raumboote* steam after it, and the officer in charge orders it back by shouting at it through a megaphone."

"They do that at night, too?" I asked. "Guided by the light that the sardine-boat wears?"

"That's it," said the brigadier.

"They come within thirty or forty yards?" I was beginning to see the outline of his scheme.

"Closer than that. Both vessels have their engines running. They have to come very close to make themselves understood."

"I see," I said thoughtfully. I glanced at him. "A very easy target."

"Yes, a very easy target," he repeated. "As you know, we've got several of these sardine-boats in this country. We want to send one over with a special crew and with a special armament and let it mix in with the fishing fleet during the hours of darkness. It should not be very difficult to draw the *Raumboot* alongside and deal with it."

I smiled a little. "Who thought of that idea?"

"The young man I was speaking of. Captain Simon."

I said: "Is he one of the ones who go over to the other side?"

"Yes. It was he who gave us most of this information."

I paused for a moment, and fixed the name in my memory. "He's an Army captain, I suppose?"

The brigadier hesitated. "Well, yes. We had to regularise his position. He holds the rank of Captain in the Royal Engineers seconded for special duties, of course."

I thought about that answer for a minute, then put it on one side and reverted to the operation. "It seems to me," I said thoughtfully, "that it's going to be pretty difficult for your sardine Q-ship to get away. The noise of gunfire will attract the other *Raumboot*, and any other German ships that there may be about." I eyed him, and then said more positively: "I shouldn't think your ship would have a chance of making her escape, even if she should sink her *Raumboot*. And quite frankly, sir, I'm not at all convinced that she would sink it. What armament would you propose to give her for the job?"

He said: "A flame-thrower—one of the big ones. A flame-thrower and a few Tommy-guns.

I was silent for a minute re-arranging my ideas. When I had spoken I had been thinking of a conventional sea battle, an ill-considered venture, a desperate affair of young fools in a fishing-boat with little guns attempting to engage a powerful, well-armed motor vessel twice their size. I had been ready to veto anything so suicidal. But there was more behind this thing than that. There was some thought behind it—genius, perhaps.

I knew about these modern flame-throwers. I had been to a couple of Staff demonstrations, and had seen them belch out their disgusting fury in a violent, cherry-coloured spout enormous in diameter, ploughing and devastating the bare earth far, far from the gun. I had seen them smother and envelop a tank in a furnace. I had seen the sickening effect upon a dummy man.

I stared at him. "That's not a bad idea," I said very quietly. "There might be something in that one."

He smiled. "I must say, it attracted me," he said candidly. "It's something different, you see. I think that they would get their *Raumboot* all right, and I don't think that the other ships would interfere with them. You see, it's something new."

"It would light up the whole sky," I said.

"It would. But from a distance it might well look like a spontaneous explosion of the petrol-tanks. In any case, it would be . . . puzzling. And in the general confusion, I think our ship would get away."

"I think she might," I said. "It would certainly be devastating if it came as a complete surprise."

"Well, yes, I think it would. We're really getting quite keen on it over in our office."

I asked: "Have you worked out any tactical plan of how it would be used?"

He said: "We thought of mounting it amidships, with the fuel-tanks in the bottom of the boat. The flame gun would stick up above the bulwarks, camouflaged as a heap of nets." He paused. "In action, the first thing to do would be to get rid of the forward flak—open up first upon the forecastle of the *Raumboot* and burn up the gun crew. Then traverse aft and give the bridge a good dose to get rid of the officers, and then train aft to the machine-guns, and the flak crew at the stern. It ought not to be very difficult."

"It should not be," I said. "I imagine that you'd clear the decks all right. But you'd still have the crew within the hull to cater for, and the *Raumboot* would still be under way. What would you do next? Would you board?"

He said cheerfully: "Oh, I don't think so. There'd be no

need to run that risk, you see. You'd treat her like you treat a tank."

I glanced at him in enquiry.

"Give her a good hosing with the oil unlit. Get it well down into the cowls and ventilators and hatches, and let it drip down well inside. Then give her a burst of flame, and light her up."

All war is a grim business and we had had two years of it, but I shivered a little.

"That ought to work all right," I said mechanically.

"I think so, too," he said. "I can't see any flaw in it. In fact, over at our place we think it's worth a trial."

There was a pause. I sat in silence for a little time, trying to think up some fresh argument against this thing. I did not want to stop it now, but I wanted to bring all the possible difficulties up for discussion before I put it to my chief.

He said: "You see, it's something new. That is of value in itself. And it's something rather horrible to happen to the German crew, exactly what the French would wish to happen to them." He leaned towards me. "That's what concerns us most, of course. A thing like that will have a wonderful effect in Douarnenez as soon as it becomes known."

I said: "If it's successful, if you destroy your *Raumboot* without survivors, it may never become known."

"Oh yes, it will," he said, and smiled a little. "We'll see they get to know about it on the other side."

That was his business and not mine, and my mind swung to another aspect of the matter, one which was really more my concern. "This sardine-boat that you want to use as a decoy," I said. "You're thinking of using one of the ones at Falmouth, I suppose."

He shook his head. "Not one of those. There's another one at Dartmouth." He paused, and then he said a little diffidently: "As a matter of fact, we've already requisitioned her."

I thought to myself: "Oh, you have, have you?" It was not the first time that the Army had displayed an inclination to set up a private Navy, and I knew that my admiral held strong views upon that subject. But I kept my own counsel, and all I said was:

"What's her name?"

"*Geneviève*," he said. "She was a Camaret boat really, but they're all very similar."

"What about manning her?" I asked. "Have you thought about that?"

He said: "That's one of the things I wanted to talk over with you. Simon himself has a fair knowledge of the sea—yachting, you know. I suppose that's what turned his mind to an adventure of this sort. It was he who discovered this boat at Dartmouth, the *Geneviève*. And as a matter of fact, he's been in touch with two of your young officers down there. He wants to work them in."

I said aloud this time: "Oh, he has, has he?"

The brigadier said: "I really felt, when I heard that, that it was time I came to see you people." He smiled charmingly. "I didn't want you to feel that we'd been trespassing outside our territory."

I smiled back with equal charm. "Oh, not a bit," I said. "Who are these naval officers?"

"They're both of them lieutenants in the R.N.V.R.," he said. "One of them, Boden, is in a trawler that goes mine-sweeping from Dartmouth. The other one is in some technical shore job down there—Boom defence, or something of the sort. His name is Rhodes. He's in the Special Branch, I think. He has a green stripe between the wavy rings."

"That's Special Branch," I said. "He's probably some kind of a technician."

The brigadier said: "He's the one who knows about the flame-thrower."

I made a note of the names on my pad. "If this thing should go forward," I said carefully, "I see no reason why we shouldn't loan those officers to you, if you really want them. Was it your idea that Captain Simon should go in command?"

"That is what we should like," he said. "The proposal came from Simon, he's the man who knows the local conditions over on the other side, and we have confidence in him. But since this has to be, in its small way, a combined operation, we should want to agree the commander with you people."

I nodded. "Who's going to do the navigating?"

"Couldn't Boden look after that part of it?" he asked. "He's in a trawler now."

I made a slight grimace. "It's better to be safe than sorry. Getting to the right place at the right time on a strange coast in the middle of the night takes a bit of doing. Especially with the tides that run round there."

He said: "We should want help from you upon a point like that. But Simon wants to work in those two if he can. He says they've got the right idea about fighting with fire."

I stared out of the window at the bricklayers for a moment. I did not notice them much; my mind was on V.A.C.O., Admiral Thomson. This thing did not conflict with anything that we had going on. It was obviously in tune with Cabinet policy. There was no reason why the old man should obstruct it. It seemed to me that my job, pending the decision of V.A.C.O., must be to try and help the thing along.

"I think you want a Sailing Master," I said slowly. "A really good professional navigator."

I picked up the telephone and asked for the Second Sea Lord's office. "Lovell," I said. "This is Martin here, speaking from V.A.C.O.'s office. Tell me, do any of your temporary officers want to use fire against the Germans? Do you get anyone like that? Or wouldn't you know?"

He said: "Oh yes, we get one or two of those. It's cropped up a good bit in the last few months—five or six times, perhaps. They usually put it in the column for 'Preferred Employment' when they join."

"Do you think you could find a really good navigator who wants to do that?" I asked. "Somebody we could depend upon. First or second officer from a merchant ship, or someone of that sort?"

"I don't know about that," he said. "Those chaps are pretty busy in these times. I'll get my girl to have a look through the card index, and give you a ring back if you like?"

"I wish you would," I said.

I put back the receiver and turned again to the brigadier. "What about ratings, sir?" I asked. "Would you want us to provide those too?"

He shook his head. "From every point of view, we should prefer to use Free French. I've been in touch with the de Gaulle headquarters. I think we could pick out half a dozen Breton lads of the right type, and lads who are accustomed to that sort of boat."

"I see."

He glanced at me across the table. "How do you think your admiral will take it?" he enquired. "You know most of it now."

I paused before replying, wondering how to put it when I saw him. I had to tell my admiral that the Army had proposed a naval expedition, to be commanded by a pseudo-Army officer of curious past history, sailing in a fishing-boat manned principally by foreigners, armed with an unconventional and utterly disgusting weapon, with the object of stiffening morale over on the other side. It was certainly an unusual proposal.

I said slowly: "I've really got no idea how he will take it. It may be that he will like it and let it go forward." Privately I was pretty certain that he would.

The brigadier leaned forward and tapped the table. "Look," he said. "We may be starting something bigger than we think. There are queer streaks in the German character, and one of the things that they can't stand is fire. That's why they were the first to think of *Flammenwerfers*."

"That's fairly common knowledge," I said thoughtfully. "The Germans don't like fire." I smiled a little. "Nor do I."

I glanced across the table at him. "There's just one matter that we haven't touched upon," I said. "Are you in a hurry, sir? Or may I ask a few more questions?"

"By all means," he replied.

I said: "What sort of people are the men who want to do this thing?"

2

CHARLES SIMON was almost exactly half French and half English. He spoke both languages perfectly, and he spoke both with that faint trace of a foreign accent which betrayed him as a foreigner in either country to the discerning.

His father had been a British wine merchant who did a good deal of travelling in France, and liked the country. His mother was a girl from Lyons. Though technically English by her marriage she was never anything but French in fact. They called their son Charles because that could be pronounced in either language, making it easy for the relatives upon both sides.

They lived in Surbiton from 1904 to 1911, not very happy years for the girl from Lyons. Simon then died, and within a fortnight she was back in her home town, taking the boy with her. She had not been happy in the strange land across the Channel to the north, but she had loved her husband and respected him. Within a few years she had shaken off her British nationality and had become French again in law, but it had been his wish that the boy Charles should be brought up as an Englishman. In spite of the protests of her parents, she sent him to a preparatory boarding school near Oxford, and later on to Shrewsbury, his father's school. She knew that the English valued this peculiar form of education.

Simon grew up an odd mixture. He spent all his holidays with his mother and his relations in Lyons, but made few friends there of his own age. The French boys and girls he came in contact with regarded him as a foreigner, and a queer fish. His time in England was spent in the monastic society of a British public school; he made a few close and enduring friendships with English boys, but he never met an English girl at all, nor spent more than a single night at a time with an English family.

He left school at eighteen. He had shown some aptitude for drawing and for architecture, and with the help of his mother's family he became apprenticed as a draughtsman to an architect in Lyons. For some years he worked hard, and liked his work.

Those were the years from 1923 to 1930, when France was leading the world in the technique of ferro-concrete bridge construction. Charles Simon mastered this technique, and having an eye for line became something of a bridge designer. He changed his firm two or three times, each time with a rise in salary; before long he was sent on his first business trip to England.

He was passionately fond of England. He knew little of the country beyond the unreal idealism of his public school, so that for him everything English was rose-coloured. He was English by nationality and to that he clung; his work was in France, but he thought of himself as a foreigner working in a foreign land. Whenever he got a holiday he went to England, and in 1930, when he joined the Société Anonyme des Fabricants de Ciment, the great organisation at Corbeil, he began travelling to England as a technical representative.

He married soon after that, in 1931, when he was twenty-six years old, an English girl from Tunbridge Wells. Within a year she left him.

I don't know why that happened. It was ten years before the time of which I am writing, and it had no bearing on his war-time occupations, so there was no reason why any of us should know much about it. But thinking back, one can string together a few contributory facts which throw a little light on it, perhaps.

As I have said, he was a queer fish. His only real interest outside his work in ferro-concrete was his enthusiasm for England and for all things English, but his knowledge of England was

14

confined to his own public school. It was a queer, limited, ignorant enthusiasm. He made occasional short business trips to England, but his work lay in Corbeil. Corbeil is a small manufacturing town rather to the south of Paris, a desperately dull little place unless you happen to be deeply interested in ferro-concrete.

She must have found it hard to bear, that girl from Tunbridge Wells. It may have been the ferro-concrete that got her to the stage of breaking up their marriage, or it may have been the endless, uninformed prattle of England, or it may have simply been Corbeil. But whether it was one of those, or some quite different trouble, she left him and went back to Tunbridge Wells. He never lived with her again.

He gave up his business trips to England after that. It may have been from choice, but by that time the work was falling off. Britain and America knew quite as much as France about concrete bridges. Moreover, fortification work was growing and absorbing the attention of French concrete firms, and there was less need for them to seek foreign contracts. Simon from that time on spent much of his time in fortification work upon the Maginot Line.

What was he like? He was a lean man, fairly tall, with dark hair that hung over his forehead. He was quite a merry chap who liked to grease his work with a salacious joke. People liked working for him; he never had any trouble with his staff. In peace-time that was all that one could say about him; it never became apparent till the war was two years old that he was a natural leader of men.

He did not change his way of life much after his marriage had collapsed. He went on living in Corbeil, went on with his work. His trips to England ceased and he became more French to all appearances; he wore French clothes and stopped buying English newspapers and magazines. Gradually the people of Corbeil and the factory forgot that Simon was in a fact a British citizen; only the police knew that, and the director of the firm who dealt with military business.

And yet, there was one thing. Charles Simon—pronounce the name in French or English as you like—Charles Simon kept a boat. He kept a little four-ton cutter at St. Malo, fitted with an auxiliary engine, and in the summer when he took his holiday he used to make timid adventures in this thing, to the Channel Islands or to Lesardrieux, picking his weather with the greatest care. I know a naval officer who met him once before the war in St. Peter Port and spent the evening with him. This chap said that he was quite alone. The ship was reasonably clean, as well she might be, because Simon had been swinging at his anchor for ten days of summer weather waiting for the perfect day, the day of days when there would be a dead calm sea, a cloudless sky, a rising glass, and a very gentle breeze from the north to waft him safely back to St. Malo.

Did he do that because he liked it, or because he felt that it was English to go yachting, or just for some hereditary urge towards the sea that had to be obeyed? I don't know. I only know that it seemed to me when I heard about it to be a typically English way to take a holiday, rather uncomfortable and rather frightening.

*   *   *   *   *

He did not get his yachting holiday in the summer of 1939; the work upon the fortifications was too intense. The Société Anonyme F. C. de Corbeil was working night shift by that time, and all the staff were working twelve hours a day in a wishful endeavour to make ferro-concrete serve as substitute for an offensive strategy. They laboured through the winter and on into the spring of 1940; they went on working till the refugees were streaming through the town and the Germans were within thirty miles. Then they stopped, and Corbeil joined the throng of refugees.

Charles Simon stayed behind in the works, together with the managing director, M. Louis Duchene, and a foreman or two. Duchene stayed because he had built most of the factory, and because he could not visualise a life away from it for more than a short trip to Paris; his wife and family had left for Pau a week before. The foremen stayed because the factory was their livelihood, and because they shrewdly thought that whether France was ruled by Germans or by French, concrete would be needed and their jobs were safe unless they ran away from them. Charles Simon stayed because he felt himself to be an officer, and because he was ashamed to go while old Duchene still sat on in his office.

He went up to the old man in his room. "It seems that the Germans will be here within an hour now," he said nonchalantly. "You will receive them, monsieur?"

"But certainly," said *monsieur le directeur*. "Watch for the first officer to come in at the gate, and have him brought up here with courtesy. And, Simon, get out the general arrangement plan of the works, and bring it to me. No doubt the officers will wish to see it."

It never crossed their minds that they should destroy any of the buildings or equipment to prevent them falling into German hands. Such a course had never even been suggested, and would have been ridiculed if it had been. One did not throw good money down the drain.

Simon hesitated. "I will bring the plan." He coughed. "May I raise a personal matter, monsieur?"

"Assuredly." The old man looked at him with curiosity. "These are difficult times, Simon. You need not stay here if you wish to go."

The designer said: "I would like to stay with you, monsieur. But you will remember that legally I am an Englishman, a foreigner. That may make difficulties for me with the Germans when they come."

Duchene said: "I never think of you except as French."

Simon said: "Most people think of me as French, but I am still a British citizen. Would it be possible for you to forget that I am not a Frenchman, Monsieur Duchene? If the Germans did not know, I could stay on working here. They will need all of us to run the factory."

The old man stared at him. "Does anybody else know, who would betray you?"

"I do not think so. It is many years now since I went to England."

"But your papers—your *carte d'identité*?"

Simon said: "At this moment, monsieur, that perhaps can be arranged."

He left the office, and went out of the factory into the town. Corbeil was singularly empty. A car or two with dry, empty tanks were parked by the roadside, and a cart with a broken wheel stood abandoned in the main street, the mule still in the harness. The place was still, empty, and desolate that hot summer afternoon, as if it waited breathlessly for the coming of the Germans.

He went to the Mairie. The door stood open, all the office doors were open. Everyone had fled. He passed on to the Gendarmerie; one door was locked. He withdrew a few steps and ran at it and stamped it in. There was nobody about at all.

He had lived so long in France, had visited the Mairie so many times, that he knew just what he wanted. First he extracted his card from the little card index of foreigners, burnt it with a match, and scattered the ash outside the window. He found the blank identity cards. He found the register of births, and made a hurried parcel of four volumes; later in the afternoon he thrust these into the furnace of the steam plant at the factory. He made himself a new birth certificate. He was at the Mairie barely twenty minutes and he left it a French citizen, proof against any superficial investigation.

Later that afternoon the Germans came. There was no fighting near Corbeil. They rode in on their motor-cycles first, followed by armoured cars and a few tanks, and streams of motor-lorries full of infantry. They occupied the railway station and the Mairie and the waterworks and the power-house and the gas-works; in the late evening three officers and thirty soldiers drove in to the factory to find Duchene still waiting for them, gravely courteous, with Simon by his side.

In three days the factory was working, on a much reduced basis. A month later, fortified by fresh supplies of troubled and bewildered labour drafted by the Germans, it was in its stride again.

The Maginot contracts were a thing of the past now. The German Commission of Control dictated their activities; aero-drome runways, new strategic roadways to the Channel ports, and above all air-raid shelters formed the new work of the S.A.F.C. de Corbeil. Duchene and Simon worked like Trojans to satisfy their new masters, and for a time they were too busy in the work to appreciate the implications of the new regime.

It was only slowly that they came to realise their true position. At first everything seemed to go on normally; the German troops were civil and even ingratiating. There was plenty of money in the town, for the soldiers spent freely, and there was plenty of work. All the evidence of prosperity was there—for the first three months. If you did not think too hard about the position of France, or read too many newspapers, it was quite a good time. Duchene and Simon were too busy to do either.

The first real shock they had was when Paul Lecardeau was arrested, tried, taken to the barracks, and shot, all within an hour and a half.

Simon knew Paul quite well, and had often played a game of dominoes with him at the Café de l'Univers. Paul ran a fair-sized draper's shop in the route d'Orléans, and he was a notable spitter. In the café he could hit a cuspidor at any range up to

three metres with accuracy, and he was gifted with what seemed
to be an inexhaustible supply of ammunition.

Paul discovered, when his shop was all but empty, that fresh
goods were unobtainable. His business was mostly in household
linen and women's clothes. The German major who now sat in
the Mairie brushed aside his plea for a permit to buy stock in
Paris, but displayed a good deal of interest in Paul's own
capacity for work upon the roads. It was with difficulty that
Paul evaded immediate conscription as a labourer.

With little left upon his shelves to sell, Paul took to sitting
in the Café de l'Univers hour after hour, gloomily smoking and
staring at the Germans as they passed upon the pavement.
Presently he took to spitting when a German came into the café;
it was an amusing game, because the big brass cuspidor rang
like a gong to each impact. A German *Feldwebel* stalked up
to him and warned him—once. Next day, the brassy note of
the gong was the signal for his arrest. Ninety minutes later,
Paul was dead.

Simon faced old Duchene across the table of the office which
they now shared. "It is intolerable, that," he said uncertainly.
"Paul was an honest man. He was *jocrisse,* that is all."

Duchene stared at him in bewilderment. "But why did they
do it? All Corbeil is co-operating with the new regime, as the
Marshal has said. There is not a de Gaullist in the town. Why
must the Germans do a thing like that?"

It was, of course, because they were Germans, but neither
Simon nor Duchene had yet come to appreciate that point.

From then onwards things grew worse. The shortage of goods
and even of foodstuffs became general, and the tempers of the
people of Corbeil grew short in sympathy. They became critical
of the Marshal's new order; the old confusion, they said bitterly,
was more tolerable. Before long young people of both sexes
became hostile to the Germans. It was good fun, if you had
no responsibilities, to creep out in the night and let down the
tyres of their bicycles, or pour a little water in a petrol-tank
and watch the car stall half-way down the road. Once or twice
a German officer, infuriated, whipped out his automatic and
took a shot at the dim figures giggling in the shadows. This was
great fun and gave the young people a sense of importance. They
began to talk about de Gaulle, and to dignify their little exploits
with the name of sabotage.

Presently the Germans arrested M. Chavaigne, headmaster of
the boys' school, and tried him for complicity in these affairs.

19

The evidence was inconclusive, so they sentenced him to ten years' forced labour and sent him away to Germany to work it out. With the removal of that restraining influence the sabotage increased, and even adults began secretly to listen to the British radio and to talk about de Gaulle.

Soon after that the cross of Lorraine made its appearance daubed in paint or clay upon the walls of the factory. The German Commission of Control, visiting the works one day, demanded furiously that these signs be removed and Simon, with apologies, set labourers to work.

"I am desolated that this should have happened," he told the Germans. "It is the boys who do it—the irresponsibles, who do not think. Boys are the devil."

The *Hauptmann Pionier* in charge of the Commission stared at him arrogantly. "Boys do what their parents do. In Germany the boys work hard, and do not insult the Government. It is not so here. If I see this again, I will have this town of Corbeil taught a lesson."

Simon said: "I will attend to the matter personally. This will not happen again."

The German turned away, and they went on with the work.

Simon reported the matter to Duchene as soon as they were gone. "There will be trouble before long, monsieur," he said. "The people are becoming restless."

The old man said: "I will not have trouble in these works. We do not mix with politics here, in the factory. See that the walls are cleaned each day, and the lavatories also. It is there that they write things."

"I will see to that, monsieur."

"Why must they do these things. It can only lead to trouble. What is the matter with the men?" the old man asked.

Simon shrugged his shoulders. "It is the war," he said. He glanced over his shoulders at the closed door. "You listen to the English radio, perhaps, monsieur?"

The old man said: "I have no patience with the English since they ran away. As for the radio, it does not amuse me, and there is no news. Is it that that is the reason for the trouble?"

Simon said: "It is the stories of the German losses in the air that the men hear upon the radio that makes the trouble. That, and the speeches of that man de Gaulle." He bent to the *directeur*. "A hundred and eighteen German aeroplanes were shot down yesterday," he said in a low tone. "And seventy-one

20

the day before." He paused. "That is the real trouble with the men."

Duchene stared at him. "Somebody told me something about that, but I did not believe him. The figures are too big. It is an English lie."

"I do not think it is a lie, monsieur. When I was at Caen on Tuesday the foreman said that nearly a hundred aeroplanes took off on Sunday, but less than seventy came back. The officers there have become very surly, and they will not talk to me, or to any civilian. It is quite different from what it was a month ago."

The old man said: "Sacred Mother of God! If the English can shoot down Germans in that way, why did they not do it when they were fighting with us? They are playing their own game. They have betrayed us."

Simon shook his head. "I cannot understand the turn the war has taken," he said soberly. "If they betrayed us, we are now betraying them in turn. These runways we are doing for the aerodrome at Caen—they are to make it possible for Heinkels to take off with double bomb load, to drop on English towns. But we were allies, once."

Duchene said: "It was they who began it. . . ." He turned back to his desk. "No more of politics—that is not our affair." He picked up a paper. "This invoice from Mensonnier—I will not pay for crates. Mensonnier knows that. See the accountant, and have that crossed off."

It was not altogether easy for Duchene to free his mind from politics, in spite of his preoccupation with the factory. He had lived and worked in Corbeil for over forty years, since he had come into his father's business as a lad. In that forty years, inevitably since he was the managing director of the largest business in the town, he had become associated with a variety of local charities and enterprises, most of which were now in difficulties and troubles. He cared little enough for most of them; in the changed times they must adjust themselves. He could not free his mind, however, from the affairs of the St. Xavier Asile des Vieux at Château Lebrun.

Château Lebrun was a village about five miles from Corbeil, and Duchene was a trustee of the Asile des Vieux. The asylum was an organisation with a religious flavour, partly supported by a subsidy from the municipality of Corbeil, partly by local charity, and partly by small sums extracted from the relatives of the occupants. The Vieux were of both sexes and many of them were feeble-minded, all being sixty years old or more. It was a useful and on the whole a kindly institution, which collected destitute and unwanted aged people from a wide area of country and saw them unhurried to the end.

About seventy of them were accommodated in wards in a big, rectangular stone building on the outskirts of the village. The land was flat about Château Lebrun, and suitable for a dispersal aerodrome: a fact that the Germans were quick to grasp. They took the building as a barrack for the air mechanics. The Maître d'Asile came early to the Maire and to Duchene for help, and Duchene rang up the Commission of Control, only to get a short answer. The building was required for military purposes. The inmates would be moved by the German Field Ambulance Service; it was not permitted for civilians to accompany them. All asylums in the occupied zone were to be cleared, and the inmates would be accommodated in the Vichy area. Relatives would be told the new address in a few days.

So the old people were removed, feebly protesting, in a convoy of field ambulances. Thereafter nothing happened. Most of the relatives dismissed the matter from their minds; they had seldom been to see *Grand-mère* and had more important matters now to think about. A few became insistent and began to bother the Commission of Control with demands for the new address. One by one these received an intimation, with regrets, that the person in question had succumbed to the fatigue of the journey.

One by one they came to Duchene, at his house or in his office at the factory.

Worried, he went to the Commission and got a sharp rebuff. Such things were apt to happen, in their view. They could not tell him the location of the new asylum yet; in due course an information would come through. In the meantime, he would kindly not waste the time of German officers with trivialities, but attend to the manufacture of cement.

Anxious, and a little frightened, he began to make enquiries of his own. The manager of a large industry invariably has ways of getting information which are not available to ordinary men, and in the concrete business Duchene's influence spread wide. Gradually, in bits and pieces, the truth came to him. The old people had got no farther towards Vichy than the German hospital at Sézanne. There all had died by hypodermic as they lay strapped upon the stretchers in the cars, and had been thrust into a common grave with lime, on the same night.

Shamefaced, white, and shaken, the old man blurted it out

22

to Simon in the office late one night. "One does not know how to behave now," he muttered. "One does not know how to address a German officer. It is the act of barbarians, that. Even the beasts, the animals, do not do things like that."

Simon was silent.

Duchene's voice rose a little. "But it was murder! Seventy-two people."

Charles Simon said: "I know that, monsieur. They are murderers, every one of them, if it will serve their end. They did not want to feed these old ones, or to care for them. That is all."

The old man said, distressed: "But that is not civilised. That is what savages would do, in the black jungle."

Simon smiled sourly. "I think that we are now in the black jungle, in Corbeil. And only now have we begun to realise it."

That was all that was said that night, and Duchene went back to his empty *appartement* in the town. He did not even go to bed that night. He sat primly in a gilded, plush-upholstered chair all night, his hands resting on the table, smoking cigarette after cigarette, staring unseeing at the ornate wall before him. At dawn he got up, pulled aside the black-out, and opened a window to let air into the stuffy, smoke-filled room. An hour later he went down to the works.

Simon came early to his room that day. "The Commission comes at eleven o'clock," he said. "Lunch as usual?"

M. le directeur drummed nervously upon the table. "I will not see them," he said irritably. "You must tell them I am ill."

Simon looked at the old man for a moment, silent. Then he said quietly: "It is understandable, that. But they will know that you are here, monsieur, and that may make a difficulty. Perhaps you could go home till they have gone."

Duchene raised weary eyes, clouded with doubts, to his designer. "I am going to close down the factory," he said, but there was irresolution in his voice. "I will not have my people working for those German swine."

Simon said gently: "Leave it for to-day, monsieur. Let the car take you to your house when it goes in to fetch the Germans." They still had a tiny drain of petrol for the works car for station trips.

The old man flared out: "I will not work for them, myself, not after this. Not one more kilogramme of cement shall they have from me."

Charles Simon dropped down on to the chair before the desk.

and leaned towards the older man. "You are tired now," he said. "You do not look well at all. Did you sleep badly, monsieur?"

The old man said: "I did not go to bed. I was thinking of . . . all sorts of things."

They had worked together for ten years, and Simon knew his chief very well. "Listen, monsieur," he said. "We cannot do that, now. It would not help at all for you to close the factory. It would be open within the hour with Germans in control, and all that would be gained would be one hour of our production lost to them. And you would be held in a concentration-camp. That would not benefit Corbeil, or France."

Duchene passed a weary hand across his eyes.

"One must go on working for the present," said the younger man.

M. le directeur said: "I have been thinking over what you said the other day, about the runways at the aerodrome at Caen. Each ton we send out is a blow at England, and although I do not like the English, at any rate they are still fighting in a way against these German swine. How do you feel about that, Simon?"

"I do not like it, monsieur."

"I do not like it either. The English are still fighting in their way against these filthy murderers, and you and I are fighting in our way against the English. Does that make sense to you—you who are an Englishman yourself? Hey? Does that make sense?"

"No, monsieur. It does not make sense. But there is nothing we can do about it."

Duchene sat brooding for a time, in silence. "I would rather that the factory had been blown up and stood in ruins than that it should be used like this."

"That is what we should have done," said the designer. "It is too late now, but we should have blown it up ourselves, before the Germans came."

The old man stared at him. "Who could have guessed these Germans were not people like ourselves?"

"We were told often enough," said Simon grimly. "All the world told us that the Germans were a murderous and an uncivilised people, without decent codes of conduct. But when they conquered us, we thought they would be people like ourselves."

There was a long silence. When Duchene spoke again his voice had lost all its vigour; he spoke as a very tired old man.

"I do not know what happened to France," he said wearily. "I have been thinking and thinking, and I cannot understand. We *knew* that the Germans were like this in the old days—we knew it, and we fought them with the British as our allies, and we beat them down. And then we lost our faith. . . ."

He stared at the designer with tired eyes. "It is as if all France had lain under a spell," he said slowly. "From that place at Berchtesgarten there has spread an influence, malign, like a miasma, that has sapped our will. So that we laid down our arms, and never fought at all, and so became mere tools for evil in the hands of evil men. . . ."

He got up wearily from his chair, swaying a little as he stood. "One thing alone saved the English from our lot," he muttered, half to himself. "Running water—twenty miles of it, salt running water of the sea. That is why the English are still brave to fight, as we were once. No spell, no sucking weakening influence sent out by evil people can cross running water. When I lived in the country as a boy, everybody knew that much."

Presently Simon got him downstairs to the car. He took him to the *appartement* and gave the old man over to his housekeeper, before he went on to the station in the car to meet the Germans coming down from Paris on the midday train.

At that time there was construction work of every description going on along the whole length of the Channel coastline of France. The little watering-place of Le Tréport, amongst others, was undergoing a radical reorganisation of its harbour under German supervision, with a view to making it more suitable for barge traffic. A fortnight later, Simon was summoned to a conference at Le Tréport, to deal with certain engineering problems at that port and at Saint-Valery-sur-Somme.

It was not the first time that the Germans had used him in this way; indeed, the vast extent of their conquests made it necessary for them to use technicians from the countries they had overrun. Simon went with mixed feelings. He disliked open work on military matters; it did not seem so bad when one was working in the office at Corbeil, when he could forget the use to which the product would be put. On the other hand, the trip to the sea coast was a change and something of a holiday; he could spin it out over three days.

He went on a Tuesday in late October, and spent the first afternoon walking round the watering-place and studying the little docks. Wednesday was spent with the Germans. They made a quick tour of the harbour in the morning, then settled

to a conference on material supplies. They finished about four
o'clock.

Gathering together his papers, the German chairman of the
conference said to Simon: "You are going back to-night?"

The designer shrugged his shoulders. "I will go to the station
and find out about the trains. I do not think I can get through
to Corbeil to-night, and it is cheaper to stay here than in Paris.
I shall only go to-night if I can get home."

The German nodded. "As you like."

Simon went back to his hotel, the one beside the station, and
decided to stay the night. He had dined the previous evening
in the hotel and had not cared for the dinner. That night he
went out and found a café-restaurant upon the little front, and
settled down to spend the evening there.

It was not very full. He sat for an hour over a Pernod reading his paper and listening to the wireless, and passing a word
now and again with the man on the other side of the marble-
topped table, an engineer from the power station. Then he dined
and sat for a long time with a cup of coffee, running over his
notes of the day's business, planning the work involved.

He was sitting so when the swing doors burst open with a
crash. There was an instant's stunned silence as the people at
the tables turned to the interruption. Then, in a deafening
clamour in the narrow room, the fire from a couple of Tommy-
guns burst out. A group of four German non-commissioned
officers seated together at a table rose half to their feet. One
of them spun round and collapsed backwards with a crash. The
others dropped where they sat. Their bodies shook and quivered
with the impact of the bullets pumping into them.

An officer, an *Oberleutnant*, sitting with a French girl at a
table at the end of the room, ducked down behind a little wooden
table fumbling for the automatic at his wrist. He never got it
out. The wooden splinters flew from the table and bright holes
spread in a pattern over it; one of the splinters gashed the girl
across the eyebrow as she stood screaming with her hand up to
her mouth. Behind the table the officer fell forward as a sodden
weight, and a thin stream of blood ran out on to the floor.

Suddenly the firing stopped. With a little brassy tinkle the last
shell rattled to the floor.

One of the men at the door shouted in French: "Don't any
of you move!" Then, to the white, terrified proprietor behind
the bar: "Any more Germans in this place?"

The man shook his head, unable at first to find words. Then

26

he gulped, looked at the bodies, and said: "Only those.

The man at the door said in English: "Go right through the place, lads. Ben, stay with me."

Three men rushed in, and made their way through into the back quarters. They were hard, violent young men in British battledress. They each carried a sub-machine-gun; they had two revolvers each, worn on light webbing harness from the shoulders; the same harness supported a belt with pockets for Mills hand-grenades. A large electric torch hung at the waist. They wore British tin hats.

The other two, one of whom wore sergeant's stripes, came forward from the door, their guns at the ready. The sergeant said again, in accented, ungrammatical French: "Don't any of you move! Put your identity cards out upon the tables."

The man called Ben stayed by the door. The sergeant began to move methodically from table to table looking at the cards displayed, his gun always at the ready.

There was silence in the café, broken only by the tramping of the men upstairs as they ransacked the house, and by the noise of light gunfire intermittently outside in the night. Once there was a heavy, thunderous explosion, as of a demolition. The girl who had been sitting with the dead officer had stopped her screaming and stood motionless, her back against the wall. her hands pressed palms against the wall behind her, staring at the devil with the sergeant's stripes advancing slowly down the room, his gun held at the ready.

To Charles Simon, in that tense moment, came the realisation of what he had to do. This was an English raid, this violent gangster-like affray. This was his chance. With sudden, utter clarity it came to him that this was the turning-point of his whole life, and he must take the turning.

He did not produce his card, but turned out letters, bills, receipts, all the contents of his pockets on the table before him as if he searched desperately, but the card stayed in his hip pocket. The man with the gun came to the table and paused, merciless, thrusting his gun forward.

Charles Simon raised his head, and said in a low tone, in English: "I seem to have lost my card. You'd better arrest me, and take me to your officer."

The man said: "Are you English?"

Simon said: "Don't be a fool. Arrest me, and take me outside."

The man lunged forward, thrusting the barrel of the Tommy-gun against his chest. "Outside, you!" he said in French. "Get up!" He swung round to the man at the door. "Here's one, Ben," he said in English. "Take him outside, and keep him till I come."

Simon walked the length of the room, most conscious of the guns directed at him. Outside the night was full of rifle fire; from the small docks the red glow of a fire was growing bright; the street seemed full of British soldiers, heavily armed, purposeful, intent. Overhead there was the noise of many aeroplanes, and the dull thunder of their bombs upon the roads that led into the town mingled with the rumble and crash of demolitions at the docks. The place was rapidly becoming an inferno.

The man Ben stood Simon up against the wall outside the door, covering him with his gun. The tension, in the half-light of the growing fires, was intense. It was a night of murder unprovoked, of arson and rapine; a night of war.

Simon said to his guard: "Look, I'm an Englishman. You must take me to your officer."

The man thrust his face up close. "How do I know you're not a mucking Jerry?"

"If I was one I couldn't hurt you," Simon said. "You've got all Woolwich Arsenal to back you up. I tell you, I am English. You've got to take me back with you; they'll want to question me."

His guard was a sharp, intelligent young man, picked and trained for this work. The sergeant came out with the other three men; in a few moments Simon was at a mustering point, a busmen's shelter on the front. There was a subaltern there, a dark figure in battle-dress indistinguishable from the rest but that he carried no gun. The sergeant reported his prisoner in terse, short sentences; the officer flashed a shaded torch on Simon.

"You are a British citizen?"

"Yes, sir. I've been working in France."

"What at?"

"Concrete construction work. Bridges, aerodrome buildings and runways, things of that sort. I came here for a job upon the docks."

"What is your Company?"

Simon told him.

The subaltern said: "I am taking you to England as a prisoner. Do you come with us willingly?"

"Yes, sir."

28

"All right. Stand over there."

Simon said: "May I write a letter and post it?"

The torch flashed into his face again; he felt suspicion rising up against him in the darkness. "What sort of letter? Whom to?"

"I want to write to the head of my firm. It's just possible that you may want me to come back here when you've heard what I have to say. I want to write to the firm and say that I have gone for a week's holiday to the south of France, to see my mother in the Vichy territory."

There was a short silence. The officer made up his mind with a quick decision that Simon could not but admire. "You may write a letter like that," he said. "Have you got paper and an envelope?"

"Not here."

The subaltern called one of the men, a sharp, keen-faced lad, and gave Simon over to him. The boy took him to an empty, deserted café, where they found stationery behind the bar, and there Simon wrote his letter while the guard made a light for him to write by with his torch and kept him covered with a heavy black revolver.

Simon said:

Dear Monsieur,

It is with pleasure that I can inform you that the Commandant in Charge has been so kind as to grant me a permit to visit my mother, who as you know lives in the neighbourhood of Lyons. It is now nearly a year since I saw her, and as this permit to pass into the Vichy territory is for ten days only from to-day I am leaving at once for Lyons, and trust that I may be allowed this short vacation. I will write particulars of the contracts that I have to-day negotiated from there; in the meantime we should keep up deliveries of the fifty tons a week to Tréport provisionally demanded.

Accept, dear monsieur, the assurance of my deepest respect.

CHARLES SIMON.

The guard took the letter from him and read it slowly, now and then asking the meaning of a word. He passed it and Simon sealed the envelope: then they went together through the fire-lit darkness to the Bureau de Poste. He slipped the letter in the box. A naval officer in blue pressed by them; he wore a white scarf around his neck and a revolver in a belt at his waist. In his hand he carried a tin bedroom utensil, white-enamelled. Painted on it roughly was A PRESENT FROM TREPORT.

Simon and his guard stopped and turned to watch. The lieutenant went to the counter where the scared postmaster was handing over a sack of registered mail to a couple of desperate-looking thugs in battle-dress. The officer said, in bad French:

"Pardon, monsieur. I have a parcel to despatch." He slammed the enamelware down upon the mahogany slab and pulled the revolver from his belt. "I will pay the postage, and you will put it in the mail."

The man looked at it uncertainly, and then at the revolver, now pointing at his belly. "For the mail?" he said.

"For the mail," said the naval officer. "Be quick; we have not long to waste. How much is it?"

The postmaster put it on the scales, then looked at the label tied to the handle. Then he laughed. "Adolf Hitler, Bierhalle, Munich," he said. "Seventeen francs, monsieur."

The officer threw down half a crown. "English money," he said. "Is that all right?"

The man shrugged his shoulders. "I will keep it as a souvenir." Under the levelled guns he stamped the label and dropped the pot into a mail-bag.

Simon and his guard left the Post Office and hurried back to the mustering-point through rose-coloured, firelit streets. The fires had got firm hold upon the town, especially in the region of the docks. From somewhere in the outer darkness machine-guns were firing down the lit streets, enfilading them; the range was great and the fire scattered and inaccurate. Outside the town, again, the noise of battle had grown; there was more happening now on the outer roads than bombs from aeroplanes. It was quite clear to Simon as they hurried to the sea-front that unless the British meant to hold the town, it was time to go.

*　　　*　　　*　　　*　　　*

He landed in England in the earliest light of dawn, having crossed the Channel in pitch darkness in a strange, small boat with fifty other men. There were seven wounded in the boat with him, lying upon the bare deck, uncomplaining; one died in the middle of the night. In that boat there were no other prisoners, but he had reason to believe that ten or twelve Germans and civilian French crossed in another boat. It occurred to him that he was being segregated.

They landed in a muddy, tidal creek between fields. He never learned where it was. There was a wooden jetty and a few brown corrugated iron sheds; it might have been a little yacht-yard in peace-time, or something of that sort. The men with him stretched stiff, tired limbs, unloaded Tommy-guns and pistols, and passed soldiers' jokes about ham and eggs and a good kip.

They landed at the pier and the men formed up in a rough order and were marched away towards a wood; there seemed to be a camp among the trees. Simon was ordered by the subaltern to wait; he was taken into a little hut by a guard, and stayed there till a small lorry with a canvas-covered back drove up.

He rode in this for half an hour with the subaltern to a large military camp. Here he was shown into an office, where he was interrogated shortly by a major. They were kind enough to him, and after ten minutes' questioning took him to a room and offered him a bath and a shave. Then he had breakfast, English breakfast that he remembered from his schooldays, where you were expected to eat porridge as well as meat or fish, and then very thick toast, and the orange conserve that they called marmalade. Already he was feeling that his English was a little rusty.

In fact, it was. It was grammatically correct and the accent was not very noticeable, but his schoolboy slang called attention to his speech and then you noticed his accent. It is not natural to hear a man of thirty-five in serious conversation use the word "topping" to express appreciation of the treatment that he had received, nor does he generally refer to his food as "tuck". Charles did both because his English was like that, and then you noticed him and wondered who he was.

They put him in a car again after breakfast, and by noon he arrived at a large, rather dilapidated country house, full of soldiers. It was not very far from London, but Charles had no means of knowing that; he never learned where it was. And here he came before a major in the British Army and a *capitaine* of the Free French, and he talked to them freely for three hours.

In the middle of the afternoon the major said: "I'm going to call a halt for to-day, Mr. Simon, and have some of this transcribed. I may want to have another talk with you to-morrow."

Simon said: "Right-oh, sir. I'll stay here, shall I?"

The British officer said gravely: "It would be very kind of you if you would stay with us to-night. We can make you comfortable." In fact, Simon was as much a prisoner as if he had been German, but he did not care to realise it. He was too happy to be back in England.

"I'd like that ever so much," he said.

The major smiled slightly. "Tell me, Mr. Simon," he said. "Have you got any relatives or friends in England?"

Charles said: "Not very many. There are my wife's people, of course . . ." He had told them about her. "But I don't much want them to know that I'm over here."

"Of course not," said the other easily. "Whom do you know best—whom would you go and stay with when you leave here?" He smiled with disarming frankness. "You see, you've come to England rather—unconventionally. We may have to help you to make up a story to tell."

Charles laughed. "I would like to see the Beak," he said. "He was my housemaster at Shrewsbury. I think I'd go and stay with him for a bit, at the school."

The major asked: "What's his proper name?"

"Mr. Scarlett. He's retired from the House, but he lives just opposite the cricket-ground."

The major handed him over to a subaltern, who took him and gave him tea in the mess. Charles was immensely pleased. He had never before had a meal in a real mess, with officers just like grown-up versions of the boys that he had been at school with. It was all very, very good.

The mess waiter was just bringing him his second cup of English tea when, two hundred miles to the north, a camouflaged army car drew up before the little house opposite the cricket-pitch. Three minutes later a young officer was explaining his errand to a white-haired old gentleman.

The old man said: "Oh dear me, yes. I remember Charles Simon very well. He was a good oar, a very good oar; if he had gone up to the Varsity he might have done very well. Not the Blue, you know, but I think he would have got into the College Eight." The young officer listened patiently; his job was to listen. "He rowed three in my First Eight in 1923, the year that we made three bumps and finished up third boat on the river. It was a good year, that."

Mr. Scarlett paused thoughtfully. "He was French, you know, but a nice boy all the same."

The subaltern said: "Would you know him again?"

"Know him again? Whatever do you mean? Of course I'd know him again! Besides, he came to see me here in this very room only nine years ago, after that unfortunate business with his wife."

The subaltern said: "He's over here now, sir. I understand that he is in confinement."

The old man looked at the boy searchingly over his spectacles. "What for?"

"I don't know. I had to tell you that we want you to come down to London to identify him."

"When?"

"To-night, sir. Right away."

Charles Simon had a game of billiards with his companion, and he had several glasses of English gin and bitters, and he had dinner in the mess and talked to the colonel about France, and he listened to the nine o'clock news with the officers, and he listened to them talking about the war. He was staggered at their nonchalant assumption that they were going to win the war. It was obvious that their country was being terribly battered; he had driven that morning through one blitzed city that he fancied was Southampton, and the desolation of it, and the stillness, had seemed to him to be the hall-mark of defeat. In dumb amazement he listened to the officers discussing what should be done with Germany when the war was over; the words "if we win the bloody thing" passed as a joke. It was an eye-opener to Charles.

About ten o'clock there was a raid warning, and most of the officers went out to their duties. His guide stayed with Charles Simon. "We don't sleep on the top floor in a raid," he said. "But you'll be all right—you're on the first floor. There's a shelter if you'd like to go down there."

He said: "Are you going?"

The other said: "Not unless they start to drop stuff round about. We all used to go at first, but we don't now. I'd go to bed, if I were you. I'll call you if it gets hot."

"I think I will."

He went upstairs to bed, and by the light of a candle got into the pyjamas they had lent him. He lay awake for a long time, tired though he was, listening to the drone of German bombers passing overhead, the distant concussion of the bombs, and the sharp crack of distant gunfire. And as he lay, a wonderful idea formed in his mind. He was a British subject, an Englishman for all his long years in a foreign country. He had been at a good English school. If he played his cards right he might become a British officer like all these other officers, and be made

33

one of them, with military duties and a khaki tunic with patch pockets and a beautiful Sam Browne belt, deep brown and polished, with a revolver holster buckled on to it. And with that uniform he felt there would come peace of mind, the calm assurance of the future unaccountably possessed by these young men.

Presently, dead tired, he fell asleep.

He had breakfast in the mess next morning with his guide, and at about ten o'clock he was taken back into the office where he had been interrogated on the previous day. The British major was there alone; he got up as Charles came in, unobtrusively pressing a bell button on his desk.

" 'Morning, Mr. Simon," he said cheerfully. "Sleep all right? Raid didn't keep you awake? That's grand."

Behind Charles the door opened, and an old man came in. Charles Simon turned and stared. "Mr. Scarlett!" he said. "I say—whatever brought you here, sir?"

The old man said: "The soldiers brought me here. Well, Simon, been getting into trouble? What have you been up to?"

"I've not been up to anything, sir." He spoke as a small boy.

"Well, what have they got you here for? You're under arrest, aren't you?"

The major interposed. "I think there is a misunderstanding," he said. "Mr. Simon is not under arrest. But he arrived in this country in a peculiar way, and we had to get a positive identity for him. You know him well, I take it?"

"I was his housemaster for four years," the old man said. "If that's not knowing him well I'd like to know what is."

There was little more to be said. Simon was allowed a quarter of an hour with his old housemaster; then the old gentleman was politely put into an army car and taken back to London to his club, slightly bewildered at the rapid, curtailed meeting. Simon was taken back into the major's office, but this time there was a brigadier with him, a smartly dressed officer with red staff tabs, with greyish hair and china-blue eyes. That was the first time Simon met McNeil.

For half an hour they went over his information of the previous day. He had told them a good deal about the aerodromes at Caen and other places, and about the coast defences around Calais, so far as he had knowledge of them from the concrete contracts. To-day they wanted to pursue the matter further. They wanted information about Lorient in Brittany.

34

He wrinkled his brows. "Yes," he said. "There is a good deal of cement going there. And steel reinforcement, although we don't handle that."

"How much cement a week?"

"Oh, a good deal. Two hundred tons a week, I dare say, sir."

"What do they want with all that in a little place like Lorient?"

Simon said: "I really couldn't tell you. You see, most of our Brittany contracts pass through our sub-office in Brest. We have an agent there who takes the orders and passes them to us in bulk at Corbeil. We only know the destination of the trucks."

The brigadier leaned forward. "I can tell you what that cement is used for, Mr. Simon. Would you like to know?"

Charles stared at him.

"The Germans are building shelters for their U-boats operating from Lorient. Did you know that?"

He shook his head. "I knew that they had U-boats there. But—shelters?"

"Bomb-proof, ferro-concrete shelters over the submarine docks," said the brigadier. "That's what they're doing there. They plan to make those docks completely safe from our attacks by air. Then with their submarines they plan to close the English Channel to our shipping—and they may do it, too. It's really rather serious."

He turned to Charles. "If you were back in Corbeil, in your office," he said quietly, "could you find out the thickness of the concrete roof, and the amount of reinforcement? Could you get hold of the design of the roof of the shelters, so that we can adapt our bombs to penetrate it?"

There was a silence in the bare little office. The officers sat gazing at the man from France.

"I couldn't find out anything about that in Corbeil," he said at last. "I'd have to think up some excuse and go to Lorient. I could tell you at once if I could have a good look at the things."

"And could you manage to do that?" the major asked.

There was a long silence. From the next room there came the clatter of a typewriter; from the fields outside the rumble of a tractor on the farm.

Charles said heavily at last: "If I went back to Corbeil I could get to Lorient all right."

The two officers exchanged a glance. The major said softly:
"But you don't want to go back."

There was another pause.

The brigadier leaned forward. "What do you want to do,
Mr. Simon?" he inquired. "Did you come over here to join
the forces?"

Charles turned to him gratefully. "I suppose I did," he said.
"You see, I didn't know what things were like here till I landed
yesterday. It was on a sort of impulse that I said they'd better
take me from Le Tréport, if you understand. I knew, I knew
the sort of things you want to know, and I've always been
English, when all's said and done." He struggled to express
himself. "I mean, I was never naturalised French, not in all
those years. I've got a French identity card, but I made that
out myself. I told you."

The major said: "I know. And there's another thing. As I
understand it, the way is pretty clear for you to go back to
Corbeil and take up your work there again, if you want to."

"If I could get across the Channel."

"Oh . . . of course."

Charles Simon raised his eyes to them. "I was thinking about
all this last night," he said. "I was thinking, I'd like to stay
over here and join up, now that I'm here. I'd be of some use
to you—in the Royal Engineers. I know quite a lot about
fortification works in ferro-concrete." He hesitated, and then
came out boldly: "Do you think I should be able to get a
commission?"

The brigadier glanced at the major, and the major at the
brigadier, and each waited for the other. The brigadier spoke
first. "I think you could get a commission," he said, "if that
was the best way to use you. But quite frankly, I would rather
see you go back to Corbeil."

The major said, a little bitterly: "My job is in the army.
I've been in the army all my life, and wars don't come very
often. I thought this war was my big chance to make a name.
In the first week of it I found myself in this job here, simply
because I'd worked hard during the peace and learned six
languages. All my contemporaries have got battalions. One of
my term at Sandhurst is commanding a brigade. And I'm
stuck here, and here I'll stay till the war ends. Then I shall be
retired on pension."

He raised his head. "I don't want you to think that I'm com-
plaining. But I tell you that, because so few of us get what we

36

want. So few can go and fight. So many have to stay and work."

Charles pulled out a packet of *caporal*, extracted one of the last two, and lit it. He blew out a long cloud of smoke. "If I did go back," he said, "it might be months before I could get down to Lorient. Some very good excuse would have to be contrived, and that would all take time. But when I had secured the information that you want, what then? How should I send it back to you?"

The brigadier said: "We'll look after that."

Charles said: "That would be espionage, wouldn't it? I should be shot if I were caught?" He eyed them narrowly.

The brigadier looked at him straight, bright blue eyes in a tanned, brown face. "Yes," he said directly. "If the Germans caught you they would shoot you. That's one of the risks you would have to take."

The designer said: "I don't mind so much about that part of it."

He was silent for a minute, while the officers stared at him. "It's just the going back that is the worst part. I don't know if I can explain it." He dropped his eyes and stared at the thin, dirty smoke arising from the ragged ember of the cigarette. "France is a beastly country now," he said quietly. "I never realised just how beastly it all was until I got over here. Everything—everybody over there . . . they go round as if they were in a dream, or tied up in a nightmare. There is a disgusting influence that has sapped their will to work, their will to live. They move about in lassitude, half men. They are tools for evil, in the hands of evil men. And the best of them know it. And the worst of them enjoy it . . ."

There was a long, long pause.

Charles Simon raised his head. "If I went back and did this job for you," he said, "could I come back to England afterwards and be a British officer?"

The brigadier said: "Yes, I think you could. In fact, I'd go so far as to promise that."

"All right," said Charles, "I'll go. How are you going to get me back to France?"

They spent the rest of the morning priming him with all he had to know. It was not much to memorise. There was the name and address of a small tailor on the quays of the Port du Commerce at Brest and the simple little phrase: "I want red buttons on the coat." There was a corn-chandler in the Rue

Paul Feval in Rennes down behind the station, and the head
waiter in the Café de l'Arcade in the Boulevard de Sévigné in
Paris. Through one or other of these friends he would return
to England, but how they would not say.

In the late afternoon he was driven to an aerodrome to meet
his pilot had to learn his parachute. With the pilot and a large-
scale map of France he planned the flight. "That's where I
mean," he said. "Ten miles north-east of Lyons, by that little
place Montluel. Anywhere just round there, within a mile or
two."

The squadron-leader who was to pilot him drew a pencil
circle big and black around the place upon the map. "That's
quite okay," he said. "We'll take a Blenheim. If you come
over with me now we'll get you fitted for the parachute, and
then we'll go and have a look at the machine."

The flight-sergeant fitted and adjusted all the heavy webbing
straps around his body. "Now when you come to jump," he
said, "you just counts one—two—three after you starts falling.
Not onetwothree quick—but deliberate, like; one—two—three.
And then you pulls the ring and be sure you pull it right out,
wire and all, case any of it's holding up. And don't go thinking
that you've bust it when it comes away in your hand, because
you haven't."

His manner robbed the business of all fear. Simon had little
difficulty in grasping the technique of landing. There were
obvious risks of injury, but those did not distress him. He
passed on with the squadron-leader to the aircraft where they
met the young sergeant who was to serve as navigator with
them, and for half an hour longer he examined the machine
and the means of getting out of it.

"I shall pull her back to about ninety-five," the pilot said.
"You won't have any difficulty."

With the major from the interrogation centre, he had tea in
the Air Force mess. Then they went back in the car and he met
the brigadier again in the bare little office that had seen all their
business. McNeil had not been idle.

"Fix things up with the Air Force?" he enquired. "It's all
right for to-night, is it? Fine. The sooner you're back in
France the better. Here are your papers."

He passed an envelope across the table. It contained a pass
made out in German and in French, signed by the *Oberstleutnant Commandant* of Le Tréport authorising the bearer, M.
Charles Simon, to pass into Vichy territory for the purpose of

visiting relatives, and to return into the occupied zone within ten days. An oval rubber stamp in purple ink defaced it— *"Vu à l'entrée, Chalon"*, and the date.

Charles studied it carefully. "Is that the real signature?" he asked.

The major smiled. "We got a good deal of his correspondence in the raid."

There was no more to be done, and no more to be said. Charles dined with the major in the mess, and then went up and lay down, fully clothed but for his boots, upon the bed. He lay awake for a considerable time, wondering what lay before him. Presently he grew drowsy and slept for an hour or two.

At one o'clock in the morning they came to wake him. He got up and put on his shoes and went down to the mess; they had thoughtfully prepared for him a drink of hot coffee laced with rum and a few sandwiches. Then he was driven to the aerodrome. On the tarmac the Blenheim was already running up, the exhausts two blue streaks in the blackness of the night.

"All ready?" said the squadron-leader. "Well, let's go."

Charles turned to the major and held out his hand. "I'm terribly grateful for all you've done for me, sir. Don't worry if you don't hear for a month or two. It's going to take a little time."

The other said gruffly: "Wish I was going with you, 'stead of sticking in this blasted job. All the very best of luck."

The pilot and the navigator were already in the Blenheim. Charles was assisted up on to the wing, clumsy in his parachute harness, and settled into the small seat behind them. The hatch was pushed up behind him and snapped shut. The Blenheim moved to a burst of engine, and taxied out into the darkness of the aerodrome.

A few faint lights appeared ahead of them; the engines burst into a roar, and they went trundling down the field. The lights swept past them, the motion grew more violent, then died away to a smooth airborne rush as the lights dropped away beneath them and behind. The pilot bent to the instrument panel and juggled quickly with his massed controls. They swept round in a long gentle turn and steadied on the course for France, climbing as they went.

Charles remembered little of that flight. He sat there for two hours, gradually getting cold, watching the computations and the plotting of the navigator in the dim, shaded cockpit light. In the end the sergeant turned to him. "About ten minutes more," he said. "Are you all ready to go?"

Charles said: "All ready."

The pilot swung round in his seat. "You'll see to land all right," he said. "The moon's just coming up." Charles had watched it rise over the pilot's left shoulder.

The pilot and the navigator conferred together for a moment. Then the sergeant got up from his folding seat and turned round to Charles. "He's going to slow her down," he said. "We'll open the hatch, and I'll help you get out on to the wing. Then when it's time I'll give you a clap on the back . . . and just let go."

The roof hatch dropped down, and the night air blew a keen, cold gale around him. With the assistance of the sergeant he clambered slowly out. The wind tore round him, dragging his legs from the slippery surface of the wing. Far, far below him he could see the dim line of a river and the faint shadow of the woods upon the patterned fields. His heart was pounding in his chest, and he thought: "This is death. I have only a few minutes left to live."

The sergeant, standing in the hatch helping to support in the violence of the rush of air, shouted with his mouth against his ear: "Just take it easy and count one, two, three after you go. Put your hand upon the ring—that's right. Wait, now . . ."

They both stared at the pilot, intent on the instruments. They saw him glance at his watch, and back to the instruments again. Then at his watch. . . . He turned in his seat and nodded, smiled at Charles, and said something which was never heard. The sergeant shouted in his ear: "Okay, and the best of luck. Off you go."

Charles felt the grasp upon his arm released and a heavy clump upon his shoulder. He dared not show his fear. He turned his body to face aft and the wind took him; he slipped, lost his hold, and bumped heavily upon the trailing edge. A dark shadow that was the tail-plane swept over him, and then he was head downwards and rotating slowly, seeing only the dim earth below as the wind rose about him, tearing at his clothes. The fear made an acute pain in his throat.

He forced himself to think, and counted slowly. Then desperately, with all his strength, he pulled the ring. It came and something snapped behind his back; he pulled at the wire following the ring with both his hands. For a sickening moment he went on falling; then came a rustling rush and the harness plucked violently at his shoulders, hurting him with the buckles of the straps. He came erect and saw the sky again; the wind had gone and he was hanging there suspended in the quiet peace of the night. For a few moments he hung limp and shaken, exhausted by his fear.

Presently he regained control of himself, and set to steering the parachute gingerly away from the woods and into open country.

He fell into a pasture field close by a hedge. He fell down heavily on knee, thigh, and shoulder as he had been told to do and got badly shaken up again. The parachute collapsed beside him on the grass. He stayed there for a quarter of an hour, gradually calming down. He was not hurt at all.

Presently he got up, made the parachute and harness into a bundle, and did with it what he had been told to do.

An hour later he walked into his mother's house, with a story that he had walked from Lyons, having come from Paris by the night express.

*　　*　　*　　*　　*

He got back to Corbeil after a few days and settled down to work again. Duchene took his absence as a matter of course, and no word of the raid upon Le Tréport seemed to have penetrated to the factory. Charles fell back easily into his humdrum daily round, and for a time everything went on normally.

Three weeks later he appeared one morning in the office of *M. le directeur,* bearing certain test samples of cement, odd-shaped little twin bulbous bricks. "I regret, monsieur," he said, "that there is trouble with the samples."

They bent over the fractures; they were granulated and short. "These are the figures," said the designer. "See for yourself, monsieur." The failing load of the test-pieces was forty per cent below the specification strength.

Duchene glanced at the figures. "This is very bad," he said. "What is the reason?"

Simon produced a paper bag of powdered cement. "This is the sample." They dipped their fingers in it; the powder was rough and gritty to the touch. "It has passed once only through the kiln," said Duchene. He fingered it again, with forty years' experience behind the touch. "Or—some of it. Half—more than a quarter and less than half—has passed once only. Has any of this stuff gone out?"

Simon said: "This is from Batch CX/684, monsieur. I regret infinitely that much of it has been already shipped. I trust that this is not a true sample of the rest."

The old man bit his lip. "Where did the shipment go to?" he enquired. This was a serious matter for the prestige of the company.

Charles said: "It was sold through Brest. Much of it was shipped to Lorient, and some to Audierne, Douarnenez, and Morgat. It has all gone to the same district."

They discussed the distribution for some little time. It was a major crisis, and most serious to them commercially. "I will ring up the Commission of Control," Duchene said in the end. "They must know about this first of all, and quickly, in case they think that we have made a sabotage. Then they must arrange at the ports that every sack is put in quarantine till we have made a test-piece from that sack and broken it. Every sack is to be tested. I will not take a risk in matters of this sort."

The designer nodded. "I will go and see to it myself," he said. "They cannot say that we are taking this lightly if I go myself to do the tests."

The old man beamed his approval; he was fond of Charles. "That is a very good suggestion," he said. "I will tell the Commission that I am sending my chief engineer to make this inspection. You must be ready to start immediately, and make my apologies to all the commandants concerned. Telegraph immediately what replacements are required."

The Commission were annoyed, and naturally so, but somewhat mollified by the suggestion that the S.A.F.C. de Corbeil proposed to send their chief engineer in person to inspect the defective batch. Half a dozen telegrams were sent without delay isolating the material, and Charles was given all the necessary permits for his journey and told to get off at once. He travelled up next morning to Paris, a city of desolate, dirty streets and closed shops. He lunched sadly in a little restaurant and took the afternoon train for Brittany.

He went first to Brest. At the station he took the common hotel bus, an ancient horse-drawn vehicle, and asked to be put down at the Hôtel Moderne. The driver looked at him curiously. "Monsieur has not visited Brest recently, perhaps?" he said. "The hotel is closed."

He found that it was closed indeed, or rather that it stood wide open to the sky. There was much bomb damage in the town; he was fortunate to get a room in the Hôtel des Voyageurs.

He went to the agent next day, and sat in conference with him for an hour. Monsieur Clarisson was much concerned about the defects of Batch CX/684, and said he could not believe that there was really much wrong with it. He himself had taken samples and had tested them as soon as the news reached him, and all his samples had come out in strength well above specification. The two engineers drank several cups of coffee in the office, bitter stuff tasting of acorns, and gloomed over the samples that Simon had brought with him from Corbeil. Monsieur Clarisson gave Charles the names of all the local German commandants that he would have to see, and expressed his irritation that he would not be able to accompany Monsieur Simon on his trip from town to town along the coast. The German regulations in that part were very strict.

"I should warn you, monsieur," he said confidentially, "that here in Brittany it is necessary to be most discreet." He hesitated. "You will not mind if I say this? Coming from Corbeil, you may not know quite how things are here with us."

Charles nodded. "There are difficulties here?"

The man said: "Not here in Brest. Here we are business people, and we understand that circumstances change. But in the country districts people are more stupid. They are always trying to do things against the Germans, and that makes trouble. In the café, monsieur, they are always talking. You will hear the English radio quite openly." Charles drew in his breath; this was asking for it. "You must be very careful not to get involved in their stupidity. It is trouble—trouble—trouble all the time."

Charles said: "I am deeply grateful, monsieur, for the warning. These places I am going to—Lorient, Audierne, Douarnenez, and Morgat—are they bad?"

The agent said: "Not Lorient, nor Audierne. Morgat is too small for much to happen there. But in Douarnenez, monsieur, it is most difficult. Those fishing people will not understand the new regime. Each week there is some new trouble, each week there is an execution by the Germans, sometimes several. And it has no effect . . . But for the fishing industry and for the food that they bring in, the town would have been bombarded by the Germans from the air, and razed down to the ground. I have heard German officers say so."

"It is as bad as that?"

"It is bad as it could be, monsieur. Life is terrible for people in Douarnenez just now. You must be very, very careful there."

Charles went that afternoon to Lorient, put up at the Hôtel Bellevue, and reported himself next morning to the German commandant. He was coldly received, and was informed that work of great importance was completely stopped. He was questioned sharply about the day that he had spent in Brest: it did not seem to the Germans necessary at all that he should have wasted time in visiting his agent. They gave him a good dressing down, then took him to the harbour in a Renault van

The cement was stacked in heaps in its sacks in a shed over looking the estuary. He set to work with one Breton lad to help him, numbering the sacks, making a sample briquette in a little mould from each sack, and leaving it to dry. He worked all day Once or twice, when nobody was looking, he mingled a little of the sample powder from Corbeil into a briquette.

In the late afternoon he was taken down to see the sacks upon the job. He passed along new quays and under arches of new concrete, stepped over piles of girders and steel reinforcement, walked round great heaps of wooden shuttering. He dared not glance in each direction more than once; that one glance was sufficient, if he could remember. His mind was crowded with the detail he observed. He must, must keep it clear. With each glance he tried to memorise the picture of what lay before him so that he might reconstruct it in the night.

They took him to the ready-use cement store, and he set to work again to make briquettes of the sacks there. As he performed the simple job he indexed in his mind what he had seen. Seven bays each holding two U-boats, held up on columns one metre twenty-five square section, each with two I beams in the centre, each I beam forty-five by fifteen centimetres, wrapped round with twenty-kilogramme reinforcement. Each bay a hundred metres long and twenty metres wide, and six columns to each bay. The weight of roof could be deduced from that alone. But keep that detail in his mind, treasure it. God, let him not forget!

His task finished, he was free to go till the next day; it took twenty-four hours for the briquettes to dry. He walked back up the quays. Fifteen-metre girders, each one metre twenty deep— they would be the longitudinal horizontals between columns. Each girder built of webs and angles, each angle twenty centimetres by twenty, each web twenty-two millimetres thick. Mary, Mother of God, help him to remember!

Shuttering for the arches of the twenty-metre bays—radius of arch thirty to thirty-five metres, each arch about one metre eighty wide. He glanced up casually to the half-completed job, and looked down at the quay. Say two tons eighty of forty kilogramme reinforcement to each arch. Fifty by twelve I beams for the purlins between arches, ten or eleven purlins to each arch. Over the purlins, six layers of twenty-kilogramme reinforcement buried in the concrete of the roof, the layers separated by about fifteen centimetres. Jesus, give him a clear head to sort out and disentangle all that he had seen!

He did not dine that night because food dulls the brain. He went up to his room in the hotel and lay down on the bed, staring at the ceiling in the hard light of the one unshaded lamp. He would not, must not think of anything except design. This was no amateur erection that he had seen. He knew that at a glance. Whoever had designed it had had much experience in structures of that sort. That made Charles Simon's job more possible, for everything would have a reason. Each girder and each column would be made sufficient for the loads imposed upon it and no more; the strength of one part would show him the strength of the rest, when he had understood the matter rightly. And all in turn would lead him to the weight and thickness of the roof, as yet unbuilt, if he could keep a clear mind and remember all that he had seen.

He set himself to find the gaps, the links in the chain of the structure that he had not thought to look at. The list of points that he must memorise to-morrow, his last visit to the quays. Then he got up and wrote in pencil on a little ivorine tablet all the dimensions he had noticed, and set to work to learn what he had written off by heart, as he had learnt poetry when he was a boy at Shrewsbury. Finally, at about midnight, he expunged what he had written from the tablet with a wet corner of his towel, and lay down on his bed, still repeating his lesson to himself. Presently, in the middle of his repetition, he dropped off to sleep. When he woke up at dawn, alert and desperately hungry, he was still repeating it.

He went down to the main cement store later in the day and started to break his briquettes with a little shot weighing machine that he had brought with him. A German officer of Pioneers was there to watch him as he worked. Of about two hundred sacks, seven proved to be defective, with fractures much below the specification strength for the briquette. Charles had the offending sacks sorted out and opened one at the neck. He took a handful of the cement, rubbed it between his fingers, smelt it, and nodded.

He turned to the German officer. "I regret this infinitely, *Herr Oberleutnant,*" he observed. "But there it is. See for yourself."

The German rubbed some in his hands and nodded wisely.

"Such things happen in any factory from time to time," said Charles apologetically. "But all the rest may now be cleared for use."

Seven sacks of perfectly good cement were sent down to the breakwater to form part of the sea wall, sacks and all. Charles was taken down to the ready-use store again.

Footings for the columns seven metres by seven metres, apparently on sand or gravel bottom. A squad of carpenters knocking up one-metre-eighty shuttering—would that be the depth of the roof? Great boxes full of thirty-millimetre bolts—where did they go, what members did they join? And what were all these tons and tons of angles, all fifteen-centimetre angles. Where did they come in? And all those seven-millimetre strips?

In the ready-use store every briquette passed its test well above specification strength, possibly because Charles had been under close supervision the previous afternoon, down there upon the job. The German officer was very pleased, and genuinely cordial as they walked back along the quay.

One last look round. An indication of something similar in a very early stage of construction upon the other side of the river; exactly in a line between the church of Plouarget and the tall chimney at the gasworks. A boom across the entrance to the river between Plouarget and Creusec, turned back for ships to enter, and with one guard-ship. What seemed to be an oil-tanker beside the quay two hundred metres down-stream from the bridge. Five naval motor-launches. Two large twin-engined float seaplanes moored out to buoys. Two salvage ships . . .

He left Lorient that afternoon and went to Audierne. He must go through with his trip in all sincerity, for on the coast of Brittany he was under observation the whole time. There was only a matter of five tons or so to test at Audierne. He condemned three sacks, apologised to the commandant on behalf of the S.A.F.C. de Corbeil, and left for Douarnenez two days later.

It was February, and though the days were beginning to get longer, it was still quite dark by six o'clock. From Audierne to Douarnenez is not much more than fifteen miles, but the direct railway line was closed to all civilian traffic, and Charles had to make a long detour through Quimper. Here he had a long, indeterminate wait upon the station platform for a train that was indefinitely late.

He went into the buffet and drank a cup of bitter coffee. The place was ill-ventilated, smelly and cheerless outside the night was mild, even warm. It was fine and starry. He went out on to the platform and began walking up and down.

Presently he fell into conversation with a priest, a man perhaps fifty years of age, in shabby black canonicals.

They talked as they walked up and down. The priest, Charles learned, was travelling to Douarnenez from a seminary at Pontivy; he was on his way to take up a new cure in the great Church of Ste-Hélène in the middle of the town. He told Charles quite simply the reason for the vacancy that he was to fill. His predecessor had been executed by the Germans.

"You understand," he said ingenuously, "that in my calling one is sometimes in a difficult position, more difficult than I anticipated when as a young man I joined the Order."

In the dim light of the stars Charles glanced curiously at his companion. Was this just the folly of an unworldly old man, or was it—courage? He could not resist the endeavour to find out.

"A middle course is usually possible," he said. He was mindful of the warning that he had received in Brest. "The Germans, after all, are men like ourselves. It is not necessary always to be finding means to irritate them."

The priest said very quietly: "The Germans are not people like ourselves. They are creatures of the Devil, vowed to idolatry, and followers of Mithras. If you deny that, you deceive yourself, my son."

Charles did not wish to argue; they walked a few paces in silence. Then the priest spoke again.

"I am not one of those who consider matters of the earthly sphere," he said. "Our life and our hope of things to come lie not in this world. I do not think it matters very much who exercises dominion over these fields of France, whether our race, or the Germans, or even the English, who in bygone times ruled here for a century. The Church does not concern herself with conquests of that sort. We fight against the conquest of the soul."

Half-heartedly Charles tried to turn the conversation into safer channels. "The Germans have their Lutheran religion," he said. "The English also, and the Americans, and the Dutch. I do not see much difference."

The man said: "The English are not members of the true Church. They worship Jesus Christ in a foolish and misguided way, and as a social usage rather than a true belief. Yet they

47

do worship, and they have no other gods. And so it is with all the other countries that you name. But not with Germany."

"So much the worse for them, father," said Charles.

"You do not understand, my son," the priest replied. "To gain their temporal ends the Germans first destroy the souls of men. The Church thinks little of the temporal end. The Church will fight to save the souls of men from everlasting torment, and by the Grace of God she will emerge victorious."

There was no turning him, Charles thought. There were few people on the platform in the night, and none at all at the far end beneath the signal lights, where they were pacing up and down under the stars.

"Lies and deceit in every form," said the old priest. "Sexual immorality weakening the body, bribery, false witness, selfishness, corruption, sloth, and all the petty minor sins that weaken character. These are the things that Germany has sown in Frenchmen, save in small corners of the country such as we have here. These are the weapons with which Germany fights wars. First they destroy the souls of men and then they occupy the country. Against that we are set; against that we will fight.

"And do not think," he said, "that these things come from facile cleverness called Propaganda. All in this world, my son, descends from God, or it ascends from Satan in the Pit. These things that I have spoken of, these things that Germany has put into the souls of Frenchmen, do not come from God, whose servant I have been for forty years. They come from Satan and his messenger at Berchtesgaden."

They walked on in silence for a minute. Charles was deeply impressed, yet with shrewd realism it seemed to him that there might be another vacancy at Douarnenez before so very long.

"These things are bred of sheer idolatry and witchcraft," the priest said presently. "They have cast out and persecuted their own Lutherans. They make sacrifices of living goats to Satan on their hill-tops in the night; they bow down to the false gods of war, to Mithras and Moloch. In their unholy Sabbaths they sit down in conference, and from their conference are born the sins and infamies that they now call political warfare. But these are works of Satan; black magic, and the products of the Pit."

A little wind swept past them in the starry night. Charles said: "But, father, what can simple people do?"

"Pray to Almighty God in all humility," the old priest said. "Turn to the Faith, and watch that you fall not into the pit that has been digged for you."

They paced up and down in silence for a few minutes. A cool, fresh wind blew inland from the sea; the stars were very bright and quiet above. "Mother Church," the old man said at last, "has given us no guidance upon the matter temporal. Yet age by age the wisdom of the Church remains unaltered, my son. There is not one truth in one century, and then another in a later age. Truth, and the Laws of God, endure through all the ages of the world. That is so, is it not?"

Charles said quietly: "That is true. If it were otherwise we should be lost indeed."

The old man nodded his agreement. "Each one of us must seek for his own guidance, and at Pontivy in my retreat I have spent many, many days and weeks praying to God for guidance on the road that I must tread. And presently, my son, it was revealed to me that since Truth must endure it is not necessary for guidance to be given more than once. Mother Church speaks once, and that truth then endures through all the ages of the years for those who seek in humbleness to find it."

They paced on. Charles did not speak.

The priest said: "So humbly, and in long, long hours of prayer I sought for guidance in the matter temporal, where evil men are dominant, perverting the souls of men for their own ends by sorcery and the black arts that they have studied to perform. And presently I saw that this was no new thing, this struggle against heresy arising from the East. Black magic and the foul infamies of Satan have arisen in past ages, and in past ages Holy Church has called up spiritual powers, and weapons temporal, to beat them down. It is all in the old books, for those to whom faith gives the faculty of understanding."

Charles said: "I have not gained that faith, father, nor that understanding." He spoke very quietly. "Is there a weapon temporal for me?" As he spoke there came a fleeting image of the man in Brest and of the warnings that he had received. He knew himself to be venturing among great risks, and he dismissed them from his mind.

The old man said: "I do not know, my son. Yet in past centuries the Church wielded one great cleansing weapon against heresy and infamy and all idolatry, a weapon that sweeps all before it, before which Anti-Christ and all the devils of the Pit recoil. That in past ages was the wisdom of the Church, my son. It is the wisdom still."

"What is this weapon temporal, then, father?"

The priest said: "It is fire."

49

He turned and faced Charles Simon. "So in the past the Holy Inquisition fought the battle against heresy, idolatry, and witchcraft, with faith in God and with the weapon temporal of fire. With that faith and that weapon they beat down the devils seeking to destroy the souls of men. Through that faith and that weapon men's souls may again be saved from all the dangers that beset them now."

The priest, facing him, laid his hand upon the designer's arm. "That is the truth of God," he said. "For the weak in faith there is an evidence." He dropped his voice and glanced round furtively. "Listen, my son, and I will tell you what I know."

In the dim light they bent together. "There was a brother of my Order," said the priest. "He was in Belgium, at Ostend, in September last, four months after the Occupation. For those four months he watched the Germans as they trained their troops to sail in barges for the invasion of England—men and guns and motor-bicycles and cars and tanks, and men again, all entering and disembarking from the barges. And finally, my son, the day arrived—September the 16th."

Charles said in a whisper: "What happened then?"

"God in His mercy laid His hand upon the English," the priest whispered in the dark. "They are not of the true Faith, but the Lord God is generous to all sincere misunderstanding, and He led them to the weapon temporal. The barges were three hours from land when British bombers of the Royal Air Force came upon them and dived on the barges, dropping upon them drums of oil and small incendiary bombs. Wave upon wave of aeroplanes came out from England strong in the power of the Lord, oil and incendiary bombs, oil and bombs. And the drums burst on the barges and the oil flowed into them, and the bombs set all on fire so that they blazed fiercely on the water, and the English dropped more oil into the flames."

Charles drew in his breath sharply.

The priest drew back a little. "For ten whole days the bodies came ashore upon the beaches," he said in a low tone. "Choked in the blazing oil, burned, suffocated, and drowned in their vile sins and infamy. Hundreds upon hundreds of them, every day, and the Germans buried them among the sand-hills of the beaches like dead animals, that none might know how they had met their end. Yet it was known all over Belgium and all through the German armies of the Netherlands within a day."

There was a short silence. "Before that power of fire all powers of heresy, idolatry, and witchcraft must recoil," the old

50

man said. "It is not given to us to understand the choice of the Lord's instruments, why He revealed His mercy to the English rather than to us, any more than it is given to us to understand His choice of the Hebrew race in ages past. I only know that by that temporal power the Germans suffered a defeat, the first that they have suffered in this war. Before that power the powers of Mithras were thrown back."

He bent close again. "There was a mutiny," he said in a low tone. "A mutiny in the German Army, because the Nazis ordered that the troops should sail again for England. And there was mutiny . . . it is true what I say. A hundred officers and men were shot in Antwerp at the rifle-range on September the 29th. And after that, and gradually, the troops were moved away."

They turned and resumed their pacing up and down. "The lesson of the ages has been taught again," the priest said quietly. "No other weapon purges evil from the earth and rids men from their bondage to the powers of darkness. Only the simple elementals can avail against the elemental foe—faith in the Power of God and in the cleansing power of fire."

The train came shortly after that. They got into a crowded third-class carriage and travelled together to Douarnenez. At the station their ways diverged; before turning into the Hôtel du Commerce Charles stopped his companion.

'What is your name, father?" he enquired.

"Augustine," said the old man. "Augustine of the Church of Ste-Hélène."

In the hotel Charles went up to his room, washed, and went down to the dining-room for a late meal of tunny fish, garnished with onions and potatoes. As he was eating a steam hooter from a factory near-by blew a long blast, taken up all over the town by other sirens. A number of people came hurriedly into the hotel from the street.

Charles asked the waitress: "Is that the air-raid warning?"

She said: "It is the same hooter. But that is for the curfew."

It was half-past eight. "One has a curfew here?" he enquired.

She nodded. "You must not go outside now, in the street. Or, if you have to go, go very carefully in rope-soled shoes and be prepared to run for it. They shoot if they see you, but they do not shoot well."

Charles said that he was tired and thought that he would stay at home.

He went down to the café after dinner, bought a bock, and

settled down to read his paper. The *patron* and his family were there and a few travellers; presently they turned on the radio and tuned it to the British news in French. They heard of fresh advances by the Greeks into Albania and the news of the British entry into Benghazi. That was before we got chased out again.

Presently the *patron* came over to the table at which Charles was sitting. He was a heavy man of about forty-five, but still vigorous. He said: "Monsieur is not from these parts?"

Charles shook his head. "This is the first time I have visited Douarnenez. I come from Corbeil, in Seine et Oise."

The man said: "Then, possibly, monsieur would drink a glass upon the house to celebrate his first visit to Douarnenez?"

Charles was very pleased, and they settled down together with the Pernod. Presently he told the innkeeper that he had travelled from Quimper with a priest called Father Augustine.

The man said: "So, he has arrived?" His face grew black. "The father told monsieur, perhaps, the reason for the vacancy?"

Charles said gently: "Not in detail. I know that you have had great trouble here, monsieur."

"And there will be more." There was a short, grim pause.

"I will tell you about that," the man said presently. "In Seine et Oise, from all I hear, you are great friends with the Germans, but it is not so here. In August thirty people of this town were shot—thirty, in two batches, in one day. Two cousins of my own and my wife's brother. What do you think of that?" He bent towards Charles, trembling with anger.

The designer said: "It is terrible."

"One day, presently, when they are weak and beaten, we shall get at them with axes and with billhooks," the innkeeper said.

He drew back. "I was telling you. Our children are not very well in hand," he said. "It is understandable, that. There was a boy of nine—a little boy, monsieur—a bad boy whose father is at Toulon with the fleet. A bad boy, monsieur—but a child still, you will understand. It was his way to go out in the dark night in the curfew and pick up the horse droppings in the street. Then he would creep up in the darkness to a sentry and fling what he had collected in the German's face and run. Many times he did that."

Charles nodded. It was not a very edifying tale.

The man said: "One night, as he ran, there was another

52

sentry in the way with a fixed bayonet. He lunged at little Jules as he came running past, monsieur, and he ran him through the chest beneath the left shoulder. Then the two sentries together had to pull his little body off the bayonet. Then, one took each arm and they walked him between them towards German head-quarters in the market-place. All the way, monsieur, he was coughing up his blood. We found it on the *pavé* in the morning. But he was not dead."

Charles did not speak.

"Father Zacharias was our *curé* then," the innkeeper went on. "He also was out that night, but that was allowed, for he had taken the last Sacrament to a sick woman. There was a moon that night, and in the Rue Jean Marat he met the German soldiers as they dragged the little one along between them, and he stopped them and upbraided them, ordering them to take him into the first house and go to fetch a doctor. All this was heard, monsieur, by Marie Lechanel outside whose house they stopped. There was a great pool of blood there in the morning to prove her story, where they stopped and argued."

He paused. "They would not listen. The father grew angry, and he said: 'If you do not release that little one and fetch a doctor for him, the Fire of Heaven shall come down and strike you, and you will perish unshrived in your sin.' But they would not listen. They said: 'We are taking him to the officer. He will make an example of this one.'

"And Father Zacharias said: 'I shall come with you, and if that boy dies you both shall be denounced as murderers.' So he went with them to headquarters of the Gestapo, monsieur. And in the night, there in a prison, the little boy Jules died, monsieur. And they took Father Zacharias away to Rennes in a motor-car, and three days later he was shot for treason, and for inciting the people to revolt. That was the reason that they gave, and there was not one word of truth in it—at least, not that the Germans knew."

Charles Simon said gently: "I am desolated, monsieur. This is very, very bad."

"Aye," said the man heavily. "It is bad indeed here in Douarnenez."

A quarter of an hour later, after another glass of Pernod, the innkeeper said: "I was in Brest, monsieur, when the English left. It was incredible to us, you understand—unreal. I had stopped for a glass down in the Port du Commerce at the Abri de la Tempête. There were still English ships in the harbour, and two officers of the Royal Navy came in also to drink a glass. And I went and asked them, monsieur, if it was true that the English were going away and leaving us.

"And one of them said: 'It is true indeed. It is now three days since you have signed an armistice with the Germans and we must go, for we are going on with this war even if you are not.' And three women in the café began sobbing, monsieur . . . That was the start of our bad time."

Next day Charles reported to the German commandant, and was taken to the cement store, where he worked all morning taking samples from about fifteen tons of cement in stock. He discovered that there was no cement at Morgat, since all distribution took place through Douarnenez; this meant that when he left the fishing port he would be able to go back to Corbeil.

He returned to the hotel for *déjeuner* and was free for the rest of the day; his samples took twenty-four hours to set hard. He wandered down to the harbour in the afternoon; it was a warm, sunny day of early spring. He was very fond of ships and shipping, and deeply interested in fishing-boats. For a time he stood and watched the sardine-boats and tunnymen from the quay. Presently, with a chance word and a cigarette, he was down in one of the sardine-boats helping a deft-fingered, gruff old man called Bozellec to find the holes in a blue gossamer net.

He stayed there for two hours, and in that time he learned the whole operation of the sardine fleet. A German *Raumboot* came in from the sea, turned the end of the sea wall, and came alongside, just astern of them; Charles studied her with all the interest of an amateur yachtsman. The old fisherman looked at her for a moment, saw that a German officer was noticing him, and spat ostentatiously into the sea before resuming his work. The sun beat down upon them on the boat, pleasantly warm. As they worked on, Charles learned the tactics of the *Raumboot*. Presently he awoke to the value of what was being told to him and set to work to memorise the facts, and to fill in the gaps in his information by direct questions.

The job finished, they strung their net up to the mast-head to dry and air. "A little glass, perhaps?" Charles said.

A little glass, the old man thought, would be a very good idea. They got up on to the quay and walked to the Café de la République overlooking the harbour.

They went in and sat down, and Charles ordered Pernod for them both. He told his companion a little of himself, and

54

of the defects of the batches of cement. And presently he said casually:

"Do you have much trouble with the Germans here?"

"No more than any other lice," the old man said.

There was a short silence. "Lice," the old man said again, "and as lice we treat them. I have told them so."

Charles said: "Is it . . . wise to say things of that sort to them?"

The fisherman shrugged his shoulders. "The other night," he said, "in the boat we had a *Bootsmannsmaat*, a German, as a guard, and so we had the shade over our lamp. And this man said to me, what would I do when the war ended? Would I go on fishing? So I told him what I would do, in memory of my dead brother who was murdered. I said that I would put on my best clothes and go to watch the young men tie the Germans up in bundles and pour petrol over them and light the petrol. That is the way to deal with lice, I said. With a blow-lamp."

Charles stared at him. "Does one talk so to the Germans in Douarnenez?"

"He started it," the old man said. "He asked me what I was going to do, and I told him."

There was nothing to be said to that, and Charles sat on in the café, smoking and talking, till the hooter sounded for the curfew. He heard all that he wanted of the life of the town. It was a sad, pitiful tale, of desperate insults on the one side, of mass executions and torture on the other. It was a town in which the Germans seldom ventured out alone or without arms, a town in which each glint of light in the black-out received an instant shot from rifle or revolver. It was a town of sullen hate and brooding superstition, a town turning in despair to the old country spells and witchcraft for help against the oppressor. They did not hesitate to let the Germans know of these activities, moreover. Charles heard a story of a little waxen figure of the German commandant, finished and painted with the greatest care, found on the *Oberstleutnant's* desk one morning. The feet of the little image were partially melted away, and the bowels were transfixed with a pin; it was common knowledge that the *Oberstleutnant* suffered from gout and from an internal disorder.

The truth of what he had been told in Brest was evident to Charles. This town continued to exist simply and solely because the Germans could not do without the food that it produced. But for that fact the Germans would have wiped out every house. The people of the town knew this quite well. They played their cards up to the limit, venting their scorn and hate upon the Germans in a thousand ways and purchasing immunity with the loads of tunny and sardines that they brought in.

At curfew Charles went back to his hotel. He slept little that night; once or twice he heard the sound of shots that echoed down the streets. There was an atmosphere of brooding evil over all the place that left him utterly appalled: in his experience of France after the occupation he had come on nothing similar to this in any way.

Next day he broke his samples of cement and condemned four sacks, made his report and the apologies of the firm to the commandant, and left for Paris on the midday train. He got there very late at night, turned into a small hotel, and slept heavily and well.

On the following morning he went for coffee to the Café de l'Arcade in the Boulevard de Sévigné. The head waiter served him, an elderly man with a drooping grey moustache. He wore a faded green dress suit.

Charles said: "That is a handsome suit that you have on to-day. It only needs one thing to set it off. If I wore that I should want to have red buttons on the coat."

The man shot a quick glance around the room. Then he said quietly:

"Monsieur Simon, I presume."

*　　　*　　　*　　　*　　　*

Charles Simon landed in England forty-eight hours later. He had spent part of the intervening time in the cellar of the Café de l'Arcade, and he had spent part of it beside the driver of a German ammunition lorry, going north. In the dark night he had commenced his flight and had landed shortly before dawn at an aerodrome in Berkshire, a very frightened man.

A subaltern was there to meet him with a car. He was given a light meal of sandwiches and coffee in the mess, and in the early light of dawn they started on the road. It was February, and a wet, windy dawn; the air was cold and raw. They spoke very little in the car. Once the subaltern passed him a silver hunting-flask of whisky and they both took a long drink; the neat spirit heartened him, and he felt better for it.

At about ten o'clock they drove up to the same dilapidated old country house that he had been taken to before, full of the same soldiers. It seemed to him that he had hardly been away

56

a day, though it was a full two months since he had been there. He was taken into the same mess and given breakfast. Then he was shown into the same bare little office, and interviewed by the same major and the same *capitaine* of the Free French.

The major rose and shook his hand; the *capitaine* rose and bowed stiffly from the waist. The major said: "Did you get to Lorient?"

The designer nodded. "I was there on Thursday of last week."

"And did you see the shelters?"

He said: "I saw the shelters." Very briefly he outlined to them an account of his journey through Brittany. "I think I saw all that you want to know," he said.

The major passed a sheet of paper across to him, with a pencil. "You'd better sit there quietly, and put down the details of the structure."

The designer demurred. "I cannot think like that," he said. "Even if I could, that way would not be useful to your engineers. Get me a drawing-board and a T-square, and a good roll of tracing-paper. In twenty-four hours you shall have proper working drawings of the thing that any engineer can understand."

They got him these things in an hour or two, and gave him a table in a quiet office. He took the tools of his profession eagerly; they made him feel at home. He spread the backing-paper with a light heart and pinned it down, spread the thin tracing-paper, and began to work.

He worked on till he was called for lunch, snatched a quick meal, and went back to the board. He was happy as he worked that afternoon, unburdening his memory and putting it all down on paper. As the lines of the structure grew before him the pieces of the puzzle fell together; it was quite clear now to him what the fifteen-centimetre angles did and where the seven-milli-metre strips came in. They filled the missing links of structure, evident now that it was down in hard, neat pencil lines, in black and white.

From time to time the officers came in and stood behind him, watching the drawings growing under his neat fingers. They brought him tea and pieces of cake to the drawing-board; he would not stop again to eat. In the early evening Brigadier McNeil came in and Simon had to stand up at the board to answer a few questions and expound the drawing; it irked him to interrupt the currents of his thought, but he did not dare to offend the man who had promised to secure him a commission as a British officer.

The brigadier looked critically at what he had done. "The Air Ministry must have a print of this immediately . . ." He paused, running his eye over the unfinished details. "You make a beautiful drawing, Mr. Simon."

The designer smiled faintly. "Is it good enough," he asked anxiously, "to get me a commission in the Royal Engineers?"

The hard, china-blue eyes of the brigadier looked at him, noting the lean, intelligent face, the straight black hair, the quick, rather nervous movements of the artist hands. "I think it is," he said. "I'll get a paper going about that to-morrow, Mr. Simon."

"Thank you, sir." He hesitated. "I really do know a good bit about coastal fortifications that might be useful to you." He turned again to the drawing and became immersed in it; the officers watched him for a time and then left him to his work.

He worked on far into the night. At about two in the morning he finished the third and last sheet of details, drew a border round the edge, and handed in the lot to the British major. Together they put them in an envelope and gave them to the despatch rider; then Charles was taken to a bedroom. In a quarter of an hour he was deeply asleep, exhausted and relieved of the burden of his work.

They left him to sleep late. At about ten o'clock in the morning he awoke and lay for a few minutes staring round the darkened room, till he remembered where he was. Then he got up and went down to the mess, and managed to secure a cup of coffee. It embarrassed him to find that he had no money whatsoever, barring unnegotiable francs, as he discovered on asking for a packet of cigarettes. He went to find the major in his office.

An hour later they had him in for another interview, the major and Brigadier McNeil. This time they wanted a complete account of everything that he had seen and done in France since he had made his parachute descent. He told them everything that he could remember.

At the end the brigadier said thoughtfully: "Douarnenez seems to be in a queer state."

Charles said: "It is a town that is going mad."

The major said: "What do you mean by that?"

The designer shrugged his shoulders helplessly. "I don't know that that's the right word to use. But they don't seem like ordinary people there, at all. They don't seem to think in the same way, even." He paused, noticing that neither of the soldiers really understood what he was driving at. "I mean, like when that old man said you had to deal with lice with a blow-lamp. . . ." His voice tailed off into silence.

The brigadier said: "Their minds seem to run on fire. The priest at the railway station, and your fisherman both talked of fire."

"And the little waxen image of the commandant," said the major. "That had its feet melted away—by fire."

There was a little silence. The brigadier said: "Can you imagine anything behind this talk of fire?"

Charles shook his head. "I think it's simply hate," he said. "Burning and scorching are the most painful, the most horrible things that they could do to Germans, so their minds are running in that way. And in the background of their minds that thought of fire, subconscious, colours everything they do or say. I tell you, sir, they aren't like ordinary chaps."

The brigadier nodded. "That's probably the truth of it. We'll just have to leave it at that."

I do not know a great deal about the next three months of Charles Simon's life. He was commissioned almost immediately into the Royal Engineers as a first lieutenant, and shortly after-wards he was promoted to captain. He worked for a time at Chatham upon coast-defence projects, but the next thing I really know about his movements is that he was sent down to Dart-mouth, at the beginning of May.

He had a job of work to supervise there on the foreshore, just outside the mouth of the harbour. What it was I do not know. It kept him down there for about a month, and for that time he lived in a billet half-way up the hill towards St. Petrox.

He was still slightly uneasy in his uniform, though desper-ately proud of it. He knew that he was foreign in his ways and he sought out the company of other officers to study them. Dartmouth at that time was stiff with officers, mostly young naval officers who came into town each evening from trawlers and M.L.s. The Royal Sovereign on the quay was the hotel they favoured most, and Simon was usually to be found in a remote corner of the bar, sipping a pint of heavy English beer, watching, and learning. He did not very often talk to anybody.

He was there after dinner one warm summer night, sitting in his usual corner. The bar was nearly empty and a little group

59

of R.N.V.R. officers near him were chatting about their work. One of them came from a destroyer, fresh from a sweep over to the other side.

"Never saw a Jerry plane the whole time," he said. "I don't know what's become of them."

"Got them all over in the East," somebody said. "He's going to go for Russia."

"Wouldn't be such a fool."

The first speaker said: "We went right close in shore, east of the Ile Vierge. You could see the people working in the fields and everything. Broad daylight, it was."

"See any Jerries? '

"Not a sausage."

Somebody said: "Did the people you saw look downtrodden and oppressed beneath the Nazi heel, like it says in the *Times*?"

The first speaker took a drink of beer. "They looked just like any other people in the fields. I don't believe the occupation means a thing to them. Not to the ordinary run of people in France."

The Army captain in the corner stirred a little, but he did not speak.

"I don't suppose it does," another said. "I don't suppose they know there's a war on—any more than our farm labourers over here do."

"Ours know it all right," said another. "And how! Three quid a week I see they're going to get."

Somebody said: "It'll be just the same over on the other side. Farm labourers always do well in a war. Win, lose, or draw— they get their cut all right."

"So does everybody else. Look at the chaps in the aeroplane factories. They're the ones that make this shortage of beer."

The barmaid pushed half a dozen brimming tankards to them across the bar. One of the naval officers threw down a ten-shilling note, and harked back to the subject.

"I wish one knew what it was really like over there," he said thoughtfully. "Tantalising, just seeing it and coming away."

Probably it was the beer; he had already had two pints. Charles Simon stood up suddenly. "I'll tell you what it's like upon the other side," he said vehemently. "It is terrible, and horrible. You cannot know how terrible it is."

They all turned to stare at him, a little startled at the queer choice of words and at the foreign accent, always more noticeable in moments of excitement.

One said: "I suppose it must be pretty bloody for them."
He thought the Army chap had had quite sufficient beer, and
wanted to conciliate him.

Simon said: "Even so, you fellows do not understand. It
it . . . simply foul. I will tell you." He stood there before
them, the dark hair falling down over his forehead, deadly
serious and rather embarrassing to them. "In Douarnenez, in
January of this year, only four months ago. Only just across
the sea from here—a hundred and thirty miles, no more. There
was a little boy of nine called Jules that used to pick up—what
you call it? Droppings of the horse, and throw them at the
German sentry in the night." There were faint smiles all round,
and somebody said: "Red hot!" Simon went on: "And they
ran him through the body with a bayonet, but he did not die,
and the priest who came by told them to fetch a doctor, but
they would not. And in the night, in prison, the little boy,
he died. And three days later they shot the priest also, because
he would not keep quiet."

In the bar, dim with cigarette smoke, the impact of this story
left a silence. Somebody said: "Who told you that?"

"It is true," said Charles. "I tell you—cross my heart. I
was there only a month after. I heard everything."

Another said curiously: "Are you French, sir?"

Charles said: "I am a British subject. But I have worked
in France for many, many years—oh, the hell of a time. I was
at school at Shrewsbury. And I tell you chaps, if you think
that things go easily there, over on the other side in Brittany,
you are making the hell of a mistake. It is not Vichy, that."

They clustered round him. "Will you have a drink, sir?"

"Did you say that you were over there in February?"

He said: "Oh, thank you. Half a pint of beer."

"Did you mean, February of *this* year?"

Charles, said: "My French tongue slipped away with me.
What I said was true, you chaps, but we will now forget it.
Excuse me, please. . . ."

He stayed with them for half an hour, but resolutely refused
to talk about the other side. He talked to them about the war
in France, and about the French Army and the French Fleet,
and enjoyed their evident pleasure in him as a mystery man.
And then, feeling that he had drunk as much beer as he could
carry satisfactorily, he left them and went out on to the quay.

There was still an hour and a half before dark, in the long
daylight hours of war-time England. He strolled on idly beside

the river, and presently turned to a step behind him. It was a lieutenant in the R.N.V.R., one of the officers who had listened to him in the bar.

This was a tall young man, not more than twenty-four or twenty-five years old, with red hair and the pale skin that goes with it, and a strained, puckered look about his face.

He said: "Look, sir. I want to have a word with you. I was in the pub just now, and I heard what you said about the other side. Do you mind if we have a chat some time?"

There was an urgency in his manner that compelled attention. Charles said: "Right-oh. I do not think that I can talk very much myself, you understand. But if you wish to talk to me, I am entirely at your service."

They turned, and strolled along together. "I want to say first that I know what you said is true," said the young man. "The Germans do that sort of thing. They do it for a policy, because they think it makes people afraid. And if we mean to win this war we must do horrible, beastly things to them. Torturing things, like they have done to us."

Charles glanced at the strained face of the young man beside him, interested. He had not heard that sort of talk since he had come from France.

"So . . ." he said quietly.

"There's a thing going on down here," the young man said in a low tone, "that one or two of us are trying to work up. But we've never been able to find anyone who could tell us what things are like on the other side. If we let you in on what we want to do, will you keep it under your hat?"

"Of course. And I will give what help I can. But there are matters that I cannot talk about, you understand."

The naval officer hesitated. "Look," he said. "It won't take more than half an hour. I want you to come across the river with me and see a boat. Would you do that? And then we can talk over there, where it's quiet."

They went down to the ferry close at hand. As they were crossing the young man said: "My name is Boden, sir—Oliver Boden. I'm in a trawler here."

3

OLIVER BODEN was the son of a wool-spinner in Bradford. George Boden, his father, was well known in the West

Riding as a very warm man and the firm that he founded in his youth, Boden and Chalmers, as a very warm firm. Henry Chalmers was, of course, the young man's godfather.

The two partners, in fact, exchanged the function of god-father fairly frequently; George Boden having two girls and three boys and Henry Chalmers having three girls and one boy. The Chalmers lived in a large greystone house in Ilkley and the Bodens lived in a large greystone house in Burley-in-Wharfedale. The Chalmers, having mostly girls, had a hard tennis-court and the Bodens, having mostly boys, had a river running through their garden. Each of the partners took five thousand a year out of the business as a matter of course, and each lamented the disastrous state of the wool trade.

They were very happy people.

The partners used to stop on the way home sometimes, and drink a couple of pints of beer at a roadside pub, while their expensive motor-cars grew cold outside. It was at these times of relaxation that they swapped stories about newly-married couples, did their football pools, and talked about the education of their children. They were quite agreed about the boys. Boys had to work, there must be no nonsense about educating them. None of the Eton and Harrow stuff for the young Bodens or the young Chalmers. The boys would have to work in Bradford all their lives; it would only unsettle them to put ideas into their heads. Chalmers favoured Leeds High School for his sons and Boden favoured Bradford Grammar School, but they agreed that there was not much in it.

About the girls they were completely at sea. Each of them felt, inarticulately, that only the very best was good enough for the girls, but what the best was they were not quite sure. Henry Chalmers, turning in his perplexity to the guidance that had never failed him, came to the conclusion that since the best goods cost most money, Crowdean School near Lympne, on the south coast of England, must be the best school in the country for girls. He sent all three of them there. They came out four years later polished till they shone, but thanks to the sturdy simplicity of their parents, quite unspoilt.

Boden, yielding in his perplexity to the opinions of his wife, sent his two to an academy for young ladies in Harrogate. Then, at the age of sixteen, he sent them to a finishing school at Lausanne in Switzerland, for two years. He spent the next ten years kicking himself for a mug.

Oliver Boden, the second son, was born in 1916. He started

working in the business in the autumn of 1934 when he was eighteen years old; to console him for the loss of liberty he was given a Norton motor-bicycle, capable of an incredible speed. The first day he had it he rushed round on it to show it to Marjorie Chalmers, then fifteen years old and home on holiday from Crowdean. He always wanted to show things to Marjorie. She went off on the back of it with him far up into the hills, to Malham Tarn among the bleak crags and the moorlands. It was a fine, exciting day. They were late home for tea.

During the years that followed he showed Marjorie a twelve-bore shot-gun, a Harley Davidson motor-bicycle, a trout fly-rod, a Jantzen swimming-suit, a Brough Superior motor-bicycle, the inside of the Piccadilly Hotel in London, a Morgan three-wheeler, most of the dance-halls in Yorkshire, and how not to fly an aeroplane. He showed her everything he got as soon as he got it, and she was always interested. The parents looked on with amused resignation. It was quite obvious to everybody what was going to happen, and most satisfactory The wool trade was built up on unions like that.

It was in 1936, I imagine, that he took to racing outboard motor-boats. He had a little thing more like a tea-tray than a boat that the two of them could just squeeze into, with a very large racing engine pivoted on the stern. To get it moving Boden used to open out the engine full and then stand up and rock it up on to the step, while Marjorie lay out upon the curved deck of the bow to bring the weight forward. Then it got going and they grabbed the steering-wheel, slipped back on to the thwart, and went flying down the river to the first turning-point. They raced a good deal, that summer. Frequently they upset at a turn and had to swim ashore; each time that happened the engine took a long drink of cold water at six thousand revs and had to be rebuilt. They thought it was tremendous fun.

Islanders have curious traits in them that break out in the oddest places. Neither the Bodens nor the Chalmers ever had much truck with the sea; for generations they had lived and worked in the West Riding. But presently it came to Oliver and Marjorie that there were more amusing ways of playing with the water than just flying over it upon a skimming-dish before a racing engine. Somewhere or other they saw a fourteen-foot International sailing dinghy, a beautiful, neat, delicate little thing, and longed for it with all their souls. The skimming-dish went on to the scrap-heap; in 1937 Boden got his dinghy and learned to sail it, more or less, before Marjorie came home for the holidays. It was another thing for him to show her, that, and a new electric razor.

Racing the dinghy took them to the tideway, and they began to learn something about mud and moorings and gum-boots. And presently, one day in September, they were staring thoughtfully at a two-and-a-half-ton sloop, a little yacht in miniature. She was Bermudian-rigged and had a little engine and a little cabin with a little galley, and berths for two. She was not much bigger than the dinghy, really.

"You could go anywhere in her," Oliver said thoughfully "I mean, you could sail her round to Bridlington or Scarborough."

Marjorie said: "Do you think one'd be sick?"

"I don't know. I wouldn't mind trying. You'd have to have charts and things."

"And a sextant," said Marjorie. "That's what they have in books."

They crawled all over it, opening all the lockers, examining the warp and anchor, enormous to their eyes. They were enchanted with the little boat. "It would be good fun to have a thing like this," said Oliver. "Fancy anchoring off somewhere for the night, and getting up and cooking breakfast in the morning!"

"All very well for you to talk like that,' said his young woman. "I'd never hear the last of it from Mummy."

They stared at each other in consternation. Both of them realised that they were up against a major difficulty. They always had done things together in the holidays, ever since they could remember. One day, they both knew, it was extremely probable that they would marry, but that time was not yet. It seemed such a soft, unenterprising thing to do to go and marry the kid next door, just because you'd known each other all your lives.

"We could get over that one somehow," said Boden unconvincingly. "Anyway, there's an awful lot of day sailing we could do."

The International dinghy went, and by the Christmas holidays he had his little yacht. She was all new and shining, with stiff white sheets and halliards, and tanned sails. She was laid up that holiday, but they had fun with her all the same. They called her *Sea Breeze*, a name which they considered was original, and were only slightly dashed when someone showed them seven others in Lloyd's Register. They bought charts of the Humber and the Yorkshire coast, and binnacles, and patent logs, and signal flags, and a foghorn, and distress flares, and all the books that they could find in Yorkshire dealing with yacht cruising. They had a fine time that holiday, quite as good as if they had been sailing.

Sea Breeze was laid up at Hornsea, rather more than eighty miles from Ilkley. If anything, that made her more attractive still. Two or three days each week—the firm was generous to young Oliver Boden during the school holidays—he would get up at half-past six and drive over to Ilkley. A sleepy maid would let him into the big greystone house, and Marjorie would come down and they would drink a cup of tea. And then they would start off. He had a little Aston Martin at that time, a two-seater very low upon the ground and capable of a high speed, pretty with French blue paint and chromium plate. In the half-light they would set off with a thunderous exhaust and step on it to York, where they used to stop for breakfast at the Station Hotel. Then on to Hornsea, to paddle about in gumboots all the day, painting and varnishing and doing minor carpentry. They would have tea in Hornsea and be back in Ilkley by seven o'clock, in time to change their clothes and join a party to go dancing at the Majestic in Leeds. They were never tired.

The Easter holidays came round, and the fitting-out season, and the spring. They got *Sea Breeze* afloat before Easter, and for a week the firm saw nothing of young Oliver. He was over at Hornsea every day, ecstatic at his new possession, and every day Marjorie went with him, because there was always something new that he wanted to show her. And if he wanted to show her something, she just had to go. It always had been like that, ever since they could remember.

But there were complications now.

It occurred to Oliver Boden that his Marjorie had changed, disturbingly. All his life he had taken her for granted; she was just Marjorie, somebody that he might marry one day if he couldn't find anybody more exciting and if she didn't marry someone else. He could hardly have described her, unless to say that she had short brown hair and danced quite well. He knew she smoked De Reszke minor cigarettes, because that was what he paid her when he lost bets with her, and he knew that she liked ices, but that was all he really knew about her tastes.

Now, rather to his own embarrassment, he found himself glancing furtively at her long, slim, silk-stockinged legs as she got into the car, at the line of her figure, and at the nape of her neck. She had filled out since Christmas and had changed a lot; she was nearly nineteen and she was leaving school at the end of the summer term. She was learning to wear pretty clothes. She was still the same old Marjorie, but Boden was forced to admit that she was turning into a very pretty girl, and a most disturbingly attractive one. He did not know what might not happen if the night was warm, and the moon shining on the water, and soft music in the distance; certainly something that he had never before associated with Marjorie.

It was all very difficult.

They did a good deal of sailing together during the Easter holidays, in short, timid ventures of an hour or two on calm days between Hornsea and Bridlington, and they did a good deal of dancing. Then Marjorie went back to Crowdean in the south to complete her education, and Boden began to venture farther each week-end upon the deep. Sometimes he took young Freddie Chalmers with him, Marjorie's brother, but Freddie was frankly bored by sailing and only came for the sake of driving the Aston Martin. By the end of the summer term they had worked the little yacht round to Brough haven, in the Humber. That was in the summer of 1938.

Marjorie came home then for good, and as soon as Oliver Boden set his eyes on her he knew, deep down inside him, that there would probably be trouble before the summer was out. Marjorie's mother had the same feeling, and for all I know Marjorie had it herself, but nobody seemed to be able to do much about it. They plunged into the usual round of dancing and sailing together. And presently, the inevitable happened. They went sailing too far down the Humber and got stuck on the mud at about seven o'clock at night, upon a falling tide. At least, that's what they said.

They turned up at Ilkley the next morning at about ten o'clock looking rather sheepish. I do not know what Mrs. Chalmers said to Marjorie; I only know what Marjorie's father said to George Boden in the pub that night.

He said: "Eh, George, what's this I hear about your lad and my lass beating t' starter's pistol?"

"I dunno. Do you think they did?"

"I dunno. Do you?"

"I dunno."

There was a long, slow pause. Two more tankards were pushed across the counter to them.

"Don't like going home to-night," said Henry Chalmers. "The wife's got precious fussed about it all."

"It's all your lass leading my lad into evil ways," said George Boden. "He'd never have done a thing like that upon his own."

"He couldn't have," said Mr. Chalmers simply. "But next time he wants to, I'd just as soon he didn't pick my Marjorie."

"I spoke to Oliver. He said they didn't do nothin'. But who's to tell?"

"That's what Marjorie said to the wife. Flew into a proper temper when the wife suggested it, and said she wished they had."

"Aye," said George Boden. "So does young Oliver, I'll be bound."

They stood gloomily discussing it for a quarter of an hour. Finally common sense asserted itself.

"Well," said George Boden, "either they did or they didn't. If they didn't, then there's no harm done and the less said the better. If they did, well, they're both right young folks and they'll want to be married. I shan't stand in their way."

"I'd like to see you try it on," said Mr. Chalmers, "if your young Oliver got my lass into trouble."

So the row simmered down, but left behind an atmosphere of uneasy expectancy in both families. The old relationship between Marjorie and Oliver was obviously a thing of the past, and nobody quite knew what would succeed it.

And then ten days later, I'm blessed if they didn't go and do it again. This time they hadn't even got the decency to turn up early. They arrived home at three o'clock in the afternoon, arm-in-arm and beaming all over their faces in a most discreditable manner. They said cheerfully that they had been stuck on the mud all night, and they'd slept late, and they had talked things over and they wanted to get married.

"And about time, too," said Henry Chalmers. His daughter turned and made a face at him.

They were married in October, 1938, when she was nineteen and he was twenty-two. They were married in Ilkley and there was a reception in the Magnificent Hotel in Harrogate, which most of the wool trade attended. They left from there in the little Aston Martin for their honeymoon in the Lakes, and everybody heaved a great sigh of relief that they were safely married without any scandal getting out.

They came back after a month, and settled down into a little flat in Harrogate. The Boden family had given Marjorie a little coupé as a wedding present, and this made her free to run around and meet her family and meet her friends when Oliver was at work with the Aston Martin. They had a fine time in those last few months before the war. They ranged the country in their little cars, motoring, sailing, dancing, and having fun together with a young crowd of their friends. All Yorkshire, and all life, was open wide for them.

Then the war came. A war is not at all a bad time for young people; it brings movement to them, travel, and adventure— all the things that young people long for. In the Yorkshire set that the Bodens moved in there was great excitement. Most of the young men wanted to go into the Air Force and be pilots; Oliver Boden was unusual in that he plumped for the Navy. He knew a little about navigation and the tides by this time, and the thought that one day he might rise to command a trawler as a naval officer thrilled both Marjorie and Oliver. A trawler was a real tough, man-sized job; better than sitting in a mouldy aeroplane and dropping things.

He got his commission in October, 1939, and went down to Brighton for his training, to a large, new municipal casino newly christened H.M.S. King Alfred. Marjorie went with him and stayed in a hotel on the sea-front which was his billet, thrilled to the core with all the uniforms and signs of war at sea. For the five weeks it took to turn him into a naval officer they had a lovely time. The work was not too strenuous and he could spend each evening with her in their billet. They drank a good deal of beer and saw a good many pictures, and they met a great number of young R.N.V.R. officers from all corners of the world. They felt that they had never had such a good time before.

He passed out of King Alfred after five weeks, a full-fledged sub-lieutenant with a wavy golden ring upon his arm. He had put in for trawlers, and a trawler it was that he got, though not the sort of trawler that he had envisaged. He was posted to a very old, decrepit ship at Portsmouth that tended the buoys in the swept channel; her name was *Harebell*. She could do six knots after a boiler clean, not quite so much before it. She was commanded by a very old R.N.R. lieutenant who kept a little newspaper shop in Southampton in the days of peace, and her duty was to waddle out and replace buoys in the approaches to the harbour that had been blown out of place.

Young Boden knew it was a dud job, but it thrilled him to

be doing it. He knew that it was an apprenticeship for better things. He went at it in the right frame of mind, humbly learning from his captain the rudiments of his trade—how to handle stiff wire ropes and how to handle ratings with a grievance; how to read a hoist of signal flags and Admiralty Fleet Orders.

Marjorie went with him to Portsmouth and lived in the Royal Clarence Hotel in some considerable luxury. Each morning he would have to go off at about seven o'clock unless he had had a night on, when he did not come home at all. Each morning she would walk down to the Battery and watch the ships going out; usually she would see *Harebell* waddle out at half the speed of other ships, with Oliver very noble in a duffle coat upon the bridge, or standing over men who worked with ropes and winches in the well. In the late afternoon she would walk down to meet him at the dockyard gate; then they would go back to the hotel and have a few drinks with their friends, and a grill, and then perhaps the pictures.

He went to Portsmouth in December, 1939. In April, 1940, *Harebell* was blown up, and sunk in three minutes.

Oliver Boden never had a very clear idea of what really happened. A couple of Heinkels had paid their nightly visit to the Solent to drop magnetic mines, and the trawlers had been out at dawn as usual and pooped three of them off. *Harebell* had pottered out in the forenoon to shift a buoy and Oliver was up upon the bridge with the skipper as they passed the Elbow. He remembered saying "Starboard Five" down the voice-pipe, and then he glanced ahead. He saw the water cream on both sides of the ship beside the well, and he felt through the deck a tremendous jolt beneath his feet. He saw the well deck split, and a vast mass of water coming up towards him; then the blast took him and threw him back against the binnacle, breaking two ribs. He remembered falling from a height into the water, and a great pain in his chest, and the salt down in his lungs. Then he was up again upon the surface coughing and choking, and feebly trying to blow air into the life-saving waistcoat that Marjorie had given him to wear instead of a Mae West. There was the mainmast of the *Harebell* sticking up out of the water near to him, and eight men of a complement of twenty-one struggling to reach it with him. There was no sign of the skipper. A motor-pinnace picked them up in a few minutes, and took them all direct to Haslar Hospital.

Marjorie heard about it from the Captain of the Dockyard. She was having lunch alone in the hotel when she was called

to the telephone, and suffered a succession of irritating com-
mands to wait a moment, please. She could not understand
who was calling, or what they wanted, but a vague apprehen-
sion grew in her. It could not be that anything had . . .
happened.

Then Captain Mortimer himself came on the line. She had
met him once at a sherry party, and she was rather frightened
of him. He said: "Look, Mrs. Boden. We've had a bit of
bother here this morning, I'm afraid. Your husband is in
Haslar Hospital, but he's not badly hurt." There was a silence.
"Are you there?"

She said: "I'm here. What was it—what happened?"

"I don't want you to ask that, Mrs. Boden. You know how
it is these days. I don't talk about things that happen here,
and you've not got to, either. Your husband's got a couple of
ribs broken, but they tell me he's quite comfortable. You can
see him for a very short time this afternoon at about four
o'clock. Do you know where to go?"

He told her, and impressed on her again the necessity for
reticence. She rang off, and went back to her lunch in the
dining-room, but she ate nothing more. Presently she went up
to her room, and threw herself down upon the bed. There were
nearly two hours to wait till she could go to Haslar.

In that two hours she changed a good deal. She was only
twenty and life had never hit her very hard. The war had
been a great game up till then. People got killed, of course;
she knew that in the abstract. But not people that you *knew*,
people that really belonged to you. For the first time she faced
the fact that Oliver might have been killed that day—in fact,
had probably escaped it very narrowly.

Later she went to Haslar, and heard from an over-garrulous
sick-bay steward that two-thirds of *Harebell's* complement had,
in fact, been killed, including the captain. She saw Oliver for
about two minutes, white and motionless in bed, his head red
on the pillow, smiling at her with his eyes, but drowsy with
the drugs that they had given him for shock. Then she went
back to the hotel.

She sat for a time in the lounge, hoping that some other
officer's wife would come in that she knew, that she could talk
to. But no one came, and presently she went and dined alone.
By nine o'clock she was in bed, but not to sleep.

The appalling nature of the disaster that might have come
to her shook her very much. She came of Yorkshire stock,

71

accustomed to face facts; she now faced the fact that she had very nearly lost Oliver. She might still lose him; she had heard of deferred shock. She simply could not visualise what life would be like without him. Oliver had always been there, ever since she could remember. They always had done things together, all their lives. All their lives they had given their spare time to each other. All of their lives, unknowing, they had been in love.

She lay for hours, blindly miserable, hating all ships, and the war, hating the Royal Clarence Hotel, and the grill-room, and the drinks, hating Portsmouth and the Navy. If only they could be back in Yorkshire as they had been once, forgetting all this beastliness! All their lives they had been so happy there. She saw Chalmers' greystone house, and she saw the Bodens' greystone house, and she remembered all the fun that they had had together, with all the fathers and mothers and brothers and sisters, for so many years. And now, in contrast this. . . .

She cried a little into her pillow, and presently she cried herself to sleep.

She did not sleep for long. She was awake again by about four; she got up and sponged her face. Then she lay down again, grave and thoughtful. She knew quite well now why everything had been fun up in Yorkshire in those days. It was because her father had been in love with her mother, and George Boden had loved Mrs. Boden, and there had been lots of children. People without children lived in flats and places like the Royal Clarence Hotel, but when you had a family you had to do things differently. A family meant you had to have a house, and the bigger the family the bigger the house—a big greystone house in Ilkley or in Burley, with lots of children and young people in and out of it. That was what she wanted now, with all her heart and soul.

They had avoided children; she now felt that they had been very wrong. Marriage without kids was a silly business, an affair of flats and cocktail-bars that held no solid Yorkshire happiness. A family mean home and happiness. And anyway, she thought with grim realism, if they had a baby there'd be something left for her if Oliver were—killed.

Oliver did not die; in fact, he made a very quick recovery. She used to go and sit with him each afternoon; he had a cabin overlooking the garden quadrangle, bright with spring flowers. And suddenly one afternoon she said: "Nolly, I vote we have a crack at a kid pretty soon."

There was a pause. "They slobber," he said gently.

"I know they do."

"And they get sick all over you."

"I know." She was holding his hand.

"It must be pretty lousy for you, all alone and doing nothing all day," he said. "If that's what you want, it's all O.K. with me."

She said: "You'd like it too, wouldn't you? I mean, it'd be rather fun."

He temporised. "They smell just terrible . . ." he said.

"Not if you manage them right." She made an appeal to his better instincts. "I mean, it'd be just like having a puppy and seeing it grow up into a decent dog."

"You wouldn't like to have a puppy instead?" he enquired. "You'd see the results quicker."

She said: "I won't be fobbed off with a puppy."

He said: "All right—have it your own way. I was only trying to help. If we don't like it we can always leave it on a doorstep, and get a puppy."

Presently he was up and about, walking with difficulty, and later they went back to Yorkshire for three weeks' leave. In that time the battle of Flanders reached its climax and everybody who was fit to handle a boat went over to Dunkirk; in Yorkshire they knew little of what was going on. Oliver was irritated and upset when he discovered from the newspapers what he had missed. His leave, which had been pleasant enough when it began, now irked him, and he began to write letters to the Admiralty for another ship.

He applied this time to be posted to a trawler in the Humber or Mersey area, in order to be closer to their home if Marjorie were going to have a baby. He did not get it; he was posted instead to a trawler in the Forth, based on Port Edgar. Marjorie went up there with him and stayed in the Lothian Hotel, overlooking the Firth of Forth, with the other naval officers' wives; Boden was able to spend about two nights a week on shore with her.

The work was more interesting, and more what he had joined the Navy to do. His ship was H.M.T. *Grimsby Emerald*, and the commanding officer, a middle-aged lieutenant R.N.V.R., was a bank manager in civil life and had been in trawlers in the last war. They used to go sweeping up and down the Forth in pair with another trawler, and now and again they had the satisfaction of creating a shattering explosion on the sea bed.

Then they would heave-to, drop a bucket over the side for the harvest of stunned fish, repair the sweep, and go on, hoping to do it again. It was pleasant enough during the summer months of June, July, and August. From time to time Marjorie would go in to Edinburgh and come back with a copy of the *Nursing Times* or else a little book on Infant Management; these she would read in bed at night and sometimes read out bits of them to Oliver if he were there.

Presently it became necessary for her to go to London, to visit a particular shop in Bond Street. This, she explained to Oliver, was all part of the ritual. Only the experts of the Radiant Cradle Company Ltd. knew the ins and outs of this most difficult and intricate affair, and if you got the wrong sort of wool, for example, the baby would develop something horrible and die. Then they would have to start all over again, which would be troublesome.

Oliver said again: "Much better have a puppy. They're hardier," and took her in to Edinburgh to put her in the sleeper for London. The Battle of Britain was then just beginning, and London had had about a month of raids. Oliver's sister, Helen Boden, had a little flat up at the top of an old house in Dover Street, and Marjorie had reckoned to stay with her there. On account of the raids, and at Oliver's insistence, she changed her plans and sent a telegram to a school friend who lived outside at Harrow to invite herself to spend a couple of nights with her.

There was no answer to that telegram before she left Edinburgh, but that did not worry them. Oliver took her to the Waverley grill-room and they split a bottle of burgundy to make her sleep, and then they went to the train together. In the cramped, delicately furnished little sleeper he took her in his arms and kissed her.

"So long, old thing," he said. "Look after yourself."

She said a little tremulously: "So long, Nolly. Don't go and bump another mine before I get back."

He left her, and the train carried her away into the night. He went back to his duty in *Grimsby Emerald*, and Marjorie arrived in London next morning, fresh and cheerful after a good night. The train was three hours late, on account of the raids, and everybody seemed to think that it had done very well to lose so little time.

She had heard nothing from her friend at Harrow, and so rang her up. It seemed that there was trouble; mother had bronchitis and there was a trained nurse sleeping in the spare room. Marjorie was really very glad. Honour was satisfied; there was now no alternative to sleeping in Helen's flat in Dover Street, and it would be great fun if there was a raid.

She went to Dover Street and saw the caretaker who lived down in the basement, a Mrs. Harrison. Helen, it seemed, had gone to Yorkshire for a few days, but she had left word with Mrs. Harrison that Mrs. Boden might turn up to use the flat, so that was quite all right. Marjorie went up to the top floor and unpacked her things; she had slept there before. Each time she used the flat she envied Helen again, for living free and independently in London in a real flat of her own, in Dover Street.

She went out, and walked down Piccadilly, looking in the shop windows. She bought a warm blue scarf for Nolly in the Burlington Arcade because it took her fancy, and she bought a little silver cigarette-lighter at Dunhills', which she would keep for his birthday in November. Then she had lunch at the Chinese restaurant, partly for the novelty and partly because it was quite cheap, and she was Yorkshire bred.

And after lunch she went to the Radiant Cradle Company in Bond Street and spent two hours with them. She came out a little dazed, having spent a good deal of money on little bits and pieces that were obviously necessary. Having a baby, she thought was a terribly expensive matter, but quite fun. Everybody in the shop had been so very, very nice to her. Her heart warmed to Radiant Cradle Company.

She went back to the flat and made herself a cup of tea, feeling rather at a loss. It was fun to be alone in London, but she felt she wouldn't like to have too much of it; she was almost glad to be going back to Port Edgar the next day in spite of the boredom when Oliver was at sea. It would be awful fun if he could come to London next time with her. She could not think of anyone in London at that moment that she knew, so when her tea was finished she went out and saw a film.

She came out of the cinema at about seven, on a warm September evening. There had been a raid warning while she was in it, but ten minutes later the All Clear had sounded, and when she came out there was nothing unusual to be seen. She knew little about London restaurants except the Piccadilly Hotel, and she did not feel like going there alone. So she went back to the Chinese restaurant again and had another peculiar meal, and so back to Dover Street in the gloaming.

The warning sounded again as she went in, at about nine

o'clock, and gave her a tremendous thrill.

It was hot in the flat beneath the roof, though all the windows were wide open. She took off her shoes and her dress, put on a kimono and went and leaned out the window. There were a few searchlights stabbing the evening sky and a low rumble of gunfire in the distance to the south; she listened to it with pleasurable excitement. Perhaps it would develop into a real blitz, with fires and bombs and everything; something to brag about when she got back to the Lothian Hotel. In the street below her people seemed to be scurrying quickly to their homes.

The blue sky darkened into night; at about ten o'clock the first bombs fell. Overhead, very distant, she could hear the faint noise of an aeroplane; from that time onwards the drone was continuous. Whatever aeroplanes they were, she thought they must be flying at a very great height, five or six miles, perhaps. She wondered if they were German bombers or British fighters; there was no means of telling which.

Presently bombs began to fall all over London, some not more than half a mile away, it seemed to her. There was a glow of fire towards the east, and several times from Piccadilly she heard the clang and rumble of fire engines coming from the west. The gunfire from the park not far away was continuous; each time that one particular gun fired her window rattled and the floor shook a little beneath her feet. Splinters of shell fell down from time to time upon the roofs with a sharp rattle, and once a large piece, probably a fuse, fell with a great crash of slates not far away. She kept back under cover after that, and only gazed diagonally upwards through the window at the little bursting stars spattering the sky above.

After a time it seemed to her that her top room was not the safest place of all to be in at that time. She opened the door of the flat and went downstairs in her kimono to see what anybody else was doing. She found a little knot of people sitting on the stairs of the bottom flight; there was no cellar or shelter to the house. She went upstairs again and fetched a cushion and her eiderdown, and came down again to join them, sitting most uncomfortably upon a stair.

The raid went on and on, the detonations sometimes distant, sometimes very close at hand. She stayed down there on the cold stairs for over two hours, weary and bored and rather cold, and most uncomfortable. At about one o'clock the bombing and gunfire died away, and for the first time there was no sound of aircraft overhead.

Somebody said at last: "Sounds like the end. Give it another ten minutes." Ten minutes passed, a quarter of an hour. There had been no All Clear, but people started drifting up to bed; Marjorie went up too, took off her clothes and put on her pyjamas, and slipped thankfully between the sheets. In five minutes she was asleep.

A second wave of bombers came half an hour later, and the gunfire began again and woke her up. She did not stir from bed, being very tired. She lay and listened to the raid for nearly an hour, and presently dozed off again, accustomed to the noise.

She woke to the shrill scream of the bomb that hit the house next door, an instant before it burst. She had no time to do anything, hardly time to realise what the noise denoted, before the appalling thing happened. Her bed was lifted bodily up into the air and slammed down again upon the floor, and a great pressure blast came on her that made her cry out with the pain in her ears. Then, as she watched, the solid wall at the end of her room split and crumbled and dissolved in shreds of plaster, and was gone, and a thick, choking cloud of dust was over everything that made her gasp for breath. She lay petrified with fright in bed; then something happened to the roof above her. A half-ton coping stone came crashing through the ceiling and fell down on to the lower half of the bed. The bed collapsed down on to the floor and she lay pinned there, stunned with the shock and with the pain in both her legs.

She struggled to sit up and the pain bit and gnawed her legs, piercing, unbearable. She lay back white and trembling, and fearful of what this might mean to her. She thought: "This is the sort of thing that gives people a miscarriage"; indeed, it seemed to her that people had had miscarriages for something rather less than she had got. She felt that she must try to lie back quietly, and rest. Presently, when she was a little calmer, she would cry out, and somebody would come.

Below her, in the street, there were confused noises of men shouting and the rumble of falling masonry and brick. Slowly the thick choking dust began to settle; it settled thickly on the ruins of her bed, upon the sheets, upon her arms, her face, her hair. As the cloud slowly cleared she found that she could see straight out ahead of her where the wall used to be; she looked into a torn, incredible gap, vacant, that had been the house next door. Above the shattered roof of the next door but one she could see the stars pin-pointing in a deep blue sky.

Suddenly, from the stairs outside the door behind her head

there was a sound of scrambling, and a man's voice. It was calling:

"Is anyone up there in the top rooms? Is anybody up there?"

She answered weakly: "Yes, please. Me. I'm here."

"Which room are you in?"

"In the front, on the top floor."

"Can you get out on to the landing, where I can see you? Come carefully, because the stairs are down."

She said: "I can't move. There's something lying on my legs."

There was a momentary pause. Then the voice said: "All right, lady—take it easy. I'll come up to you."

The scrambling noises recommenced. She heard a voice say: "Bert, there's a woman up on the top floor. I'm going up. Stand from under, case the whole bloody lot comes down." And presently, crawling upon his belly on the floor that swayed and teetered beneath his added weight, a man came to her.

She saw him faintly in the starlit darkness, through the fog of dust. He was a very dirty man, in a tin hat and a blue boiler-suit, with an armlet bearing the letters A.F.S. He was a man of about fifty, still lean and athletic. He said: "This floor isn't quite what it might be. Come on, lady. Let's get out of this toot sweet."

She said: "I can't move, I'm afraid. I think both my legs are broken. Look."

He switched on an electric torch and examined the wreck of her bed. He tested the weight of the coping stone with his hands: it was utterly beyond his power to shift it. In three weeks of intensive raids this man had learned a great deal, had amassed a sad store of experience. He knew that there was only one thing that could save this girl. A doctor must come up, alone, because the floor would bear no more than one, and amputate both legs where she lay. And he must do it quickly.

He said: "Look, lady, I'm going down to fetch my mate to give a hand with this. We'll get you down okay. Just lie there quiet and stick it out, and don't move round more'n you've got to. I'll be back inside ten minutes."

Then he was gone, and she was left alone again.

She heard him slithering and scrambling down the staircase well. His visit had comforted her, had eased her fears; she knew now that everything was going to be all right. The little noise of the incendiaries, the six or seven quick plops as they fell among the wooden ruins of the roofs and floors, passed her unnoticed; she heard the growing clamour in the street, but did not understand.

A sharp, bitter smell of smoke was blown to her. In sudden fear she raised her head and saw, arising from the ruins of the house next door, a tongue of flame. She stared at it dumbfounded. Then she realised it meant the end.

In those last moments she was agonised by thoughts of Boden, and of their dependence on each other. She cried: "Oh, Nolly dear, I've góne and let you down! Whatever will you do?" The smoke came pouring up the staircase well and gushed around her, products of combustion, stifling and merciful. In a few moments she lost consciousness.

The fire shot up into the starry night, enveloping the ruined houses, violent, uncontrollable. It made a flaming beacon in the night a hundred feet in height; the Germans took it for an aiming point and sowed the area with bombs. It was two hours before the sweating, cursing firemen got it down.

*   *   *   *   *

The news came to Boden forty hours later, in this way. H.M.T. *Grimsby Emerald* came in at about seven in the evening and dropped anchor off the trawler base. A lamp began to flicker from the signal tower. The captain stood in Monkey's Island beside the signalman and spelled it out.

He turned to the lad. "All right. Nip down and tell Mr. Boden."

The signalman went up to Boden on the forecastle. "Captain said to tell you, sir, there's been a signal. You've got to report to the captain's office, on shore. They're sending the launch out for you."

Boden glanced ashore; already the launch was casting off from the quay. "My Christ!" he said. "I'd better go and get clean."

Ten minutes later, in a collar and his best monkey jacket, he slipped over the side into the launch. He landed at the harbour steps still straightening his tie. There was an officer he knew slightly waiting for the Ferry, an R.N.V.R. serving in *Rodney*. To this chap Boden remarked "Baa", according to the custom of the service at that time, and passed on to the Naval Centre and the office of the captain (Mine-sweepers).

In the outer office he asked the secretary, another R.N.V.R. officer: "What does he want me for?"

"I don't know, old man." Instinctively, Boden knew that he was lying.

He went into the inner room, his hat under his arm, and there was his father, standing with the captain.

"Eh, lad," George Boden said directly. "I've brought bad news, and you must take it like a man."

And then, in plain unvarnished terms he told him what had happened.

The next few days passed in a horrible, unreal dream. He went in to Edinburgh with his father and they caught the night train down to London. His captain with unobtrusive naval kindness had telephoned to C.-in-C. Rosyth, the admiral himself, explaining the position, who in turn had telephoned demanding sleepers at an hour's notice, so that on the first night young Boden had a chance of sleep. His father dosed him well with allonal, and he slept fitfully to London.

They went to Dover Street and saw the blackened ruin of three houses, with men working to dislodge the crumbling, tottering walls in clouds of dust and filth. They went to the A.F.S. station, a garage in a near-by mews, and there they interviewed an awkward, embarrassed man of fifty with grizzled grey hair, still wearing a tin hat and a dirty boiler-suit. They gave a statement to the police for records. There was nothing more that they could do in London, and they went home to Yorkshire.

Oliver Boden stayed there for three days. Then, because there was nothing for him to do there, and because he ached to get away from everything, he took the train north to Port Edgar, and reported back for duty.

He made two more sweeps in *Grimsby Emerald*. They anchored off Elie, on the north side of the Firth, one evening; the captain let a few of the ratings go on shore to stretch their legs. He pressed Boden to go with them, but the boy refused.

"I don't feel like it, sir, if you don't mind," he said awkwardly.

The late bank manager went himself, and walked about the little greystone town for an hour, and had a drink at the hotel. And coming back on board in the twilight, he saw Boden standing alone up in Monkey's Island, and went up to him.

"Fine night," he said, for want of something to say. "Anything doing?"

"No, sir." The boy hesitated, and then said: "Sir, would you mind very much if I put in to leave the ship?"

The older man said: "I should mind the hell of a lot. Probably help you over the side with the toe of my boot." Boden smiled faintly. "Still, I'd probably get over it. If that's what you want, I'll see the captain for you, if you like. What do you want to do?"

"I don't know. But I want to get away from here."

The other nodded. "I know. Not much fun going on shore."

"No, sir."

Two days later he was saying the same thing to his captain in the Naval Centre at Port Edgar. "I don't like coming on shore here, sir," he said awkwardly. He was flushing, and fumbling with his cap. "Do you think I could get in some ship going overseas?"

"I don't know about that. Sit down, Boden. Have a cigarette." He made the boy comfortable, and a little more at ease. "You've only been in trawlers, haven't you?"

"Yes, sir. I was in a ship called *Harebell* before this."

"I remember," said the captain directly. "She was sunk. You haven't had much luck."

"No, sir."

"I don't think you'll get overseas at once, Boden. You're not a gunner, and you're not a navigator. You're a trawler officer. I tell you what I can do for you, though. I can put you forward for an anti-submarine course, and you can go on in an A/S trawler on the west coast somewhere. Would that suit you, do you think?"

"I'd like that, sir." Boden hesitated, and then said: "I'd like to do something a bit more active than just sweeping up mines all the time."

The older man nodded. "If you go in now for anti-submarine work, and if in a year's time you still want to go overseas, you probably won't have much difficulty in getting a destroyer or a corvette, as a qualified A/S officer. I think that's your best course."

They talked about it for a time, and the senior officer gave him a cup of tea. In the end:

"All right, Boden," said the captain. "I'll put you in for that course right away. You'll probably be going in two or three days' time—I'll let you know."

The young man got up to go. "I'm terribly sorry to be leaving," he said awkwardly.

"I'm sorry to lose you, Boden," said the other. "You've done very well, and I shall say so in your record. I'm very sorry that you've had this bad luck. I think you're doing right to make a change."

"Thank you, sir."

A week later he left *Grimsby Emerald* and travelled to a far part of the country, to a place that he had never seen before, where nobody knew anything about him. Here he began his anti-submarine course, and for a month he learned the technicalities of Asdic and of depth charges, and of the methods of attack. He passed out well, and found himself with a second stripe upon his arm, a full lieutenant. Having been in two ships already, and been sunk in one, he found himself regarded as an officer of some experience.

He was posted to a trawler based on Dartmouth, H.M.T. *Gracie Fields*. His captain was another officer of the last war, a printer in civil life, who ran a little business of his own in Exeter. He was a pleasant, easy-going man and reasonably competent. Boden settled down to his new work with him quite happily; that was in November, 1940.

The work absorbed him; the long hours of watching, hunting, were a pleasure to him and an occupation for his mind. Three or four times in those first winter months they made a contact and dropped depth charges with indeterminate results. Once, with an M.L. and another trawler to assist, they kept the contact for two hours, and started leaks in their own ship with the continual detonations of their charges. They produced a wide slick of oil upon the surface of the sea and a great mass of bubbles in the dusk of a winter afternoon. The water was too deep for sweeping to investigate effectively, and at the conference on shore the team was credited with a "probable". Young Boden got the keenest pleasure out of that.

His days on shore were much less satisfactory. He was awkward and lonely, and he never settled down to his new life. He was unable to adjust himself . For many years he had looked only to Marjorie in his times of leisure; he could not now take any pleasure in dances, and even cinemas now seemed to him artificial, tinsel things, and rather painful. He liked the company of men of his own sort in hotel bars as much as he liked anything, but he did not care to spend an evening upon beer and cigarettes. In short, nothing that in his loneliness he found to do on shore pleased him so much as his work. Killing the Germans was the greatest fun of all, chasing them, listening for the ping, making fierce detonations all around them in their narrow steel hulls. He lay night after night in his narrow bunk, picturing how the hull would split, the lights go out, and the air pressure rise intolerably round trapped and drowning men. That was the line of thought that gave him most real pleasure at that time.

Presently the problem of his off days on shore became acute. As the days grew longer it became imperative to him to find some outlet for his restlessness on shore, something to do. Once in April, casting around to try something different, he took a little sailing-boat and set off up the Dart upon a voyage of discovery.

It was a warm afternoon of late spring, with a gentle southerly breeze. He went up-river on the flood from the trawler anchorage off Kingswear, in between the wooded hills beyond the town. The quiet, easy progress of the boat rested and contented him; in spite of all his painful sailing memories, it was good to be sailing again. He went up past the Naval College, past Mill Creek. He skirted by the Anchor Stone, and so came to Dittisham, with its whitewashed and thatched cottages straggling down to the creek.

Just below Dittisham his eye caught a ship, and his interest was aroused. She was a very large, black fishing-boat, perhaps seventy feet in length. She had an enormously high, straight bow and a great sweeping sheer down to the stern; forward there was one short, thick mast in a tabernacle, now struck down and lying with the truck down aft. The mast and some of the upper works were painted light blue, and there was a little white moulding running down her sheer. On her transom, picked out in white, was her name and port, *Geneviève—D'Nez*.

She was lying at a mooring in the river, and there was an ancient rowing-boat streaming behind her on a length of painter. That meant that there was somebody on board. Boden eyed her appreciatively as he swept past; she had something of the lines and figure of a drifter, but without the funnel or the upper works. Above the sheer-line there was little of her showing. Probably, he thought, she had a great big engine in her; indeed, he noticed an exhaust-pipe like the town drain sticking through her side. She must, he thought, be a fine sea boat with those lines.

He tacked upon an impulse, and stemmed the tide up towards her from the stern to have another look at her. The little bow wave of his boat made a small noise, and a man stood up on

deck and looked towards him. It was a naval officer, an
R.N.V.R. sub-lieutenant.

Boden knew the man by sight, but did not know his name.
He was a dark-haired young special branch officer; that meant
that for some reason he was classed unfit for watch-keeping
at sea, and that he wore a green stripe below the wavy golden
ring upon his arm. He worked in some shore job in the
N.O.I.C.'s office. Boden was a little bit surprised to see him in
a ship.

He sailed up very close to the black topsides, slowly creeping
past her up against the tide. "Just having a look at your ship,"
he said. "There's plenty of her."

The other said: "She's not my ship. I'm just having a
look at her myself."

"Whose ship is she."

"I don't think she belongs to anyone. She's French."

"Has she got any accommodation?"

"Not so as you'd notice. Come on board and have a look."

Boden hesitated. Then he said: "All right. Take my painter
and I'll drop astern."

He eased his sheet and threw the painter over the black
bulwarks; the special officer took it and made it fast. Boden
lowered and stowed his sail; the other pulled his boat alongside
again, and he stepped aboard the Frenchman.

He looked around her as he stepped on deck, and liked what
he saw. There was a small forecastle hatch forward of the tabernacle, probably for gear. The well of the ship was split into
two holds, covered by hatches. Aft there was a companion,
and a tiny skylight indicated some sort of cabin or bunk-room.

"What sort of motor has she got in her?" he asked.

"Ruddy great Sulzer Diesel." The other paused. "They
say that these boats go like hell. They do about twelve knots."

They walked around the deck together, and looked down at
the engine in its section of the boat. "What's her history?"
Boden asked. "What's she doing here?"

"She came over with a lot of refugees last summer, I believe,"
the other said. "They all left her, and the Harbour Master had
her moved up here. We want a launch down in the Boom
Defence, and I knew that she was up here, and I thought I'd
come and look at her, and see if we could snaffle her. But I'm
afraid she's much too big for what we want."

They stared around them. "Yes," said Boden. "She's a real
sea-going boat. Pity she can't be used."

The special officer said slowly. "I believe she could be used, if people only had the guts."

Boden glanced at the man beside him curiously. He noticed that he had dark, smooth hair and keen, thin features; he looked rather a delicate man. He was about twenty-four or twenty-five; they were much of an age.

"How do you mean?" asked Boden. "How do you think she could be used?" He lit a cigarette with the quick, nervous motion that had become customary with him in the last few months. The other filled a pipe.

The special officer said diffidently: "Oh, I don't really know. But I think *something* could be done with her. She's French-built. I believe you could go anywhere in her and never be questioned. Over on the other side, I mean."

"What'd you do when you got there?"

The other shrugged his shoulders. "I don't know. It's only a crack-pot idea I had." He laughed awkwardly. "We chaps who stay on shore get frightfully brave."

"I suppose you're some kind of a scientist," said Boden.

The other nodded. "I couldn't get into the Executive—I'm colour-blind." He hesitated, and then said: "You're in a trawler, aren't you? I think I've seen you in the pub."

"That's right. My name is Boden."

The dark-haired special officer said: "Mine is Rhodes."

4

MICHAEL SEYMOUR RHODES was the son of a doctor in Derby, who died when he was fifteen. His mother was left in rather difficult circumstances, but she sold capital to finish the boy's education. He went to Birmingham University at a younger age than usual, and passed out when he was nineteen with a degree in chemistry.

He got a job with the great chemical combine, British Toilet Products Ltd. at their works at Bristol. The concern employed nine thousand hands at Bristol and about twice that number at the Preston works. They demanded about fifty young industrial chemists from the universities each year to feed the great machine with new ideas. Most of the young men left them six or seven years later, finding promotion to the higher grades completely blocked, but there were always new ones coming on to fill the gaps.

Rhodes was one of these, and as one of the team he left a little mark upon the country's modes and manners. It was his idea to put the stuff into Titania foot tablets that gave a faint brown tinge of tan to tired feet, making them more becoming and toning down the angry redness of the aching corn upon a dead white foot. The slow effervescence of Blue Grotto bath-cubes, protracted over half an hour, was one of his. In the field of basic research he did good work upon the solubility of solid organic perfumes in soya oil which influenced both soaps and face creams considerably in 1938 and 1939. He was, in fact, a very competent if rather inexperienced young industrial chemist.

He lived in a bed-sitting-room in a little house in a suburb of Bristol, and he lived quite alone. His landlady was a widow who looked after him quite well; on his part, he made very little trouble for her. He was a very shy young man. He was good company in the office and quite popular with the staff, but outside office hours he had little contact with his fellow-men. He joined no sports clubs because he was not interested in sports. He did not go to dances because he felt himself to be shy and awkward with young women, and consequently he had an idea, that they were laughing at him. He did not drink at all before he joined the navy, and he smoked very moderately. In consequence of these ascetic habits he was rather a lonely young man, and that loneliness made him more shy and more awkward still. He spent most of his evenings and week-ends in long, solitary walks, or brooding on the solubility of substances in soya oil. Occasionally he went to the pictures.

In the autumn of 1937, when he had been at Bristol for about a year, a great interest came into his life. He had been to Derby for the week-end to see his mother, and returning late to the little house outside Bristol on Sunday night, he was surprised to find a very large black dog upon the doorstep. It slunk away into the front garden as he entered the front gate. He looked over his shoulder at it, curiously and uneasily, as he let himself in with his latchkey. It was a very big dog indeed, and very black and fierce-looking.

His landlady met him in the hall, fussed and a little frightened. It seemed that the dog had been standing up against the front door for the last two hours and blowing through the letter-box; in that position he could look in through the little windows of the door like the Hound of the Baskervilles.

The snuffling snorts in at the letter-box, the blood-curdling whines, and the fierce glaring eyes had troubled her considerably.

Rhodes went to the door, opened it, and looked out. The dog pushed past him and stalked into the sitting-room, wagging his stern. He saw the gas fire and sat down in front of it, beaming up at them. He took up most of the hearth-rug.

"Coo, look at that!" said the woman. "Makes himself at home, don't he?"

They stood and marvelled at the dog. It was a very large black Labrador perhaps three years old, short-haired, with a great dripping jowl, brown eyes, and a permanent expression of perplexity. It weighed a good six stone. They very soon became accustomed to it; indeed they had to, for it obviously meant to spend the night with them. They tried it with a bit of bread and it ate that ravenously; it ate the rest of the loaf and the rest of the cold lamb and a lump of suet pudding and a good many biscuits, and asked for more. It made no objection when Rhodes scrutinised its collar, but there was no name on it.

In the end, of course, it stayed for good and Rhodes paid his landlady another five shillings a week for its food. He took it next day to the police, who offered to destroy it for him. He took it to the local veterinary surgeon, who told him that it was a Labrador but much too big, and did not recognise it. He kept it for a few days in constant trepidation that an owner would turn up and take it from him, but no owner came.

After a fortnight he gave the dog a name. He called it Ernest, after its expression; he bought it a new collar with his own name on it, and paid seven and sixpence for a licence. The police saw to that.

From the first it slept in his bedroom, curled up on a rug in the corner at the foot of his bed. Out of the office it became his constant companion. His walks grew longer and more regular; each evening after tea he started out for his three miles with Ernest ranging on ahead of him. There was frequent trouble. Ernest, too old to learn new ways, chased everything that ran, from sheep to partridges, with gleeful abandon. Rhodes used to thrash him for it without any noticeable effect; his hide was thick. Grieved words of reproach could reduce him to abject misery, but only for five minutes. He needed constant watching, and this in itself was an occupation and an interest for the young man.

The dog, in fact, became Rhodes's principal spare-time

interest. The regulation of his diet and his exercise, and the tending of cut paws and cat scratches, the daily grooming and the occasional major operation of a bath took an appreciable proportion of his leisure after the daily work. On his part the dog became dependent on his master, as dogs will. He developed an engaging trick of sitting in the sitting-room window in the late afternoon, watching the road. As the first men came streaming past from the factory soon after half-past five Ernest would go scratching at the door to be let out; released, he would bound up the road till he found Rhodes among the crowd, snuffle his hand, and come back at his heels.

Rhodes took the dog everywhere with him. At week-ends when he went back to Derby to see his mother he took Ernest with him sitting beside him in his Austin Seven; with some difficulty he took Ernest on a fortnight's summer holiday in Cornwall. He liked summer holidays in Cornwall, poking about among the fishing-boats in the little harbours, from Helford to Port Isaac, from Padstow to Polperro. Like most young men in England, he had a genuine affection for the sea, though when he was out upon it he was frequently sick. He could manage a harbour rowing-boat and he knew something of the rudiments of sailing, but till he joined the navy he had never been more than a mile from shore.

Rhodes had had Ernest for the best part of two years when war broke out. He was settled deeply in his Bristol groove. His salary was increasing much more slowly than he once had hoped; still, there was a perceptible increment every year, and it was sufficient for him in his modest style of life. He calculated that if the rate of promotion were maintained, after forty years' service with British Toilet Products Ltd., he would be getting nearly seven hundred a year, and that, he thought, was quite a decent salary. War, when it came, was not a bad thing for Rhodes.

At first, the war did not affect him; indeed as a scientific worker in industry he was classified at first as in a reserved occupation. The Company had a very considerable export trade throughout the world, and in the autumn months of 1939 it was common ground that the war could not be paid for unless export trade were maintained. On the outbreak of war those of the Company who were territorials were called up at once, but they were not numerous. A few of Rhodes's fellow-scientists sneaked off and joined the Royal Air Force. Everybody admired them for their disregard of danger, but there was a feeling at the luncheon-table that they had taken the easy path regardless of the real interests of the country. The hard path was to go on with the humdrum task that lay to hand, devising cheaper and more fragrant bath-salts, foamier shampoo-powders and shaving soaps.

This attitude of mind lasted for nine months or so. Then in May, 1940, the Germans invaded Holland, Belgium, and France; in June the British Army evacuated from Dunkirk.

In those weeks of troubled humiliation Rhodes went through the spiritual changes that were common to most people in the country. It seemed to him that all this talk of export trade to pay for armaments was bunk. If things went on the way that they were going there would be no need for further armaments, for the country would be beaten by the Germans. Not all the toilet soap in Bristol, Rhodes concluded, would prevent the Germans landing on the coast of England in the next few weeks. The only things to stop them were young men with guns, and he himself was young.

It became clear to him that whatever the pundits of the luncheon-table in the Middle Staff Room might declare—and they were not now giving tongue so readily—his study of the solubility of substances in soya oil was drawing to a close. He could not bring himself to concentrate upon it, and he did not want to. When Rotterdam was bombed he knew in his own mind that he would have to go and fight, but it was three weeks more before he actually handed in his notice to the Company.

For that three weeks he hung on, miserable, irresolute, desperately hoping that in some way the cup might pass from him. And the reason for his trouble was simply this: that he had nobody with whom he could leave Ernest.

Rhodes was a sensible young man, and he could face up to the fact that Ernest was not everybody's cup of tea. He was now about six years old, growing a little grey about the muzzle and a little more portly, as a Labrador will in middle age. He was a very large dog indeed, and though for Rhodes he had the imperishable affection of a dog, there was no denying that he was sometimes a little short with the neighbours. There were complaints about Ernest growling and frightening people from time to time, which had to be smoothed over. He now ate over a pound of meat a day, which took some finding in a time of growing scarcity, and if he had less he got eczema. He was also subject to a more indelicate internal trouble.

In those weeks Rhodes searched desperately for a solution to

this problem, while at the same time he found out particulars
of entry into the Royal Naval Volunteer Reserve. If he had to
go and serve he wanted most of all to be a naval officer; his
holidays in Cornwall had done that for him. But Ernest was
an obstacle that seemed insuperable. He could not leave Ernest
with his mother; it would not be fair on the old lady. His landlady, although she tolerated the dog and liked him well enough,
could never cope with an ageing dog of that size in the difficulties of war-time rationing That, as Rhodes realised in sick
despair, would not be fair to Ernest.

A lonely man who has a dog grows almost as dependent upon
him as does the dog upon his master. In the end, in the tension
that came after Dunkirk and nerved by the words of the Prime
Minister, Rhodes did what many people had to do. He took
Ernest on his last walk to the People's Dispensary for Sick
Animals and paid ten shillings to a sympathetic veterinary
surgeon, with a muttered request that he would make it snappy.

He walked home alone. Ten days later he was a sub-lieutenant in the R.N.V.R. at H.M.S. King Alfred undergoing
training.

The loss of Ernest made a great gap in his life, that the new
interests crowding on him failed to fill. He was unused to
spending evenings with other men. He did not mind the change
of circumstances that was imposed on him; indeed he felt that
it was not unhealthy to be shaken from his rut. He was most
bitterly resentful of the sacrifice imposed upon him in the loss
of his dog. He brooded over this, until a hatred of the war and
of the Germans who had made the war became the main preoccupation of his mind. A girl could have got him out of that
obsession, possibly, but he was too diffident a man to have much
truck with girls.

The naval duty to which he was eventually posted only made
things worse. At his medical examination the surgeons very
soon found out a fact that secretly he knew already; that he
was colour-blind. A naval officer who cannot easily distinguish
red from green is not much use in the executive, and they told
him so. In view of his experience as a scientist they offered him
a commission in the Special Branch, which meant that he would
spend the war mostly on shore, wearing a green flash between
the gold bands on his arm and working upon technical matters.
Indifferent in his unhappiness, he took it.

He spent five weeks at King Alfred, and was drafted out.
And two weeks later he found that he was living in a shore job

down at Dartmouth, and quite likely to stay there for the dura-
tion of the war. He was billeted in rooms just like the rooms
that he had had at Bristol, but here he had a good deal more
leisure time. His work was necessary and useful but not
strenuous. Most of his fellow-officers kept dogs for company.
If Ernest had been alive, he could have had him in Dartmouth
perfectly well, with more time than ever to look after him.

The thought of that weighed on his mind, making him sullen,
bitter, and morose. He felt that he had done a cruel, beastly
thing; he had taken the dog who loved him and depended
utterly on him, and he had had him killed, unnecessarily and
wantonly. It was the war that had tricked him into doing such
a thing, a thing he would not have dreamed of a year pre-
viously. The war was made by Germany. He had joined the
navy to fight the Germans and here he was, stuck in a shore
job on the coast of England, never to see a German, likely as
not. He had been tricked all round, and Ernest was dead, and
he was desperately, desperately lonely.

I do not want to paint him as a very tragic figure, though in
those first months of his naval service he was not a very happy
one. The work absorbed him and occupied a good deal of his
waking thoughts, and if in leisure moments he was moody and
distrait, so much was true of many temporary officers whose
lives had been disrupted by the war. The long dark months of
winter dragged by in anxiety and preparation for invasion.
Rhodes spent his time divided between working in the office,
working at gear disposed about the harbour mouth, in launches
or on shore, often wet and often in some danger, and watching
and waiting for the enemy in a little stone control hut on a
headland.

Loneliness, and the aching void caused by a personal loss,
do not endure for ever. Old wounds heal; new friendships and
associations come as anodynes. In the spring, Rhodes got a
rabbit.

I am not joking; that is literally what happened. His landlady, a Mrs. Harding, took to breeding rabbits for the pot to
eke out the meat ration. She had a very small back-yard to
keep them in, and in a short time had acquired three breeding
does. A buck was evidently necessary if the flow of little rabbits
was to proceed according to the plan, and she got a large grey
buck for ten shillings in the market. His presence in a hutch
adjacent to the does did not induce the quiet contemplation
proper to a maternity home, and for three days there was wild

excitement in the hutches, culminating in the death of three tiny, rat-like rabbits through neglect. Mrs. Harding discussed the tragedy at length with Sub-Lieutenant Rhodes, who offered to accommodate the buck in the yard of the net defence store down the road. This yard was a naval establishment, lately a motor-bus garage, and was forbidden ground for Mrs. Harding. That did not matter much because Rhodes went there every morning and could take a bowl of apple cores and cabbage stalks and potato peelings to the rabbit in a little covered basket. An elderly torpedo rating undertook to clean the hutch out once or twice a week, and everyone was satisfied.

This rabbit became an interest to Rhodes, and filled to some extent the gap left in his life. He did not forget Ernest, nor did he change his mood about the war. But after a day spent in a boat heaving on wet, slimy wire ropes or changing detonators with chilled wet hands, it was amusing to spend half an hour in the net store, smoking a cigarette and playing with the rabbit. He found that if you teased it with a bit of Brussels sprout stalk or some other delicacy it made little grunting noises and pranced forward, playing with mock ferocity. He found that it would eat an apple core held for it right down to his fingers. Knowing that he usually brought food, it used to come out of its hay-box when it heard his step, which pleased him very much. It grew quite tame and playful with him.

After a week or two he came to the conclusion that it was a rabbit of character, and deserved a name. After some thought he gave it the name Geoffrey, because its face reminded him a little of a cousin of his own. By the end of the month he was letting Geoffrey out each evening for a run upon the little patch of waste ground enclosed by the fence around the store, keeping a watchful eye over him for fear of cats.

Rhodes's section of the defences was under the command of an old lieutenant-commander called Marshall. They were equipped with one old motor ferry-boat and two row-boats for all the business that they had to do about the port, and as that business grew their need for boats became more pressing. "What we want," said Marshall, "is a decent twenty-five-foot motor-boat with a big open well. If you see anything like that, make a note of it. There might be something over at Torquay."

Rhodes said: "There are a lot of yachts up-river here, sir."

"There's nothing of that sort. The Air Force cleaned up all the launches at the beginning of the war."

Rhodes was not convinced, and made two or three trips up the river on his off days, looking inexpertly at boats. He did not find the boat that he was looking for, but he discovered a French motor fishing vessel called *Geneviève* moored up by Dittisham. He saw her first from shore from some considerable distance. He did not realise her size, and to his inexperienced eye she seemed at least a possibility. It was on his next visit, when he borrowed a row-boat from a fisherman to go and board her, that he came to the conclusion that she was unsuitable.

There was a faint flap of canvas by her while he was on board, and a faint ripple of water. He looked up and saw a sailing dinghy pass, with a red-haired naval officer alone in it. He knew the officer by sight; it was one of the chaps from the anti-submarine trawlers based on the port. Rhodes watched the dinghy tack and stem the tide back to him. They passed a few words across the intervening water; presently the red-haired officer was on board with him, and they were examining the fishing vessel together. It seemed that the newcomer was called Boden.

They talked about her for a time. "It's quite right what you say," said Boden. "A boat like this would be a gift for somebody. She really should be used."

Rhodes said: "Surely to God she isn't going to lie there rotting all the war."

They sat there smoking for a little. Presently the trawler officer remarked: "The fishing fleets still go out round about Ushant, somebody was telling me. You might be able to mix in with them by night. But if you did that, I don't see that it would get you any further. It isn't those we want to scrap against."

Rhodes nodded. "No," he said. "But if you could mix in with those you might sail right back into harbour with them. You could put one ruddy great gun in her, in the forward fish-hold there, and camouflage it in some way."

"And shoot up anything that you could see when once you got inside?"

"That's right. In Brest, or in some place like that."

There was a short pause.

Boden said: "I wonder how in hell we'd get the gun?"

The other glanced at him. "Do you think there's anything in it?"

"I don't see why not. If there were would you want to be in on it?"

93

Rhodes said: "Yes." He hesitated, and then said: "If I could have got in one of the fighting branches, I'd rather have done that."

The other nodded. "I think I know the way to set about it," he remarked. "The first thing to do is to think up some reasonably plausible scheme, and put it up in writing to our captains."

Rhodes nodded. "That's the way to handle it. You ask the captain to forward it for the consideration of Their Lordships."

"Is that what you say?"

"I think it is."

In the days that followed they spent a good deal of time together, sometimes in the cramped ward-room of the trawler, but more often in the sitting-room of Rhodes's lodgings on shore. In the end they evolved a scheme, sufficiently good, as they thought, to put forward in a letter.

I saw that scheme a couple of months later, with the comments of the Plans Division on it. It was not a very good idea, but there was enough good meat in it to keep it on the secret list, and so I shall not go into it here. The attitude of the Staff was broadly that for certain reasons it was only an even chance if the raid would produce the results that were anticipated in the paper. The authors admitted in their paper that the prospects of the vessel coming home again were small. The Staff did not consider that the prospect of results justified the certain loss of the vessel and her crew. They said that the officers concerned should be commended for their zeal, and that they should be encouraged to put forward any further proposals for the employment of the vessel in question that might occur to them.

This all took some time, and by the time this answer came to Rhodes and Boden the spring was well advanced. They set to work to recast their ideas, for to each of them the French ship represented the chance of fighting in the way they wanted to. They became friends in a limited, reserved way, but neither of them confided in the other. Boden let slip one day that he had once been married, and that his wife was dead, but said no more about it. Nothing would have induced Rhodes to tell any living man about his grief for Ernest.

They worked and cudgelled their brains through April into May to revise their plan in order that they might submit it again. They were much hampered by a scarcity of information about the other side. Obviously, it was extremely difficult to work out an operating plan without access to intelligence reports from which to learn the objects which could reasonably be attacked, and they had no such access. The whole thing might have fizzled out and died if Simon had not come upon the scene.

Rhodes was not present at the first meeting between Boden and this unusual, half-French army officer. Boden, it seemed, had met this Captain Simon in the private bar of the "Royal Sovereign" and had taken him at once to see the French fishing vessel that they had come to regard as their own property. She had been moved from Dittisham and had been towed down to a little shipyard on the Kingswear side; Rhodes had contrived that for their mutual convenience.

Next day they all met at the shipyard and talked for some time in the boat-shed, sitting on upturned dinghies. "I see what you mean to say, you two chaps," said Simon presently. "You mean this war goes too bloody slow for your liking."

"Put it that way if you like," said Rhodes. "There's the boat and here we are, and the Germans over on the other side. The Admiralty will give us guns for her if we can thrash out what we want to do. They as good as said so."

"And what is it that you want to do?"

There was a little silence. "That's the devil of it," Boden said. "We're working blindfold. But surely to God there must be something you could do with that sort of a boat."

The Frenchman looked across the sunlit water of the estuary towards Mill Creek. "You want to fight a battle," he said quietly. "I think you have got hold of the wrong end of the stick. You cannot fight a battle against German ships in a French fishing-boat. Your Admiralty have told you that, and they are right. I think you have been looking at this thing all wrong."

Boden said: "What do you mean?"

Simon looked at them and smiled. "Look, you chaps," he said. "I have been over on the other side. I must not talk about it, but I know what I am saying. You do not want to fight a battle in that fishing-boat. It is not suitable for that. But it is suitable for . . . secret things. In that you can approach the other side without suspicion. You can take photographs, land agents, even lay a mine or two, perhaps, before you slip away. You may work secretly for months and never fire a shot. That is the proper way to use a fishing vessel like that one."

Boden said: "You may be right in that. But that's a bit out

of my depth. That turns it into a—a sort of an intelligence job."

"Yes. That is what it would be."

Boden said moodily: "I don't know that I'd be much interested in that."

The army officer said quietly: "It is interesting work."

"Not to me."

"What would you rather do?"

"I'd rather stay on in my A/S trawler. It's a bit slow at times, but it's definitely killing Germans."

Simon glanced curiously at the strained white face. "So?"

Boden said: "Look. Take a contact that we made last month. We put down fifteen charges set for various depths, and *Louise* put down thirteen. We got a lot of oil up to the surface, and the hell of a lot of air came up. And we could hear the muggers tapping—hammering at something. We *heard* them on the hydro-phones. The noise went on for nearly half an hour, and then it got fainter and stopped."

He turned to them, eyes glowing. "They were trying to get out, or something, right down there on the bottom in seventy fathoms, in the darkness and the mud and slime. I reckon we split the pressure hull right open, and there were just a few of them trapped in one end, up to their necks in water, smothered in oil, trying to get out. I expect the lights were out and they were trying to get out in the darkness. They'd probably got just a little pocket of air above the water-level, and as they breathed up that they died off one by one. Or else the pressure killed them, or the chlorine fumes. But I swear we got the lot of them. I swear we did."

There was a little pause.

"So?" said Simon again.

Rhodes spoke up. "Can you think of how this vessel could be used if she were turned over to intelligence, as you say?"

The other said: "I could find out about that from—from my friends."

They settled that he should do so, and presently broke up their meeting. It was not satisfactory to any of them, but it seemed the only thing to do. Boden was definitely not interested; in the job that he was in he knew that he had killed some Germans, distant and unseen as they might be. He had no intention of giving up that mode of life for a less active one. To Rhodes it seemed that if the vessel were employed as Simon had suggested, there could be no place for him in the scheme. If she were to do no fighting there would be no place in her for a colour-blind Special officer; it would have been difficult enough for him to go with her, anyway.

Simon went up to London some days later, Boden went to sea, and Rhodes went on with his routine jobs at the harbour mouth. He was depressed about the vessel he had been the first to find, and a little morose. It had seemed at first that he had found an opportunity for active combat with the Germans; now that was slipping from him. Other men with better eyes would take *Geneviève* upon whatever secret mission she was destined to perform, and he would only be an onlooker. It seemed that it was not his lot to fight the Germans in this war; he could have served his country just as well or better by staying on with British Toilet Products, now switched entirely to war work. He could have still had Ernest with him.

He did not regret altogether his decision to become a naval officer, but the remembrance of his dog affected all he did or thought about. He became morose and rather bitter in regard to the trivial defect in his eyes.

Marshall, his elderly commanding officer, made short trips now and then with other area officers of the defences to see demonstrations of new methods of attack for which the coast defences must prepare. Sometimes these took the form of confidential lectures in some hall in Plymouth; at other times there were actual demonstrations of real weapons in the field. He went down in the middle of May with acute lumbago; after a day of pain and bad temper in the office he gave up and went to bed. He sent for Rhodes in the stuffy little bedroom of the hotel where he lived.

"Look, Rhodes," he said. "This show at Honiton the day after to-morrow. I fixed up with N.O.I.C. I'd take the little Austin van because the place is five miles from a railway station. But I shan't be fit. You'd better go instead of me, and come back and write a report that I can send in all about it. It's eighty miles there and eighty miles back, and I can't stand that with this damn thing I've got."

Rhodes said: "I'm very sorry, sir. What is it you were going to see?"

"Didn't I tell you?"

"No, sir."

"Well, it's flame-throwers. I don't know what the ruddy things are like, but the Germans have them in the invasion barges, so we've got to know what we'll be up against. They're going to show a lot of different sorts of them, I believe."

"I see, sir. Then we've got to see if we can cope with them?"

"That's right. You make a full report of what you've seen, when you get back, and then we'll see just what it means to us."

"Are these our own flame-throwers that they're going to show or German ones?"

"Oh, these things are our own. The Army do a good bit with them, I believe."

Marshall gave him instructions how to find the place and a roneoed, numbered pass for entry to the show. Rhodes asked: "Shall I take the van myself, sir?"

"No, you'd better not do that. The Naval Stores are sending a Wren driver. It'll take you all of three hours to get there in that thing; you'd better make your plans to get away from here by eight o'clock at the latest. The show's at eleven."

"Very good, sir."

Rhodes went into the naval garage next day and spoke to the petty officer in charge of transport, looked at the battered little khaki-coloured van with the canvas top, and decided to start at half-past seven. Punctually at that time next morning the little vehicle drew up outside his rooms driven by a dark-haired girl, a Leading Wren.

He put his raincoat on and went out to it. " 'Morning," he said a little awkwardly. "Have you had your breakfast?" He was oppressed by the knowledge that he was bad with girls.

She smiled at him and said: "Yes, thank you, sir. I had mine in the Wrennery before I came out."

He got into the bucket seat beside her. "All right. You know where we've got to go to?"

She slipped the gear in and the van moved down the road. "I think I know the place," she said. "They marked it on the map for me last night."

The morning was bright and fresh, the sun shone, and the little birds chirped at them from the hedges. The old under-powered van ground its way very noisily and rather slowly up the long steep hill out of the town.

Sub-Lieutenant Rhodes said diffidently: "She doesn't get along so fast, does she? Do you think we'll make it by eleven?"

"I think so, sir. She does a steady thirty on the level."

"I suppose she's very economical in petrol."

The Wren said: "She does about twenty-five to the gallon. That's why she doesn't go so fast, I suppose."

They relapsed into shy silence. The old van trundled noisily through the Devon lanes to Totnes and on towards Newton Abbot. Once Rhodes lit a cigarette and offered one to his driver, not quite certain in his own mind whether he was violating the King's Regulations by doing so. The Wren refused the cigarette and drove on in silence; the relationship between officer and rating was maintained, though the awkward tension in the van increased.

Rhodes did not dare to turn and look at his driver. He became very much aware, however, that the Wren was rather an attractive girl. He thought it was a pity that she was so shy.

They reached their destination with a quarter of an hour to spare. It was a bare, scorched hill behind a little country house that had been taken over by the Army and neglected; there was a small camp of hutments in the field beside it. They passed two sentries who scrutinised their passes and drove the van into the car-park.

Immediately it became most evident to Rhodes that this was not a party of his grade at all. The cars that came into the park disgorged colonels and brigadiers, air commodores and group captains, admirals and captains in profusion. They parked diffidently between the Bentley of a divisional commander and the Packard of a vice-admiral. There seemed to be nobody there lower in rank than a commander. Sub-Lieutenant Rhodes got out of the van awkwardly and looked around, trying to brush the dust from his jacket.

He said to the Wren: "You'd better hang about here. I don't suppose it'll last more than an hour."

She said: "Very good, sir." She watched him as he made his way towards the demonstration, suddenly rather sorry for him. He looked terribly diffident and out of place, she thought, amongst all those high officers.

Twenty minutes later the show was in full swing.

*　　　*　　　*　　　*　　　*

By noon the show was over, and the Packard and the Bentleys were sliding out on to the road, bearing their admirals and generals back urgently to their more humdrum work. The little Austin van was the last left in the car-park, but it was nearly one before Rhodes came back to it. A subaltern walked with him to the van; the Wren heard the last words of their conversation.

"It's terribly good of you to give me all this dope," said

Rhodes. "If I think of anything else I'll give you a ring."

The army officer said: "Okay—you've got the number?" He dropped his voice. "If you think any more about that other thing, come up again and have a chat about it."

Rhodes said: "I will do that. Thanks so much for your help."

He got into the van. The Wren pressed the starter and they moved out on to the road. As soon as they were clear of the sentries he turned to her.

"I say," he said enthusiastically. "Did you see the big one?"

She said: "I saw them all. I got a good view from the bottom of the hill."

"Aren't they the cat's whiskers?"

The Wren hesitated. She did not quite know what to say. Never in all her life had she imagined such appalling, terrifying things as she had seen in the last hour. She could not force herself to think of them as—weapons.

She said weakly: "What are they supposed to be for?"

He said: "Burning up Germans."

She was silent for a moment, sick and horrified. Presently she said: "Are you allowed to do that to . . . to people?"

"The Germans use them. As a matter of fact, they're all right in the Hague Convention." He paused. "But did you see the *distance* that the big one goes?"

She said vehemently: "But they're beastly things."

He turned and glanced at her; she was flushed and rather pretty, evidently feeling strongly about it. He shrugged his shoulders.

"The Germans started using flame-throwers—at any rate, in modern times. If we can build more horribly, outrange them, smother them with their own blazing oil . . . so much the worse for them."

He relapsed into silence, thinking moodily about his dog. He knew that he had offended the girl. He was not surprised; indeed he had expected it would happen some time or another; he was bad with girls. The only thing that he was really good with was animals, he thought. The little friendly creatures that depended on you, that had to be cared for, that must never be let down. Those were more satisfactory companions than any girl.

The Wren drove on in silence, shocked and hurt. She had not been in the Navy very long, and this was the first time that she had seen the use of weapons and what they entailed. She was twenty-two years old; in civil life she had kept the books and acted as cashier in a shop in Norwich, run by two aunts. The aunts had created a high-grade business in antique furniture and art fabrics; the shop itself was an old Tudor house, carefully and rather expensively modernised. The Wren had led a very sheltered life until she joined the Navy, mostly with women. With men she was usually on the defensive; she did not understand them. Generalising, she considered men to be brutal and insensitive. Sub-Lieutenant Rhodes confirmed her views.

I am sorry to say that their high sentiments broke down before the pressure of their baser appetites. At twenty minutes past one Rhodes said awkwardly:

"Have you had lunch?"

"No, sir."

"We'd better stop and get something." And then he realised that he had forgotten all about his cheque the day before. He had meant to cash it, and he hadn't. He fumbled awkwardly in his trouser pocket, feeling the milled edge of the coins; he had about four and sixpence. This was terrible.

The Wren was a girl of his own type, although she was a rating. He had never had anything to do with Wrens before, but it seemed to him to be essential that he should offer to pay for her lunch. Four shillings and sixpence might possibly buy lunch for one at one of the hotels along their route; it certainly would not provide for two. He wrestled in silence with this problem for a few minutes as they drove on; then said casually:

"We'd better stop and get a snack at the next pub we come to. Bread and cheese and beer."

The Wren said: "Very good, sir," a little distantly.

Presently they came to the "Coach and Horses"; he made her pull up outside it. "This'll do," he said, getting out. "I expect they can fix us up with something here."

The girl did not move from her seat. She smiled at him brightly. "I'll wait till you're ready, sir."

He was appalled. "But won't you come in and have something to eat?"

"No, thank you, sir. I'll just wait here."

"But aren't you hungry?"

She was very hungry, and she was getting very much annoyed with this young man. She said curtly: "I'll just wait here, if you don't mind, sir. We aren't supposed to go drinking in public-houses with officers.''

He was very much embarrassed. He stood there looking at her, slowly blushing; even in his confusion it did not escape him that she grew prettier than ever when she was angry. Knowing that he was blushing, he grew irritated himself.

"There's no need for you to blow that kind of raspberry at me," he said. "I was offering to pay for your lunch, but I've only got four and sixpence on me, so this is the best I can do. I forgot to cash a cheque before I came away." He withdrew his hand from his trouser pocket and looked at the contents. "Four and eightpence halfpenny, to be exact."

She felt suddenly that she had been very rude, but she did not know what she could say. "It's frightfully kind of you to want to pay for my lunch," she said. "But I've never been inside a public-house in my life."

He said: "I say, I'm awfully sorry. You'd rather go on till we find a café, would you?"

"But you want beer, don't you?"

"Not specially."

She knew he wanted a glass of beer; men always did, so she believed. She was awkward and embarrassed in her turn, and uneasily conscious of two pounds ten shillings in a note-case in her pocket. He had done his best to be friendly, after all. She said:

"Do you have to drink whisky and beer and stuff like that in there?"

"No—you can have something soft. Would you like a glass of lemonade? I expect they've got that."

She got out of the car. "All right," she said. "Which door we go in at?"

He took her into the private bar; it was deserted and empty. Rhodes ordered a pint of mild, a lemonade, and bread and cheese for two. The girl glanced around her at the clean wiped tables, the varnished woodwork, and the brewery advertisements, vaguely disappointed. She had expected to see a haunt of vice; instead it was all rather like a church vestry.

Rhodes brought the plates to her at the table. "I say," he said. "Would you mind telling me your name? Mine's Rhodes —Michael Rhodes."

She said: "I'm called Barbara Wright."

They talked for some little time about the road, and Dartmouth, and the Navy. Presently she came back to the subject that was troubling her.

"Those things you went to see this morning," she said. "We aren't going to have them in Dartmouth, are we?"

He did not answer that, mindful of security; moreover, he did not know. He said: "The Germans will be using them against us when they invade. We've got to be prepared."

She said: "We aren't using them—on our side—are we?"

Again he did not answer her directly. He said: "The more we do with things like that the sooner the war will end. It's a good weapon, that. Put a dozen of those up at the head of a beach and hold your fire till you can get the first detachment landing. Then turn up the wick on them and frizzle them up. The others will think twice about coming ashore."

She said no more. The memory of the violent spouts and gusts of burning oil that she had seen, the intense red flame, the clouds of billowing black smoke, sickened and disgusted her. People who worked out weapons of that sort, she thought, were pagans, far remote from mental contact with all ordinary people.

Presently they went out to the car, and got going again.

A quarter of an hour later one of the little tragedies common on the road occurred to them. A flight of sparrows rose up from the hedge in front of them and flew forward and across the path of the van. The quick flight of the birds made it impossible to help them, and three of them disappeared squarely between the front wheels below the line of the radiator. The Wren was startled to feel the officer beside her flinch and turn to look back through the canvas body of the van. She turned with him and looked back at the road behind. A little heap of feathers was fluttering and leaping in the middle of the road.

They both drew in their breath together; instinctively the girl had slowed down as she turned. Rhodes said: "I say—I hate leaving it like that."

She was amazed. "Would you like to stop, sir?" she enquired.

He said eagerly: "Would you mind? I won't be half a minute." The officer got out and went back down the road, stooped and deftly tweaked the sparrow's neck. It collapsed and lay still. When he looked up, the Wren was at his side.

He said apologetically: "I hate leaving them kicking. You can't help hitting them, but I always feel you ought to stop and do your best for them. If you aren't in too much of a hurry."

She said: "I feel like that, too. I hate leaving them."

He picked up the limp body and laid it on the grass verge by the roadside; together they walked back up the road to the van in silence. The girl was bewildered and a little confused. She felt that this young officer was behaving very oddly; she knew him to be a callous and insensitive man, full of enthusiasm for the most devilish things. It simply was not in the picture that he should have any feelings for the gentle things in life.

Through the hot afternoon they trundled back through Devonshire towards the coast. They were talking more freely now, telling each other the story of their lives. Rhodes told her all about his work on soya oil and Titania foot tablets, but he said nothing about Ernest; that lay too deep. The girl listened with interest and satisfaction; her first judgment had been quite correct. This, she thought, was a young man of no account. The things that he was interested in were either rather nasty, like soap and foot tablets, or they were loathsome, nightmare matters that she would not think about. He was a pleasant, well-set-up young man, she thought, but not one that one would care for as a friend. There was no depth of feeling in him.

She told him, as they drove, about her life in the old Tudor house in Norwich. She told him about the famous authors and artists that came to her aunts' shop, and how nice it was when Queen Mary came shopping in Norwich, from Sandringham, and how her aunts had put up Dr. Cronin for a night when he was on a lecture tour. Rhodes listened, politely making the appropriate comments, wondering how anyone could put up with a girl for company when they could get a dog—or even a buck rabbit. He thought it was a pity that such an attractive young woman should be interested in such footling things. He was slightly resentful because he had thought that she looked intelligent, and she was patently not so.

By the time they reached Totnes they were on terms of amused tolerance, each feeling very much superior to the other, which was satisfactory for both of them. And then Rhodes gave the girl another jolt.

They were creeping on low gear up a fairly steep hill between high banks fringed with foliage. As they neared the top he turned to her and said:

"Would you mind stopping for a minute at the top?"

Men were horrible, she thought; as if he couldn't wait. She said: "Very good, sir."

He explained: "I just want to get a bit of that cow parsley. I won't be a moment."

She turned and stared at him, and noted a faint colour in his face. "Cow parsley?" she repeated.

He said awkwardly: "It's for my rabbit. It's a chance to get him something different, coming out like this. I'm only just going to get a little. I won't be long."

The van drew into the side of the road. "I'm in no hurry," she said. "Do you mean you keep a rabbit?"

He said: "He's my landlady's rabbit, really, but I look after him. He lives in the net defence store."

He got out in the road and began pulling up handfuls of the weed from the grassy bank. The Wren got out in turn, watched to see what he was picking, and picked a little for him.

"Thanks awfully," he said. "That's enough. It makes a change for him, you see."

They put the heap of foliage in the back of the van and drove on. Again Miss Wright suffered that feeling of bewilderment. "Do you feed him on what you pick up in the hedges?" she enquired.

Rhodes said: "Oh no. He only gets that as a treat. He lives on Brussels sprout stalks and potato peelings, and that sort of thing." He turned to her. "It's so difficult being in uniform," he said. "You can't go out and come back through the streets with an armful of cow parsley. That's why I wanted to get some now."

She comprehended that; an officer had to behave as one. She said without thinking: "I'm out in this van somewhere every day. I'll get cow parsley for you, if you like."

He took her up eagerly. "Oh, would you? It'd be terribly kind if you did that. A rabbit ought to have a lot of green stuff, much more than he's been getting."

She felt it was absurd; the juxtaposition of the flame-throwers and this rabbit simply did not make sense. "You think a lot of your rabbit," she said curiously. "Has it got a name?"

He said: "Well, I call him Geoffrey."

"Have you had it long?"

"Not very long," he said shortly. He did not want to talk about his rabbit much. It was decent of the Wren to offer to get cow parsley for him, but he was not sure that she was not laughing up her sleeve at him, and this made him reticent. He felt that a girl whose interests lay with books and arty things would be scornful of the practical matters that pleased him, such as the care of a buck rabbit or the solubility of organic solids in soya oil.

They drove down into Dartmouth to the net defence store; he got out there and put his foliage just inside the gate. He dismissed the Wren, and she drove back to the Naval garage. It was time for tea. Rhodes walked back to his rooms and washed his face, had a quick cup of tea, and went out to report his visit to Lieutenant-Commander Marshall.

An hour later he was in the ward-room of H.M.T. *Gracie Fields* drinking a glass of gin with Boden. They were alone together; the captain was on shore. "I saw the devil of a thing to-day," said Rhodes. "I believe it might be useful in our racket."

"What sort of thing?"

"A flame-thrower." He told the trawler officer briefly what he had seen.

Boden said thoughtfully: "A flame-thrower . . ." He stood staring out of the scuttle at the tide flowing past, bright in the evening sun. He was silent for so long that Rhodes looked curiously at him, noting the staring auburn of his hair, the white strained face, the rather sunken cheeks. Boden wasn't looking quite so good to-night, he thought. Sometimes he looked about sixty.

Boden turned to him. "Is it a big flame?" he enquired. "Big in diameter, I mean—not just in length."

Rhodes told him.

"I mean, if you turned it on anyone—a German—he wouldn't be able to jump back and get out of it?"

"Lord, no," said Rhodes. "You ought to see the thing."

"And is it all blazing oil inside the flame, in all that width?" He paused. "I mean, what would happen to anyone caught by it?"

"It wouldn't do him a great deal of good," said Rhodes decidedly. "It's flame temperature, of course, the whole of it. But there is solid oil all through it, I think, in a sort of spray form, burning as it goes. Your German would get blazing oil all over him, and when he gasped he'd get it blazing down into his lungs. He wouldn't come up for a second dose."

Boden said: "Were you thinking we could have one in *Geneviève*?"

"That's what I had in mind. I sounded out the chaps up there about the possibility of getting an equipment. They said they thought there'd be a chance."

They spent some time together, talking it out in detail. To Boden the suggestion came like the opening of a door. It gave

a form and substance to the whole proposal to use *Geneviève;*
he ached to use a weapon of that sort against the Germans.
Anti-submarine work was all very well, but it needed so much
imagination. You could not actually see them smothering and
perishing deep down in the black sea, trapped in a bubble of
chlorine-polluted air in the split hull. Sometimes, if you were
lucky as he had been, you could hear them tapping as you
listened on the hydro-phones, but then you had to build up all
the rest with your imagination. With this new thing, if you
could bring it to the enemy, you would be able to see them curl
up and burn and die before you as you watched.

"The difficulty will be to bring it to the enemy," said Rhodes.

Boden said: "Well, that's our same old tactical problem.
But this puts a new angle on it altogether. I think we ought to
have another talk with Simon soon as possible, and see what he
thinks of it. I must say I'd be in it right up to the neck myself
if there were any chance of using anything like this."

"Simon's in London," said the Special officer. "He isn't
coming back until to-morrow night."

There was nothing much more to be done that night. Rhodes
stayed and had supper in the trawler, then went on shore again.
He walked up to the net defence store to give his evening meal
to Geoffrey; rather to his surprise he found a few stalks of the
cow parsley already in the hutch. He wondered if it were the
Wren who had been there to feed his rabbit.

He did not object to that. He had a little sixpenny book on
rabbits which informed him that a rabbit liked a full stomach,
and Geoffrey had given him no cause to disbelieve that statement. He stayed there for a quarter of an hour in the dusk,
teasing the rabbit with the cow parsley, playing with it, and
stroking the furry little coat. It was a playful, friendly little
beast and he had grown very much attached to it, but it would
never be to him what Ernest had been; it would never have
the faithful devotion of a dog. He still missed Ernest terribly.
If only this flame-thrower business could come off!

Two days later he met Captain Simon, alone, because Boden
was at sea on a routine patrol. They met in the boom defence
office; Rhodes showed the army officer the finished report of his
visit to Honiton, and told him of their plan to put a flame-
thrower in *Geneviève.*

In the hour that followed Rhodes and Simon got to know
each other better than before. Hitherto Rhodes had regarded
Simon as an odd, dilettante Frenchman, romantic, like most

foreigners. Simon had regarded Rhodes as a dreamy, ineffective young officer. He now became aware that this young officer was very much alive to the technicalities of flame-throwers, that he was an industrial chemist with a good background of experience, and that he had considerable knowledge about what could and could not be done with oil. Once launched upon his own subject he showed an energetic and a penetrating mind. Simon very quickly revised his views about Rhodes. This was a young man who could be used in war.

In turn, Simon displayed himself as a keen manager, accustomed to quick decisions upon the basis of hard technical facts. He asked the right questions, he asked all of them, and he asked them in short time; when he had got his data he made the right decision without further ado. He was obviously a man who was accustomed to control an engineering business; the sort of man, Rhodes felt, that he would like to work under.

They talked over the report for an hour. In the end Charles Simon leaned back in his chair in the bare, whitewashed little office. He lit a cigarette, blew a long cloud of smoke, and stared out of the window at the sunlit street of the small Devon town.

"So . . ." he said, half to himself. "Here is the temporal weapon that crops up again, the sacred weapon of the Holy Church."

Rhodes said: "What's that?"

Simon turned to him, deadly serious. "Listen, my friend," he said quietly. "This thing that you have now suggested—it is frightfully important. How much, you do not know. But now I shall tell you secret things which you must keep under your hat, that happened to me on the other side, not many months ago."

He leaned forward to an ash-tray, and brushed the ash from the cigarette. ":Listen to me," he said. "You know, I was employed and worked all my life in France. I used to be chief engineer of a cement works, in a town called Corbeil. . . ."

Three days later Simon was back in London sitting in Brigadier McNeil's office in Pall Mall, at the conclusion of a long discussion.

"There is the matter, sir," he said at last. "This is the way to help the people of Douarnenez." He paused for a moment. "Their minds are running upon fire," he said. "Let me bring fire to them."

The brigadier sat for a minute deep in thought. "We'll have to get the Navy interested," he said.

5

TWO days later I went down to Newhaven with Brigadier McNeil to see my admiral about the proposal. Admiral Thomson was a young man for a vice-admiral, not much over fifty; on the morning of our visit he was much engaged on a forthcoming operation, and had little time to spare for fishing-boats with flame-throwers. Yet he had found time to read the memorandum I had sent him; he discussed it with us for about ten minutes, and asked one or two questions.

In the end he said: "All right—I have no objection." He turned to McNeil. "I wish you all good luck with it," he said, "and on our side we shall do all we can to help. There are one or two restrictions that I have to make. It must not conflict with any major naval operation, and I must be the judge of that. And then, it must stand on its own feet. I can't promise you any naval support. I can't send destroyers up to the front door of Brest to help you out if you get into trouble. But you don't want that."

McNeil shook his head. "That isn't the idea at all. The expedition is a minor one, and I don't want to see it grow into a major operation. But it will serve a useful purpose, I assure you, sir."

Vice-Admiral for Channel Operations was silent for a moment. "I think it will," he said at last. "I hope it does. I think there is some danger that you'll lose your vessel and her crew."

McNeil shrugged his shoulders. "We have to take that risk each time we send a party over to the other side."

"Of course." Admiral Thomson turned to me. "I shall leave all the details in your hands, Martin. I shall inspect the ship before she sails in operations. See Captain Harrison about her routing when the time gets near. Keep me informed from time to time how it is getting on."

I said: "She will require a navigator, sir. An R.N.R lieutenant would be suitable. Can I get her one?"

"See the Second Sea Lord's office. That will make three of our officers in her—there are two R.N.V.R. already?"

"Yes, sir. A lieutenant in an A/S trawler, and a sub. in Boom Defence. Both in Dartmouth."

"And the ship is at Dartmouth, too?"

"Yes, sir."

"What is her name?"

"*Geneviève.*"

He turned away. "Very good, Martin. Do everything that you consider necessary, and keep me informed."

McNeil said: "It's very good of you to give us so much help, sir."

"Not at all. I wish your venture every success."

We left him dealing with far more important matters, and we took the next train back to London. I parted from McNeil at Victoria; when I got back to my office I found a note upon my desk asking me to ring the Second Sea Lord's office.

I rang up Lovell at once. He said: "That navigator you were asking for, who wanted to do fire. Do you still want him?"

I said: "I do indeed. I've just got permission from V.A.C.O. to take him on."

He said: "Is it for a major war vessel?"

"No," I said. "It's for a very minor one. One of these harum-scarum shows."

"I see," he said. "I've got a very good navigator, but he's not everybody's kettle of fish, if you understand. He might be suitable for you. He's ringing me again this afternoon; would you like to see him?"

"Certainly. Send him along. Is he R.N.R. or R.N.V.R.?"

"Oh, R.N.R. He holds a master's ticket."

"What's his name?"

"Colvin. A lieutenant."

Lieutenant John Colvin came to see me in my office next morning. He was a man of about forty-five, a fine-looking chap. He was over six feet tall, a lean, hard-looking man. He was deeply bronzed. He wore the ribbons of the last war on his shoulder. He had a fine head with short, curly, iron-grey hair, and he carried himself well. He had a firm chin, a humorous twist to his mouth, and grey eyes. When he spoke it was with a marked American accent.

I made him sit down. "Well," I said. "What have you been doing so far in this war?"

He said: "I was in an ocean boarding vessel, sir." He told me the name. "We paid off last week, on account of the repairs that had to be done," and I knew about that, too.

"I asked: "Were you Number One in her?"

"No, sir. Lieutenant Johnson, he was Number One." I glanced at the papers before me, wondering a little. On paper, Colvin's record should have made him first lieutenant. It might, of course, be whisky—but a glance at him convinced me that it wasn't.

"Did you join her at the beginning of the war?"

"No, sir. I joined her in February, 1940." There was a momentary silence and then, as if feeling that some more explanation was required, he said: "I had quite a way to come."

"Where were you when it started?"

"I was in 'Frisco, sir. I was Marine Superintendent with the Manning Stevens Line."

I did not know the name. "Where do they run?"

"Down to Chile, and around. Nitrate tramps, under the Chilean flag. Five of them, there were."

I nodded. "Did you come back across the States?"

He shook his head. "I hadn't that much jack," he said softly, smiling a little. "I worked a passage home as deck-hand on a tug."

He told me that the Salvage Department had been in the market for tugs all over the world, and they had bought a thing called *Champion* in San Francisco at the beginning of the war. She was not very big, she was twenty-three years old, and when loaded with a deck cargo of coal for the Atlantic crossing she had fourteen inches freeboard. They left San Francisco in November, 1939, bound for Liverpool.

Her auxiliary machinery gave continuous and increasing trouble. They came by Rosario and Acapulco to the Panama Canal, and from there by way of Kingston in Jamaica to Bermuda. Here they waited for a fortnight to join a convoy. Sailing with the convoy they blew a gasket out of the condenser pump when they were three days out, and had to stop engines while they made repairs, rolling their fourteen inches freeboard under twice every twelve seconds. Six hours later they were going again and chasing on to catch the convoy up, and nine hours after that they blew the gasket out again. They turned and steamed back slowly to Bermuda to face up warped castings in the dockyard shops.

When they were ready to start off again they were routed up to Halifax to join a convoy there. It was January by that time, and a tug with fourteen inches freeboard in the North Atlantic in mid-winter is no joke, especially for the deck-hands. They elected to try it, however, and sailed with a convoy for Liverpool as soon as they arrived. Nine days later in longitude twenty-eight west the condenser pump passed out again, this time with a bi. .n piston. They were about six hundred miles from Ireland.

The convoy went ahead and left them, and they followed after it thirty-six hours later. They sailed unescorted into London-derry in the end, rested for three days, and completed the trip to Liverpool to hand the vessel over to the Salvage Department.

"A very good show," I remarked.

He smiled gently. It was quite a trip," he said. "I'm glad we made it all right." I was coming to the conclusion that this was rather an attractive man.

I turned again to his papers. "I see you put down here that you wanted to be employed in fighting with fire," I said casually. "That's rather unusual. What put that into your head?"

He said: "Oh, that was just a fool idea I had at the beginning of the war. That doesn't mean a thing."

"What sort of fool idea? I'd like to know."

He glanced at me curiously. "The Germans used *Flammen-werfer*, in the last war, an' I think we should have done. It's what you want to give these Nazis."

I said: "Have you ever seen a *Flammenwerfer?*"

"I did see one once," he said. "It seemed to be rather an unwelcome subject."

"Where was that?"

"In the United States."

"When?" He was telling me no more than he had to.

"About 1927, it must have been."

I wrinkled my forehead, trying to think of an easy way of extracting what I wanted to know. "Was that a demonstra-tion?"

"That's right," he said. "A kind of demonstration."

I had no time to waste in going on like that. "I want to know about that flame-thrower you saw," I said. "How did you come to see it?"

He seemed very reluctant. "I was in the import business," he said at last.

"Import business? What were you importing?" And sud-denly I saw the answer to my question, and smiled. "Rum?"

He looked confused. "Hard liquor," he admitted. "It was mostly rye. I'd been going through a bad patch, sir," he said.

I grinned at him. "I don't suppose that you're the only ex-rum runner in the Navy," I said cheerfully.

"I know damn sure I'm not," he said.

"About this flame-thrower," I reminded him. "Was that in a ship?"

He said: "It was in a ship it happened. Off the coast of Massachusetts, way back in twenty-seven."

I nodded; he was easing up. "What ship was that?"

He hesitated. *"Heartsease,"* he said. "Or . . . it might have been *Judy*. They changed her name," he explained. "She was called *Oklahoma City* in the end."

"I see," I said. "How did she get mixed up with flame-throwers?"

He told me the whole incident, and it took a quarter of an hour. I didn't cut him short, partly because I was curious, but also because I wanted to know all I could about John Colvin. And what he said was this:

Rum-running in those days was an affair of queer, tortuous politics. In the beginning ships used to arrive in Rum Row and used to sell cases of liquor indiscriminately to the fast motor-boats that came out from the shore to them; there was never much difficulty in disposing of the cargo in this way. Presently the shore end of the trade became more organised as the small individual operators were amalgamated into powerful groups, were squeezed out and murdered, or were taken by the law officers. The repercussions of this development upon land were felt upon the sea. Sleek, Italianate gentlemen began coming out in fast armed boats and bought options on large parcels of the cargo. The old customers would come along next day and would be told that no Scotch was for sale, or else no rye; that it was all reserved. Then there would be trouble. Sometimes the two parties would meet on board and there would be a show-down, usually with a settlement to the profit of the Italians.

Occasionally the settlement was not so amicable. Shots were exchanged in *Heartsease*, once in the saloon and once in a desperate running battle round about the bridge that lasted for a quarter of an hour and left the ship with a good deal of washing down to do before returning to Nassau. John Colvin disapproved of this, as did his captain, but there was nothing much that they could do to stop it.

It was at this juncture that they had their trouble with Bugs Lehmann.

Colvin had known Bugs Lehmann for some months. He was a German American, they thought; at any rate he spoke with a thick German accent. They were lying anchored some miles off

Cape Cod at that time, and had come back to the same place for a number of successive trips. Bugs came out with half a dozen other men in a big launch; he paid cash on the nail with never any trouble. He did not buy large quantities, but he was a good, steady customer. They thought he came from one of the little harbours on the north side of the cape; his trade was almost certainly in Boston.

It was only when it was all over that they came to know the origin of his name, Bugs. It was, they found out later, short for Firebug.

Bugs Lehmann came on board one day just after an Italian that they knew as Mario had left. Mario had bought an option for a week on the remainder of their cargo of hard liquor, and had paid good dollars for his option. About five hundred cases were involved. When Bugs arrived in an empty launch, there were five hundred cases staring at him from the open hatches. but all they had to sell him were three barrels of Algerian red wine, an unwanted sample that they had carried with them for some months and proposed shortly to dump overboard.

Bugs Lehmann was a very angry man. He argued for some time and was exceedingly unpleasant, but the ship's officers were obviously armed and he had only three men with him. Presently the captain, a red-headed Ulsterman, took him down to his cabin and split a bottle of whisky with him. They were rather sorry for Bugs Lehmann in their way; there were no other ships about and it was clear to them that this option was one move in a shore battle of the gangs which would end in his elimination from the Boston trade. But there was nothing they could do to help him out.

He went over the side to his launch after a couple of hours, sullen and silent.

The captain stood with Colvin by the rail, watching the launch as it drew away. "That's another of the little chaps," he said. "We won't see him again."

"I reckon Mario's got his number," said the mate.

"Aye," said the captain. "Mario's got his number. Got his tombstone ready for him, like as not."

Colvin laughed. "Maybe. In any case, we deal with Mario from now on."

But they were not quite right in that. In the late afternoon three days later, Bugs came to them again. He came with six or seven men beside him in the launch. Colvin met them at the head of the companion ladder; the captain was in his bunk.

Before Colvin realised what was happening he found himself covered by a Thompson gun.

He was not greatly worried. He said: "Say, Bugs, you don't have to act like this."

The German said: "I haf no quarrel with you, eider with the captain. You chust keep quiet, and you don't see nodding, and you don't say nodding. Nor de crew eider."

The captain came up, and was covered similarly immediately he stepped on deck. Their guns were taken from them and they were locked into the chart-house; the crew were ordered below and went very willingly.

From the chart-house windows Colvin and his captain had a good view of the head of the companion, and could see most of what went on on deck. They saw a queer harness brought up from the launch, comprising a back pack of tanks and cylinders; there was a length of hose that terminated in a long metal pipe or nozzle. They watched as this equipment was buckled on to Bugs Lehmann by his satellites.

"What in the name of God is all that gear?" whispered the captain. "Is it for squirting gas?"

"I reckon it must be," said Colvin. "Do you think it's Mario they're laying for?"

"Must be Mario. I didn't expect him till to-morrow. I wish we'd never got mixed up in this."

They waited for an hour, as dusk fell. Then from the mist towards the shore they heard the deep rumble of a heavy launch. "Mario," the captain whispered.

They watched from the chart-house, tense and apprehensive. Bugs Lehmann's boat was evidently lying off some distance from the ship, because the new launch circled normally to the companion. They could see Bugs crouching down behind the bulwarks, uncouth in his equipment, the nozzle poking out towards the ladder.

There was a hail from the launch. *"Heartsease?"*

One of the men on deck, dim in the evening light, hailed back in a good English voice. *"Heartsease* it is. Watch out for our companion as you come alongside."

There was a pause, tense and pregnant.

And then a horrible thing happened. A violent blast of cherry-coloured flame shot out from the long nozzle down the companion ladder, crowded with six or seven men coming up the side. They saw Bugs Lehmann rising to his feet, directing the jet of fire full on the bodies of his Italian enemies. A burst of

Tommy-gun fire followed from the bulwarks down into the launch; there were hoarse, tortured screams, and a loud sighing, windy noise of flame. The fire lit up the whole ship with its light, died, and burst out again in sudden, dreadful jets, hideous, devastating, and inhuman.

In the chart-house the two officers watched, utterly appalled. The jets of fire, full twenty yards in length, went on and on; they could not see all that was happening over the ship's side. But in the end it stopped, and there was only the faint smoky flame of the burning companion ladder, and the blaze from the launch burning upon the water, and drifting away astern.

Presently they were released from the chart-house by an exultant gang. "I guess you got whisky to sell me to-day?" said Bugs Lehmann grimly. "That Mario, he ain't going to need it now, I t'ink."

He showed them his equipment with great pride; they examined it with horrified interest. It was a German type pack flame-thrower, and he was tremendously proud of his prowess in handling it. It seemed to mean nothing to him that he had just murdered seven or eight men horribly. Colvin got the impression from something that was said that Lehmann had served in the world war as a German *Flammenwerfer* soldier, and that he had built the equipment himself from the German model.

They sold him all the liquor that he wanted, about two hundred cases. It was slung down into his launch and in an hour he was away, and they were left to cut away the burnt companion ladder and remove the scars of fire from the ship's side before returning to the Bahamas. They sailed that night, resolved to work on the Virginia coast thenceforward and to give New England a long rest.

A fortnight later they saw in a newspaper that the body of Bugs Lehmann had been discovered in a ditch between Chatham and Hyannis.

Colvin told me all this, sitting in my room at the Admiralty; I was too interested to cut him short. "It was just a fool idea I had," he said apologetically. "But it stuck in my mind these fourteen—fifteen years; the proper way to treat them Nazis. Treat 'em the way they understand. So when the admiral asked at my interview if I had any preference in my employment, I just upped and said what I thought, and it went down like that in the record. But you don't want to pay any attention to that, sir."

That, of course, was my affair, not his. Before I took him

into my confidence, I wanted to know one or two more things about him.

"Are you married?" I enquired. One must give some weight to that sort of thing.

"No, sir," he said. He said it with just that momentary hesitation that convinced me he was lying; it was, I thought, the first lie he had told me in the interview.

"About to be?"

"No, sir."

His private life was no affair of mine, of course, and he had given me the answers that I wanted to hear. It seemed to me that I could safely leave it at that.

"Well now," I said, "the duty that you are proposed for is a special operation in a very small vessel. It's something rather in the nature of a Commando operation on a very small scale. A good navigator is needed, and that's what you've been recommended on. The vessel will be under the command of an army captain; if you accept the job you would be a sort of sailing master under his command. There will be one other deck officer under you, a lieutenant R.N.V.R. Most of the crew will be Free French."

He said quickly: "I learned some French, one time up in Quebec." He seemed keenly interested.

"That helps," I said. "Does that sort of thing line up with what you want to do?"

"And how," he said. "I got a bellyful of ocean boarding vessels."

He said: "This means some close-up fighting with the Jerries, I suppose?"

I nodded. "It's genuine Commando stuff. There is some risk in it—in fact, a lot of risk. There always is in this short-range fighting. It'll be practically hand-to-hand. Essentially it's a job for volunteers."

"Well, I'm a volunteer for anything like that," he said. "I guess that's why you asked if I was married?"

"Yes," I said dryly. "It's as well to know."

"Sure." He thought for a moment. "Say, is that why you wanted to know all about the *Flammenwerfer*?"

This was a first interview. "That's as it may be," I replied. "Plenty of time to talk about that later on."

"Okay," he said. "I certainly would like to have a job like that.

I thought about it for a minute or two. I liked the man quite well myself, but I wasn't in the party. "I'm going to send you down to Dartmouth," I said at last. "A little ship like this has got to be a happy ship; before you get this job you've got to meet the commanding officer, Captain Simon." I told him how to get in touch with Simon at the port. "You'd better take the next train down."

"Sure," he said. "But I can work with anyone. I never get no personal trouble in a ship."

That was confirmed in his record. There was one question I had forgotten to ask.

"You are a British-born subject, are you?" I enquired.

"Surely," he replied. "I was born in Birkenhead."

Colvin went down to Dartmouth on the evening train, and got to Kingswear in the middle of the night. He reported at the Naval Centre and they fixed him up with a bed. Next morning he reported back to the Naval Centre after breakfast, and there Simon went to find him.

McNeil had arranged the release of Simon from his coastal defence work some days before, and he had been putting in most of his time upon *Geneviève;* the shipyard were already working on the vessel. He had made two visits to the place at Honiton. On my part, after finishing with Colvin, I had spent the remainder of the afternoon telephoning other Admiralty departments and visiting the Second Sea Lord's office, with the result that signals went off late that night releasing Boden and Rhodes for special duty.

Simon met Colvin in the Naval Centre, where these two unusual men took stock of each other. Nobody had thought to tell Colvin that Simon was half French. They walked together down to the ship, and as they went Simon was asking questions about the other's navigational experience. What he heard satisfied him; Colvin, I think, was taciturn and wary.

They reached the quayside, and Simon indicated *Geneviève*. "There is the ship," he said bluntly. "That is what you are to work in and to navigate, if you come with us in this thing."

Colvin was startled. "What in hell kind of a ship is that?" he asked. "A fishing-boat?"

Simon said: "Certainly—a fishing-boat from Brittany. In that sort of a boat one can sail unquestioned anywhere upon the other side."

The other looked her over, noting the high bow, the steep sheer and the sloping deck, the wide beam, and the sharp-raked transom. "Sure," he said at last. He turned and smiled at

Simon. "Well, try everything once."

He jumped down on the bulwark from the quay, and so to the deck. In one quick tour from bow to stern he took in everything, noting the heavy timbers of the vessel, and her powerful engine. Then he turned to Simon.

"Say," he said quietly. "Nobody told me yet just what it is this ship is supposed to do."

Simon said: "There is the cabin, what they call the cuddy in the shipyard here. Suppose we go down there."

They went down there for an hour, the July sun streaming down upon them through the l'ttle skylight. "There is the matter," Simon said at last. "That is the job that this ship has to do."

"The oil-tanks, and that, go down into the fish-hold, I suppose?"

"That is the place for them," the other said. "There is room there for everything, for all the oil we shall require. Only the gun itself, the flame-gun, will show up above the deck, and that we shall pile over with a net."

He glanced at Colvin. "This is the way I want to fight the war, myself," he said simply. "It may not be the way for you. If it is not your way, then you should say so now."

Colvin said: "Sure it's my way. The way I look at it"— he paused and sought for words—"if you're going to have a fight there's no good sticking to the Marquess of Queensberry's rules, if you get my meaning. If the other chap's out to hurt you, why then kick him in the belly and have done with it. That's how I look at it. And this fire racket is as good a way of hurting Nazis as any that I know."

Simon got up. "So—then we are agreed. It is a terrible weapon," he said reflectively. And then he smiled. "Almost good enough for the Germans."

They went up on deck. "A little can of beer?" he said politely to his navigator.

That afternoon Colvin met Boden, released that morning from his trawler. He met him in the ship. "They're reckoning to put me into this as Master," Colvin said, "as near as I can make it out. In that way you'd be working under me. But as I understand it, this was your idea right from the start."

The other said: "Don't worry about that. I've never had command."

"What have you been doing in the Navy?"

"I've been in trawlers—about eighteen months."

Colvin grunted; it was not a bad recommendation. An R.N.V.R. who could stand trawler life was obviously no pansy. "I reckon we'll make out all right," he said.

They talked about the ship for half an hour, going over every part of her in detail.

"This army chap, this Captain Simon," Colvin said at last. "Where does he come from, and who is he? Is he French?"

Boden said: "He's an Englishman by birth. He's a pretty fine sort of chap, I think. He's done at least one spying trip upon the other side."

Colvin said: "It's certainly a change from ocean boarding vessels."

6

MCNEIL was very busy in the next few days, and I was not idle myself. He got the flame equipment down to Kingswear in forty-eight hours from our meeting with the admiral, and installation started in the shipyard. I went down there to organise accommodation about that time. I saw the Naval Officer in Command, an elderly retired commander, much puzzled by the unorthodox and secret nature of the party that had been established on his doorstep, but willing to help in any way he could.

After a short talk with him, I decided to put the party up the river, at Dittisham, three miles above the town. It was a quiet, isolated country district for one thing; for another, there were a few empty houses there. I got a couple of modern villas standing side by side; one was already empty and we requisitioned the other at twenty-four hours' notice. Messing had then to be arranged, and finally transport.

Sitting in N.O.I.C.'s office I came to this one. "Transport," I said. "While they are out at Dittisham, say for two months, they'd better have a light ten-horse-power truck with a Wren driver. That should make them independent of your organisation." I made a note. "I'll get an extra driver and a truck appointed to you right away," I said. "In the meantime, for the next few days, can you help them out?"

He said: "Of course. I've got an Austin van that they can have the use of. It's usually pretty busy; we shall want another."

The old commander played a typical old-stager's trick over that van. Up at the Admiralty next day I thought it out and came to the conclusion that the lightest sort of truck might not do all they wanted in the way of transporting all the various stores and ammunition that they might require. I went one size larger, and sent them down a new, fifteen-horse-power truck with a very efficient young woman as a driver. This outfit was attached to N.O.I.C. for administration, of course; when the old commander saw it it appeared to him to be a gift from heaven. He put it straight on to his routine work, and attached the little old Austin van with Leading Wren Barbara Wright as driver to work for Captain Simon's party.

Colvin knew all the details of the exchange within twenty minutes. He went to Simon in great indignation. "What d'you think?" he exclaimed. "That bohunk up there in the office went and pinched our truck! Commander Martin sent us down a dandy truck from London, a new one, bigger'n this. I just seen it in the garage. What say, we go and have a showdown with the old bastard?"

Simon said: "It is very wrong, and we are very much mis-used, but we will not make a quarrel over it. If we have too big loads for this one, or if this one breaks, then we will ask for our own truck again. But N.O.I.C. is helping us in many ways; we will now let him get away with this."

Colvin grumbled. "I wouldn't let him get away with it."

Simon smiled. "Think of the junior officers, and do not spoil the fun. That other woman with the big truck, she has a face like a boot."

They were on deck, with shipyard men all around them; the old truck stood on the quay. A gang of men were unloading cans of cooper's grease and drums of tar from it. Rhodes, newly promoted to a lieutenant, was standing talking to the driver.

She said: "I put some cow parsley inside the gate last night, sir. Did you find it?"

He said: "Oh yes—it was frightfully good of you to bother. I gave him half last night, and the other half this morning." He hesitated, and then said: "I was away at Honiton the day before yesterday, with Captain Simon. Somebody fed him while I was away. Was that you?"

She said: "I wasn't sure if you were coming back that night, so I thought I'd better. Mrs. Harding isn't allowed in there, is she?"

"No. It was very kind of you to think about him."

She flushed a little, and said: "Oh, that's all right. I let him out for a little run, but I was scared of him getting under that heap of depth charges, so I didn't let him out for long."

He was immensely grateful to her. He had been very worried on that trip to Honiton that they would not get back in time for him to take Geoffrey out for his daily constitutional, and now, it seemed, he need not have worried at all. Miss Wright, as a naval rating, had access to the net defence store at any time, and she was willing to look after Geoffrey in emergency, it seemed.

He said: "He can't get under the depth charges if you put the plank up across the ends. Didn't you see the plank?"

She shook her head.

He said diffidently: "If you like to come down there this evening when I'm feeding him, about seven o'clock, I could show you how it goes. Then if you want to have him out again, you can."

She said: "All right. I've got to go over to Brixham this afternoon, so I'll be able to get some more cow parsley. I'll bring that along with me."

"Fine—I'll be there."

There was a little pause.

"You've got another stripe," she said. "That makes you a full lieutenant."

He smiled self-consciously. "I get a bit more money now."

"Did you get it because of this show?" She inclined her head towards the vessel at the quay.

"I was about due for it anyway," he said. He hesitated, and then said: "Are you going to be attached to us now? I mean, we're going to have a truck with a Wren driver."

"I think I am. It was to be the new truck with the Wren who drove it down from London—Miss Roberts, I think she's called. But they seem to have switched things round."

He said a little shyly: "It'll be fun if they keep it like that." And then he said quickly: "I mean, it'll be interesting for you, seeing the whole thing right through from the start."

She said: "I'd like to see it all, I mean, having seen it at the very beginning." She coloured slightly. "I must go now, or I'll be late."

He stood back from the van. "If you're not doing anything, I'll be down there about seven."

He was there before her, standing over the rabbit as it hopped about the little yard of the net defence store, eating the dandelions. She found him there cleaning out the hutch.

"Good evening," she said. "I see you're busy."

He straightened up, pan and brush in hand. "I do this in the evenings," he said, "because then the ratings aren't about."

She said: "Is this the hay you give him?"

"That's right," he said. "That goes in his sleeping quarters."

"I'll do that," she said.

They worked together for ten minutes, making a boudoir for the rabbit between the Oropesa floats and the depth charges. He showed her the plank that he had set up across the ends of the depth charges to prevent the rabbit getting in between them and eluding capture.

She said, half laughing: "You aren't afraid that any of these will go off?"

"They're not fused," he said. "We couldn't keep them stacked like this if they had pistols in."

"Does that mean that they're quite safe?"

"I think so," he replied. "Just how safe they are, I'm not quite sure."

They stooped down together to the rabbit, and began feeding it young carrots. Geoffrey nibbled them seriously right to their fingers; he was very tame. "He *is* fun," said the girl. "Have you ever kept rabbits before?"

Rhodes said: "No, I've never had a rabbit." And then he said: "I had a dog once, but he died . . ."

She said: "You seem to know all about rabbits."

"Well, they're decent little beasts," he said. "I mean, it's something ordinary to have, to look after. He isn't really mine, of course," he said. "He belongs to Mrs. Harding."

"But you look after him, don't you?"

"Oh yes," he said. "She hardly ever sees him."

The girl turned to him. "I do think you're funny," she said.

He was immediately on the defensive, and a little hurt. "Because I like rabbits?" he said. " 'Pansy' is the word you want."

She said quickly: "Not like that. But things like flame-throwers—and rabbits—they don't seem to go together."

He shrugged his shoulders. "I can't help that. If that's the way you are you can't help it."

"No," she said, "I suppose that's so."

They fed Geoffrey the remainder of the carrots. "Was that the flame-thrower that they were putting in this afternoon?"

she asked. "All those tanks and things?"

He nodded. "We're going to move up to Dittisham the day after to-morrow, to finish off the job up there."

"Is that because it's more secret up there?"

"That's right," he said. "We don't want this equipment in the shipyard for too long."

She indicated the rabbit. "Will you be able to come down here and look after him from there?"

He said: "I've been thinking about that. I can get the trot boat down each evening, or else come in with you in the van."

She said: "You don't need to worry about him. I shall be living in the Wrennery and coming out to Dittisham every day, so I can always do him if you can't."

He said warmly: "I say, that's awfully nice of you."

They moved up to Dittisham one Thursday, and went on a mooring two or three hundred yards above the landing. The four officers moved into one of the houses requisitioned for them, the other being held in reserve for the crew. Simon spent most of his time away in London at Free French Headquarters during these days, interviewing and picking his crew. The bulk of the work of getting the ship fit for sea fell inevitably upon Colvin and Boden, and they worked solidly from dawn to dusk each day.

Colvin found Boden to be unlike any R.N.V.R. officer that he had met in this war or the last. Most of these amateur seamen had definite shore interests, seldom shared by the R.N.R. Boden, it seemed, had no such interests. He never seemed to want to go on shore; he had no correspondence to speak of. He never seemed to want any relaxation; he seldom read a paper or a magazine. Colvin himself was no great reader, but he liked the *Daily Mirror* and he liked looking over the pages of *Picture Post* in the evening. The other officers very soon discovered that what this handsome, grey-haired merchant seaman really liked was pictures of bathing girls. Sometimes he would find one in a periodical and hold it up for their inspection. "Say . . ." he would breathe, "just get a load of this! Ain't she a dandy?"

"I knew a girl one time that used to sit for them pictures," he said once. "Miss Oregon, she was. Her real name was Susie Collins."

Rhodes said curiously: "How did you get to know her?"

"I was one of the judges," Colvin said simply. "A guy what knows his way around can always get to be one of the judges in a beauty contest. Ankle competitions, too."

Simon laughed. "And then you can take your pick!"

Colvin was a little offended. "You don't want to talk that way," he said. "This was all regular. I used to go visiting with her folks."

They tried to get more detail out of him, but he was put off by their ribaldry, and would tell them nothing more.

The man who got to know him best was Boden. Boden had very few interests outside the ship, and in the ship his duty lay continually with Colvin. He grew to admire the middle-aged merchant officer immensely; he was the first really competent and efficient commanding officer that Boden had served under. He learned continuously from Colvin. If they had had much paper work on board the defects of the older officer would have become apparent, but their constitution was such that there was practically no paper work of any sort to do. What little there was in the way of requisitions and indents, Colvin was content to leave in Boden's hands.

On his side, Colvin had never had a junior officer so hard-working as Boden, or one with so few shore interests. After a week or so it seemed to him that there was something almost queer about the lad. Rhodes he could understand; Rhodes was running after the Wren in the truck, a reasonable occupation for any young chap in Colvin's opinion. Boden, it semed, had no such inclinations.

Ten days after they began it was a Saturday. Three or four Breton lads had joined them under the command of a petty officer called André, who spoke a little English; Colvin arranged that they should knock off work at five and that André should take these lads on shore. Rhodes, they knew, would be in Dartmouth; Simon was in London.

Colvin turned to Boden. "Let's you and I go into Torquay an' see what's to be found," he said.

"I don't know about me," said Boden. "Think I'll stay on board." .

The older man looked at him, puzzled. "Say," he said. "You'll get enough of sticking around here before we're through. Come on into Torquay, an' make a break I don't want to go alone."

The last remark bore weight with Boden. "If you like," he said.

He would genuinely rather have stayed on board. Six little long green boxes had arrived on board that day, containing six Thompson guns; other crates and boxes had arrived with them full of drums and ammunition. Boden had never handled any weapon of that sort; to prepare for it he had bought a book about the Thompson gun. He would rather have sat all evening in the cuddy with his book and with the gun and with a handful of clean rag, learning, assimilating. Still, Colvin wanted to go to Torquay, and didn't want to go alone. In his loneliness he was becoming fond of Colvin.

They got to Torquay at about six o'clock. Boden had no particular wish to go anywhere or do anything; he was content to let Colvin take the lead. He suspected that Colvin was on the look-out for a bathing beauty, for Miss Torquay. If he achieved his end, thought Boden, he would make off and leave him to it; he could get back to the ship and have an hour with the sub-machine-gun before bed.

They strolled from the station down the front towards the town. There were young women by the score there, sunning themselves; most of them turned and glanced at the two naval officers. The white-faced, red-haired young R.N.V.R. was commonplace, but they looked very long at the tall bronzed officer beside him, with the ribbons on his shoulder and the iron-grey hair.

"Get anything you want to here," said Boden presently.

The other gave a little snort. "I don't go in for them kind," he said. "All giggles an' silliness, and in the end you get what you don't want, as like as not."

Boden was surprised. "I couldn't agree with you more," he said. He had never picked up a girl on the beach and didn't want to start; it warmed him to find that Colvin held the same views.

The R.N.R. officer said presently: "What say, we find the best hotel and have a drink or two, an' then a durned good dinner—oysters and that?"

"Suits me," said Boden. "What about the Metropole?"

"Is that where you get the best food?"

"The food's supposed to be better at the Royal Bristol, and that's got a garden. But it's full of old ladies."

"They won't hurt us any."

They found their way to the Royal Bristol Hotel, and had a couple of pink gins on the terrace overlooking the garden and the sea. It was a quiet, pleasant place. The service was unobtrusive and efficient; the sun was warm, the garden bright with flowers. As Boden had foretold, it was full of well-to-do elderly people.

"I call this a dandy place," said Colvin. "It must cost a

raft of money to live here, like all these old Buddies do."

Boden knew something about that. "I had an aunt who came here once. They took eight guineas a week off her."

"Sure. Was that with a bathroom and a sitting-room, and that?"

"Not on your life. She had just a bedroom."

"Nice business, if you can get it."

They sat in silence for a minunte or two. Then Boden said: "Have you ever fired one of those Thompson guns?"

"Not against anyone. I fired them once or twice at barrels and that."

"What's the muzzle velocity?"

"Oh shucks, I dunno. Fifty to a hundred yards, that's all you want to use them at. It's only a little bullet, like an automatic has."

His mind was evidently not on the subject. Presently he indicated a couple of chairs in the lounge over to their right. "I bet that Jane don't see much life," he said.

Boden glanced over and took in the scene. A very old lady dressed in black was sitting primly in a chair, knitting. A girl, or woman, perhaps thirty years of age was sitting by her reading the evening paper aloud in a low tone. She wore no rings. She had a blonde, fair head and a resigned, bored expression. Once she must have been a beautiful girl; now she was growing old before her time.

Boden shrugged his shoulders. "She looks after Mother," he diagnosed. "Somebody's got to look after Mother."

"Sure," said Colvin. "And when Mother dies the girl gets all the berries."

"Probably."

The gong for dinner rang, and the old lady and her daughter went in almost immediately. Colvin and Boden followed them ten minutes later. At the entrance to the dining-room the older man paused, reading a notice. "Got a dance on here to-night," he said thoughtfully. "Fancy that!"

They did not get oysters with their dinner, but they dined quite well. They talked very little, both occupied with their own thoughts. Boden was still preoccupied with the sub-machine-gun; if the shells were really automatic pistol ammunition, then the muzzle velocity was probably quite low, which agreed with the short range that Colvin had in mind. That, probably, was what made the gun handy to fire; there would not be very much recoil.

Colvin was also absent-minded. Half-way through dinner he said to the waitress: "That old lady dining over there. What's her name?"

"That's Mrs. Fortescue, sir."

"She live here?"

"She's been here since March."

"That her daughter sitting with her?"

"Yes, sir. That is Miss Fortescue."

"Okay."

The waitress moved away; Boden awoke from his ballistic reverie and cocked an eye at his companion. "What's all this about?"

Colvin smiled. "I was just thinking," he said, "that it was quite a while since I went dancing."

Boden shook his head. "You'll get us both thrown out if you try that."

But he had underrated Colvin. They finished their dinner and went through into the lounge for coffee. The old lady and her daughter were sitting a little way away from them; presently the old lady wanted something from her room. The girl went to fetch it. Colvin, who had been watching, immediately got up and crossed over to Mrs. Fortescue. Boden sat still, appalled.

He had great charm of manner, an air of distinction. He bent slightly towards Mrs. Fortescue and said: "You must forgive me, ma'am. Would you consider it all out of order if I asked your daughter for a dance to-night?" He smiled charmingly. "I've been out of England a good many years, and I've rather forgotten the way things go back home here, socially. I didn't want to do what folks might think was rude—but I don't know anybody here . . ."

The old lady looked at him and took him all in, the firm, handsome features, the grey eyes, the iron-grey hair. He looked like an ambassador in naval uniform. "I am sure my daughter would be delighted to have a dance," she said. "Sit down and talk to me."

He sat down readily, retrieving her spectacle-case from the floor as he did so. "That's very, very kind of you," he said. "My name is Colvin. One gets kind of lonesome when you don't know anybody in a place."

"I am sure you do," she said. "Have you been here long?"

"Only a week or two," he said. "Before that I was in the North Atlantic on patrol since war began, with convoys and that. And before that again I had a job in San Francisco for a raft of years. It's fifteen—seventeen years since I last lived in England.''

She dropped her knitting to her lap. "And did you come home all the way from San Francisco to fight in this war?''

"Yes, ma'am.'' He had a good story to tell without departing from the truth, and he told it with modesty and humour. Half-way through the girl returned carrying a shawl; she approached them with surprise and interest giving new life to her face. Colvin got up as she approached.

Mrs. Fortescue said: "Elaine, my dear, this is Mr. Colvin. He has been telling me such a marvellous story of his journey home from San Francisco. Quite thrilling!''

The girl smiled at him and they all sat down together. Boden watched from his seat a few yards away; it had been a smooth, competent piece of work which increased his respect still more for his commanding officer. He did not want to join them. If he left in half an hour he could get back on board *Geneviève* by half-past nine, with an hour's daylight still to go in which he could become acquainted with the gun. In the meantime, he would sit and smoke.

Presently there was the sound of a dance band from the dining-room and Colvin took Miss Fortescue through to dance; a faint flush of colour in her cheeks made her attractive. The colour had deepened when Boden passed them in the corridor on his way to the cloakroom for his cap and gloves. He overheard her say:

"You mustn't call me Wonderful, Mr. Colvin. My name is Elaine.''

He said pleasantly: "Oh shucks, that's my American tongue running away with me. You don't want to worry about that.''

Boden treasured up that one to tell Rhodes.

I went down to Dittisham for the gun trials a few days after that. The installation of the flame-thrower was complete and the full crew of ten Free Frenchmen and two Danes were on board. One of these Danes spoke English and was an engineer in civil life; Rhodes took him as his second-in-command upon the flame-gun, and trained him in the rather complicated mechanism. I got to Dartmouth early in the forenoon, having spent the previous day at Teignmouth on another job. Simon met me at the station with a little shabby truck, driven by a Wren. He wore the uniform of a captain in the Sappers, battle-dress; he saluted me very smartly.

I paused before I got into the truck. "Is this the lorry I sent down?" I asked. It seemed so old.

. Simon laughed. "It is not the same," he said. He told me the circumstances as we started off. "He is very pleased with us because we got him a new truck," he said. "We can get anything we want now—ropes, paint, anything."

I grunted; there was nothing much to say, and Simon went on to detail to me all that still had to be done before the ship was fit to sail on operations. We got to Dittisham in about ten minutes, and drew up outside the officers' villa.

I got out. Simon said:

"I am going to change my clothes before we go to sea." He paused, and looked me up and down, hesitant. "We do not call attention to ourselves, or to the ship," he said. "We usually go out in rough clothes, as fishermen. I could lend you an old pair of trousers and a jersey . . ." And then he added: "But you can wear your uniform if you like, sir. It does not really matter."

"Not a bit," I said. "I'll do whatever you do."

I went and changed with him in his room; when we went down to the boat on the hard a quarter of an hour later I was the complete fisherman, in blue jersey with S.Y. *Arcturus* in white letters on the chest, rather torn and old, blue serge trousers and gum boots. It was the first time I had ever done a gun trial in those sort of clothes.

Colvin met me as I scrambled over the side. They were all dressed as fishermen, and their salutes were humorous in their incongruity. I spent about ten minutes going round the ship with them; then we cast off the mooring and got under way.

We slipped down past the town, out by St. Petrox; at the harbour mouth we set a course south-east out into the West Bay. We steamed on on that course for an hour or so; I did not want to do our stuff within sight of land. I was busy all that time, because I had to satisfy myself that they would be ready for the admiral's inspection. I went around the ship with Colvin and with Boden making a list of the defects that they still had to rectify. I spent some time in the engine-room, crouched in the confined space beside the pulsing Diesel. Then on deck I had a long talk in bad French with André, the C.P.O. in charge of the Free French and Danish crew. He was a decent, fresh-faced, smiling sort of chap who had been in the French Navy for eight years, much of the time in the *Dunquerque*. His home was in St. Nazaire; he said his wife was there still.

That put an idea in my head, and I asked him if any of the

crew came from Douarnenez. But Simon, I found, had considered that point carefully. None of them came from anywhere closer to Douarnenez than Audierne.

I left André, and found the ship's armament laid out on deck
for my inspection; six Tommy-guns and several revolvers. They
were all well oiled and cared for; we put a barrel overside and
cruised around it, firing a few rounds from each. Then we turned
to the flame-thrower.

We did not fire that at a target; I did not want to draw attention by creating a blaze. We had a good look round the sky for
aircraft, waiting a quarter of an hour till one away over to the
west went out of sight. Then Rhodes slipped into the little bucket
seat, we pulled away the camouflaging nets, and I gave him the
word to open up.

He fired three shots of three or four seconds each, traversing
as he fired. The thing belched out its flame in a great terrible
jet that dripped blazing oil upon the water underneath its fury;
above it thick black smoke wreathed up into the sky. On deck
the heat was intense; one could hardly bear to keep one's face
exposed to it. He fired three times, and each shot plunged its
burning, lambent tip into the sea many ships' lengths from us.
Rhodes seemed to have no difficulty in training and in elevating
the weapon.

I stopped him then and got into the little seat myself. He
stood beside me till I was entirely familiar with the controls;
then he stepped aside and I fired three shots with it myself. The
heat was very great, but not unbearable, and the view of the
target seemed to be fairly good. Within the limitations of the
thing it seemed to work all right, and I could pass it off for
service. I told Rhodes that he must have a pair of goggles up
upon his forehead to pull down if firing had to go on for a length
of time. Three shots was all I wanted without some protection.

That was the end of our gun trials, and there was a great
column of black smoke above us towering up to show what we
had been doing, six or seven hundred feet high. We turned and
steamed towards the north end of Torbay at our full speed to
get away from it, re-arranging the camouflage as we went in case
a Heinkel or a Dornier came up to have a look. But nothing
came except a Hudson of the Coastal Command, which circled
round us at a hundred feet, obviously puzzled. We had an Aldis
lamp in the little wheel-house, and I made a signal to him:
Admiralty to Hudson—Go away. He waggled his wings at us
and went off up Channel.

We held on our course till we were within a couple of miles of Hope's Nose, then altered course for Berry Head and Dartmouth, making a wide circuit to prevent our return being associated with the dark cloud that we had made at sea. We entered the river and passed up by the town at about 15.30, picking up our moorings at Dittisham a quarter of an hour later.

We went on shore, changed back into our uniforms, and had a cup of tea in the ward-room. Then I got into the truck and the Wren drove me back to Dartmouth to catch the evening train to London.

I sat beside the Wren. During the short drive I said to her: "Are you with this party permanently, or do other drivers share the duty with you?"

She said: "I'm the only one that ever comes to Dittisham, sir. They put me on to this job when it started. I do nothing else but this."

I nodded. "You know a good deal of what's going on, then, I suppose?"

"I think so, sir. I've driven them to Honiton three times."

"I don't suppose I need to tell you not to talk," I said. "One day this party will be going over to the other side. If through some careless word of yours the Germans get to know about it, they may be killed. That's a real danger now, and you don't want to risk it."

She said: "I know that, sir. Lieutenant Rhodes warned me to be very careful."

I was mildly interested; everything to do with that party was of interest to me. Rhodes was the technician. I said: "Who gives you your orders—tells you what to do?"

"Captain Simon, sir. When he is away, Lieutenant Colvin or Lieutenant Boden."

I said idly: "But it was Rhodes who told you about secrecy?"

She said: "Oh well . . ." and stopped. I glanced at her, and she was flushing a little. Then she laughed. "I get the food for his rabbit," she said. "He told me then."

"Does Rhodes keep a rabbit?"

"Yes, sir. In the Net Defence Store." With a little urging she told me all about it; that is how I came to know about Geoffrey."

She took me to the station; I crossed to Kingswear and took the evening train to London. Next morning from my office I rang Brigadier McNeil and told him that the gun trials had been satisfactory.

He said: "I'm very glad to hear it. I say, you've got a very smart young officer upon that thing." We were speaking on an outside line. "That chap Rhodes."

I was pleased. "I think he's pretty good," I said. "He's colour-blind, but I don't think that matters for this job."

"He's some kind of an industrial chemist, isn't he? In civil life?"

"I think he is," I said.

"They were very much impressed with him at Honiton. They seemed to think you'd picked a really good man for the job."

"Well, that's pure luck," I said. "It was he who brought it forward in the first instance. We didn't pick him; he picked us." And then I went on to talk to him about the admiral's inspection of the ship.

I saw V.A.C.O. a couple of days later and told him, amongst other things, that *Geneviève* was ready for him to inspect.

"Very good, Martin," he said. He turned to his engagement diary. "Sunday—I am meeting Captain Fisher at Torquay to see the M.G.B.s for Operation Parson. Suppose we say Saturday afternoon for *Geneviève* at Dittisham? I should like Brigadier McNeil to be there, if he could make it convenient."

"Very good, sir. Will you stay the night in Torquay?"

"I think so. The Royal Bristol is very comfortable. See if you can get rooms for us there, Martin."

I did, and when the day came we travelled down to Torquay in the morning, arriving soon after lunch. I had arranged a car, and when we had dropped our bags at the Royal Bristol we started off in it for Dittisham, Admiral Thomson, Brigadier McNeil, and myself. We got there about four o'clock. Simon was waiting for us with a little motor-boat to put us on board the vessel; we were not taking her to sea, so everybody was in uniform and very smart.

N.O.I.C. was there. I imagine that they had been consulting him on etiquette, because a boatswain's pipe shrilled out as the admiral clambered up the short rope-ladder that served as a companion on *Geneviève* and swung his leg over the bulwark. I never saw such a variety of salutes upon one ship before. Simon saluted army style, of course, and the naval officers in navy style; nine of the Free Frenchmen saluted the same way and one differently because he had been a rating in their *Armée de l'Air*. The two Danes saluted differently again.

The inspection followed upon stereotyped lines. The admiral found a cat on board. That was my fault; I knew that idiosyncrasy of his and I should have warned the ship. "I have no objection to animals on board—within reason—in harbour or in time of peace," he said weightily. "But in a ship sailing against the enemy they are out of place, and may even cause the loss of valuable lives. People do stupid things, go back to save them when the ship is sinking. A great many seamen have lost their lives in that way—yes, and officers too." He turned to Colvin. "See that it is put on shore before you sail."

"Very good, sir."

He was interested in the flame-gun, and got down into the seat to handle it while Rhodes explained the mechanism to him. "Yes," he said at last. "A very dreadful weapon if you have your enemy within its range. Unfortunately, he isn't always there."

The ship's armament—what there was of it—was laid out on the hatch. He picked up a Tommy-gun, handled it for a moment, and put it down again; then we went aft. He turned to Simon. "I understand you are the officer who got the information which you hope will lead you to the enemy," he said.

Charles Simon said: "I was in Douarnenez in February, sir. I went there on my way back from Lorient."

"Yes—I remember. Tell me now, in your own words, what you hope to do. I have heard it from Commander Martin, but I want to hear it from you."

Simon said: "On this first trip, sir—it is just reconnaissance. If we can find the fishing fleet, mix in with them, and get away without detection—that in itself is of much value. That way we can land agents, open up communications with the country." He paused.

"I do not want to make contact with the enemy, at any rate on this first occasion," he said. "I would prefer we . . . how do you put it? Find our feet—yes, first find our feet." He smiled deprecatingly. "And, anyway, we cannot make a contact with the enemy even if we want. We have twelve knots at the most, and a *Raumboot* can do twenty. It is for him to make the contact with us."

V.A.C.O. said: "That's very true. And if the enemy makes contact with you?"

"Then he is almost certain to come up to shouting distance," said Simon. "He can do nothing else, because to him in the night-time we are a fishing-boat, that cannot read a signal. If he comes close, then we burn him up."

"And get away into the darkness quickly?"

"That is the way. We must be many miles off shore before the dawn."

They talked about it for some little time, standing there in the calm summer afternoon, the admiral and the cement engineer from Corbeil. The tide slipped by us between wooded hills under a clear blue sky; in the trees the wood-pigeons were calling. It was very quiet and peaceful there.

"What English port will you sail from?" the admiral asked.

"From Penzance, if we may. That makes the shortest crossing of the sea and the least risk of observation by the German aeroplanes."

"Very good." The admiral looked up and down the length of the little vessel. "All the luck in the world," he said at last. "Come and report to me when you get back."

We went over the side into the boat, and he followed us down the ladder; we were ferried ashore. On the hard we turned and looked back at the ship; they had draped the netting over the flame-gun again. But for the men in uniform moving about on board she was every inch a fishing vessel.

We got into our car and were driven back to the Royal Bristol Hotel. I had to be with the admiral next day in Torquay; McNeil was going back to London, but had missed the afternoon train. So we all stayed that night in the Royal Bristol Hotel.

It was a Saturday, and I remember noticing as I went through the entrance lobby that there was a dance that evening. I went up and washed and then came down and sat with the others in the garden till dinner, looking out over the bay.

We dined rather late. As we sat down to dinner I noticed Colvin sitting with an old lady and a younger woman, probably her daughter; he seemed to be keeping them amused, because I heard the girl laugh more than once. They got up shortly after we went in and went through into the lounge for coffee.

Admiral Thomson had noticed them. He said: "Wasn't that the first-lieutenant in the ship we saw to-day?"

"Yes," I said. "His name is Colvin."

"A handsome-looking chap," said McNeil.

The admiral said: "I'm sure I know the old lady. Her husband was Chief of Staff in Malta just after the last war. I was in *Tiger*. They used to ask us up for tennis." He wrinkled his brows. "Now what the devil was the name?"

He asked the wine waiter when he came. "Mrs. Fortescue, sir," the man said.

"That's it—General Fortescue. I must go and talk to her after dinner."

When we went out into the lounge he crossed the room to where the old lady was sitting with Colvin and the daughter. Colvin got to his feet as the admiral went up, looking a little awkward.

V.A.C.O. said: "Mrs. Fortescue, I'm sure you won't remember me. But years ago—in 1919 or 1920—we met in Malta. You were very hospitable to my ship, and you came to a dance we had on board."

She looked at him from her chair. "Of course I remember you," she said. "Commander . . . Commander—is it Thomson?" He nodded, smiling. "But I see it's not Commander any longer—something much grander. I'm sure I don't know what all those gold bands mean. Do bring your coffee and come over here and join us. This is my daughter and Mr. Colvin."

V.A.C.O. bowed to the daughter and nodded to Colvin. "I have met Mr. Colvin," he said. "Is this the little girl you had at Malta?"

He sat down with them and began reminiscing with the old lady. Colvin was looking awkward still; I moved over to him.

"I say," I said in a low voice, "I'm damn sorry about that cat. I ought to have remembered what he thinks of cats and warned you."

He said: "That's all right, sir. I'm glad that was the only thing he found to bawl us out on."

"There was nothing else," I said. "I think he was very pleased with what he saw."

We sat chatting about this and that for a quarter of an hour; then dance music sounded from another room, and Colvin took the girl through to dance. I heard the old lady say to the admiral:

"What a nice man that Mr. Colvin is! Is he under you?"

He said: "In a way he is. Commander Martin here knows more about him than I do."

She smiled at me. "Elaine and Mr. Colvin are great friends," she said. "He comes and takes her dancing whenever there is a dance. It's very good for Elaine. Living as we do in hotels like this she meets so few young men. Sometimes I feel it's rather selfish keeping her with me."

The conversation shifted on to something else, but I had heard enough to make me just a bit uneasy. I was fairly certain Colvin had been lying when I had asked him if he was married;

at the time I was quite glad, because that was the answer that I wanted. I watched when they came back after two or three dances. The girl had got a colour in her cheeks and she was as radiant as a bride.

Geneviève was due to sail on operations in a few days' time. A damn good thing, I thought.

I went back to London with the admiral the next afternoon, Sunday. That was some time at the beginning of September, and the nights were long enough for what she had to do. I made the necessary arrangements, and they sailed her round to Penzance on the Thursday and Friday, working up as they went.

There was a full moon that week, and the weather was perfect, much too good for them. I wasn't going to be any party to sending them over to the mouth of Brest upon a blazing moonlit night half as light as day. I talked it over with McNeil, and we kept them there at Penzance for the best part of a week before we let them go. By then the moon was waning, and we got a forecast of unsettled, rainy weather. That was more the sort of thing we wanted, and I went down to Penzance with McNeil overnight.

That morning, Thursday morning, was grey and dreary with a light rain falling. *Geneviève* was anchored just outside the harbour; I went to the Naval Centre and got a boat out to her. Colvin had been ashore to report when they got there; apart from him none of them had left the ship. They had been out each day exercising in Mount's Bay, but it was very cramped quarters in the ship for the full crew, and they were anxious to get away.

I had a conference with them in the cabin that forenoon, Simon, Colvin, McNeil, and I. By the shortest route they had about a hundred and ten miles to go to a point half-way between Le Toulinguet and the Ile de Sein, where they might reasonably expect to find the fishing fleet. I wanted them, however, to keep clear of Ushant by ten miles or so; that made their route about a hundred and seventeen sea miles. At their comfortable cruising speed of ten and a half knots, that meant a bit over eleven hours.

I did not want them to get to the rendezvous before midnight, in order that they should have plenty of darkness in which to approach the coast, and I told Simon that he ought to get away soon after three in the morning.

Colvin marked off their course upon the chart and measured

it carefully. "Get under way at one o'clock," he said. "Hands to dinner at twelve. I'd better tell the cook." He went out to the galley.

I turned to Simon. "If you can make it, come to Dittisham direct on your return," I said. "I shall go back to Dartmouth and wait for you there."

Brigadier McNeil said: "Is there anything more that you want? Anything we can do for you when we go ashore?"

Simon brushed back the long, dark hair that had fallen over his forehead. "There is nothing that we want," he said. "We now have everything. Only if you are going back to Dartmouth, would you do one thing for me?"

He said: "Of course."

"These Frenchmen that I have here in the ship," said Simon. "In England they can none of them afford to drink the French wines, and they do not like the heavy English beer. When we come back, in two days or in three, they will be very happy. I would like that they should have each a bottle of French wine to their dinner—cheap red wine, like Pommard, or the St. Julien that English people drink. I will pay, but will you find the wine for me?"

The brigadier said: "I'll look after that. I'll have it there at Dartmouth waiting for you."

I straightened up above the chart-table. "Well, away you go," I said. "Wish I was coming too."

We went on deck; the boat was waiting for us at the side. I took a last look round. Rhodes was there, and he came up to me.

"You going back to Dartmouth, sir?" he asked.

I told him that I was.

"If you see that Wren, Miss Wright," he said, "would you remind her to be sure and feed my rabbit? She's the Wren that drives our little Austin truck."

"I'll do that," I said. "Anything else?"

He grinned and said casually: "Give her my love."

"I'll do that, too," I said. McNeil was already in the boat, and I went over the side and joined him, smearing black, tarry paint over my bridge coat as I went. We pushed off, returning their salutes, and made our way back to the harbour in the rain.

It was nearly twelve o'clock. Neither of us wanted to leave Penzance or to sit down to lunch till we had seen them on their way We went into a pub beside the harbour and had a couple of whiskies in silence; neither of us could think of anything to talk about except what could not be talked in a public-house. At a quarter to one we went out and walked up and down on the sea wall watching the ship.

At five minutes to one we heard the rumble of her Diesel motor over the water and saw that she was shortening her cable. The anchor came up to the hawse, and she turned to the south. She put on speed, and very quickly vanished in the rainy mist.

7

I WENT back to the Naval Centre and made a cryptic signal to V.A.C.O. to tell him that the ship was on her way. Then we had lunch and got on to the train; we arrived back in Dartmouth late at night and slept in the Naval College.

I say we slept, but speaking for myself, I was awake for most of the night. I had been intimately concerned with this venture from the beginning, and I had come to know the officers if not the ratings more intimately than was usual in operations that I had to do with. It makes it difficult to sleep when you possess that knowledge; you lie awake hour after hour, wondering whether, sitting at your desk, you could have thought more deeply for them, organised them better, made them safer in the perils that they had to face. It's really not so good to know a ship so intimately as I knew *Geneviève*.

We did not hurry in the morning. By the shortest route, close round by Ushant, it is a hundred and seventy sea miles or so from the rendezvous where they expected to find the fishing fleet, to Dartmouth. Assuming that they left the area at two in the morning, they could not possibly arrive before six o'clock in the evening; in all probability they would be out another night unless they put into some nearer port. There was nothing for us to do all day but to keep within hail of the telephone in the Naval Centre.

We made our way down there after breakfast. Outside the door the little Austin van was parked; the Wren driver was walking up and down disconsolately outside. She brightened when she saw us coming up the street, and went and stood by her car.

I stopped for a moment. "Miss Wright," I said. She came to attention, which rather put me off. "I had a message for you from Lieutenant Rhodes. He wanted me to remind you to be sure to feed his rabbit."

She coloured a little. "Very good, sir," she said formally. And then more humanly she asked: "Did they go?"

This girl already knew sufficient to blow the gaff if any gaff was to be blown, and had known it for weeks. "They got off yesterday," I said in a low tone. "They should have done their stuff last night. They may be back here late to-night or very early to-morrow morning."

She said: "Thank you, sir, for telling me."

"Keep it under your hat," I said. "And don't let Rhodes come back and find his rabbit hungry."

She smiled at that; she was really quite a pretty girl.

I turned away, then stopped. "Oh, and one other thing," I said. "He asked me to give you his love."

She blushed suddenly scarlet; it seemed that I had hit the bull's eye quite unwittingly. "He did what, sir?" she muttered.

I grinned. "You heard me the first time," I said, and turned and went into the Naval Centre with McNeil.

I rang up V.A.C.O. and told the duty officer where I was in case any news came through, and I did the same with C.-in-C. Western Approaches. It was then eleven o'clock in the morning, and there was nothing to do but sit and wait for news.

It's very trying when you have to wait like that. McNeil and I did not talk much; we sat there smoking our pipes, trying to read and concentrate upon our newspapers in the bare little office. So many things could have happened to them, apart from enemy action. It had been a dark night up till two o'clock, though it had not rained much; at Dartmouth visibility had been poor, and it was probably much worse around Ushant. We had sent them in in the dark night to close a coast that was unlit and sown with reefs. To the north of their area ten miles of half-tide rocks run out from St. Mathieu to Ushant; to the south the Saints stretch a great tongue of reefs westward fifteen miles off-shore. In the middle of the area the reefs outside Le Toulinguet stretch two or three miles out; in amongst all that mess they had to find their fishing fleet. The tides were strong round there; in places they ran four or even five knots. If in the darkness and the run of tide they were five miles out in their position at the end of a hundred-and-thirty-mile trip, they might have met disaster absolute.

I sucked my pipe and tried to read the news, which was all bad. The Russians were being driven farther and farther back, and now the Germans were approaching the Crimea.

McNeil and I went out to lunch in turn, one of us staying by the telephone. We walked up and down outside the office after lunch in the fitful sunshine between bursts of rain; the Wren was still there waiting with her little truck. At about four o'clock I went and saw the secretary, an R.N.V.R. lieutenant.

"There's the Watch Point up on the cliff, sir," he said. "We've got a direct line to that. Your Wren knows where it is, and I'll have any call that comes put through to you there."

I went down with McNeil and got into the truck, telling the Wren to take us to the Watch Point. She said eagerly: "Are they coming in, sir?"

"It's not time," I said. "They can't be here much before dark."

The Watch Point was a little camouflaged hut on the cliff-top, half sunk in the earth. There was an old petty officer in charge and a signalman with him; they had a good big telescope upon a stand and a couple of pairs of field-glasses. Three hundred feet below us lay the sea, grey, dappled, and corrugated with wind. It was a better place to wait than in the office.

The signalman made tea, and I had the Wren in and gave her a cup. She sat in a corner silent, waiting with us. We waited on there, smoking patiently, talking very little, hour after hour. And in the end they came.

The signalman first saw them at about half-past seven, when the light was beginning to fade. He saw a vessel through the telescope many miles out, heading for the harbour. We all had a look in turn, continuously; even the Wren had a look, the signalman helping her with the focusing. When they were three or four miles out and we were quite clear it was *Geneviève* I rang through to the duty officer and told him they were coming in.

"Make them a signal to go straight up to their mooring at Dittisham," I said. "I shall go round and meet them there."

"Very good, sir."

I sent a message to their mess steward at Dittisham to get a meal ready, and then we left the hut and got into the truck. Half an hour later we drew up outside the villas, left the Wren there to help with the meal, and walked down to the hard.

The vessel was already in sight down the reach, coming up in the last of the evening light. Down at the water's edge there was an R.N.V.R. surgeon-lieutenant waiting in the boat, who had come out from Dartmouth on a motor-bicycle. A rating rowed us out towards the mooring as the ship drew near, and we scrambled over the side before she was secured.

Simon met us and helped us over the bulwark. He was in fishing clothes, dirty and unshaven, and very, very tired.

He said: "We got a *Raumboot* with the flame-gun, sir."

McNeil said: "You did get one? God, that's fine! Did you sink her?"

He shook his head. "I do not know. I think she may have sunk in the end. She was all burning end to end when we had finished, but we did not stay around. And then the rain came down again, and we lost sight of her."

McNeil went on with Simon; Colvin came up to us. "This is a damn good show," I said. "Did you get any casualties?"

"Not one," he said. "They never got a single round off at us. That fire-gun surely is the goods."

I asked a few more hurried questions, but the men were obviously very tired and I wanted them to get ashore. The full report could wait till they had had a meal and some sleep; there was no urgency. I told Colvin to get everyone ashore and hand over to the shore party for an anchor watch.

Boden said: "What about the Jerry? Do we take him too, or leave him here?"

Colvin said: "Leave him here the night. He's all right as he is."

"Do you mean a German?" I asked, startled.

"Sure," said Colvin. "We picked one up out of the water, but he died pretty soon." He paused. "We put him down alongside the fuel-tanks. Do you want to see him?"

I turned to McNeil. "They've got a dead German," I said: "Do you want to have a look at him?"

"So I hear. I think perhaps we'd better, and then take him ashore to-morrow."

Colvin took us down into the hold beside the tanks. There was a long figure lying covered by a blanket. "He's not a pretty sight," said Colvin. "He was pretty well burnt up before he got into the water."

He removed the blanket.

"No," I said, "he's not."

McNeil asked: "Had he any papers on him?"

Colvin shrugged his shoulders. "I dunno," he said. "To tell the truth, we didn't kind of fancy going through his clothes. We reckoned that was the shore party's job."

He replaced the blanket and we went on deck. The ratings were being ferried on shore in batches. I found Rhodes and said:

"This is a damn good show. Did you have any difficulty?"

"Not a bit, sir. It went exactly as we planned."

"Fine. You'd better get on shore now and get a hot meal and some sleep. We'll make out a report in the morning."

"Very good, sir."

He turned away; I stopped him. "I gave your message to the Wren," I said.

"Thank you, sir."

"I should bloody well think so," I replied. "Next time you want a go-between, just you give the job to Brigadier McNeil."

André was there. I spoke a few sentences to him in my lame, halting French, telling him to tell the ratings that they had put up a damn good show, and that the admiral would be very pleased with the ship. He replied with a volley of which I understood one word in five, and we beamed at each other, and then it began to rain.

It was practically dark and there were only a few of us now left on board. Boden was at my elbow, obviously very tired. I said to him: "I expect you could do with some sleep."

"I'm not tired, sir," he said. And then he said: "It's a fine thing, that flame-thrower. There were three of them on the bridge, and they were just blotted out. And the two by the aft gun—they just disappeared." He paused. "I think it was one of them we picked out of the sea."

"Very likely," I said. "We'll make out a report in the morning."

"Will we be going out again, sir?"

"I don't know. We'll have to think about that."

"We ought to go again, sir. It's a fine game this—better than anti-submarine. I mean, you can see what you're doing."

The boat came back again. "Go on down," I said to him. "The thing to do now is to have a meal and some sleep." And a bromide for him, I thought; the surgeon would provide that. Boden went down into the boat; I followed him, and we were ferried ashore in the darkness and the rain.

In the two villas most of them were at supper. I told Simon that I would be out in the forenoon, and I had a word with the surgeon-lieutenant about bringing the dead German ashore and about the bromide.

He nodded. "Two or three of them can do with something of the sort," he said. "I'll look after that—I've got some stuff with me. I'll stay here for an hour or two."

McNeil and I left them; they would not settle down while we

were there. We went back in the little lorry driven by the Wren to the Naval Centre, and I put in a telephone call to V.A.C.O. The admiral was still in his office and I spoke to him and gave him the substance of what had happened.

"That's very satisfactory," he said. "Give the ship my congratulations, Martin—no, I'll make them a signal. And I should like to see the commanding officer, that Captain Simon, as soon as he has finished making out his report. I shall be here for the next two days."

I rang off and we went back to the College for a late, scratch meal before bed. Next morning we went back to Dittisham and settled down with Simon and Colvin in the ward-room to hear the full story. And what it amounted to was this.

They left Penzance at about 13.00 in a squall of rain. It was warm and rainy all the afternoon, with visibility varying between one mile and five miles. They saw two aircraft of the Coastal Command and flashed their code sign at them with an Aldis lamp; they saw no enemy aircraft. They kept their speed meticulously, doing ten and a half knots in each hour by the log and plotting their tidal drift each hour with wind corrections. They set their course to pass seven miles to the west of Ushant, and as darkness fell they were approaching the island.

They had a bit of luck there, because the fog-signal was going from the lighthouse at Le Jument; they heard it faintly in the distance. It was too distant and too faint to give them more than an approximate bearing, but what they got out of it checked more or less with their dead reckoning, and they changed course off Ushant according to plan.

They were then upon a course as if to enter Brest, and they were perhaps twenty-five miles from the entrance to the Rade. There was some danger that they might meet a patrol vessel, so they put on their red and green sidelights and slung a white light half-way up the mast, fishing-boat style. At the same time they manned the flame-gun and made ready for action.

They were not intercepted. Visibility was poor, with occasional showers of rain. They had time in hand, and slowed to eight knots, at which speed their engine was much quieter. They stopped two or three times to take a sounding, and went on upon a course for Cap de la Chèvre.

They ran two and a half hours, about twenty miles upon that course, into the region which the French call L'Iroise. At any point in that course they might have met the fishing fleet, but they saw nothing of it. What they actually saw, at about 23.45, was a flashing light, which they identified as a minor light-house called Le Bouc, upon a rock about two miles west of La Chèvre.

Simon and Colvin bent over the chart-table together. "That's the boy," said Colvin. He put his pencil on the rock. "Just about where he should be, and if that's not a bloody miracle, I'd like to know what is."

Simon stared fixedly at the little pencil-line that marked their course. "The light must mean that there are vessels out to-night," he said. "So much is certain; they would not have the lighthouse alight unless it was necessary to them." He turned to Colvin. "This lighthouse, is it useful to ships going in and out of Brest?"

The other shook his head. "It's right out of their way. It only serves ships going to Douarnenez."

"Then it must be alight for the fishing fleet, or for their *Raumboote.*"

"Seems like it."

Their course for the last twenty miles had been south-east, parallel with the string of reefs that runs from Ushant to La Chèvre, broken by the entrance to Brest. The fleet could not be to the north of that course, therefore if it was out at all it must be either ahead of them in the bay of Douarnenez or to the south down by the Chaussée de Sein, which we call The Saints. They stood on into the bay, still burning all their steaming lights.

Visibility was a bit better by that time. They saw the great bluff of La Chèvre and went on past it right into the Bay of Douarnenez. They were in the enemy's waters with a vengeance then, in range of batteries that could have blown them out of the water with the greatest of ease. They must have been seen from La Chèvre; in all probability their steaming lights protected them.

They got within about six miles of Douarnenez at about one o'clock in the morning. There was no sign of the fishing fleet in the bay. They turned and steamed along the south shore of the bay, about two miles from land, heading back towards the west.

Near Beuzec, suddenly, a searchlight leaped out at them, and caught and held them in its glare. From the wheel-house Simon shouted out in French—"No firing. Two or three of you wave your hands at them. So—that is good." The white light lit up every detail of the ship, blinding, intolerable. They puttered on upon a steady course towards the west, each moment expecting a shell.

Then the light went out, and for some time they could distinguish nothing in the inky darkness.

Simon turned to Colvin. "We must look very like a fishing-boat," he said.

"Sure," said the other. "If we didn't we'd be looking like a butcher's shop by now."

At about one forty-five they saw a light ahead, and slightly to the north, low down upon the water. Then there were several lights, and presently a number, scattered rather widely in their course.

Simon and Colvin bent together over the chart. "They're all around the end of the land," said Colvin quietly. "I reckon that the flood is bringing the fish up through this bit they call the Raz de Sein. . . ."

They were all on their toes as they approached the fleet. Coming from the direction of Douarnenez their approach was natural enough, if it was ever natural for a vessel to come out from harbour in the middle of the night to join the fleet. They moved on towards the swaying lights, and saw no sign of a patrol vessel. Then it occurred to them that the *Raumboot* would be to seaward of the fishing fleet, while they were approaching from the land.

Presently they could see the hulls of the vessels. All had their bows towards the south and their engines ticking over as they stemmed the flood-tide, keeping their station with the coast, trailing their gossamer nets in a wide, gentle bag not far below the surface. All of the vessels wore a light upon the mast; about thirty per cent of these were orange lights, and the remainder white.

They took station with the fleet, extinguishing their red and green sidelights, leaving their white light burning on the mast. With bows towards the south they rode for a time at the tail of the fleet. The nearest boat, burning a white light, was within fifty yards of them; they avoided the neighbourhood of the orange-shaded lights, the boats that held the German petty officers. They rode like that for half an hour, tense and waiting developments. But nothing happened at all. It would have been very easily possible for them to go alongside one of the boats wearing the white light, to exchange messages or to land an agent. The first object of the reconnaissance was proved.

146

The officers discussed the position in low tones. Simon said: "Now we should slide away, and make for England again. Next time we come, it will be with a purpose."

Boden said: "We're not going home without having a crack at a *Raumboot*, sir, are we?"

Rhodes was still at the flame-gun, growing a little tired, with the thought of Ernest brooding darkly in the back of his mind. Colvin said:

"This sliding away. Do we put the light out here, where everyone can see us put it out, and then slide? Or do we slide away with our light on? Seems to me we get the *Raumboot* on us either way."

Simon thought for a minute. "We will slide away with the light on," he said definitely. "I think you are quite right. In either case the *Raumboot* will come to us, but if we drift away towards the north with the light on we shall be some distance from the other ships, and what we hope to do may then look like an accident."

He turned to Colvin. "Drop backwards very slowly with the tide," he said. "Let it seem that we lost position accidentally, keeping the bows to the south."

"Okay," said Colvin. "Now for the fun."

The slow beat of the engine dropped still lower, and the boats near them began to draw ahead. In the dark night, misty and wet with a light rain, they waited, peering over the water. Boden, in charge of the six Thomson gunners, crouched down behind the low bulwarks on the wet deck, tense and listening. An alarm gong, sounded from the little wheel-house, would bring them into action; till then they were to remain concealed.

Colvin was at the wheel himself, the engine controls at his hand. By his side was Simon, with a speaking-tube to Rhodes at the flame-gun.

Nothing happened for a quarter of an hour.

They dropped further and further back from the fleet; by the end of that time they must have been over a mile from the nearest of the fishing-boats. Five minutes more went by, in unendurable tension.

"Don't believe there's any *Raumboot* here at all to-night," grumbled Colvin.

Simon said: "Well, you are wrong. She comes now, over there."

He pointed at a white light over to the west, and the faint glimmer of a green light. A vessel was coming northwards under power, heading towards them. A faint buzz of whispers ran around the decks.

Simon asked, whispering: "How large is she?"

Colvin measured the height of the lights from the water with his eye. "She's only a tiddler," he said. "Not much bigger'n we are." In fact, she was nearly twice their size; he meant that she was not a destroyer.

She passed a quarter of a mile away from them; the green light broadened and a red appeared; then white and red alone were visible. "Coming up along our starboard side," said Colvin. "I'll give her a sheer in a minute, so as we get right up to her."

Simon bent to the speaking-tube. "She comes up now upon the starboard side," he said. "You see her clearly?"

Rhodes said: "I see her."

In a minute Simon said again: "Rhodes, listen to me. There is nobody on deck in front of the bridge. If there is a gun there, it is not manned. Fire first at the bridge, and then to the aft gun, if she has one."

"Aye, aye, sir. Fire first at the bridge."

The tension was unbearable. The *Raumboot* came up on their quarter about fifty yards away; they heard the clang of her engine-room gongs as she slowed. Her bow came level with their stern. . . .

Colvin stooped and jerked the throttle half open, and gave the wheel a twist to starboard, to close the gap between the ships. "Fire when you like now, Bo'," he said laconically.

Simon shouted down the speaking-tube: "Rhodes—fire!"

A jet of blazing oil leapt out from the camouflaging nets, setting them well alight. It lit up the *Raumboot* coming up alongside them, dark grey in colour and now only thirty yards away. Appalling, fascinating, the jet seemed to travel slowly to its target. It was a horrible, yellowish-red writhing spear; it carried at its point to strike the enemy a dark blade of un-burnt oil, ever consumed and ever sailing nearer to the bridge. Its light went on before it, and in that light they saw a bearded officer in an oilskin, leaning over the rail towards them, mega-phone in hand. In an instant that stayed etched in Colvin's memory they saw him staring at this frightful thing sailing through the air at him, horrified and immobile.

Then it hit him, and all sign of the bridge vanished in a terrible furnace of bright flame. For three or four seconds the flame played upon the bridge with a hoarse, windy noise, then it

trained aft to the petrified gun crew at the stern. It came very
swiftly on them. They hesitated; there were three of them. Then
they broke and left the gun. One of them dived for a hatch
and may have got below; the others went down in a violent belch
of fire.

Colvin, watching intently, saw the *Raumboot* start to fall
astern. He spun the wheel and sheered away from her; she
dropped further astern, and Rhodes could no longer bring his
fire to bear upon the gun. He traversed up her decks again as
she fell further back. Then he cut off his fire, and black darkness fell on them, lit only by the burning camouflage nets on
Geneviève and the blazing oil fires on the *Raumboot*.

Simon roared out to the Breton crew, speaking in French, to
get the net fire out and to take down the mast-head light. Then
he looked astern. There were men upon the foredeck of the
Raumboot; there was another gun there.

"Turn quickly," he said to Colvin. "Or they will shoot us
up." And down the speaking-tube he said: "Fire at the forward
gun, upon the foredeck, when you can. There are men there
now."

The gun was evidently stowed and unloaded; a long immunity
had made the Germans casual. The fire burst upon them as
they were fixing a drum to the breech, and they were hidden
from sight in the violence of the flame. In a few seconds Rhodes
trained back on the bridge.

The *Raumboot* was now stopped. Colvin continued with his
turn across her bows, slowed, and drifted down her starboard
side as she lay burning.

Simon said down the speaking-tube: "Rhodes, give her oil
now." The flame died away; there was a moment's pause, and
a great hosing jet of black oil burst from the gun. Where it fell
upon a flame it blazed up and fire ran along the deck; in other
parts it made great dripping, smearing pools.

"Now the fire."

The flame blazed out again and trained the full length of the
ship; she became a furnace from end to end.

The fire from the gun ceased, and they lay rocking by the
burning ship, watching what they had done. "Time we were out
of this," said Colvin tersely. "What say, we get going now?"

There was no sign of life now on the *Raumboot;* nothing but
a great sea of flame. She was alight down to the water's edge.
She lay between them and the fishing fleet; they were well placed
to get away towards the north. Moreover, it was time. Other

ships must be making for the burning *Raumboot* at full speed;
it could only be a matter of a few minutes before they were discovered in the light of the blazing ship.

They put on power and began to draw away. Almost immediately one of the Bretons shouted from the bows; there was a
body in the water ahead of them. Simon spoke to Colvin and
shouted a command to André. They reversed engines to check
way upon the ship beside the man, now seen clearly floating in
the water by the topsides. In urgent haste they made a bowline
on a rope and lowered one of the Bretons down into the sea;
he made a rope fast round the body and it was unceremoniously
hauled aboard. They put on speed again at once and drew away
towards the north; they were barely a quarter of a mile distant
when they saw other vessels coming up behind the burning ship.

Colvin said: "Let's hold on this way for a couple o' minutes
more. Then, what say we jink a bit?"

They went on for half a mile or three-quarters, doing their full
twelve knots. Then they turned sharply to the west, and in a
few minutes turned again and made for the south-west. Several
vessels were around the burning ship, and amongst them was
at least one other *Raumboot*. They went on, tense, expecting
every moment to be picked up by a searchlight. But no light
came, and presently they altered course again towards the west.
They saw the blaze upon the water till they were distant about
five miles from it; then it was blotted from their sight by a rain
squall. The glow on the horizon lasted for half an hour.

After a time they turned to the north-west.

Boden came up to the wheel-house presently. "That German
that we picked out of the water died," he said.

Simon said: "Died? Was he alive at all?" He had risked
waiting by the burning ship to pick the body up because he
wanted to bring home a trophy of some sort, something to show
for certain that they had engaged the enemy.

"He was alive, within the meaning of the act," said Boden.
"Caspar gave him a shot of morphia with the hypodermic."
Caspar was one of the Danes who had been a chemist in his
previous existence. The morphia he gave was a full lethal dose,
and presently the body on the deck found peace.

"Where had we better put him?" asked Boden. "I suppose
you want to take him home with us."

"Sure we do," said Colvin. "What do you think we stopped
to pick the mugger up for? Sure we take him home."

"What'll we do with him?"

They were well clear now of the burning ship, which showed as a faint, distant glow on the horizon. Colvin called André to the wheel and handed over to him. He went forward with Boden, and surveyed the body on the deck.

"Two of you get him down the aft hatch and lay him between the fuel-tanks," he said. One of the Danes translated into French. "Then get a blanket to put over him, the way that we won't keep on seeing him."

So they brought him back to England. I do not think that anybody in the ship was much affected by the sight of him, unless perhaps Colvin himself. Bitterness had warped most of the rest of them; if they had any feeling in the matter it was satisfaction.

Certainly Boden displayed no regret. He squatted on the steering-cable case in the lee of the wheel-house with Colvin, just before the dawn. They had been ten miles off Ushant by their reckoning at 04.30 and had set a course for the Lizard, planning to get as far as possible from the French coast before day betrayed them. In the east a greyness was beginning. They had empty mugs, which had contained hot cocoa, on the deck beside them. It had stopped raining, but the decks were wet and their oilskins hung in stiff, clammy folds. It was rather cold; there was the strong saltiness of a small ship at sea.

Colvin said: "You'd better go down and turn in for a spell. I'll call you in a while."

"I'd rather stay on deck. I don't want to turn in."

"Not sick, are you?" There was some motion on the vessel, but though Colvin had watched for it he had never yet seen the R.N.V.R. officer seasick. His time in trawlers had hardened him.

"I'm not sick, sir. But I shouldn't sleep if I went down. I'd rather stay up here. You go on down; I'll call you if we see an aircraft."

"Why wouldn't you sleep? You're not thinking about that dead Jerry, are you? You don't want to think of that."

Boden said: "Just what I do want to think about."

"What's that you said?" The older man was puzzled.

Boden turned to him. "I don't mind looking at that Jerry. I wouldn't mind a hundred or so like him, all stretched out in rows and stinking." He paused, and then he said: "I was married, you know."

Colvin glanced at him in wonder. "I never knew that."

"I don't tell people, much." He hesitated. "She got burned

to death in one of the first London blitzes. She had to go to London because we were going to have a kid. And the Jerries got her. . . ."

He stared out over the dim sea. An early gull rose from the water at the bow, wheeled crying above their heads, and soared away into the murk.

Colvin said: "Say, I'm sorry. It's tough when a thing like that has to happen. I never knew a thing about it."

Boden said: "I sort of keep it under my hat."

Presently Colvin asked: "How long ago did that happen, lad?"

"Just a year—almost exactly." He turned to the other. "I'd rather that you didn't tell the others," he said. "I sort of like to keep it to myself. I wouldn't have told you but for something that you said."

"I'll not say anything." From the depths of his experience the older man sought for something that was comforting. "Was you married long?"

"Nearly two years."

"How old was you then, when you got married?"

"Twenty-two. She was nineteen."

Just a pair of kids, the merchant sailor thought. It was plenty tough. "Had you known each other long?"

"We'd known each other all our lives. Her father and my father are partners in the firm, you see." He turned to Colvin; for the first time in a year he was speaking freely. "We very nearly didn't get married at all, because of that. We'd always done things together, all our lives, and it seemed so—so unadventurous to go and marry somebody that you'd known all your life as soon as you were old enough. As if we might miss something. And then we thought we might miss something bigger if we didn't. . . ."

Colvin said: "I guess you had all your eggs in the one basket."

"What?" And then he said: "Well, that's so. I never got much fun out of going around or dancing with anyone else."

The older man said: "It's just dandy if it happens to work out like that. But then when something happens, like it did with you, you're in an awful spot."

"I know."

The dawn was grey now, over a cold grey sea that foamed past them and slopped in at the scuppers as they rolled. "I never got so deep as that with any one woman," said Colvin.

152

"Maybe I'm not the kind for a great lover. Maybe I think too much of myself."

Boden glanced curiously at the handsome, middle-aged man by him. "Were you ever married?"

"Lord, yes," said the other. "I was married earlier'n you, way back in the last war when I was twenty-one. I been married five or six times, maybe more. Over'n over again. But it never took."

For the first time in a year Boden was intrigued, taken out of himself by interest in someone else's affairs. He said: "What used to happen?"

"Most times I lost my job," the merchant sailor said. "That happens pretty frequent in the shipping business. Like when I was in Halifax, Nova Scotia, in the import trade. Then they repealed the prohibition law, and we was all on the beach, all the lot of us together. Well, some stuck around in Halifax till they were down and out, but that was never my way. I just drew all I had and gave it to the wife—and there was quite a wad, close on two thousand dollars. I took fifty of them and skipped out to look for work some other place—shipped as a deck-hand on a freighter going south. Three months later I was master of a coaster sailing from Shanghai. Chinese, of course, but better'n nothing."

He paused. "Well, there you are," he said. "I never was much of a hand writing letters, nor was she. After saying I was quite well and was she quite well and the weather was lousy I was finished, 'n you can't keep married upon that when you're eight thousand miles apart. Even the Pope of Rome himself couldn't keep married that way."

"No," said Boden. It seemed the only thing to say.

"It's the way things are in the shipping business," said Colvin. "Mind you, I'm not saying that I'm not to blame. guess I always wanted to go places and do things more'n I wanted to stay home with the wife. And then you get stuck down in some foreign place like Shanghai that I was telling you about, or else maybe in Sydney, and every month you think that you'll be on the beach again, and it drifts on for years. And then maybe you get a notice that you've been divorced for desertion, or else maybe you get so God-damned lonely that you just say what the hell, and go and marry someone else. And in a year or two it starts again all over."

Boden said: "You never felt like chucking up the sea and getting a job on shore, and settling down?"

Colvin laughed. "I did do that one time," he said. "I got a shore job in Frisco; I was Marine Superintendent of the Manning Stevens Line. Not a lot of jack attached to it, but I don't need much. We got a little apartment out in Oakland, and everything was dandy while it lasted. But it didn't last."

Boden asked: "What happened?"

"The bloody war came," the older man said simply. "Just another thing, like happens all the time. It didn't work then, going on in Oakland. I stuck it long as I could, 'n then I gave her all the jack I'd got saved up, about six hundred dollars, and skipped it back to England in a tug."

"Where is she now?"

"I dunno. Eight or nine months since I had a letter. She don't write much. Time she's got the ink and the pen and the paper all together in one place she's forgot what she wanted to say and lost the stamp."

Boden grinned. "When did you last write?"

"Oh shucks, I couldn't say. Longer ago 'n that."

There was a long silence.

"I did think, one time, I was settled down for good," Colvin said. "The job was steady and all regular, not like it was in Halifax. The last marine superintendent that they had held it down till he was sixty-eight, 'n only quit then because he wanted to. And one time I was all set to do the same. We was even talking about having kids, which is a thing I never held with in my way of life. But now, it's just the same as it's been all the time—I dunno why. Two years since I skipped out of Oakland, 'n six thousand miles—maybe seven."

He sounded tired and depressed. Boden said gently: "Why don't you write and get her over here?"

The other shook his head. "It wouldn't be practical," he said. "Junie's a small town girl from a burg called East Naples, in Arkansas. Maybe she's gone back home by this time. I did think once that I might try and save the jack to get her over. But when you come to think of it, I'd have been a sap. Like as not by the time she got here I'd have been in Capetown or some other place; we went 'most everywhere in my last ship before we settled down to convoy duty. And then she always did have a bad break if it was possible to get one; like as not she'd have been sunk coming over, or if not that, then I'd have been sunk by the time she got here and then she'd be stuck here with not enough jack to get back to East Naples. You got to be practical."

Boden nodded.

Colvin laughed. "As for this bloody racket that we're in on now," he said, "she'd likely be a widow before ever she left Oakland to come over."

He got stiffly to his feet. "Toss you which of us goes down and has a caulk."

"You go on down," said Boden. "I shouldn't sleep."

"Okay." He fumbled in his oilskins and pulled out a watch. "Send someone down to give me a shake at twenty to eight, 'n tell the cook I'll want a mug of tea and a hot sausage ten to eight. Give you a spell at eight o'clock."

"All right," said Boden. "I'll give you a call if we sight anything before."

"Aye. I don't want to miss nothing."

They rolled on steadily towards the north, over a grey sea covered by low cloud. We had picked our weather well; they saw no aircraft until shortly after noon, when a Hudson picked them up and took the identification signal which they flashed at him. At 12.30 they sighted the Lizard about ten miles to the north and altered course up Channel. They entered Dartmouth at about 20.30, shortly before dark.

*   *   *   *   *

Simon wrote out his report and I had it typed that morning by one of the Wrens in N.O.I.C.'s office. At midday, McNeil, Simon, and I left for London. V.A.C.O. was at his office on the coast; we got there very late that night and saw him first thing in the morning.

He was very pleased with the ship, and listened very carefully to Simon as he was telling him about the raid. He was interested in the state of unreadiness of the *Raumboot*. "You mustn't expect to catch them in that state again," he said. "The Germans are very quick to pick up points of that sort."

McNeil said: "It seems very doubtful if there were any survivors from the *Raumboot* to pass on the information."

Presently V.A.C.O. asked: "Well now, what is the next move? Are we going to pay off the ship, or have you any plans for going on?"

Simon said quickly, before anybody else could speak: "My officers and crew, they all want to go out and do it again. I think we ought to go again, sir."

McNeil said: "I agree with that, in principle. But before any operation of that kind is planned, we must have information about this one. I should oppose doing it again if the Germans are aware that it was a British ship operating a flame-thrower, for example.''

I said: "I agree absolutely with you there."

McNeil said: "If the Germans are ignorant of that and treat it as an accident, then I think it might be done again. At some later stage we can arrange to tell the people of the town that it is British and Free French action against the Germans. But first of all we must have information."

V.A.C.O. said: "I should think you're right. Well, go ahead and get your information, and when you want to do another operation let me know." He turned to me. "You will see that the ship has everything she may require, Martin, and keep in touch with Brigadier McNeil. Then, when you're ready, come and talk to me again."

We went back to London, to my office in the Admiralty. There Simon said to McNeil: "I have been thinking about getting information, sir. I see that it is necessary; I do not want to see my crew lose all their lives. I know Douarnenez, myself. In one day I could find out everything. If I could be put on shore one night, from *Geneviève*, not very far away, and picked up the next night, I could learn everything."

I said: "Who's to say that you wouldn't land straight into the arms of a German patrol? Then the ship might be caught as well."

McNeil said unexpectedly: "I think we could avoid that, with the information that we have."

I was silent. He said to Simon: "I was thinking rather on those lines myself."

McNeil turned back to me. "I should explain," he said, "that we have been paying more attention to Douarnenez recently. It comes into our Class A category, the places that are ripe for armed revolt. The situation in the town is very tense."

"Apart from that," he said, "a landing in that neighbourhood is not difficult. We have done that several times recently."

I knew nothing of the work of his department. "You have, have you?" I said. "Isn't the coast guarded by the Germans?"

He said: "Oh, well, it's guarded against an invading force. That is to say, there are patrols and strong points on the beaches, at the ports, and at all points where troops or armoured fighting vehicles could land. But, obviously, the Germans can't even patrol the whole extent of coastline that they have to cover from the North Cape to the Pyrenees. They guard the salient points, and they keep strong reserves at nodal points inland ready to concentrate at any place that may be attacked. But in between the cliffs, where no landing in force could take place, those places are unguarded usually. They simply haven't got the men."

"I see," I said.

"There is no difficulty in putting one man on shore from a row-boat in the night, upon the rocks at the foot of the cliffs between the Saints and Beuzec," he said. "We have done that more than once. The only danger is the fishing fleet and the *Raum-boote;* you've got to keep away from them."

"All this is really rather outside my province," I remarked.

He nodded. "Let me have a day or so to work upon it," he said. "I think we could arrange an operation to put Simon on shore there and fetch him off again without too great a risk, say in a week from now."

He went away and took Simon with him, and I set about the arrears of work that had piled up while I was away. I worked on at the Admiralty till ten o'clock on other matters; from time to time my mind drifted uneasily to *Geneviève* and had to be jerked back to the work in hand. And over a late supper in my flat before I went to bed, the matter crystallised. I was not happy about what we had decided, not quite content. *Geneviève* was a slow ship, though fast for her type, and we were proposing to send this slow ship right back into the same area where she had done much damage. She was a very vulnerable ship, unarmoured and almost unarmed, except for the flame-gun. A *Raumboot* would only have to withdraw out of range of our ship's flame, which it could do easily with its high speed, and then we would be at its mercy. It could lay off and sink *Geneviève* at leisure.

We were getting terribly dependent upon secrecy, much too much so. We had had luck with a surprise attack; we must not overplay our hand.

If she could have a gun as well as the flame-thrower, a gun that would sink a *Raumboot,* that would enable her to fight it out on even terms, handicapped only by her less speed. Couldn't we possibly install a 20-cm. cannon in her—for example, an Oerlikon or a Hispano?

These thoughts raced round in my head all night and spoilt my sleep. The matter seemed so important to me in the morning that I passed the rest of my work over to my runner and went across to Naval Ordnance, and got a handbook and an installation drawing of the gun. By midday I was in the train again upon my way to Dartmouth, to see if we could not possibly find room for it, somewhere, somehow.

I got there too late in the evening to do anything before dark. I had arranged for a naval constructor to meet me on the ship at Dittisham next morning, and early in the morning the truck called for me to take me out to Dittisham, driven by the Wren.

" 'Morning," I said, and got into the truck. "How's the rabbit?"

She smiled and flushed a little. "He's very well, sir," she replied.

It seemed to me that I had pulled her leg a little clumsily, and so I said:

"I used to keep a rabbit when I was a boy. They're rather fun. But I haven't had much to do with them since then."

We turned out of the College grounds into the main road. "This one is tremendous fun," she said. "He's very tame with Lieutenant Rhodes. You ought to see them having a boxing match together. I've never seen a rabbit play like that. He plays just like a dog."

I said: "Rhodes is very good with animals, I suppose."

"I think he is," she said. "He gets very much attached to them. He had a dog once that he had to put away when he joined up. He's still very much cut up about that."

We drove on to the ship, where I met the constructor. I had a short talk with Colvin about the gun; he was enthusiastic for it, but doubted if they could find room for it. He got hold of Rhodes and we went down to the hard and were put on board the ship; Boden met us at the gangway.

It was a disappointing forenoon. I had hoped that we could have sunk the gun down the aft hatch; I had forgotten how much gear the ship already had on board in the shape of extra fuel-tanks and the equipment of the flame-gun. We worked over the problem for an hour, and came at last to the conclusion that it was insoluble. For the gun to have any field of fire at all it would have to stand up clear above the deck, betraying the nature of the ship. It was impossible to fit that gun and still maintain the appearance of a fishing vessel.

In the middle of this rather gloomy conference the air-raid sirens went in Dartmouth, and in a very few minutes planes were overhead.

At that stage of the war a daylight raid in any force was quite unusual, but there were eighteen aircraft in a squadron for this one. It was probably the last raid to be made by Ju.87s upon England. I can't imagine what the Germans did it for; there was nothing of real value to them in the port at that time and they must have known that they would lose heavily in the attack. It may be that they had wrong information of the movements of our ships.

Each of the aircraft made two dives on Dartmouth and its shipping; the first they each dropped one five-hundred-kilogramme bomb, in the second dive they dropped a pair of one hundreds. From our position three miles up the river we had a grand-stand seat of the whole thing. We saw them screaming down in almost vertical dives and saw the bombs leave the machines. In the crashing bursts of the explosions they zoomed up again perhaps to about five thousand feet, but a flight of three Hurricanes was there by then.

There was little we could do to help, but Boden and André, with a couple of men, were tumbling the Tommy-guns on deck. I said to Boden: "Those things aren't much good. Don't waste ammunition on anything but a close-range shot."

"Very good, sir."

Nevertheless, he worked on frantically to get the guns ready.

The second dive was spoilt for the attackers by the Hurricanes. The last German aircraft zooming up from the first dive saw two of his comrades shot down in savage bursts of fire, and saw the Hurricanes turning to attack again. From being a disciplined and planned attack the thing developed into something like a raid of wolves upon a flock of sheep. The Hurricanes seemed to be everywhere at once; a third 87 went down in a trail of flame, and then a fourth.

It was too hot for them. They made their last dive on the town and did not zoom again; they swept on at a low altitude, hedge-hopping across country and scattering, working round towards the sea. In that way the fighters could no longer dive on them and, coming up behind, would be a target for the rear-gunners in the 87s.

They scattered across country. One of them came jinking up the river towards us between the wooded hills. Boden said, by my side: "André. *Quand j'ai dit 'Tirez', tirez en avance par deux longueurs de fuselage. Compris?*"

The Breton said quietly: "*Oui, monsieur.* Lay off *deux longueurs en avance.*" The other Bretons nodded, fingering the guns.

There was a tense wait as the thing swept on towards us, only a hundred feet up, taking cover in the valley between the hills. Then Boden shouted: *"Tirez!"*

The Tommy-guns cracked out. I crouched down beside the wheel-house with the naval constructor. I did not think this Tommy-gun fire would do any good, but it was better than nothing. But I was wrong. The Jerry swerved and pulled up violently. He passed very nearly over us, and his rear-gunner gave us a vicious burst of fire. Nobody was hit and presently the Tommy-guns reluctantly fell silent, but as the 87 went away low across the hill towards the east it left behind it a white plume of smoke that was not there before. "Glycol," I said. "You got his radiator," and no one disagreed with me.

Later we heard that one had come down in the sea seven miles south-east of Berry Head. There was no real evidence till the body of a German rear-gunner was washed up ten days later and the surgeon found two little Tommy-gun bullets in it. I claimed the machine then for *Geneviève*, and it was marked up to the ship.

After that interlude we turned back to the problem of the gun. In ten more minutes we came to the conclusion that it was impracticable. If her camouflage as a fishing vessel were to be maintained we could not fit her with a cannon; it was not possible. The most that we could do was to give her a few Bren guns in addition to the Tommy-guns she had; I decided to see McNeil about that.

There was nothing then for me to wait for, and I had to get back to London. It was doubtful if the raid would not have stopped the train service temporarily from Kingswear, but I knew that V.A.C.O. would be interested to hear the state of the town, and so I told the Wren to take me into Dartmouth.

Rhodes came up just as I was getting into the truck with the constructor. "May I have a lift in with you, sir?" he said.

I said: "By all means," and he got into the back.

We drove to N.O.I.C.'s office through streets littered with broken glass, making a detour once to avoid a great heap of debris and dust strewn across the road. At the Naval Centre I dismissed the truck, and Rhodes drove off in it with the Wren in the direction of the net defence store.

In the office I got the reports of damage as they came in; I stayed there for about an hour. It was not a very bad account, considering the determination of the Germans. An M.L. had been sunk by a near miss, but it was in shallow water and she could probably be raised. Two lighters had been sunk, and a number of ships slightly damaged. The total of naval casualties was about thirty, of whom ten or twelve were dead. Among civilians the casualty list was heavier. None of the schools had been hit, but there was a fair list of damaged dwelling houses. One bomb had fallen in the almshouses, and some of the old people had been killed. And they had killed one rabbit!

Blast had burst down the doors of the net defence store yard, and had thrown down the hutch. Within it the little furry body was stretched, hardly cold; it had been very sudden, for a part-eaten frond of cow parsley was clenched between the teeth. The body was unmarked, the fur unruffled. A rabbit does not stand blast very well.

The naval officer took out the body gently, but it sagged limp in his hands; there was nothing they could do. The girl said unevenly: "He couldn't have known anything about it, Michael. He wasn't even frightened. Look, he was still eating."

Rhodes turned to her, and she was shocked at his expression. He was dead-white, and tears were streaming down his face.

"They had to pick this street, of all the streets," he said.

There was a pause; the girl did not know what to say to help him. Very carefully he laid the body down upon the grass and stood erect, thoughtful. Mechanically he got out his handkerchief and blew his nose.

The problem of burial occurred to her. She looked up at him. "What had we better do, Michael?"

"I'll have to go to Honiton," he said. "I'd better go to-morrow. I'm going to do something horrible to them for this."

8

I MET McNeil in his office a few days later, at his request, and he told me the arrangements he had made for Simon's journey to Douarnenez. "There is this family, Le Rouzic," he said. "Once he gets to the farm he should be quite all right."

I asked: "What name did you say?"

"It doesn't matter. They'll look after him, and take him in with them to Douarnenez. They go in every Sunday morning. Most of the farmers go into Douarnenez on Sundays. I'm told that as many as fifteen hundred strangers from the country go in in fine weather."

"We don't want that," I said, thinking of the approach to the coast.

He agreed. "What we want is a nice wet, misty Saturday night."

"What does the fishing fleet do on Saturdays?"

"Goes into harbour, late at night. They never go out on Sunday. They sail again on Monday morning, very early, before dawn."

"The *Raumboote* go in too?"

He nodded. "The coast should be quite clear around the Saints late on Saturday night. It would be sheer bad luck if they ran into anything."

We discussed the arrangement for a little; given the right weather, it seemed pretty safe. The weather had broken up nicely, and it looked as if we were in for a good long spell of rainy, unsettled stuff coming in from the Atlantic.

Presently he said: "I saw Major Carpenter, from Honiton, on Tuesday. They're very busy with the new stuff for the flame-thrower."

I said: "What's that?"

He grinned. "I thought you knew about it. They're going to run the thing on Worcester Sauce."

I stared at him. "What's Worcester Sauce? I thought they ran on oil."

He said: "Well, oil is still the basic part of it, of course. But they've got this sort of cocktail now—oil with a lot of solids in solution in some way. Carpenter was giving Rhodes a pretty good boost over it, as a matter of fact. Making solid things dissolve in oil is what he knows about, it seems."

I thought about the perfumes and the soya oil. "That's true enough," I said. "That is his line in peace-time."

"It all sounds very complicated," he said. "They do it during the cracking process. I didn't understand, but the result is Worcester Sauce."

"How does it differ from oil?" I asked.

"It's hotter, and it leaves a nice warm glow behind," he said. "That's why they call it that."

I did not smile. "What's it got in it?" I enquired. "What are the solids that they put into the stuff?"

He told me.

I sat in silence for a minute. I am no chemist, and I don't know much about what those things do to you. "That's pretty nasty stuff," I said at last.

"Well," he said, "I wouldn't like to get a burn with it myself."

"It's all right—internationally—is it?"

He shrugged his shoulders. "It's not gas and it's not an acid. But anyway, if the *Boche* had thought of it first he'd have used it against us fast enough."

There was no denying that. All I said was: "Well, they'll have to be damn careful in handling it that they don't burn themselves."

I went away soon after that, but I was troubled about Worcester Sauce. I went down to the club for lunch and there I saw Margeson, the surgeon-commander. I got him on one side in the smoking-room. "Look," I said. "There's something I want to ask you. Keep it quiet, though."

"What'll you have to drink, old boy?"

"I'll have a gin."

They came, and then I told him about the oil and the other things. "Suppose you got a little splash of that on you," I said, "burning. Would it be very bad?"

He stared at me, gin in hand. "You mustn't do that," he said. "You'd be better off if you drank it."

"It makes a very nasty burn?"

He laughed shortly. "That's putting it mildly. I don't believe that it would ever heal at all."

"I mean, just a little splash, about the size of—that," I said.

"Small or large, it'd go septic right away. And it would go on going septic for a very long time. It's horrible stuff, that."

"It'd heal in the end?"

"It might do, if it didn't start a cancer."

We went in to lunch.

I went up to the library that afternoon, still troubled in my mind, and got a copy of The Hague Convention, and took it down to my office. I read it through that evening. But in those far-off days before the last war nobody had even thought about flame warfare, so it seemed. Certainly they had never visualised the use of Worcester Sauce against the enemy, and there was nothing in the wording to prevent the use of it. There was no paragraph to say that if you hurl a jet of blazing oil against the Germans you must use clean oil.

I took the Convention back to the library and went to bed, but I didn't sleep very well. I suppose I had been doing too much work.

About a week after that we sent *Geneviève* out again, one Saturday. The weather forecast was fairly promising, and she left Penzance about midday as before. She had definite instructions to avoid the enemy this time; all she had to do was to land Simon and stand out to sea, returning the next night to pick him up. McNeil went down to see her off; I did not go.

By midday the next day she was back again. The weather had cleared up off Ushant and turned into a fine starry night, with visibility unlimited after the rain. It only lasted a few hours, but it spoilt their game. If Simon had been ashore already Colvin would have risked going in for him to take him off; as things were they abandoned the venture and came home. I was very pleased with them for that. It was the proper thing to do, and sensible.

It meant they lost another week, however. We had planned the whole thing for a Saturday night, so that Simon could go into the town with the peasant crowd on Sunday; I was unwilling to consent to a fresh plan to save the week. I kept them where they were, kicking their heels in Dartmouth for that week. Rhodes, I know, spent a good deal of that week away with the Honiton organisation and at the refinery, so that when they finally did sail they had Worcester Sauce for fuel in the flame-thrower tanks. I shut my eyes to that. If she had been a proper naval vessel I should have had to have taken notice of it, but a fishing vessel requisitioned by the Army was another matter, and I let it go.

They sailed again on the next Saturday, this time from Dartmouth. Three weeks had elapsed since they had destroyed their *Raumboot* and the nights were much longer; it was the second of October. It was a nuisance going to Penzance, and another possible source of leakage of information; they were all in favour of sailing direct from their base over to the other side.

The lapse of three weeks had both favourable and adverse features. It would be more difficult, perhaps, to find out after that time whether the loss of the *Raumboot* was considered to be accidental—or it might be easier, because there had been more time for gossip to get out. If the Germans *were* suspicious, as it seemed to me they must be, it was clearly a good thing to go over on a night when the fishing fleet would be in harbour and the *Raumboote* too; *Geneviève* would be less likely to run into trouble on the other side, especially after three weeks. Time would have elapsed for things to simmer down a bit, and vessels which had been urgent on patrol for a week might have gone back to other duties.

The forecast for the region between Ushant and the Saints was wet mist and fog, probably lasting over the week-end. I was down at Dartmouth to see them off that time with McNeil. Simon was wearing a dirty, torn blue suit of poor cloth and a continental cut, with pointed yellow shoes, a yellow celluloid collar, and a vivid orange-and-blue tie, rather torn. He had a very old black felt hat on his head with a blue band. He looked like nothing that you ever see in this country; I hoped he knew his stuff for Brittany.

The rest of them were in their fishing clothes; as usual it was raining when they went. There was no ceremony or leave-taking. I stood on the hard at Dittisham with McNeil and watched them cast off the mooring; the little truck was close behind us with the Wren. They passed a warp from the mooring to the transom and let her swing to that as they cast off because the tide was on the ebb; then they let go and went away between the wooded hills, down past the town, out past the harbour mouth on their way over to the other side.

We turned back to the truck; they would be gone more than two days and I was going back to London. The Wren opened the door for us to get in, and I noticed she was looking tired and worn. She looked as if she wasn't sleeping well.

I said: "You don't look so grand, Miss Wright. When did you have your last leave?"

"About six months ago, sir."

"About time you had some more," I said. "I'll mention it to N.O.I.C."

She turned to me. "Please don't do that. I'm quite all right, and I couldn't go on leave just now."

"Why not?"

"Not in the middle of all this, sir. I'm quite well, really. I don't want to go away."

I thought before I spoke again. She was quite calm and not hysterical or anything like that, but she was looking rotten. The officers were used to her, of course, and that went for something; a strange driver would be just a little bit more burden upon them. And then there was security to think of too—and Rhodes.

I turned to McNeil. "We'll have to think of leave," I said. "It might do the whole outfit good if they had a spell off between this and the next operation."

*   *   *   *   *

That was on Saturday morning. I worked on Sunday at my office in the Admiralty because with all the time that I was spending upon *Geneviève* my normal work was getting in arrear. I had arranged with McNeil that we should meet at Paddington next day and go down on the midday train to Dartmouth; the ship could not arrive before Monday evening at the earliest. But at about ten o'clock on Monday morning, when I still had an hour and a half more office time before I went, McNeil rang me up.

"Martin," he said urgently. "Look. We're talking on an outside line. Something has happened in the town we know about. It happened last night or early this morning. Can you come over right away?"

I said: "I suppose I can. Is it good or bad for us?"

"Good for the war. I don't know anything about—about our closer interest."

"I'll come round," I said.

I was with him in his office about ten minutes later. He had a flimsy on his desk marked in red MOST SECRET. He passed it over to me. It said:

DOUARNENEZ. October 4th. Two *Raumboote* lying alongside the west harbour jetty have been destroyed by a violent fire commencing about 01.00. The fire involved two 75-cm. HA/LA guns mounted in emplacements on the jetty. German casualties are believed to be considerable. Allied action is suspected, and the civil population are greatly excited. Germans have been attacked and murdered in the streets. Ends.

I read this through a second time without speaking. Then I said: "This is to-day's date. This all happened only a few hours ago."

"That's right," he said. "It was early this morning."

I waved the flimsy at him. "Where did this come from?"

He·said a little shortly: "We get these reports." He screwed the flimsy into a spill and lit it with his lighter, held it until it burned down to his fingers and dropped it in the ash-tray.

"What do you think it means?" he asked. "Did they go right inside the harbour in the middle of the night to do their stuff?"

I sat there brooding for a minute or two. "If they did that, I don't see how they possibly could get away," I said at last. It was better to face the facts. "Do you?"

"No," he said heavily. "I don't."

There was nothing we could do about it, and no chance of further news. McNeil took some action of his own that was not my affair, and we went down together on the midday train as we had fixed. It was a silent, anxious journey for us both.

We got to Dartmouth at about five o'clock and walked up to the Naval Centre. The truck was parked outside it and the Wren was there with it; she stood up and saluted when she saw us. "Wait a bit," I said to her. "I shall want you." We went into the office.

Nothing had come through about our ship. It was too early anyway for us to have heard anything unless she had put in to Falmouth or Penzance, and she had not done that. I had arranged this time for her to be admitted to the port during the hours of darkness on the proper signals; the nights now were so long that that was necessary. I checked up that this was all in order, and then went outside with McNeil.

There was still about an hour of daylight. I said to the Wren: "Take us up to the Watch Point again—where we went before."

"Very good, sir."

As we drove out of the town McNeil said cheerfully: "How's the rabbit?"

She did not answer for a moment. Then she said: "He's dead, sir."

"Dead? How did that happen?"

"He was killed in the air-raid."

I said: "I'm very sorry about that." She did not answer, and we drove on to the Watch Point in silence.

The evening light was grey upon the sea when we got there; the rain held off, but it was heavily overcast. There was no report of our ship; indeed I had not expected that there would be. I had a word or two with the old petty officer and told him what we were expecting; then there was nothing we could do but hang around and wait. We should have been more comfortable in the hotel, perhaps, but after London the sea air was fresh up on that cliff.

I went aside presently and found Wren Wright sitting in her truck. "Miss Wright, I'm very sorry to hear you lost that rabbit," I said. "Was Rhodes upset?"

"He was a bit," she said. "He was such a nice rabbit." She hesitated. "I think he felt it frightfully," she said. "You see, there was his dog as well."

I hadn't heard that one, and with a little encouragement she told me all about Ernest. She seemed to know a good deal about Rhodes. She told me how they had found Geoffrey in his hutch.

"It was after that he went and worried them at Honiton to get out this new oil," she said.

"Worcester Sauce?"

She nodded.

"Did he tell you what was in it?"

She shook her head. "He only said it makes burns very bad to heal. He was terribly—bitter, sir, after the raid."

There was nothing to be said to that; it was just another little drop to swell the flood of misery that comes from war. I turned back to the Watch Point, but there was nothing new. It was now very nearly dark.

There was no object in staying there; they might come in any time during the night, or else they might not come at all. McNeil and I went out presently and got into the truck again. I said to the Wren: "Take us down to the hotel—the one upon the quay."

"The Royal Sovereign." As we drove down I was thinking out what we had better do. I felt that it was necessary for me to meet the ship as soon as they came in, whatever hour it was. I had arranged for the young surgeon-lieutanant with his ambulance to be at Dittisham all night if need be; that was fixed up. But when they came in, quite apart from wounded men, they might want anything. They might have prisoners— all the officers might have been hit—they might have urgent news for V.A.C.O.—anything. There might be any kind of an emergency demanding energetic action, when my brass hat and McNeil's red tabs would carry weight.

They could ring up the hotel from the Naval Centre when news of the ship came in. I could get the Duty Officer to do that.

We drew up outside the hotel and got out; it was dark by that time. I said to the Wren: "I shall want this truck to-night, Miss Wright, as soon as they get in. You'd better park it here and let me have the key. Then you can get along."

She said: "That's quite all right, sir. I'll be here."

"They may come any time," I said, "or they may not come in till to-morrow." It was blackly in my mind they might not come at all. "If I want the truck to-night I'll drive myself."

She said: "I'd rather wait." And then she said quickly: "It might be very awkward if they came in and they—they kind of wanted anything and you hadn't got a driver, sir."

I hesitated; there was truth in what she said, although I knew that wasn't her real reason. She followed up before I could speak.

"I'll just slip back and tell them at the Wrennery and get my coat, sir. I won't be more than ten minutes."

I said: "All right," and turned into the hotel with McNeil. We decided that the only thing to do was to have dinner and sit by the fire till something happened. I rang through to the Duty Officer and told him where we were, and then we went and washed and had a gin in the bar, and presently we had another. McNeil said: "Is that Wren of yours outside?"

It was raining in the street; I could hear it rippling in the gutter. "I expect she is," I said. I went out to the door; in the dim light I saw the dark mass of the van parked by the pavement a few yards away. I went out in the rain and tried the door, and there she was, sitting at the wheel.

"You'd better come inside, Miss Wright," I said. "It's cold as charity out here."

She said: "I'm quite all right, sir."

"You'd better come on in. Brigadier McNeil wants to buy you a drink."

She laughed shyly and got out. I took her into the hotel and took her coat; we went into the bar. McNeil was very good with her. "On a cold night like this I should think you'd like a ginger wine," he said. "With or without gin?"

She said: "Lieutenant Rhodes gives me a tomato-juice cocktail when we come in here." She was refreshingly naïve. "I think I'll stick to that."

He ordered it for her. I was not very familiar with the drink, and said: "Does that have gin in it?"

"Non-alcoholic," said the brigadier. He took it from the barmaid. "It's just tomato-juice and . . . other stuff."

"Worcester sauce," the barmaid said. "Tomato-juice and Worcester sauce, that's all it is."

That made a little silence; we none of us could think of anything to say. We talked about the weather and the war for a bit, but none of the subjects that linked us together could be talked about in a bar, and in the background of our minds was Worcester Sauce.

We took her in to dinner with us, after a little argument. "I had my tea in the Wrennery before you came," she said. Still, she managed to do pretty well in spite of that, and we gave her a glass of port to top up with, and then we settled down in long chairs before the fire in the smoking room.

We were still waiting there at midnight, half asleep.

I stirred as it struck twelve. I said: "You'd better go on back to the Wrennery and go to bed, Miss Wright. I don't suppose they'll come now."

She said: "What are you going to do, sir?"

I yawned. "I'm going to have a double whisky. I shall stay up a bit longer."

She said: "I think I ought to stay, sir. I'll go and see if I can make a cup of tea."

She went and raked out the night porter, and presently she came back with her tea while McNeil and I drank whisky. There was nothing we could do but wait. McNeil made up the fire. Then we sat on before it, half asleep, hour after hour.

At twenty-five to three the telephone-bell rang. I roused and heard the night porter going to it in the passage. I went out and took the receiver from him.

"Duty Officer here, sir," it said. "Your ship has just signalled for permission to come in."

A great load slipped from my shoulders. "Fine," I said. "I shall wait here till I hear her pass up-river; then I shall get along to Dittisham and meet her there."

I rang off; behind me were McNeil and the Wren. "Coming in now," I said. "We'll wait here till she passes and then get along."

McNeil said we'd better have another whisky, and I didn't disagree. The Wren was radiant. "It's splendid—I've been terribly anxious. It's silly, I know."

"They've done a bit of good this time," I told her. And then the telephone-bell went again.

"Duty Officer here, sir. Your ship has just made this signal: 'Requests permission to berth alongside at Dartmouth to land casualties.' Is that all right?"

"That's all right," I said. "Where will you put her?"

He thought for a minute. "It's raining so hard. The west ferry pontoon is vacant, and that's got a roof. The ambulance can back down there and we can have some light. I'll put her at the west ferry pontoon, sir."

I said: "Right. Make that signal to her. Then ring up the hospital and tell them to prepare for casualties." Behind me I could feel the Wren listening. "Ring up Dittisham and get that ambulance and the surgeon back, quick as they can get. See if the hospital can send down a few ratings for stretcher-bearers, and get a rating or two down to the pontoon to help them berth her."

"Very good, sir."

I put down the receiver and turned to McNeil. "She's got some casualties to land. She was bound to have, from what we heard. She should be berthing before long now."

By my side the Wren said timidly: "Have they been in action again, sir?"

I glanced down at her; all the sparkle had gone out of her and she was looking tired and worn. I could not tell her much. "They were in action, I think," I said. "If what we heard was true, they've done very well. But we shall know before long."

We gulped down the whisky and put on our coats. It was pouring with rain; outside it was pitch-dark and windy, a dirty kind of night. The streets and the quayside were quite deserted. The pontoon was only a hundred yards from the hotel; I sent the Wren to drive the truck round and McNeil and I walked across through the rain.

For a time we three huddled on the pontoon, finding what shelter there was in the black darkness between bales and crates, staring down over the black running water to the river mouth. Then she came. We saw her moving white mast-head light and then her red port light; we stood there watching those two slowly moving lights till she loomed up on top of us out of the darkness to the slow uneven chugging of her engine in the rain.

A truck drove up just before she berthed, and a petty officer and a couple of ratings in oilskins tumbled out of it and began fumbling with a flood-light of some sort to get it rigged. I moved up to a bollard and caught her heaving-line myself, and with McNeil pulled in her warp and made her fast. The ratings took her stern line and the light came on; then we were over the bulwark and on board.

In the shadowy light we saw that she had taken punishment. There was a gaping hole in deck and bulwarks at the bow, starboard side, close up beside the stem; they seemed to have stuffed it up from the inside with sails or mattresses. Around the flame-gun it looked as if they had had a fire. One hatch was open. Half of the little wheel-house had been carried away, and the same burst had damaged the engine, cracking one cylinder casting; they had come home on five.

Colvin came to meet me from the wheel. " 'Evening, Colvin," I said. "What casualties have you got?"

"One stretcher case," he said. "Louis Richier got a splinter in his back. Then there's two walking cases. Captain Simon lost two fingers, sir—left hand. Jules Clisson—he's got a wound in the throat and jaw."

I said: "Any dead?"

"Two, sir. André, the *maître*, he got killed right out. I made that chap Rollot *maître* in his place right away; them Frenchies won't work right without they have a straw-boss. And then Caspar, one of the two Danes, he died about midday."

It was a heavy list for so small a ship's company. "I'm very sorry you got this bad luck," I said. "Did you go into the harbour?"

He stared at me. "How in heck did you know that?"

"We got a report a few hours afterwards from somewhere on the other side. It said you got two *Raumboote* moored up against the quay."

"Sure we did," he said. "We made a proper muck of them. But then one of them little cannon, like you wanted us to have, got going and did all this to us in two shakes just as we were getting back into the rain."

"You're not hurt yourself?"

"Not a scratch, nor Boden, nor Rhodes. Rhodes got a bit of fire all round about him when they split his oil-pipe for him, but he hopped out all right. I reckon his asbestos overall saved him."

"Did he get burned at all?" I asked, thinking of Worcester Sauce.

"I looked him all over this morning myself, but I couldn't find nothing. I reckon he was too darned quick."

The rain streamed down upon us steadily; in the shadowy half-light everything was soaking wet. The ship had water in her, too; I could hear it swishing as she moved at the pontoon. "She's not taking much," said Colvin. "We pump her out each watch, 'n that's enough to keep it under."

The ambulance came slowly backing on to the pontoon, and the young surgeon came on board. "It's a fine show," I said to Colvin. "Far better than I ever thought you'd do. Now let's get these casualties on shore."

Simon, still in his blue civilian suit, his left hand grotesquely bandaged and in a sling, was talking to McNeil down aft. I had a word with him, and then set to work with the surgeon to get the stretcher case on deck and to the ambulance. I glanced aside as the stretcher was eased over the bulwarks on to the pontoon. In the dim semi-darkness Rhodes was standing on the pontoon with his Wren, in among the crates, in the wet, windy rain. He was in fishing clothes, as they all were. The two were standing very close together, holding hands, watching what went on on board the ship. They did not seem to be talking.

We got the casualties into the ambulance and it moved off. McNeil was taking Simon independently to the hospital; it was necessary that he should get his information out of Simon before the doctors got at him to dull his mind with pain or drugs. They went into the truck with the Wren driving them; I saw them off and turned to Rhodes.

"You've had a pasting," I said, "I'm very sorry. How did you come to go in there?"

He was dead-tired, almost falling over as he stood. "Simon told us when he came back," he said. "You couldn't miss a chance like that. If there'd been fifty men behind us we could have taken the whole town."

He was too tired to give a proper story, and I didn't ask for more. "As it is," I said, "you'll take a drop of leave." I turned back to the ship. Colvin was there on deck, and Boden with him. "Would you like to leave her berthed here for the night?" I asked. "I'll get you transport up to Dittisham. Or will you take her up?"

He said: "The ferry comes here in the morning. And besides, she's not just like we'd care to have the public looking at her, sir, in daylight. I'd like to take her to the mooring 'n finish off the job."

I nodded; it was better so. I went to telephone the shore party to get out in the motor-boat and meet us at the mooring with a lantern, and to telephone to the young surgeon to get back to Dittisham. Then I got back on *Geneviève;* we cast off and felt our way up-river in the darkness and the rain.

Boden was standing by me at one time. I said to him: "You're not hurt, Boden?"

He shook his head. "I was lucky. But we hurt a lot of Jerries, sir. Rhodes must have got over fifty with the flame-gun this time, on the *Raumboot* and the jetty."

"The French got some," I told him. "They seem to have risen and attacked them in the streets."

"The French did? Oh, that's fine . . ." he breathed.

I saw them all on shore and the ship safely in the hands of the base party. Back in the villas I stayed with them while they had a meal; most of them were too tired to eat and took only a drink of cocoa or of wine before they tumbled into bed to sleep. One or two wanted the assistance of the surgeon and his sedatives; I stayed there till they were all asleep. The young surgeon would stay with them till they woke, sleeping himself upon an empty cot.

It was six o'clock and very nearly dawn before I was ready to go. The Wren was waiting there for me with the truck, looking about all in. She drove me back to Dartmouth in the rain.

This is the story of what happened on their operation, made out from the official report and from what they told me in conversation from time to time:

After they left Dartmouth they set a course to pass ten miles off Ushant, and they held to that all day. It was raining practically the whole time that they were out, with only short intervals; we had chosen those conditions for their trip, of course, but it didn't make it easier for them. Apart from navigation difficulties, they were all wet after the first few hours, and stayed wet for the remainder of the time.

They saw a German aeroplane towards the evening of the first day, perhaps thirty miles from the north coast of Brittany, flying north-west. It was a Heinkel 111; it passed within a mile of them flying low and purposeful just underneath the clouds, and it paid no attention to them. No report it may have made did them any harm.

They were off Ushant at about eight o'clock at night in darkness and wet mist, and altered course down into L'Iroise. From then onwards it was tricky, anxious work for Colvin and Boden. Visibility was practically nil; from time to time they heard the foghorn at Le Jument, but not clearly enough to take a bearing of it. They went ahead, boldly trusting to their tidal calculations and dead reckoning, and stopping every now and then to make a sounding to compare with the depth shown at their estimated position on the chart.

Two hours later they had run their distance. They were making for a little rocky cove that lies between Beuzec and the Saints. The cliffs run straight along that portion of the coast a hundred feet or so in height, but at this cove a sheep-track ran down to a tiny beach, completely covered at high water. They had a good map of the country behind. Simon had studied it till he knew the way from the beach to Le Rouzic farm by heart, but now their trouble was to find the beach.

They were surrounded by a wet, clammy mist; it was pitch-dark and they could see nothing. Soundings supported their dead-reckoning position, more or less, but that meant little over a sea bottom that was generally flat. They stopped their engine and lay for a minute or two listening. They heard nothing.

They put the engine on again and went ahead dead slow, peering into the darkness, ready to go hard astern before they struck. They went on for ten minutes, stopped again to listen, and went on. Then they stopped again, and this time they heard the wash of waves upon rocks and sea-birds crying in the darkness. Immediately Colvin anchored, and they had a consultation in the tiny chart-room.

"This is the coast all right," the navigator said. "But where your beach is I'm darned if I know. It might be three miles either way of us."

Simon said: "Three miles only? Not more than that?"

Colvin shook his head. "We should be within that much." They had confidence in him.

Simon folded up the map and put it in the inside pocket of his blue civilian suit. "I will go and see if I can climb the cliff," he said. "To-morrow night I will be at the beach at midnight. If it is clear, you steam along the coast if you cannot find the beach, and I will flash the torch. If it is thick, like this, then Boden lands and comes to meet me at Le Rouzic farm; the boat waiting on the rocks. That is quite clear?"

"Okay."

"If you do not find me, you must not stay here after three o'clock. You must go back to England; I will get back in another way."

They turned out the little oil lamp over the chart-table, pulled back the hatch, and went on deck. The Bretons had put the light punt that they carried over the side; it lay against the top-sides in the running tide. Two of the Bretons dropped down into it and Simon followed them; Boden came last of all.

From the deck Colvin said softly: "All the best," and Rhodes said: "Good luck." The painter was dropped down into the bows and the punt slid astern; she vanished from their sight before the oars were shipped.

Presently, pulling straight inshore, they came to rocks on which the sea was breaking. They skirted them eastwards till they found a possible landing in a cleft, and Simon clambered out in the dim light, slipping and stumbling as he went. From the boat Boden watched him venturing towards the shore for ten yards; then he was lost to sight.

It was arranged that he should flash a series of dots with the torch from the cliff-top if he were safely up; a series of dots and dashes was a call for help. They lay off in the punt a little distance from the rocks where he had landed, straining their eyes into the darkness. A quarter of an hour later came a series of dots well up above their heads. They turned the punt and rowed out to sea, heading a little bit up-tide and steering with a dim light over the boat compass. They found the vessel with some difficulty and got the punt on board. Then they weighed, turned to the north-west to give a wide berth to the Saints, and put to sea.

Simon had little difficulty with the climb. He found a spur of rock and went straight up the ridge; it grew steeper, but presently he felt grass roots and earth beneath his hands. He went on up a steep, grassy slope, scrambling upwards with hands, feet, and knees. The darkness and the mist prevented him from seeing what he was doing, which was perhaps as well; it struck him presently that the sea noise was very nearly straight below him. Then the slope eased, and presently he could stand up. He turned, and with his torch shaded by his open coat, made his series of dots in the direction that he judged he had come from. Then he faced inland and went on.

He had a little luminous compass, and by this he made his way inland. He came to a stone wall, crossed it, and went on over what appeared to be a pasture, stumbling among gorse-bushes. Then came a field of stubble and another pasture, and then there was a wood before him.

He shaded the torch carefully and looked at his watch. It was ten minutes past twelve; he had been on shore about an hour. Counting the time that he had taken to climb up the cliff, he judged that he had come about a mile inland; half a mile farther on there should be a road running parallel to the coast.

He skirted round the wood and found the road immediately.

He stood behind the hedge with the road before him; if there were German patrols they would very likely be upon it, and he did not dare to risk a meeting. No French civilian would be innocently wandering the roads beside the coast at midnight on a night like that; an encounter with the Germans would mean certain arrest. He was uncertain which way he should go. The road ran roughly east and west; it was marked on his map, but he might be anywhere along the length of it.

He stood there, sniffing at the wind and rain. Presently it

came into his mind that he was too far to the east: he turned west and began to follow the road, skirting along behind the stone walls that bordered it, following the field. His eyes were well accustomed to the darkness by that time; he could see about ten yards through the driving rain. He was soaked to the skin.

He went about half a mile, and came to a cart-track leading into the road and a ruinous barn beside it. He gave the barn a very wide berth; it might well be a German strong-point full of enemy troops. Two hundred yards farther on he huddled down into a thicket of brambles, pulled out his map, and very cautiously examined it in a faint glow from his torch. He was all wrong. The wood and the barn and the track were shown approximately in the relationship that he had discovered, but he was a good two miles too far west. He must go back and go the other way.

At about half-past two the buildings of Le Rouzic farm loomed up before him. In London, in the office in Pall Mall, warm, well lit, comfortable, and secure, he had been told what he must do. The lad in the French uniform had told him in great detail. He must not go through the yard because the dog was there. He must be very careful in case Germans were billeted there, as sometimes happened. He must go through the orchard; in the darkness and the rain he found his way. He must leave the pond upon his left and he would come to the *laiterie;* counting from the door, the first two windows must be passed by. The third window was the one.

Simon stood there, drenched in the rain and wind, tapping in the rhythm that he had been taught.

Presently the window stirred and opened a chink. The voice of an old man whispered in the Breton dialect: "Is anybody there?"

Simon said: "I have a letter for you from your son."

The old man whispered: "There is a door along this way. Go there and I will let you in."

Ten minutes later he was sitting by the fire, newly revived with wood, stripping the wet clothes off him. A candle stood upon the table. The old man, in night-shirt and a jacket over it, was reading the letter aloud, slowly and carefully. His wife stood by him, bare feet showing under her black dress, hastily put on; the grey hair hung down on her shoulders. Hovering in the background there were other women, partly dressed, keeping out of sight, and listening.

The letter came to an end:

I send my most devoted love to *chère mama*, and to you, *cher papa*, and to my sisters and to Aunt Marie. I am well and I have been to the dentist for my teeth and I may be sent to Syria before long, which will be better because here everything is very dear and there is no wine. Help the man who brings this letter if you safely can. I am your most devoted and loving son,

PIERRE.

The old man came to the end and there was silence in the room, broken only by the crackle of the wood upon the fire. There was a long pause. Then the old woman passed her hands down her dress, evidently in habitual gesture. "Is he hungry?" she enquired. "There are eggs—and milk."

Simon turned to her: "I have eaten recently," he said in French. "I would like to sleep till dawn."

"There is a box bed." She pointed to a recess in the wall of the kitchen."

The old man said: "In the morning what will you do?"

Simon said: "I want to go into Douarnenez for the day. I have the proper papers. In the evening I will come back here, if it is safe. At night I will go back—where I have come from."

The old man said: "All the world goes into Douarnenez on Sunday. There is the bed. Leave your clothes out for them to dry before the fire. In the morning we will devise your journey; one does not start before nine o'clock. Perhaps I will come in with you myself. Perhaps we will all go, as if it is a party."

Shortly before eleven the next morning Simon reached Douarnenez.

He got there by train, in a slow train that ran along the line from Audierne, that they had joined at Pont Croix. To reach the station they had driven through the rain in a very old victoria once painted brown, drawn by one of the farm horses. They were a mixed party. There were Le Rouzic and his wife, dressed in their Sunday black. There was a Madame Jeanne with them, a formidable old lady with the makings of a beard whose status Simon did not understand. There was a little girl about ten years old called Julie, who seemed to be a great-niece of Le Rouzic, and there was a fat bouncing girl of twenty-two or so called Marie, who seemed to be a daughter of the house. She had a baby called Mimi about six months old.

Simon carried the baby. It was explained to him, and he readily understood, that it was correct in Brittany on Sunday for a father to carry his baby. He knew that very well, and he knew also that a baby was as good a cover as any spy could wish to have. He explained to them at the farm that he had never been a father and did not know a great deal about the matter, so before they started they showed him how to change its napkin.

He walked stiffly because of a strip of hoop-iron from a barrel in the farm-yard bound behind his right knee; it would not do to seem too able-bodied. So he passed through the station wicket into Douarnenez, carrying the baby, leading little Julie by the hand, and arguing with Le Rouzic about brands of cement—one of the few subjects that they could maintain an argument upon. Le Rouzic put up all his own farm buildings. So they passed the German sentry and the Gestapo official, showing their passes and continuing the argument in a slightly lower tone while their papers were glanced over. Pressed by the crowd behind they were urged forward into the street.

The rain had stopped for the moment, but it was still windy and wet. By arrangement they separated in the town. The old people went off to mass, taking Julie with them; Simon, still carrying the baby, went with the daughter down towards the harbour.

As they went he said: "Madame, in spite of everything, it would be better if you went to church with the others. There is danger for you and the little one in being seen with me."

She shrugged her shoulders. "There is danger everywhere in these times. Besides, you will spend more money for our refreshments than my father, and that will be a change for me, and interesting."

He said quietly: "Madame, I will do that very willingly."

They went down the narrow, cobbled streets towards the harbour. There were a few Germans in the streets, strolling around awkwardly in pairs or little bands. They did not seem to mix with the people or even to use the same cafés; there was an air of sullen uncertainty about them.

"Bad things have happened in this place," the girl said by his side. "There have been very many murders."

Simon shifted the baby on his shoulder and said nothing.

The harbour opened out before them, and he paused to look around, flogging his keen, retentive memory. There were two *Raumboote* moored at the stone jetty which formed the north arm of the harbour; there were no other warships in sight, though the anchorage was crammed with fishing vessels lying close-packed at the moorings, jostling each other. On the jetty there were two guns opposite the *Raumboote* pointing to seaward over the stone wall, with steel shields and concrete emplacements open to the harbour side. There was a searchlight post at the extreme seaward end of the jetty, put there, no doubt, to pick up vessels coming into port. There were no other guns or armament in sight.

He did not linger to look at the harbour; that was not in the part of a farmer from the country. Carrying the baby and with the young woman at his side, he turned into the Café de la République; it was nearly empty, with only a few fishermen in Sunday black discussing at the tables. Simon and Marie picked a table near the back of the room by the wall, set down and unpacked the basket that she carried, and commenced the domestic operation of changing the baby's napkin.

From behind the bar mademoiselle, the daughter of the house, came to them for their order and to view the operation. It had begun to rain again. She said something about the weather, and Simon replied in the French of Seine-et-Oise.

She glanced at him in curiosity. "Monsieur is from the east?"

Simon nodded carelessly. *"She"*—indicating Marie—"is Breton. Myself, I worked in a factory near Paris till the English came and bombed it flat—no higher than one metre, mademoiselle, no part of it. Now I am to work upon the farm."

The girl nodded; it was not an uncommon story. She took his order for a coffee for Marie and for a Pernod. Simon said: "Does Monsieur Bozallec come here on Sundays?"

She said: "In the afternoon. In one hour or one hour and a half. If monsieur wants to see him, he lives in the Rue de Locranon, just round the corner."

"I have a message for him from my father-in-law," said Simon. He took directions from her how to find the house and ordered *déjeuner* for them when it was ready.

Ten minutes later he was knocking at the door of a rickety fisherman's stone cottage in the narrow street, having left Marie with the baby in the café. The old fisherman opened the door to him, dressed in the usual suit of Sunday black with no collar. Simon said: "Good morning, monsieur. Have you yet tied the Germans up in bundles and set fire to them?"

The old man stared at him. "It is the traveller in cement. I remember. What do you want with me?" He stared suspiciously at Simon.

Simon said: "If we may talk in your house, monsieur." Rather unwillingly the fisherman let him in; they stood together in the tiny, littered kitchen.

Simon said: "I was a traveller in cement when I came here last time, but that is not true now. Now I come as one who has been bombed in the east, and works upon a farm out by Pont Croix. I am a wandering man, monsieur, and not quite what I seem, but I serve Brittany in my own way."

The old man said: "What way is that?"

Simon hesitated for an instant, and then took the plunge. He said: "I carry information to the English."

The fisherman glanced at him shrewdly. "To the English or to the Germans?"

"To the English, Monsieur Bozallec."

There was a silence. "I will believe what you say," the old man said at last. "But I will tell you this. If you are lying, if you serve the Gestapo, you will not escape. You come from the east; I know that by your talk. In this place we do not have Quislings. They do not live long. Remember that."

Charles Simon said: "Those who carry information to the English sometimes do not live so long."

There was a short silence. Bozallec asked: "What have you come here for? What is it that you want?"

Simon faced him. "I want information," he replied. "News for the English, so that they might fight the Germans better. I have come to you because I think you are an honest man and a brave one, and one who can find out the things I want to know. You can betray me now to the Gestapo; you can have me killed. That is a matter that lies wholly in your hands."

The fisherman said: "What is it that you want to know?"

Simon bent towards him. "There was a ship destroyed by fire," he said, "three weeks ago." The other nodded. "A German *Raumboot*. Did any of the Germans escape from the fire? Were any of them picked up?"

Bozallec said: "Three were picked up, all dead and burnt and floating in their life-belts in the water. One was a *Leutnant;* I think he was the captain. He once had a beard. I was out myself that night in my boat, fishing, and I saw the body. Then there was a *Seekadett* and a seaman. All were dead and floating in the water, burnt."

"There were no living survivors?"

"None at all."

"How do the people say the fire began?"

The old man stared at him. "It was an explosion of the fuel-tanks on board the *Raumboot*. Perhaps some idiot fired a flare into a tank, or possibly the engine went on fire."

"Is that what the Germans think?"

The old man shrugged his shoulders. "I do not keep in company with swine like that."

Charles Simon said: "Listen, monsieur. I have my duty to perform, the information that I have to find. I do not always understand the reason why the English want to know these things, hardly ever. But now I have to find out what the Germans think about that accident. Do they accept it as a simple accident? Or do they think that it was sabotage? Or else perhaps some English aeroplane had dropped a bomb? What do the Germans think?"

Bozallec stared at him keenly. "Did the English do it?"

Simon shrugged expressively. "I do not know. Only I am to find out what the Germans think. If you can help me, do so; if not, I will go elsewhere."

"And find yourself betrayed." There was a silence. "How long are you here in Douarnenez?"

"Till four o'clock this afternoon only. Then I go out by the train. I will come back again if it is necessary, but that is dangerous."

The fisherman said: "It is very short, the time. But the Lemaigne woman who cleans the offices hears much of what the German officers are saying. And also the girl in the Café Raeder . . ."

Simon left the cottage shortly after that and walked down to the quay. The *Raumboote* had not stirred; evidently they were in for Sunday with the fishing fleet, having their day off. They lay along the quay, bows in towards the shore, the nearest fishing-boots lay at their moorings a hundred yards or so from their beam. Yet there were fishing-boats at sea.

The rain was lighter momentarily and he could see a little way across the bay. There were several boats out there in the shallow water; they seemed to be trawling, though it was a Sunday. He strained his eyes, but could not see a *Raumboot* guarding them. He turned back to the Café de la République; this would require some explanation.

Marie was sitting where he had left her, the baby on the seat beside her; she was sewing some little garment made of pink linen. Mindful of his part, Simon took the baby and made a fuss of it in what he hoped was a convincing manner; immediately it wetted on his knee. He sat there with it, chatting to Marie, until their *déjeuner* was ready; he ordered a carafe of red wine, which pleased the girl. They fed the baby through the meals on bits of bread sopped in milk and wine. There was nothing that he could do but wait till Bozallec arrived.

Outside it started to rain hard, and they had coffee.

At about two o'clock the old fisherman came in, wet through, and dropped down in a chair at their table after the introduction. He glanced around the room. "This is a safe place," he said. "We can talk, but not too loud."

Simon bent towards him. "You have information for me?"

"I have information." The old man paused. "The Germans say that it is sabotage," he said, "and they are still busy trying to find evidence against us. They may do so by inventing it; it is all one to them."

"Was it sabotage, do you think?"

Bozallec shrugged his shoulders. "Not that I know of. Not by anybody here."

"Why do they think it was?"

The fisherman said: "It is interesting, that. Both Lemaigne and the girl say the same, and it is this: The Germans say that there was a long streak of flame outwards from the *Raumboot* a long, long way. It was all distant, you understand; perhaps two kilometres. It was not easy to see clearly. But several of them saw this streak of fire right outwards from the ship."

Simon said: "How could that be?"

"They say there was a time-bomb planted inside one of the fuel-tanks. When it went off it burst open the fuel-tank and possibly the ship as well, and burning oil flew outwards in a streak." He paused. "It was a good idea, and well thought of if it were true."

There was a long pause. Simon ordered Pernod for them both. Bozallec said: "That is all I could find out."

"It is all that the English wish to know at present."

They sat in silence for a time. Presently Simon asked: "Those vessels in the bay. I thought you did not fish on Sunday?"

The other spat on to the floor. "Some do. They trawl around the bay near here. The Germans pay double for Sunday fish in this worthless money."

"Are *Raumboote* out there with them?"

The old man shook his head. "There are two only in the port just now and there they are. They have their Sunday off. Each of the boats trawling has a German in it, and they are not allowed to go out far. They cannot get away, if that is what you think."

"Do they stay out at night?"

"Till eight o'clock. Sometimes all night, but not often."

"And each boat after dark must show an orange light?"

The old man nodded casually.

Simon sat staring out of the window at the harbour for several minutes, thinking hard. Presently he turned again to Bozallec.

"I see two guns upon the jetty," he said quietly. "The English will be interested in that. They are manned at night?"

"Assuredly. They are manned all the time."

"Are there any other guns about the harbour?"

"No big ones like that. Those are seventy-fives. There are more of them at Beuzec and at La Chèvre. The soldiers have their tanks and guns, and little guns, of course."

They talked about the harbour and the defences for some time. An idea was growing in Simon's mind, the outline of a game that he must play out to the end.

He said presently: "One day the English will arrive here, and they will force a landing. It will not be this year; it may not even be next year, but one day they will come. The *Gaullistes* will be with them; when that day comes France will be French again, and free. When that happens, will the people of Douarnenez assist the landing?"

Bodallec said: "If we are told the day, the people will fight like demons, with fire and nails and teeth against the Germans."

Simon eyed him keenly. "If the British sent you guns—small automatic rifles that they call Tommy-guns—they would be used?"

The old fisherman drew in his breath. "If the British sent us guns like that the whole country would fight. Not only the people of Douarnenez, but the people on the farms also."

"It would be necessary to hide them till the day."

"Assuredly."

"I will tell the English what you say," said Simon.

He bent towards the fisherman. "We have not very much more time, Monsieur Bozallec," he said. "Listen carefully to what I have to tell you now, because I shall not come again. The *Raumboot* that was burnt was attacked, and burnt up, and destroyed by the English." The old man stared at him. "I cannot tell you how they did it, but that is true. Let the people know."

"Some of the people believe that already, but it is what they wish to think."

Simon said: "I will give them proof that the English did it. Very soon now another *Raumboot* will be destroyed by fire. It may be next week, it may not be for a month, or it may be to-night. When that happens you will remember what I tell you now, that the English are killing Germans on your own door-step."

The man's face lit up. "I will remember that."

Simon said: "Now there is another thing. That *Raumboot* first will be destroyed by fire, as the last one was. You will then remember me, and believe what I am telling you. And after that a message will come to you. It will tell you what you have to do to get the guns that the English will send."

He paused and thought for a minute. "I cannot tell you how that message will arrive, or who will bring it," he said at last. "But you will know it in this way. I am Charles Simon. The message will begin: 'Charles Simon says . . .' and then will follow what you have to do to receive the guns. That is understood?"

The old man said: "Perfectly. First another *Raumboot* will be set on fire, and then the message will arrive beginning: 'Charles Simon says . . .' We shall not fail to do our part, monsieur."

Soon after that Simon left the Café de la République. Carrying the baby, and with Marie at his side, he walked back to the station through the rain.

*   *   *   *   *

In *Geneviève* the day passed very slowly. They had steamed out west-north-west from the Saints for about thirty miles in the darkness and the rain. By that time they were out of the direct route for Brest from any other port, unlikely to be picked up by patrol vessels. They shut down their engine then and set their big lug sail upon the mast, and stood on slowly upon the same course, towing a weighted drogue astern of them to simulate a trawl.

The dawn came, wet and windy. They were far out in the Atlantic by that time and their danger lay in German aircraft and in German submarines. It was quite on the cards that they would be picked up by a submarine homing into Brest or setting out upon a cruise. They had to take their chance of that. The *maître*, André, took the wheel ready to hail back in Breton to any submarine that accosted them. Rhodes flaked down a sail below decks beside the flame-thrower and went to sleep on that, ready for instant action; Colvin and Boden went down to the cuddy. Only the Free French Breton lads remained on deck. Colvin was taking no chances with the scrutiny that a submarine would make by periscope before approaching them.

In the cuddy the day passed slowly. Boden and Colvin slept, and lay awake, and ate, and slept again; the vessel heaved and strained and water dripped in through the skylight, making the place wet and squalid. Colvin had a dog's-eared copy of an American paper magazine entitled *True Stories of the West;* he lay on his back on the bunk reading about cowboys and their broncos till the light began to fail in the dim cuddy about mid-afternoon. From time to time he got up and called up to André in the wheel-house, but there was nothing to report.

He sat down on his bunk at last, idle, and stared around. "Time goes slow, don't it?" he observed to Boden.

The R.N.V.R. officer said: "Fed up with reading?"

"Aye. It's getting too dark. We ought to have a radio." It had never struck them that they would have time to listen to the wireless on operations in that ship.

Boden said: "Try the light over the chart-table. You can read there."

Colvin shook his head. "No. I like them stories well enough, but when you've read the one you've read the lot." He paused. "You didn't think to bring them poker dice?"

They had nothing, not even a pack of cards. Boden said: "Try writing letters. Use the back of the signal-pad."

"Who'd I write a letter to?"

The other said: "You might try Junie."

There was a silence lasting into minutes. "You want to keep your mouth shut about what don't concern you," Colvin said at last. He got on to his bunk and turned over for sleep, his back to Boden.

They stood into the coast with the last of the light and picked up their bearings again. In the darkness they edged in till the cliffs loomed near them and they heard the wash of waves on rocks; then they anchored, not quite knowing where they were. At about eight o'clock the weather cleared for a brief spell; the

moon was setting down near the horizon and gave light enough
for them to take a bearing on the high bluff of La Chèvre. They
got up anchor, crept a short way back westwards along the
coast, and found their cove without great difficulty.

They went right inshore there, anchoring barely a hundred
yards from the beach. Presently they put their dinghy into the
water to be in readiness.

At midnight, punctually, they saw the flashes of the torch
that meant that Simon was there. Two of the Breton lads went
tumbling into the boat and Boden followed them, carrying a
Tommy-gun in case of accidents. A few minutes later they were
back with Simon, still in his civilian clothes and very wet.

Simon went straight to Colvin. "Is all ready for fighting?"
he enquired.

The other said: "Sure it is Who do you want to fight?"

"Listen, and I will tell you." The other officers gathered by
them; he told them all that he had seen in Douarnenez. "They
are there now," he said, "moored up beside the quay. It is a
snip; we will get both of them, and also the two guns as well."

Colvin laughed. "Try everything once," he said. "How are
we going to get in the harbour without being spotted? Like as
if we was one of them trawlers in the bay, got left out late?
We'll want an orange shade over the light."

It had begun to rain again. "Can you find the entrance to
the harbour in the dark?"

"I guess so," Colvin said. "It's not so difficult, built out into
the bay the way it is. If we hit up against a rock that's just too
bad."

They weighed anchor and made off to the north in the direction of La Chèvre. Half-way there they altered course for
Douarnenez; it was raining steadily by then and visibility was
very poor. They lit their lantern, fixed the orange shade on it,
and set it up upon the mast, confident that in that weather
nobody would see the light come into being. Then they set
themselves to prepare for action.

They found the harbour without difficulty. Another orange
light appeared on their port bow converging on their course;
they guessed correctly that it was another fishing vessel making
for the harbour after trawling in the bay. It was then about
one o'clock in the morning. They slowed a little and set themselves to follow in her wake. Presently a green light showed up
through the darkness, high up and straight ahead of them.

"That's on the end of the jetty," Colvin said softly. He

turned to the *maître*. "André, be ready to get that orange light off her soon as I say."

They slowed to a mere crawl. The orange light ahead of them turned the end of the jetty under the green light and vanished behind the stonework. Simon, in the wheel-house by Colvin, bent to the speaking-tube.

"Rhodes," he said softly. "Is everything quite ready?"

"Aye, aye, sir. All ready."

"Listen then, carefully. We are going in now, and the plan is not changed at all. The *Raumboote* will be on our starboard side. We shall go past the first one and stop between the two of them, and about fifty yards away. It is quite clear?"

"Quite clear, sir. Oil first on the outermost *Raumboot*, then the inner one, and then the two casemates. That's the right order?"

"That is right. And then the flame first to the guns, because the gun crews, they will be the most alert."

"Very good, sir."

"Wait now, and do not shoot the oil until I tell you . . ."

They crept in slowly, the big engine just ticking over. The green light passed above them, and the rough stones of the jetty. There was a man standing under the green light looking down upon them, a man in uniform. He made no movement; there was no hail. The orange light upon the mast was passport for them at the harbour mouth.

The anchorage opened before them, thick with vessels. The jetty ran away from them upon the starboard bow, seen dimly in the glow of their lamp; ahead of them the anchored fishing vessels loomed dim in the rain. The transom of the first *Raumboot* appeared beside the wall, a dark mass, unlit. Colvin threw out the gear; the Diesel choked and hunted irregularly in neutral, and they crept slowly forward to the anchored ships. The bow of the first *Raumboot* showed upon the beam, and the transom of the second one; above the jetty they could see the two faint lumps that were the guns behind their shields.

Colvin put the gear into reverse to check way. Simon said down the tube: "Rhodes, can you see the ships?"

"I see the ships, sir. I'm not sure about the guns."

"Look, carefully," said Simon calmly. "Over the funnel of the inner boat there is a sort of lump upon the jetty. Do you see it? That is the one gun there."

"I see that now. There's another lump above the forecastle of the outer boat. Is that the other gun?"

"That is quite right. One moment now . . ."

He turned to Colvin. Way was off the vessel and the engine was again in neutral; they were poised motionless upon the water of the harbour. The rain beat against the ship and dripped in little quiet trickles. "Get going soon as you like," said Colvin quietly. "I can't hold her this way for long. The wind'll carry us foul of them boats."

Simon bent to the tube. "Rhodes, go on and shoot the oil now."

"Okay, sir."

There was a whistling, wet hiss. They did not see the black jet in the night, but they saw a great black splash upon the stone-work of the jetty up above the stern of the *Raumboot*. Simon leaped for the voice-pipe. "Ten feet too high," he shouted. "Down a bit, Rhodes." But Rhodes had corrected, and the oil was deluging the *Raumboot* at the quay.

Very slowly, the jet travelled up her length. It paused for a few seconds at the bridge, and then went forward, steadily and slowly. Quite suddenly, a tumult of voices became audible. The jet travelled on to the stern of the next boat and moved inshore along her length, slowly, methodically. On the jetty lights began to flash from torches down on to the vessels.

Colvin breathed tensely. "They haven't got on to it yet. Gosh, this is better'n a play. . . ."

The jet lifted from the bow of the *Raumboot* and travelled blackly up the jetty to the dimly seen lump at the top. There was an instant babel of cries and oaths from the gun's crew. It paused there second after second, a long time. Then it swept swiftly round towards the other gun.

A shot rang out, and then another one; they heard a bullet whip into the hull. Simon bent down to the tube. "The flame, Rhodes! Now the flame!"

The first burst from the nozzle of the gun and travelled in a fearful, writhing arc towards the jetty, slowly, inexorably. They saw the oil-soaked men around the guns turn towards it, watching it, appalled. They saw some of them begin to run, and some of them crouch down beside the ammunition lockers. Then it came to them, and the fire hid everything from view.

The harbour, ships, and town were now as bright as day in the huge yellow light. From the wheel-house Colvin shouted: "André—get down that mast-head light. Quick about it." Then he turned back to the jetty as the fire swung swiftly to the further gun. The firing now had stopped, and the sole noise was the hoarse rushing of the blazing oil and the hoarse shouts of men. The flame dropped to the bow of the inmost *Raumboot,* and they saw fire shoot along her decks before the jet.

Colvin heaved the gear over to reverse and lifted the brass throttle lever slowly. "Time we was out of this," he said. "Tell him to watch his training, because I'm moving out astern."

The engine of the boat plugged heavily; the water creamed in eddies back along her topsides; she moved infinitely slowly. The whole quay seemed to be ablaze, and every detail of *Geneviève* was visible. The flame poured from her midships, travelling slowly to the outer *Raumboot* and to the men upon her deck; from somewhere a few shots came whistling around them.

Simon leaned from the wheel-house and shouted to Boden, lying flat upon the deck behind the low bulwarks with his Bren and Tommy gunners. "Boden," he shouted, "watch out soon now for the searchlights, when the fire dies down. Shoot them immediately if they pick us up. Shoot them, and put them out."

The other raised his hand and nodded. Simon glanced back at the blazing boats; they were an inferno from stem to stern. The heat from them was so great that it blistered; he threw his hand up to protect his face. He bent down to the tube. "Cease fire!" he shouted. "That is now enough."

The flame pouring from the gun shut off abruptly; the truncated end of it went sailing through the air and fell blazing to the water near the *Raumboot.* They were now moving slowly astern; the *Raumboote* were ahead of them and the green light at the jetty end was now abeam. A great fire was raging on the jetty and the boats, pouring black wreathing clouds of smoke up into the dark sky in its own light. But they were farther from it now, the heat was less, and the light on board was not quite so intense. Behind them lay the friendly darkness of the bay and the safe shroud of rain.

From the shore on their port side a brilliant sheet of white light shone out behind them, and focused instantly to a sharp pencil of great brilliance, groping and searching astern of them. Another sprang out, farther along the shore, an intense white eye. In the white light Simon saw the gunners, led by Boden, spring across the hatch; the Bren guns spat and rattled and the second light went out abruptly. But now the first had found them, and from shore rifle-fire zipped over them and smacked into their sides.

They were driving astern from the harbour at a good speed now, making stern first out into the bay and the shelter of the rain. From the shore end of the jetty a stream of tracer came out suddenly, spraying around them and a little to the port side. Then, providentially and mercifully, Boden's gunners got the other searchlight, and the firing crossed them and sprayed wide upon the starboard side, bright sheaves of little yellow sparks. The white illumination vanished and they were back in the half-light of the fire at the jetty, now much farther off.

Colvin, wrestling with the wheel, made heavy with their stern-way, said: "Watch out for them searchlights." And as he spoke, a third blazed out at them on their port bow from some point above the jetty in the town. It lit them mercilessly, and in a moment the cannon fire was flying through the air at them again, bright yellow sparks.

The gun was somewhere at the shore end of the jetty, firing down its length at them. Colvin hauled madly at the wheel; a few feet more to starboard and the jetty itself would inter-pose between them and the gun. The Bren guns clattered at the third searchlight. There was a deafening crack beside them, and the framework of the wheel-house on the port side shivered and collapsed. Simon was on that side; he swung half round and his left arm flew backwards; he staggered for a moment, and recovered himself. At the bow there was a flash and flying timber. Amidships there was a flash and a bright yellow fire that sprang up suddenly around the flame-thrower, Then Rhodes, muffled in his anti-flash clothing, was rolling on the hatch; the fire ran along the deck as if pursuing him.

Abruptly there were flashes on the jetty, and the tracer that had been flying round them ceased. The Bren guns were still firing at the searchlight, and in a minute that went out. Now there were only isolated rifle shots directed at the fire amidships at the flame-thrower.

Colvin roared out: "Get that fire out, quick!" and saw Boden with a foam extinguisher. Presently there were two extinguishers in action, and the fire died down.

The engine was stopped, but the ship had good stern way upon her still. Already the blaze upon the jetty had grown dim; it was raining heavily and the rain made a curtain to shield them. Unless there were another searchlight very near they had respite for the moment. Another searchlight came on a long way to the north, two miles away, perhaps. It lit them up, but not intensely.

Colvin shouted: "Don't fire at that!" The curtain of the rain, he thought, would shroud them from the shore in that weak light.

The beam wavered, and began searching farther out to sea, and they were back in the half-light of the fire upon the quay.

By his side, Simon was holding the artery of his left arm; his hand was a mess of blood. He said: "I am all right. The engine, is that hit?"

"I dunno." Colvin turned. "André, *la voile*."

Boden answered: "André's been hit, sir. You want the main-sail?"

"Aye, get it up quick, 'n let's get out of this."

The wind was in the south-west; under sail they could do no more than reach across the bay in the direction of La Chèvre or Morgat. They could hardly beat up into the wind at all; their sail was too small for that. The most that it would do for them was to carry them out into the bay away from Douarnenez.

Colvin called Rollot to the wheel, and leaped down to the engine-room. The two engineers were uninjured and were already hard at work, but it was clear that they had a big job ahead of them. Water was pouring from the aft cylinder; a gaping hole showed in the deck above. In mixed French and English Colvin heard their diagnosis. The engine was jammed, immovable. The piston in that cylinder was cracked or seized; it would be necessary to take off the pot. There were some fractured fuel oil-pipes as well. There was no other damage. They would do all they could, but it would be, perhaps, three hours before they could attempt to start her up again.

Colvin went back on deck. The sail was up and Rollot was at the wheel; they were drawing forward. The fire upon the jetty was now less intense, and gave them little light. He spoke to Rollot about the course, then went forward. Simon was sitting on the hatch and Rhodes was putting a dressing on his hand; Boden was still watchful at the guns. One of the Danes was very badly hit. André, the *maître*, was dead up in the bows.

So, in the darkness and the rain, they drew away from land.

Two hours later they were about two miles east of La Chèvre. Searchlights were still groping for them in the bay, but the rain saved them from detection. Their quiet passage may have helped, of course, under the sail alone. They had a respite and down in the cramped engine-room the men worked like beavers. With great difficulty they got the cylinder off. The piston was cracked and useless, and the connecting-rod distorted. They took off the piston with a hacksaw, undid the big end and drew out the connecting-rod through the crank-case inspection cover, and made a fibre plate to cover over where the cylinder had been. They repaired the shattered water pipes and fuel pipes with insulating tape and cod line, and at about 03.15 in the morning Colvin heard the engine run. It ran with a good deal of vibration and a hard, uneven beat, as was only to be expected on five cylinders. But it gave them about eight knots of speed, and there were still three hours of darkness before them in which they could clear the land, and the rain held.

And that, really, is all there is to say about their venture. They headed straight out into the Atlantic, meaning to give Ushant a wide berth and make for Falmouth with their wounded. With the dawn the wind began to veer towards the north, about force 5 or 6, and settled to about north-west by 09.00. They were somewhere to the north of Ushant then, and making only about four knots through the water on their course for Falmouth against the foul wind; the prospects of getting in before dark were poor. The only port open to them in the hours of darkness was Dartmouth, so they bore away up Channel and hoisted their sail to give them a lift along. They sailed and motored slowly through the day with continual engine stoppages. They berthed at Dartmouth at about 03.00 the next morning, and moved up to Dittisham soon after that.

One personal incident occurred that morning that I heard of some time afterwards. They were going to bed in the villas; the doctor was looking after them, and I had gone back to the hotel. Colvin went in to Boden's room and found him sitting on the bed, still in his sea clothes, too tired to undress.

"Say," he said wearily. "You want to get to bed."

The lad raised his head. His face was very white at all times, and his hair a staring red; with his fatigue, in the hard light of the unshaded bulb, he looked desperately ill.

"I just sat down for a minute. The surgeon gave Rollot and Jules a draught or something. He's staying here till morning."

"I know that," said Colvin. "Did he give you one?"

"I don't need anything. I'll sleep all right."

"Let's see you do it. Give me your boots; I'll pull them off for you."

Obediently Boden stretched out his right leg; Colvin took the gum-boot and wrestled it off. "Say," he said, grasping the left one. "I spoke pretty sharp that time you said I ought to write to Junie. I ought to have clipped you on the jaw."

Boden smiled faintly. "Do it now, if you like." The other boot came off, and he lowered his leg to the ground. "Are you going to write to her?"

The older man stood silent for a moment. "I dunno," he said at last. "I dunno why you want to get me talking about Junie all the time. It don't do any good. Come on now. Get up, 'n get your clothes off, 'n get into bed."

Obediently the other got up and stripped off his jersey. "Don't you ever want to see her again?"

"I dunno. Junie's a young woman still. If she can meet up with some proper guy that has a settled job, 'n can treat her right, I'd not want anything better for her. Suppose I was to write, I'd only get her unsettled all over again."

Boden stopped in the act of pulling off a sea-boot stocking. "It gets you," he said, staring at the other. "It got me, just the same as it's got you. So that nothing's ever quite the same again."

There was a pause. Then Colvin said roughly: "Go on and get into your bed. I dunno what you're talking about."

Boden pulled off his clothes in silence. Presently he said: "How many Jerries do you think we scuppered?"

"I dunno," said Colvin. "Forty-five—fifty, maybe. Rhodes said he put eight hundred and thirty gallons of that Worcester Sauce on them, all in next to no time. I reckon we got all there were."

Boden said: "Counting the ones in the first boat, that'd make sixty or seventy in all."

"I guess so. What's on your mind?"

"Nothing." He got into his bed. "Thanks for tucking me up; I might have sat like that till morning."

"You R.N.V.R. want a nursemaid with you," said Colvin. "Good night." He switched out the light, closed the door behind him, and went to find the young surgeon.

"Look in upon Lieutenant Boden, quiet, in half an hour," he said. "If he's awake give him a sleeping dose."

9

I WENT up to N.O.I.C.'s office next morning and rang up the admiral. He asked that Simon should go to him to report. I told him Simon was in hospital, and he asked for Colvin; I promised to take Colvin to him as soon as we had got the party straightened up.

I met McNeil and had a short talk with him; then he went back to London on the morning train. I was left to do all that was necessary. I had a talk with N.O.I.C. and made arrangements for *Geneviève* to go on to the slip; she was leaking badly. While she was there we could survey her for repair.

I talked of leave to the old commander. "I'm going to send the whole ship's company away for ten days' leave," I said. "The shore party can do anything that's necessary. About that Wren who drives their truck. If you agree, I think she'd better go as well."

"If you like," he said amiably. "That's Wren Wright?"

"I think that's the one," I said. "She's refused leave recently, I understand, because she wanted to see the thing through. They may as well all go together; then they'll all be fresh when they get back."

He nodded. "What are you going to do next?" he asked. "Are you going on to do it again?"

I was silent for a moment. "That depends on what the vessel's like," I said. "I'd like to pack this party up, myself, and do something quite different. But I'm afraid that other people will decide that one."

"Why do you want to pack them up?" he asked mildly. "They seem to be a most successful ship, from what I hear."

I did not really know myself, to express it in words. I only knew that I had a feeling that they'd done enough. "They don't run under proper naval discipline," I said at last. "I don't think it's a sound arrangement to mix nationalities in a ship's company like that. It may work well enough for a time, but it can't go on."

I went up to the hospital soon after that to see Simon, but he was still asleep. I went down to the dock and had a talk with the manager, and then I went back to the hotel for lunch. I telephoned for a car after lunch, and Wren Wright came with the little truck and we drove out to Dittisham.

She was looking pale and drawn. " 'Afternoon," I said as I got in. "You're going off on leave. The whole ship's company are getting leave. Has N.O.I.C. told you?"

"They told me at the Wrennery, sir," she said. "I think I'll probably be going off to-morrow morning."

I said: "A change will do everybody good. Where are you going to?"

She said: "To Derby."

"I thought you lived in Norwich?" I said idly.

"I do. I'm going first to Derby, and then on to Norwich."

How she spent her leave was no concern of mine, but the mention of Derby struck a chord somewhere. Derby, somehow, was a part of this affair. I sat in silence for a few minutes as she drove through the lanes, and then it came to me. Derby was where Rhodes's mother lived.

At Dittisham I found them all up and about, smart and clean in new uniforms. Already *Geneviève* had disappeared, towed down the river to the shipyard by a motor-boat. I told Colvin that all the lot of them were to get off on leave. I told him that he'd got to produce the report, since Simon was in hospital.

He said awkwardly: "I'll do my best, sir, but I don't write so good. I'd rather someone else did it."

Boden was there. He said: "I'll write it, if you like."

"Aye," said Colvin, much relieved. "You write it, 'n I'll tell you where it's wrong."

I left them to it, and went on to fix up the leave of the Free French and the Danes. McNeil was arranging hospitality for them in London in conjunction with their own headquarters; most of them had nowhere of their own to go to. Presently I came to Rhodes.

"You'd better give me your address on leave," I said, "in case we want to get hold of you." I got out my notebook and a pencil.

"I shall be at Derby for the first four or five days, sir," he said. He gave me the address. "After that I'm going on to Norwich."

I shut my notebook with a snap. "I suppose I can get that one from the Wrennery," I said. He grinned, and flushed quite pink. It was odd to think that that lad had done what he had on Sunday night.

When I came round to Boden and to Colvin I ran up against a difficulty. Each of them came to me in turn and asked if he could stay at Dittisham. Boden came first.

"I don't want to go away," he said. "One of us ought to stay here to look after things. I don't want any leave."

"I want you all to get away," I said. "The vessel will be in the shipyard for ten days, and longer."

"I'd rather stay here. I've got nowhere special that I want to go to."

I knew that this lad wanted careful handling. "You've got a home in Yorkshire, haven't you?" I said. "Your people will want to see you."

He was silent. At last he said: "I suppose I ought to go and see my people. But I shan't stay there more than a day or two. After that I think I'll come back here."

"No, you won't," I said. "You won't come back here till your leave is up. That's an order." I paused. "I tell you what you can do, if you like. If you get fed up with Yorkshire there's a lot of paper work about this thing wants doing in my office. You can come down to the Admiralty and give me a hand."

He brightened; he was evidently pleased. "That's awfully good of you, sir. I'll be with you on Monday morning."

Colvin came next, and he said much the same as Boden. "I guess I'll stick around," he said.

I put that idea out of his head. "You can go to Torquay if you like," I said. "But nobody stays here."

He shook his head. "I don't want to go to Torquay." That rather surprised me. "I got no roots in this country," he said. "Not like them R.N.V.R. boys."

"You've got to come with me to Newhaven to see V.A.C.O.," I said. "After that I'll find you a job if you want one, but you don't stay here."

He grinned. In the end I sent him up to Scotland with the East Coast convoy out of London, to tell me how the double Vick formation against E-boats worked out in practice. He put in a very clear and informative report, written up for him by Boden, at the end of his leave; so that was quite good value.

I had tea at Dittisham with them, and then went to Dartmouth in the truck, with Rhodes in the back, to go to see Simon in the hospital. I found him awake and in a bit of pain from his injured hand; moreover, he was in an open ward, so I didn't stay very long. In any case, McNeil had taken his account the night before.

He told me that they had taken off the remains of the third and fourth fingers that morning, and tidied up the rest for him. "I shall not be long here, in hospital," he said. "A week—no more. Then I shall be back at duty."

It occurred to me that this was probably another one; none of these fellows seemed to have much use for leave. "I don't know about that," I said. "You won't be fit for duty, and I want everyone to have a spell of leave."

He said: "There is no time for that. As soon as the ship is repaired, we must go again, with guns. How long will that be?"

"Ten days or a fortnight." McNeil had told me something about his new idea that morning, but I was by no means sure that I agreed. "Tell me," I said, "what is it that you want to do, exactly?"

He leaned forward from his bed, tense, eager, and a little feverish. "To-day," he said, "Douarnenez will be seething hot for revolt against the Germans. We have shown them what the English can do now. The next step is to bring them arms. Seventy Tommy-guns, and about three thousand rounds for each—Colvin says that we can carry that much in the ship. Then, when we want to land a force in Brittany, we shall find them fighting at our side."

A nurse swept down upon us. "This patient is not to get excited, Commander," she said severely. "You may talk for two or three minutes longer, but not if he goes on like this." She laid him back upon his pillows and smoothed out the sheet.

"Over-enthusiasm," I said. "That's what you get, you see."

From his pillow he eyed me earnestly. "You will see Brigadier McNeil? I cannot say how important it is. They will receive the guns and hide them, secretly, to use to help us when our fellows have to land one day."

I nodded. "I'll talk it over with McNeil," I said. "Have you thought out how you'd get the guns on shore?"

He said: "The fishing fleet must take them from us, five or ten to each boat; in that way they can be hidden and smuggled on shore easily. We will arrange that there is an alarm one night, so that the boats must scatter and put out their lights." He paused. "An alarm that British raiders are near-by. Then we can make a rendezvous, in the dark night, to pass the arms to them."

If the fishing fleet would play, that was as good a way to do the job as any other. Distribution before the arms got on shore was obviously sound. "I'll see McNeil about it when I get to London," I promised him. "It's a matter of high policy, of course. For all I know, they may not want to give the Bretons arms just yet."

Simon said: "In a war like this, sir, policy depends on opportunity. And now, we have an opportunity that will not come again."

He was obviously tired, and in a good bit of pain. I left him, and on my way out stopped in the office to speak to the surgeon-commander.

"He's getting on very well, so far as we can tell at present," I was told. "We removed two fingers—oh, he told you that. Apart from that, he'll have the full use of the hand, I think."

"He said that he'd be back on duty in a week."

The surgeon snorted. "We might discharge him from here in a week if all goes well, but there's such a thing as sick leave. I shall recommend him for a month."

"You may recommend what you like," I said. "You won't get him to take it."

There was a short silence. "I agree, he seems to be difficult upon that subject," the surgeon said. "He's a funny sort of chap. Foreign, isn't he? And an army officer?"

"Yes," I said shortly.

"Anyway, he won't be passed as fit for general service for at least a month after he leaves here. If he goes back to work at all it must be for light duty only."

I left the hospital, and went down to the shipyard to see *Geneviève*. She was just coming up on to the slip; I stayed there till the cradle had gone up and we could see the underwater body. Water trickled steadily from a point by the sternpost where the planks had sprung; the foreman said it was the engine and propeller vibration that had done that. At the bow the damage from the shell hit by the stem extended to the waterline; she had taken in water there. Apart from those points she was sound enough, and they weren't serious.

I left for London on the early train next morning. Colvin came with me, and all the Danes and Bretons travelled in the next coach to us; Colvin was seeing them up safe to London. I rang McNeil from Paddington when we got in; he was in his office and I went there with Colvin before going on to Newhaven to see the admiral.

McNeil had two of the same typed flimsies on his desk; he passed them over for us to read, without comment. They were marked MOST SECRET, as before.

The first one read:

DOUARNENEZ. Riots and anti-German demonstrations continued throughout Monday. There have been many arrests. There are not more than three hundred German troops in the town, and no effective reinforcements nearer than the Panzer concentration at Carhaix. Oberstleutnant Meichen, commandant, has telegraphed Generalmajor Reutzel stating unless reinforcements are sent he cannot guarantee to control the district. Ends.

The second one read:

BREST. One officer and sixteen other ranks were executed by shooting at the Fort des Fédérés this morning. The officer was Leutnant zur See Engelmann, a native of Kassel. These men were part of the crews of *Raumboote* R.83 and R.172, stationed at Brest. It is reported that they refused duty on being ordered to Douarnenez to replace vessels destroyed by fire. Ends.

"I don't get that," said Colvin. "Was this Germans that got shot, at this place Fort des Fédérés?"

McNeil took the signals back from him. "What it means," he said, "is that you started a mutiny in the German Navy. These *Raumboote* were ordered to go to Douarnenez, but the crews had heard what happens to *Raumboote* at that port. Some of the men mutinied, and were tried and shot within a day. The *Boche* won't stand that sort of thing."

"Say," breathed Colvin. "What do you think of that?"

I said: "The other one is interesting. I had no idea that the coast was so lightly held."

McNeil said: "There are strong concentrations inland. But the control of the population is evidently worrying them. They may need more men for that."

"Well," I said, "the Russians can do without them." That was early in October, 1941, when the Russians had been retreating steadily for three months.

"That's the point," said McNeil. "That is why we must keep up the pressure."

I pulled out my case and lit a cigarette. "I haven't seen V.A.C.O. yet," I remarked. "I'm going down there now. My own view is that this vessel has done enough. She has been clearly seen now, at Douarnenez, and they know she's easy meat so long as they don't get too close to her. I think her usefulness is over."

"Is that what you're going to tell your admiral?"

"Subject to what you say—yes."

McNeil was silent for a minute. "In general," he said, "I think I agree with you. I don't think we should send her out again on an offensive operation; she's getting too well known. I think that she is valuable still because of her great similarity to the fishing vessels of the fleet. I've got in mind this gun-running that Simon wants to do."

"He told me something about that," I said. "Is it in line with your policy?"

"Yes, it is. A town that's in that state of ferment should have arms. Tommy-guns and ammunition are coming forward quite well now. I can find seventy for Douarnenez, if Simon can think up a scheme to put them in the town."

"He wants a diversion," I said. "He wants the fishing fleet to be broken up one night, so that they scatter without lights. Then he can rendezvous with them in some quiet cove, and pass the arms to them."

"From *Geneviève*?"

I hesitated. "It would be best to use a ship that looks like another fishing-boat of the fleet for the job, I suppose."

"I agree," he said. "She should be useful for some time to come for missions of that sort. But I agree with you, she should not do offensive operations any more."

"Personally," I said, "I don't care much about her doing anything at all."

"She ought to do this gun-running," he said.

I nodded. "We might let her do that. But after that is over we should give that district a long rest, or else start something different with another ship."

We left it like that; that we should review the operations of the ship again after this next trip over to the other side. I left McNeil, and went on down to Newhaven with Colvin that same afternoon to see V.A.C.O. It was dark when we got there, a fine starry night. It was fresh down by the sea, after a day of travelling.

The admiral had us in at once. He got up from his desk as we came in. " 'Evening, Colvin. 'Evening, Martin. I understand I've got to congratulate your vessel on another very good show."

Colvin flushed with pleasure. "It wasn't all that, sir," he said.

"Wasn't it? I've been getting reports all day about it. Flaps in the German Army, mutinies in the German Navy, and I don't know what beside. But first of all, how is Captain Simon?"

"He's getting on all right, sir," I replied. "I saw him yesterday. He's lost two fingers, but he'll be out of the hospital in a week."

"That might be worse." He motioned us to chairs. "Sit down, and tell me the whole thing. Smoke if you want to." He pushed forward his silver box of cigarettes.

The story took the best part of an hour in the telling, because he wanted to know every little thing, including every detail of the damage to the ship. Once launched and over his diffidence

201

Colvin told the tale quite well, in simple direct terms. He had the report that Boden had written out for him in his hand, and now and again he turned to that to check a point.

In the end the admiral turned to me. "So much for that," he said. "That brings me up to date. What's the next step, Martin?"

I said: "The next thing Brigadier McNeil wants us to do is to land those arms," I said. I told him briefly what had been proposed, that the fishing fleet should be scattered by a false attack one night, and in the confusion certain of the boats should rendezvous with *Geneviève*. "Brigadier McNeil can find the guns and ammunition," I said. "I saw him about that this afternoon. He very much wants the operation to be carried out."

He eyed me keenly. "Don't you?"

I said: "I think it should be all right, sir. I don't think that the ship should do much more after that. She must be getting pretty well known by this time, over on the other side."

"I agree that we don't want to overplay our hand. Taking this operation, though, what form would your false attack take?"

I said: "Would you consider sending a couple of destroyers in to get behind the fishing fleet, and shoot up anything that they could find, sir? It only needs a little gunfire between the fleet and their home port—Douarnenez. This would scatter them all right."

He said directly: "No, I won't. I won't even consider it, Martin."

He got up from his chair, and began pacing up and down in front of his fire, as was his habit. "I told you when this thing began," he said, "and I told McNeil. I remember telling Brigadier McNeil in this room that I wouldn't send destroyers up to the front door of Brest to help him out if he got into trouble. And now that's just exactly what you're asking me to do."

I was silent.

He turned on me, though I had not spoken. "However small the risk may seem to be, I won't do that. You must keep a sense of proportion. This is a very minor operation of war, Martin. It has to do with a fishing-boat and a few Tommy-guns. To make that operation a success you say that we should risk a million pounds' worth of ships and upwards of three hundred men. Well, I won't do it."

I knew my admiral fairly well by that time. "Very good, sir," I replied. "Could we send a couple of motor-gunboats over for the job?"

He stopped short in his pacing. "That's more like it!" he exclaimed. "All you want is something fast, to let off a few guns and make a noise. They can drop a depth charge if they want to make a bigger bang. Yes, I don't mind a couple of M.G.B.s. You'll have to see Rear-Admiral Coastal Forces, though, and see if he can work it in for you."

We settled it upon that basis, and he made us stay and dine with him. We caught the last train back to London after dinner and got back at about eleven, very tired.

I fixed up Colvin for his convoy job next morning, which was Thursday. Then I settled down to work, to clear up the arrears that had accumulated while I was away. It took me all the rest of that week to get my normal routine straight without touching any of the paper that related to *Geneviève*, so that by Monday morning I was glad to see young Boden.

He turned up bright and early. I settled him down on the other side of the table to me and got him going; he proved to be intelligent and apt at office work. In fact, he was a good deal more accustomed to it than I am; Dartmouth and life at sea don't fit one for an office chair or make it easy to dictate to a shorthand-typist. He was a great help. He took all my telephone calls when I was out and took them right, did the right thing with people who looked in to see me, and got the *Geneviève* papers into splendid shape with only minor guidance from myself. I was very sorry, I may say, when his leave came to an end.

He was sitting opposite me at the table one day when I happened to mention Colvin. "The East Coast convoy gets to Methil to-morrow," I said. "Colvin should be here on Friday."

"He'll be in time for the meeting with Rear-Admiral Coastal Forces, then," said Boden. "Do you want him in on that, sir?"

"If Simon hasn't turned up by then, I do," I said. And then I said: "I must say, you fellows have a queer idea of leave."

He smiled. "Colvin hasn't got anywhere to go to in this country. He left it just after the last war."

I wrote my name at the foot of a minute and tossed it into the out-basket. "He was going strong with a young woman at Torquay at one time," I said.

"I think that's all washed up," said Boden. "He hasn't been

203

over to Torquay for the last month."

There was a pause. Presently he said: "After this next operation, sir, the ship will pay off, won't she?"

I leaned back in my chair. "I think she will," I said. "We
haven't come to any decision yet, but that's what it looks like
to me. If we decided to pack the whole show up, what would
you like to do?"

"Do you think I could get into Combined Operations?"

"In charge of one of the landing craft?"

"That's what I'd like."

I thought about that for a minute. "It's rather a waste of
your anti-submarine training, isn't it?" I said.

He said: "That's what I'd really like best."

I nodded. "I'll remember that. C.W. Branch may get a bit
sticky; if they do you may have to go back into anti-submarine.
But I'll do what I can."

"That's awfully good of you, sir."

"Not a bit. What about the others? What about Rhodes?"

Boden said: "He isn't a sea-going officer. He's colour-blind.
I think he'd be quite happy in a shore job after this."

"Maybe," I said, thinking of the Wren. There was a pause
while I lit a cigarette. "Do you know what Colvin wants?"

The lad said calmly: "I know what he wants well enough,
but he won't get it."

I stared at him. "What does he want?"

"He wants to go back to the West Coast of America. He left
his wife out there, in San Francisco."

"I thought he wasn't married."

Boden grinned. "That's what he likes people to believe. It
may be true, legally. Probably it is. But that doesn't stop him
wanting to get back to her."

This was the Admiralty in war-time, and here we were gossip-
ing like a couple of fish-wives. I thought of that for a moment,
and relaxed. "What she like?" I asked.

"Her name's Junie," he said. "She comes from a place called
East Naples, in Arkansas. Beautiful, but dumb. She went to
Hollywood for a screen test, and got stuck there. She was a
waitress in a cafeteria in San Diego when he met her."

"How long ago was that?"

"About four years before the war. They got married, so to
speak, and went to live in Oakland, as nice a suburban couple as
you'd wish to see. That was when he had that shore job with
the line of nitrate ships."

"The Manning Stevens Line," I said. "He had that for four years. Was he still living with her when the war broke out?"

"Yes. But for the war he'd still have been with Junie and the Manning Stevens Line, snug as a bug in a rug."

"I thought of the long, difficult trip he had made in the tug before the mast, to join up; of the eighteen weary months that he had served in North and South Atlantic. "It's a rotten war," I said.

He took me up. "It's very hard on a couple like that," said Boden. "After four years of quiet, settled life, the first he'd ever had. And with people of that sort, it's such an undertaking for them to write letters. It's not like you and me. He hates writing, and Junie doesn't know what to do with a pen and ink when she gets them, so he says. And if they do write, they can't think of anything to say. . . ."

I stared at him thoughtfully. "If they can't keep together, they're sunk," I said at last.

"That's right. He made a pass at that young woman at Torquay, but then he dropped her. He's a pretty lonely man."

I glanced across the table at the white-faced, red-haired lad before me. "You think a good deal of him, don't you?"

He said: "He's a fine chap, sir. He's nice to work under, and he's a splendid seaman. I hate like hell to see a chap like that have such bad luck."

We turned back to the work.

Simon came up to London at the week-end, and Boden went back with Colvin to the ship at Dartmouth. Simon was looking well enough, but for his hand; he carried it in a sling, heavily bandaged, and came with me to the conference with Coastal Forces. There was no great difficulty about the M.G.B.s. Two of them would be available at the end of the month, both armed with Oerlikons and depth charges and capable of about forty knots in calm water. If the position of the fishing fleet could be found out for them beforehand there did not seem to be much difficulty about their job. All they had to do was to slink in behind the fleet upon their silent engines, make a noise like a couple of battleships, and beat it for home. From their point of view it was a very simple exercise.

Provisionally we fixed it for the last day of the month, October. There was a waning moon which rose at about 23.00 then; that meant that there would be a little light but not too much. We wanted good weather for this trip in order that the boats could find the rendezvous with *Geneviève*. We did not want to leave it later than that if it could be helped, because of the moon and because we wanted to get guns ashore before the fervour in Douarnenez had died away. At the same time, it seemed to me important that Simon should go on the trip for political reasons and for his fluent French; that gave another seventeen or eighteen days in which his hand could heal. It was a short time, but it was just possible he might be fit by then. Simon himself, of course, was adamant that he was fit to go.

I went to Dartmouth for a day after that meeting. *Geneviève* was off the slip, but still in the hands of the shipyard; they had repaired the damage to the bow and the wheel-house, and a couple of engine-room artificers were working on the flame-thrower under the direction of a chap from Honiton. The engine repair was the longest job; it was impossible to get spare parts and they were having to be made. The estimated date for completion was the twenty-second, so if that date were maintained the show might still take place on the thirty-first.

Simon, in the meantime, had found out from the Breton lads in his crew the circumstances that governed the position of the fishing fleet in the Iroise. He spread out the chart before me in the ward-room in the little villa at Dittisham. "On the flood-tide it is easy," he said. "The fish, the little sardines, they come northwards with the tide up from the Bay of Biscay. The tide sweeps them up the Baie d'Audierne," he showed me with his finger on the chart, "until they come to the Chaussée de Sein. Then the tide sweeps through the Raz de Sein between the Chaussée and the land—very, very quick."

"I know," I said. "It runs up to six knots through there. And the fish go with it?"

He nodded. "The tide carries the fish through the Raz into the Iroise. Always, at the first of the flood, the fishing fleet will lie in the Iroise at the entrance to the Raz, stemming the tide with their bows to the south, drifting their nets to take the fish as they come northwards on the tide. That is the way we found them on that first night of all."

"The tide was on the flood then, was it?"

"Yes. Our Breton lads knew where the fleet would be the whole of the time. But they did not know then just exactly what we wanted, and we did not think to ask them."

"What's the tide doing on the thirty-first?" I asked.

He pulled over the nautical almanack and turned the pages. "It is good for us upon that night." He showed me the entry. "Raz de Sein—the flood-tide makes towards the north at 21.40.

Greenwich time. That is 22.40 of our time."

From Dartmouth I went to Plymouth about the motor-gun-boats. I went first to the Commander-in-Chief's office and spent ten minutes with him, telling him what we wanted to do. Then I spent half an hour with his Chief of Staff, bending over the chart. It did not seem to be difficult. Zero, we decided, should be about the time of moonrise—say 23.00. That was when the motor-gunboats would begin to do their stuff. It would take them an hour to get into position on their silent engines at low speed, and five hours from Plymouth under average weather conditions. That meant that they should leave at 17.00, sunset time, which seemed reasonable enough. They would have day-light for their departure. They would be back off Plymouth at 04.30 or soon after; if the wind were in the west they might anchor in Cawsand till the port opened at dawn. We could arrange a tender for them there, in case of casualties. One of the mine-sweeping trawlers could do that.

We wrote a draft of an operation order there and then, that I could talk over with V.A.C.O. "This thing will have to have a name," the Chief of Staff said. His eyes roved around the room. There was an iron bedstead in his office, the bed made up with sheets and blankets; evidently it was his habit to sleep there upon occasion. "Operation Blanket," he said. "It's got to happen in the blanket of the dark." So Operation Blanket it became.

The M.G.B.s were in the Cattewater. I went down to see them with a young lieutenant-commander of the R.N.V.R., more for interest than anything else. Boats numbered 261 and 268 were detailed for the job; the officer commanding 268 was senior, and we went on board her. He was a lieutenant in the R.N.V.R. called Sanderson. He was twenty-two years old, and before the war had been at Cambridge studying to become a schoolmaster. He was a very tough-looking young man with hard eyes and a prominent jaw, dressed in a very dirty uniform. The officers of *Geneviève* looked like a pack of Sissies beside that chap. His Number One was a sub. of twenty with a great red beard. I never saw such a pair of pirates in my life.

Their ship was one of the new Vosper-boats, and she was very interesting. I spent an hour on board her, wishing that I'd had the chance of a command like her when I was young. She was good fun, that boat; well armed, comparatively seaworthy, and very fast. I thought a lot of her.

I went back to London, and two days later I went down to

V.A.C.O. about Operation Blanket. It was shaping quite well; indeed, it seemed to be a fairly simple little job, without great risk to anybody. McNeil was gathering his Tommy-guns and ammunition together, two lorry-loads of them. Their weight would put the *Geneviève* ten inches lower in the water and therefore slow her down a bit, but that didn't seem to matter very much. Repairs were up to time and she came off the slip to schedule. Finally, Simon's hand was getting on quite well.

Simon came up to London a few days after that, and I met McNeil with him for a discussion of the message to Douarnenez. There was an agent over there, I learned, who was to pass the message through: a man at Quimper who supplied the fish-packers with tinned steel sheets. In some way that I did not understand a message would reach him.

We settled to design the message. "Charles Simon says," it ran at last, "the English will send seventy sub-machine-guns with three thousand rounds for each. On the night of October 31st/November 1st gunfire will begin about 23.00. Fishing vessels should put out their lights and scatter. Seven vessels should rendezvous without lights in the Anse des Blancs Sablons three miles north of Cap de la Chèvre. Charles Simon will be there to meet them in a Douarnenez sardine-boat painted black and will give to each vessel ten guns and ammunition. Confirm that on that night the fleet will fish north of the Raz de Sein. Ends."

Two days later a reply came. "Charles Simon's message received and understood. Seven boats will meet him as arranged. The fleet will fish north of Raz de Sein from 22.00 to 04.00 weather permitting. Ends."

I went down to Plymouth on the twenty-ninth with McNeil; Simon met us there, and we had a conference in the Chief of Staff's office about Operation Blanket. The commanding officer of M.G.B. 268 was there, Sanderson, whom I had met before, and with him was a quiet young man called Peters, who was in command of 261. In an hour we had settled the detail of the operation. *Geneviève* would sail direct from Dartmouth as before; her officers preferred the longer journey rather than the inconvenience of making their last arrangements in a strange port. That meant that she must leave in the forenoon of the 31st. We arranged to confirm the operation by telephone that morning, in view of the weather at the time.

There was no more to be done. I went back to Dartmouth with McNeil, and we went on to Dittisham. There was a lorry down there at the hard unloading Tommy-guns in their boxes into the boat to be ferried to the ship. It would have been easier to bring her up against a quay, of course, but Simon and Colvin had preferred the secrecy of Dittisham.

I went on board *Geneviève* and made a semi-official inspection of her. She was in good shape; the damage had been well repaired and they had taken her to sea one day to test the flame-thrower. Colvin said she was as good as she had ever been.

So they went.

*   *   *   *   *

We got them away at about 11.00 on the morning of the 31st, deep-loaded with their Tommy-guns and ammunition and a full tank for the flame-thrower. I was at Dittisham to see them off; McNeil could not get down, nor was there any need for him to be there.

The weather was quite good, with high cloud and occasional bursts of sunshine. The forecast was for fine weather and moderate cloud off Ushant during the night, with only a slight chance of rain. That suited us quite well. It would make it easy for the fishing-boats to find the rendezvous; if the forecast had been for thick weather we should have been obliged to postpone.

I stood down on the hard with the shore party and watched them go. They slipped their mooring and went down between the wooded hills by Mill Creek till they were lost to sight. Then I turned away; the Wren was going to drive me back to Newton Abbot in the truck.

She was beside me. "Wish them luck," I said a little heavily.

She said: "Do you think I'm not?"

I glanced down at her, smiling in what I meant to be a re-assuring way. "They'll be all right," I said. "It's not as if they were going out to look for trouble this time." She knew well enough what they had gone to do.

She did not answer that. I glanced at her again. She seemed to have got much older in the last few weeks, much more mature. I saw for the first time that she was wearing an engagement ring, turquoise and diamonds, very little stones; a ring that a lieutenant who had nothing but his pay might give his girl.

I said: "I see that I've got to congratulate you, Miss Wright. Is that, by any chance, for any of our chaps?"

She raised her hand and looked at it. "It's for Lieutenant

Rhodes," she said. "You must have known. It's horribly conspicuous. I suppose the new look goes away after a time."

She wasn't at all excited over it; she wasn't even smiling. That seemed to me rather dreadful and unnatural.

"I'm terribly glad," I said as warmly as I could. "I hope that you'll be very, very happy."

"That's awfully sweet of you," she said. "I'm sure I hope so, too."

The shore party had dissipated; we were momentarily alone by the waterside. I did not want to go away and leave her in that frame of mind. "You mustn't feel like that," I said. "You get a double lot of troubles when you get engaged, but you get the hell of a lot more fun." It wasn't quite what I had wanted to say, but it was the best that I could manage impromptu.

She glanced up at me. "I suppose you had it in peace-time," she said unexpectedly.

I did not understand her

"Getting engaged, I mean," she said. "It must have been lovely to get engaged in peace-time, when you had time to give to it. I suppose some day there'll be a world again where people can live quietly, and fall in love, and get married, and have fun. Where you can keep a rabbit or a dog—or a husband, and not have to stand by and see them killed. Where you can think of other things than burning oil, and rain, and darkness, and black bitter hate."

I stood there thoughtful, looking out over the river. I was thinking that the Women's Royal Naval Service has its complications and its limitations. If *Geneviève* went on upon this work, Leading Wren Wright would have to be transferred to other duty.

"Don't worry too much," I said as gently as I could. "This isn't going on for ever." I turned towards the car. "Let's get along to Newton Abbot."

"Very good, sir."

We drove that thirty miles mostly in silence. She knew all the movements in Operation Blanket; she knew that I was going to Plymouth to see the supporting M.G.B.s away. At Newton Abbot station, as we drew up in the yard, she said:

"Will you be coming back to Dartmouth, sir? Would you like me to meet you here?"

I reflected for a moment. The M.G.B.s would be back very early in the morning. *Geneviève* could hardly be back before dark; as before, I had made arrangements for the port to be opened for her on her signal. I got out of the truck, crossed to the time-table upon the wall, and looked up a train. The afternoon train from Plymouth stopped at Newton Abbot at 3.40; that seemed suitable.

"You'd better meet me here at 3.40 to-morrow afternoon, Miss Wright," I said. "I shall be coming back to Dartmouth then. This is going to be another middle-of-the-night show."

She nodded. "Very good, sir. I'll meet you here at 3.40 to-morrow afternoon."

"That's right," I said. I hesitated, and then said: "If I were you I should go to the pictures to-night, and go to bed early."

She said quietly: "Thank you, sir."

I went on by train to Plymouth and got there early in the afternoon. I got down to the dock at about four o'clock. The two M.G.B.s were running their main engines to warm up, and taking on a few last-minute stores from the pontoons that they were moored to. Captain (D.) was there to see them off; I made my number with him as representing V.A.C.O. and we stood chatting for a time. At five minutes to five Sanderson came up to us, saluted, and reported that everything was ready and correct.

The captain took his salute. "Very good, Sanderson," he said. "Carry on as soon as you can. The best of luck."

The young man saluted again and went back to his boat. The captain walked up to the other vessel, 261, at the pontoon astern of 268. Above the heavy rumble of the engines he shouted to the young officer upon the tiny bridge: "Good luck, Peters." The young man smiled and saluted.

Then the boats slipped bow and stern ropes from the pontoon and moved out into the stream, great clouds of steam vomiting from their exhausts in the grey evening light. They turned down-river to the sea, and very soon were lost to sight behind Drake's Island.

I had a cabin reserved for me in the barracks, but I didn't use it. I dined in the ward-room; then, wanting to be on hand for anything that might occur, I went back to the Commander-in-Chief's office. It was a fine, starry night, without much cloud; I wondered if it were the same over on the other side.

There was no news for me in the Operations Room; indeed, I didn't expect any. The boats were bound to wireless silence except for the greatest emergency; there would be nothing for me till they came back to Cawsand at perhaps four-thirty in the morning. I left instructions with the Duty Officer to call me when anything came in, went down into the shelter, and fell asleep upon a bunk.

I woke up with a start and looked at my watch. It was nearly seven o'clock. I was annoyed; it seemed to me that the boats must have been back for some time. I smoothed my hair and uniform and went up to the Operations Room again; in the east the sky was getting grey. But there was no news of the M.G.B.s.

"Nothing has come in yet," the Duty Officer said. "There was no point in waking you."

He lent me a razor, and I went and had a shave. I got a cup of tea and stayed on in the Operations Room. It was about 09.15 when the signalman passed a message to the Duty Officer.

"That's your Operation Blanket," he said. "268 and 261 are passing Rame Head now."

He rang up Captain (D.) to tell him; I spoke to him myself and asked permission to go down to the pontoon to meet the boats. Ten minutes later I was down there watching 268 as she came first to the pontoon.

She came in rumbling thunderously, vomiting white clouds from her exhausts. From the great flare of her bow to her squat transom she was glistening with water all over; the few dry spots upon her upperworks were streaked with salt. Her two young officers wore duffle coats; they were surprisingly wide awake and fresh-looking after the rough, lumpy trip they must have had across the Channel and back.

And then I saw she had no depth-charges left in her racks. 261, following behind to the pontoon, had none either.

Captain (D.) stepped across on to the slippery little deck of 268 as soon as she was moored; I followed him. Lieutenant Sanderson nipped down from the bridge in time to salute him as he came on board.

"Good morning, Sanderson. Everything all right?"

The young man's jaw stuck out more prominently than ever. "Everything's quite all right on board 268, sir. 261 reports one minor casualty. We had to depart a little from the operation orders. After creating the diversion, at about 02.20, we carried out a joint attack upon a German destroyer with depth-charges. I don't think we sunk her."

He turned to me. "Before attacking we saw the destroyer sink a fishing-boat by gunfire," he said bluntly. "I'm pretty sure it was *Geneviève*."

*   *   *   *   *

This was his account: From the time they left Plymouth everything worked out to schedule for the first part of the night. They kept in company at about twenty knots, each clearly visible to the other in the darkness by the broad white wake they made. They were off Ushant at about 21.45 and altered course down into L'Iroise; at 22.10 they slowed to seven knots and went on upon their silent engines.

The sky, they said, was cloudless and starry, and though the moon was not yet up, they picked up the high loom of land at Cap de la Chèvre without great difficulty. The next thing they saw was the lights of the fishing fleet away to the south by the Raz de Sein, a little galaxy of yellow and white lights low down upon the water in the distance. That was all satisfactory and according to plan and they went on, meeting no opposition and expecting none.

They kept to the westward of the searchlight which, they knew from *Geneviève*, was located on the cliff at Beuzec. They closed the south shore of the bay somewhere near Goulin and reached a point about two miles off shore at 22.50. There they stopped engines and lay side by side upon the water for a few minutes, perhaps five miles from the fishing fleet, and between them and Douarnenez.

At 22.57 they started up main engines and turned to do their stuff. The wind was light and in the south-west; under the lee of the land and the Chaussée the water was fairly smooth. The boats had good conditions for high speed. They went roaring down upon the fishing fleet at thirty-seven or thirty-eight knots side by side. Their depth-charges were all set for fifty feet, and when they got within a mile or so of the twinkling lights 268 let one of them go to call attention to their approach.

It burst behind them in a great column of water, and as they closed the fleet 268 began firing tracer from her 20-mm. cannon low over the swaying lights. 261 let go another depth-charge and joined in the cannon-fire with her forward Oerlikon. The lights began to vanish one by one. They did not dare to close the fleet at that speed, fearing a collision, so they swung six points to starboard and went roaring round the north of them. Each of the boats dropped one more depth-charge, "just to help them with the fishing", as Sanderson put it, and then they swung eight points to port again.

The fleet was now behind them, and all lights were out. They drew away, still firing over where they thought the boats must be. Simon had told them that the *Raumboote* lay normally to

seaward of the fleet, and they hoped by their fire and by ramp-
ing round to seaward of the fleet that they would draw fire from
one of them and make it show itself. But if there were a *Raumboot* there at all it lay doggo; it would have been no match for
them, and probably realised it.

At 23.12 the fleet was far behind and they were getting rather
near the Chaussée. They swung right round to starboard and
headed north, slowing to twenty knots. At 23.17 they stopped
their main engines and lay upon the water side by side, their
silent engines ticking over slowly.

They had done their stuff. There were no lights now showing
from the fleet, and the moon was just coming up above the land
south of the bay. The night was fine and starry; soon it would
be very light. By their operation orders they should now have
set a course for home, but as sometimes happens, operation
orders got mislaid.

In conversation with me, as distinct from his report, Sanderson was quite frank and unashamed. "If we'd beat it for home
then," he said, "we couldn't have got into harbour before
dawn. It only meant lying for two or three hours in Cawsand
Bay. Conditions out there were so good I thought we'd lie out
there and see if the good Lord didn't send us a nice Jerry."

He said that there were several searchlights playing about the
coast, two from a point upon the mainland near the Raz de
Sein and several up on the high ground of the Cap de la Chèvre.
Several times he saw these searchlights pick up a fishing-boat
and hold it in their beam; from the disposition of the boats so
held it was evident that they had scattered widely over the
Iroise. He began to wonder about *Geneviève*. The rising moon,
white in a cloudless, starry sky, was flooding the bay with light;
they could see the land right round from St. Mathieu in the
north to Penmarch in the south. It was a bad night for any ship
to slink about the other side, trusting to darkness for her safety.

That was one of the reasons that made Sanderson disregard
his orders. He stayed to support *Geneviève* if there should be
trouble. He lay some ten miles out from La Chèvre, drifting
slowly northwards with the tide towards the rocks called La
Vendrée. It was a beautiful, calm, moonlit night. The two
motor-gunboats lay there stopped upon the water for nearly
three hours, watching the shore, running their engines now and
then to keep them warm, ready to dive inshore again to help
out *Geneviève* if there were any trouble, ready for action against
any German vessel that showed up.

They saw nothing to disturb the quiet of the night. Presently the searchlights shut off one by one; there was no sign of anything upon the waters. Simon had been uncertain of the time that he would leave the coast; provisionally he had estimated that he would have finished his transhipment of the Tommy-guns between 01.00 and 01.30. Sanderson was quite happy lying as he was and he gave *Geneviève* another hour to get clear. At 02.10 he came to the conclusion that the party must be over, and he might as well get under way. He made a signal to 261, and the two boats got going, laying a course to pass about ten miles outside Ushant, planning to reach Plymouth about dawn and go straight in.

At 02.13 there was a sudden, blinding yellow glow upon the water four or five miles astern of them. It lit up the whole sky, drowning the moon and showing up both boats in yellow light. It was not sudden as a gun-flash is. It was continuous, its origin a smoky yellow streak. There was only one thing that could possibly create a light like that.

Both M.G.B.s turned violently to starboard, worked quickly up to full speed on the reverse course, and went to action stations. They tore down to the incident ahead of them at forty knots, half their length clear out of the water, leaving a wide streak of foam behind. They each had two depth-charges left.

They could see the flashes of gunfire now. In the last bursts of flame they saw the scene; there was a destroyer there. It seemed to them that *Geneviève* was engaging her bow and her bridge with the flame; an aft gun, beyond the reach of fire, was pumping shells out on a forward bearing. The bulk of the destroyer, lying head to the north, came between them and *Geneviève;* she was silhouetted to them against the glow of flame. The engagement was going on upon her starboard, landward, side; they were approaching from the port.

As they came near the glow faded and died; a searchlight blazed out from the stern of the destroyer; in its beam the gun, perhaps a four-inch, went on firing forward up her side at the unseen target. The destroyer was on fire forward; there was fire on her bridge and wheel-house and the forward guns were silent. A machine-gun was firing from her midships.

The motor-gunboats roared into attack. It was not clear to them if the destroyer was lying stopped, or moving ahead, or going astern; there was no sign of wake or bow wave. 268 was to the north, as they ran in side by side, and 261 to the south;

so to make sure of her Sanderson attacked the bow and Peters took the stern.

The destroyer was so busy with the target on the other side, and with putting out her fires, that the motor-gunboats were not seen till they were right on top of her. Sanderson thought that the alarm was raised when they were about three or four hundred yards away. A machine-gun in the waist got off a few rounds at them as they approached, and they replied with their two Oerlikons, spraying the decks of the destroyer with little bursts of cannon shell, white and scintillating in the darkness. Then they were right on top of her.

Sanderson, in 268, attacked the bow. He approached at right angles to her length, running at forty knots; thinking that she was stopped he steered a course to pass under her bow about fifteen feet ahead. When he was right on top of her he saw that she was moving slowly ahead through the water. His fifteen feet slipped down to ten as his bow crossed her track, to seven as the bridge passed her rusty cutwater, her anchors vertically above their heads.

They dropped one of their depth-charges a few feet on her port bow, and the other a few feet on her starboard bow. The quartermaster at the little wheel swung 268 violently to starboard to clear the stern; but for that they would probably have been cut down. The transom passed the stem of the destroyer with not more than two feet to spare, and then they were running free and blazing back at the big German ship with both their Oerlikons.

They could see now what the Germans had been firing at, and what they saw was this: There was a wooden vessel, or the remains of a wooden vessel, floating bottom up about two hundred yards from the destroyer. About ten feet of her hull was showing, keel and garboards. Lying out upon this was a young man in a naval officer's cap, and he was firing at the destroyer with a Tommy-gun. Beside him was another man, hatless and in a jersey, passing him drums of ammunition. This showed up quite clearly in the light of the fires on the destroyer, and in the wavering beam of the searchlight when it came that way.

268 passed within about fifty yards of this party. There was wreckage and survivors swimming in the water, and in the background there were two or more fishing-boats, apparently coming forward to pick them up. Sanderson swerved to port to keep away from any swimmers. He was now under a heavy, concentrated fire from the destroyer, and was replying with both

Oerlikons. He said it was quite hot.

As he roared by the wrecked boat the two men upon the keel looked round at the noise, and the one in the naval cap waved cheerfully at them. They waved back, and saw him turn again to fire at the destroyer with the Tommy-gun. The searchlight went out suddenly, but who put it out, whether the Tommy-gun or their own Oerlikon, they did not know. Then their two depth-charges detonated behind them, and almost immediately there were two more explosions from the stern of the destroyer where 261 had laid her two remaining charges.

They went tearing on into the darkness, and the wreckage of the fishing-boat was lost to view. With the searchlight out, the moon and the fires still raging on the destroyer made the only light, and visibility was suddenly reduced. They circled round to port, but it was not easy for them to see what damage had been done. As the great columns of spray subsided it appeared to them that the destroyer was badly damaged at the bow; her forecastle appeared to be wrecked by the explosion of the depth-charges beneath her. She had not been going fast enough, however, for them to get under her midships section, and Sanderson did not think that she was sinking. The two that 261 had put down aft had probably done little damage other than shaking her up; she had been moving away from them.

The two boats met presently, circling in the darkness. It was obviously unwise to approach the destroyer again; she was still vicious and they had no more depth-charges to attack her with; the fire from Oerlikons could never sink her. There were other vessels near at hand to pick up the survivors of *Geneviève*. It seemed to Sanderson that there was nothing more that they could do without exposing their boats to a risk that was quite unjustifiable. So he set a course for Ushant and for Plymouth, with the intention of reporting as soon as possible in order that the Air Force could get out and finish off the destroyer.

He got back, as I have said, at about 09.20.

* * * * *

At that time, in November, 1941, it was not too easy to produce a force of bombers at a moment's notice. All we could get hold of was a flight of three Hudsons, which took off at 10.53 and were over the Iroise at 11.31. But the Germans had been too quick for us. The Hudsons found the destroyer just going into the Rade de Brest, in the part they called the Goulet, towed stern first by two tugs with another at the bow for steering.

The Hudsons had all the flak of Brest against them in broad daylight, and they dropped their bombs from a high altitude. I don't know that I blame them, but they didn't do much good. They took some photographs which got to me in London a day later; these showed the bow of the destroyer to be missing completely. It was as if she had been cut off with a knife just forward of the bridge. They got her into Brest all right and she was still there when I left the Admiralty and went to sea; I don't know what became of her eventually.

There was nothing more for me to do at Plymouth. I rang up V.A.C.O. and told him very shortly what had happened, and he told me to meet him in London to report. I rang up N.O.I.C. Dartmouth and told him baldly that *Geneviève* would not be coming back to Dartmouth for some days, and that he need not keep a watch for her that night. Then I picked up my bag and drove down to the station to catch the fast train for London.

It was not till I was sitting in the train that I realised that that was the train I should have caught in any case, that it stopped at Newton Abbot at 3.40, and that Leading Wren Wright would be there to meet me with the truck. I thought about that for a time. I could not bring myself to sit on in the train and leave her there without instructions. It seemed to me that there was very little reason to defer a nasty job; when I got to London I should have to send a note to Casualties, and they would send out the telegrams to the relatives. There was no real reason why I should not see Miss Wright.

The train stopped in Newton Abbot for less than five minutes. I got out as soon as it drew to a standstill and went through the barrier; she was there standing by the car. She smiled when she saw me.

I took her by the arm. "I'm not coming back to Dartmouth," I said. "I'm going on to London on the train. Come on to the platform in case it goes; I want a word with you."

She stared at me. "Is anything wrong?"

I did not answer, but piloted her through the barrier and to my carriage. We stood by the door, and the people and the porters and the trucks thronged round about us.

"Look, Miss Wright," I said. "We've had a bit of bad luck this time. It's not been announced yet, and until it is I don't want you to talk about it. Can you manage to do that, do you think?"

She had gone very white; her eyes were very big and dark.

218

A truck of mail-sacks came, and we had to move aside. "I think so," she said.

There was no point in beating about the bush. "They were sunk," I told her. "A good many of them were picked up by the fishing fleet, I think. I don't know any details or any names. I only know the fact. I don't want that fact talked about just yet."

"I see, sir," she said. She stood staring at a jet of steam issuing up between the carriages in the raw air. "Can you tell me how it happened?"

"They took on a destroyer," I said. "They did a lot of damage to it, but they hadn't a chance."

She asked: "How long will it be before you get the names, sir, do you think?"

I had to tell her that I didn't know. "I'll keep in touch with you, Miss Wright," I said. "I'll let you know the minute anything comes in. Keep your pecker up. It's going to be all right."

Behind us the guard blew his whistle. I got into the carriage and leaned from the window. She said: "Thank you for telling me, sir."

She had very little to be thankful for, poor kid. The train began to move. I said: "Try not to tell anybody. I know it's going to be hard, but—try."

She said: "I won't tell a soul. Thank—thank you ever so much, sir." Then I was sliding away from her down the platform, and she was standing there with tears beginning to run down her face, in the crowd and the smoke and the steam. I sank down into my seat, thanking God that that was over.

I got to London at about nine o'clock and went straight to the Admiralty. V.A.C.O. was there, and I told him the story, and then we telephoned McNeil and got him to come over. We had a long talk over it that night, but there was nothing we could do.

"I'll probably get some kind of a report to-morrow," said the brigadier at last, "—from the other side. We'll know how things stand then."

10

BUT no report came through.

We waited on, day after day, for news from Douarnenez, and nothing came at all. We got a message from the other side about the damaged destroyer at Brest; it only told us what we knew already from the air photographs. There was no news of *Geneviève* or her crew, and for some reason that I didn't clearly understand McNeil could not ask for any. "We've just got to wait," he said. "We'll get a message before long."

But when we did hear something, it was from quite a different source.

It came from the Casualties Section. They rang me up about midday on November the 7th, a week after the action. "Is that Commander Martin?"

"Speaking," I said.

"That party of yours, that we notified as missing. One of them has turned up—a lieutenant R.N.R. named Colvin. He was one of them, wasn't he?"

"He's one of them," I said. "Is he alive?"

"Oh yes—at least, he was alive when he was brought in. He was brought into Portsmouth this morning in an A/S trawler. He's in Haslar Hospital now suffering from exposure."

I said: "Where did the trawler find him?"

"He was in a boat, quite a small boat, so they said. Drifting about some ten miles south of St. Catherine's. They said he seemed to have been in it a long time. He was only just conscious, or not conscious at all. Of course, it's been very cold these last few nights."

"I know," I said. I paused. "Was he alone in the boat?"

"Yes, quite alone."

"Thanks for telling me," I said. "I'll get through to Haslar."

It is about two hundred and thirty sea miles from the Iroise to St. Catherine's. We had had half a gale most of the week, and it had certainly been very cold. I rang up Haslar Hospital and spoke to the surgeon-commander.

"I'd really rather that you didn't come to-day," he said. "He's sleeping naturally now. He'll have a bad time when he wakes up, but I think he'll be all right. He seems to be a man with a good constitution, but he isn't a young man by any means."

"I know," I said. "What about to-morrow morning?"

"I think that should be all right, if you don't stay too long. Half an hour at the most."

"I'll come down then," I said.

I went down next day to Portsmouth and over to Haslar by the ferry. I went through to the officers' block in the garden quadrangle, bleak and with a little snow lying upon the rosebeds. I found Colvin propped up in a clean white bed in a cabin to himself. He looked grey and old, and smaller than the strapping chap that I remembered from a week before.

"Say," he said, "it's real nice of you to come down, sir. We got shot up and sunk. I guess you heard about that from the M.G.B. boys."

"I was very sorry to hear it," I said. "How did it happen?" He said: "It was this way."

*   *   *   *   *

They had gone creeping into the Iroise at about 21.30, without lights, slowly and as quietly as they could. It was a clear, calm night with very little cloud; the moon was not yet up, but there was fairly good visibility under the stars. It was a bad night for them; they realised that from the start, but they went through with it according to the plan.

They had intended to anchor in the Anse des Blancs Sablons three miles north of Cap de la Chèvre before zero hour at 23.00 and let the scattered vessels of the fishing fleet come to them there. They changed that plan when the extreme visibility of the night was revealed. It was too risky for them to approach the coast alone; they would certainly be seen by the shore patrols. Instead, they hung about in the Iroise six or seven miles out to sea, waiting for the diversion that the M.G.B.s would make.

Five miles to the south of them they could distinctly see the lights of the fishing fleet clustered about the Raz. It was risky for them, waiting there like that; after the atttacks that they had made on *Raumboote* an isolated fishing vessel in those parts would have drawn immediate suspicion. They waited for an hour, stemming the tide with the engine turning over slowly, tensely watching the horizon for the first sign of a ship. But their luck held for the time, and nothing came to worry them.

Exactly at 23.00 the show started, down to the south by the fishing fleet. They saw the tracer-bullets flying through the sky and heard the crash and rumble of the depth-charges; immediately every light went out. The firing only lasted for about three minutes; searchlights came on and began to sweep the sea. Once or twice a beam passed over them but did not hold them; several times, away to the south-east, they saw fishing vessels caught and held in the white light. Some of these were heading to the north towards them, and some back to the east towards Douarnenez. In a quarter of an hour the fleet was scattered all over the Iroise, and the moon was just coming up over the hill.

They went forward then and began to close the coast. When they had come within about four miles of the rendezvous a searchlight caught and held them; they went on steadily, each man inwardly terrified and miserable. It held them for the best part of a minute; then travelled on and immediately they saw another fishing vessel outlined in the beam. She was half a mile inshore and travelling upon a northerly, converging course with them. Presently the searchlight, hunting for the enemy, picked up another one.

They held their course towards the Anse des Blancs Sablons, and twice more they were caught and held in the white, blinding light. It must have been clear to the German searchlight crews by this time that a number of the fishing vessels scattered over the Iroise were making for the Anse, and *Geneviève* went in with the crowd. Presently the searchlight ceased to bear, and they rounded up in the Anse at about five minutes to midnight.

Seven other vessels were there to meet them, as had been arranged; in the pale moonlight all the eight of them were as like as peas. They lay together in a cluster about half a mile from the white beach, manœuvring about and shouting from boat to boat. Presently one of them came alongside *Geneviève* and made fast to her with warps; they lay grinding the fenders and the work of passing out the cases was begun. Later on another came up on the other beam.

Several of the Breton fishermen came on board. Colvin saw Simon talking to an old man from the first boat. "Chummy, they were, sir," he said. "Like as if they'd met before some place. I'd say he was the one that Simon fixed up with that time he went into Douarnenez."

"Bozallec," I said.

"Aye. That was the name."

It took much longer than they had estimated to tranship the guns and ammunition. It might have been easier had they anchored *Geneviève* and let the others come alongside one by one. Colvin said they had not done that because they were certainly under constant observation from the shore, and a successive manœuvre of that sort would have roused suspicion. Instead they kept under way the whole time, stemming the tide that streamed up from the south. The fishing vessels were unhandy in a close manœuvre of that sort; there was much bumping and boring, and long delays while circling for position. The effect from shore was probably one of clumsy, innocent confusion, but it was about 01.50 before the last case had been passed and the last gulp of sour red wine drunk to seal the ceremony.

By then the moon was well up; on the calm water it was very light indeed. It would not do for one ship to strike out alone towards the west while the others turned south and eastwards round La Chèvre for home. The Bretons saw that well enough and were prepared to accompany *Geneviève* till she was off the land. They all left the Anse des Blancs Sablons together heading about south-west, as if returning to the Raz to go on fishing.

"Captain Simon, he was well in with them, sir," said Colvin. "They'd have done anything for him, they would."

The eight vessels passed outside the Bouc. It seemed then that they had gone far enough together; there was a good deal of shouting from boat to boat, and then *Geneviève* altered course to west and went on out towards the Atlantic and safety, towards Dartmouth and home.

Ten minutes after they had left the other boats a searchlight blazed out dead ahead of them, not half a mile away, and held them in its glare.

"Properly caught, we were," said Colvin grimly.

Blinded by the light, they could only see the bulk of the vessel. It was obvious from the height of the light that she was something much bigger than a *Raumboot*. She began flashing at them with a signal-lamp. There was nothing they could do but to hold straight on and try to bluff it out as stupid Breton seamen. As the vessels drew together they prepared for their last action.

All that this preparation could amount to was that Rhodes slipped into the control seat of the flame-thrower and checked his pressures. They could not man the Bren-guns or the Tommy-guns till action had commenced; their deck was flooded with white light and any preparation of that sort would have given them away at once. The Bretons played up well under Simon's guidance. The gunners stood nonchalantly, hands in pockets, cigarette in mouth, staring at the bulk of the destroyer as the vessels closed. They must have looked very like a fishing crew.

They did not answer the flashing signal-lamp; that was not in the part. In a real fishing vessel nobody would know how to read Morse. They just held on towards the enemy, and presently they were lying stopped alongside, about thirty yards away from her, opposite the bridge. She towered above them. She was only a small destroyer, somewhat similar to our V class, but to them she was immense.

The officer of the watch hailed them in bad French through a megaphone. "What ship is that? Where are you from?"

Rollot, the *maître*, was standing by Simon at the entrance to the little wheel-house. They whispered quickly together. Then Rollot called out in rich Breton dialect: "Fishing-boat *Marie et Pierre*, from Douarnenez. We left the fleet and came out here, because of the firing."

There was a pause. Then: "Come in closer and take a line and come alongside." It was very calm. "I shall send an officer on board you."

Simon turned to Colvin in the wheel-house and translated quickly. "This is the end of it," he said. "Shall we give in to them, or shall we fight it out?"

Colvin said: "I guess we'd better fight it out. The boys would like it better that way. Can Rhodes get his fire down to the stern from here?"

"No. It is too far."

"Well, let him take the bow gun and the bridge in the first place 'n then train aft. I'll see if I can work her down that way to help him."

From the destroyer a voice cried impatiently: "Come alongside, or we open fire on you."

Simon bent to the speaking-tube. "Rhodes, fire at the bow gun and then the bridge, and then work down the decks towards the stern. We shall go slow ahead. Fire quickly now as soon as you are ready."

The young man said: "Very good, sir." Their gun drill was never very formal in that ship.

The fire burst out and lit up the destroyer brilliantly. The jet curved lazily towards the A gun's crew, landed amongst them and enveloped them in flame. A great fire rose up from the forecastle of the destroyer immediately; they must have had cordite charges open for loading.

From the wing of the bridge a machine-gun opened fire on them. They replied with Bren and Tommy-gunfire, and the flame jet travelled slowly to the bridge. That machine-gun ceased to fire abruptly, but another opened up upon them from the waist of the destroyer and began to spray them. The flame paused upon the bridge, and then began to work along her length towards the gun. There was a sudden clang of gongs, and screams, and shouted orders.

The ships were lying bow to stern side by side. Colvin put on full power to go ahead towards the stern of the destroyer.

He turned to Simon. "We want to get that flame to bear on their aft gun quick as we can," he said. "Tell Rhodes."

If they had managed to do that, if they had burnt the Z gun's crew as they had burnt the A gun's, I believe they might have got away with it. The destroyer then would have had nothing but small arms and machine-guns to fight them with, unless perhaps some A/A cannon. But as it worked out, they never got the aft gun. As they went ahead she went astern; she gained speed more quickly than they did and her stern kept well out of range of their fire.

Then the Germans opened fire with their stern gun, probably about a four-inch gun, loaded H.E. There was never any doubt about it after that. The range was only about two hundred yards. The first shell pitched over them and burst behind. The second was a direct hit somewhere near the bow, and the ship disintegrated.

"She just came to pieces, sir," Colvin said. "One minute she was there all right, and next thing that I knew there was a sort of flash and all the planks and timbers were all separate, and we were in the water."

He thought there was a third shell, but he was not sure of that. He did not know how he got into the water; probably he was blown clean out of the wheel-house. All he knew was that he was in the water ten or fifteen yards from the wreckage that had been *Geneviève*, and that there was nobody else near him.

"That happened at two-sixteen in the morning," he said carefully. "I know that must have been the time, because my watch stopped, because the water got in it. And it said two-sixteen."

I nodded. "That agrees with what the M.G.B.s reported," I said. He had been talking for a quarter of an hour, and I wanted the whole story, if possible, before I was turned out. "What happened next?"

He turned his head wearily and nervously upon the pillow. "It's on the chest-of-drawers there with them other things," he said. "The watch." His eyes were turned to a small pile of personal belongings, grey with salt. "Could you get it for me?"

I got up and gave it to him. It was a silver pocket watch with a very big white dial. There was still water inside the glass. He took it gratefully.

"What happened next?" I asked again.

He said: "I'll tell you." And then his eyes dropped to the watch in his hand. "I was wondering, would you do something for me, sir? It's had water in it for a week now, 'n I wouldn't like to think that it'd never go again. Would you take it up to London to be cleaned? It was given me by somebody I thought a lot of one time."

"Of course I will," I said. "I'll take it up this afternoon and get it seen to right away."

He gave it to me gratefully. "You can see where it says on the back," he murmured in a burst of confidence. " 'Jack Colvin from Junie, September 17th, 1935.' That's what it says, isn't it?"

I glanced at the engraving. "That's right," I said. I slipped it into my pocket. "I'll get it put right for you."

"What happened after that?" I asked for the third time.

He said that he had begun to swim away from the wreckage. That was panic—instinct—call it what you like. There was a lot of light from the fires in the destroyer and from her searchlight, and he wanted nothing more than to get out of it. It was only when he had swum furiously and blindly for a hundred yards or so that he regained his senses. What brought him to himself was M.G.B. 268, which passed within a few yards of him after dropping her depth-charges at the bow of the destroyer.

He saw her bearing down on him, and saw the great wave of her wash sweeping towards him. In a quick glance around before he went down in the wash he saw the men upon the M.G.B. quite close to him as she swept past at forty knots. He saw the upturned keel of *Geneviève* with two men on it firing with a Tommy-gun. He did not know who they were.

He saw the shapes of fishing vessels in the background half a mile or more away. Then the wash came to him and he was smothered by it, clutched and spun round under water by the swirl, and thrown up gasping to the surface. He threw himself on his back for the concussion; immediately the depth-charges went off by the destroyer not more than two hundred yards away, and a great mass of water came down on him, carrying him under again.

He had his inflated life-belt on, his Mae West, as they all had; otherwise he would certainly have been drowned. But presently he came up to the surface, feebly spluttering and gasping, and it was now much darker, for the searchlight had gone out. He lay floating and winded, supported by the Mae West and recovering his senses, for perhaps ten minutes.

And presently it seemed to him that he was farther from the scene. He was farther from the destroyer. Probably she then had stern way on her to ease the forward bulkheads; in any case, she was much farther off. He could see the coast clearly in the moonlight between La Chèvre and the Anse de Dinant; it was not more than two miles away. The tide was still carrying him northwards, and would be for another two hours; from his recollection of the tidal streams he knew that it woud sweep him closer to the land as it filled up into the Rade de Brest.

And with that his guts came back to him. "I didn't fancy swimming to them fishing-boats," he said. "I reckoned if the Germans got any of us we'd be scuppered out of hand, with having put the flame on them and that." It seemed to him that he could reach the coast quite easily on that calm, moonlit night. So he began to swim.

He said that the water was not very cold, although it was November. He was in the flood-tide up from the Bay of Biscay for one thing, and that was likely to be fairly warm. He was a strong swimmer. "Living in Oakland, like I did," he said, "we used to spend a lot of time down on the beach. Besides, I been swimming all my life, one place or another. It wasn't nothing, that."

And so he swam for shore.

The tide bore him northwards faster than he swam, hampered as he was with his clothes and his Mae West. He kept his clothes on for their warmth, even in water, and because he knew that he would want them when he got on shore. He finally landed, after being in the water for about two hours, in a little rocky cove just north of Anse de Dinant, under the shadow of the island rocks that they call Tas de Pois. That must have been at about four or four-thirty in the morning. Immediately he got out of the water he began to feel the cold.

The moon was still high in the sky, flooding the coast with light. Because he was so cold he began to clamber along the rock looking for a way up the cliff. The cliffs in this part of Brittany are usually very high and rugged; where he landed he had to climb nearly two hundred feet before he got on level ground. Oddly enough, this gave him confidence to go on. "I knew there wouldn't be none of them minefields top of a place like that," he said. "There wasn't even any barbed wire." The Germans do not waste material in the defence of places which can never be invaded. Simon had found the same when he climbed up the cliffs near Goulin.

He found his way up the cliff at last, and wormed his way cautiously forward over the bare, short grass. He knew just where he was; from long study of the chart he held every feature of the coast firm in his memory. He was about two miles due south of the little fishing village of Camaret; he was on a small peninsula jutting westwards from the big peninsula between the Rade de Brest and the Bay of Douarnenez. The land that he was on was covered with heather, with occasional clumps of gorse and bracken. There were no trees.

Very soon he came to a footpath, well worn, running through the heather parallel with the cliff. He crossed it and went on away from the sea, still crawling on his hands and knees. The moonlight was still so bright that he was afraid to stand up; in that bare country he felt that he would be visible a mile away. When he had passed the footpath by about twenty yards he heard the tramp of feet; he curled up and lay still among the heather. A German soldier came in sight, marching along in tin-hat, his rifle slung over his shoulder. He was an oldish man, with rather a slovenly appearance. He went straight down the path, looking neither to the left nor the right. After a time Colvin crawled on again.

He went on for the best part of a mile, crawling all the way because of the lack of cover. This was not a bad thing, as it happened, because the effort and the use of his limbs that it entailed made him warm; his arms and legs regained their normal feeling and his clothes began to dry upon him. He had let the air out of his Mae West, but still wore it for warmth.

Presently, in the first light of dawn, he came to a stone wall dividing the moor from fields. He reached up cautiously and looked over, and found that he was looking down into the village of Camaret, a mile to the north of him. In the grey light he could see the entrance to the Rade de Brest beyond, and beyond that again the rocky coast of the north part of Brittany.

"I didn't know what was best to do," he said, fingering the sheet. "It seemed to me that I was in a jam."

On that peninsula it was dangerous to go crawling about in broad daylight with no plan. There was a big clump of bracken growing up against the wall not very far away. He made for this and crawled into the middle of it and lay down, safe from any observation but from the air. And lying there he set to work to make a plan.

He had no need for any further survey of the country; he knew exactly where he was. As he crawled there had been growing in his mind the idea that if he could get on to the north coast of Brittany, the south of the English Channel, some opportunity might arise for getting back to England. He might somehow get a boat; he might even make a raft and try to blow back on the south-west wind. In any case, the north coast was where he ought to be.

He had a terribly long way to go to get there, seventy or eighty miles, perhaps. He would have to travel eastwards on the peninsula inland into France for twenty miles or so in order to get round the Rade de Brest; after that he would have to turn north. He did not know the country or the people. He knew that the main German concentrations were usually held a few miles inland from the coast; that meant that the farther inland that he went the greater would be the risk of being taken by the Germans.

From that point of view, and because he was a seaman and had memorised the charts, he longed to stay by the coast. He felt safe there; he had knowledge of conditions and localities; the inland parts were unknown, strange, and hazardous. He thought longingly of the north part of Brittany to the west and north-west of Brest, that was in sight across the sea. If he could get there he could go on round the coast until he found what he was looking for, a means of getting back to England. On the coast he would know what he was doing.

It was only just across the way, that part of Brittany. Could he possibly . . . get there?

It meant swimming again, of course. He concentrated his mind upon the chart and on the tidal streams. It must, he thought, be about five miles across the entrance to the Rade. It was November, and resting motionless in the grey dawn he was beginning to get very cold again. The thought of going into the sea once more was an appalling one. He had just swum about two miles in two hours, and he felt now that he had nearly died of it. Another five hours might well mean the end of everything for him.

But it wasn't so bad as that. If he picked his time right, the tidal stream that swept north-eastwards in from the Iroise to fill the Rade de Brest would carry him along; it would be pretty well behind him. It ran from two to two and a half knots, that stream did. That would reduce the time a great deal. In theory he would be in the water for no more than two hours; in practice it would probably be three. That made it possible, perhaps.

He would have to enter the water about midnight, by his

reckoning, if he were to take the tide up with him in that way.

"I didn't see what else there was to do, sir," he remarked. "I reckoned that the Germans would shoot me if they got me, 'n I thought I might as well die swimming as that."

He grew very cold and hungry, lying in the bracken. He slept a little, fitfully, from time to time; in his long waking hours his mind became increasingly filled with thoughts of food. And what he thought about was American food, clam chowder that Junie made out of a tin, and waffles that Junie made on the electric cooker in the little kitchen of their Oakland apartment. And Junie herself, in a clean print frock on a warm day . . . Junie, who was seven thousand miles away from him in distance and two years in time.

It was a still, clear autumn day with a light wind from the north-east. It was sunny most of the forenoon, and that made his long wait tolerable. He was so near to Camaret that he could hear the church clock strike the hours and the quarters. As evening came on he was thankful for that clock. He had resolved to try his luck at swimming to the northern shore, but the whole matter hinged upon the proper use of the tide. If he entered the water too soon he might struggle and exhaust himself in the slack water, or be carried out to sea, and die. If he entered it too late, it might be daylight when he sought to climb the cliffs only a few miles from Brest. His watch had stopped, but now he had the clock to help him, that and the rising of the moon.

When dusk came he began to crawl towards Le Toulinguet. That is a rocky point with an automatic light on it, standing on a point of rocks down by the water's edge. He got within half a mile of it in the last light of the day, near enough to see the path that ran down to a little concrete causeway on the rocks that led to the red tower. Between him and that path there was a watch-hut, camouflaged with the heather and occupied by German soldiers. From time to time one of them came out for a natural function and went back inside again.

The dusk merged into starlight and he crept on. He passed behind the watch-hut and about a hundred yards away, moving with infinite care through the heather. "I was proper fussed about them land-mines that they stick about sometimes," he said. "They might have had some planted back of a little post like that." But if they had, his luck was with him still.

He lay through the first part of the night at the border of the heather near the path. When he heard midnight strike and saw the first gleams of moonlight on the water, he crept down to the concrete causeway. He paused to blow up his Mae West and to note the angle of the moon relative to the course that he must swim.

Then he slipped down into the water and swam powerfully from the rocks. A wave lifted him and crashed him down upon an underwater shoal, scraping his left leg painfully. Then he was clear and swimming steadily upon his course.

He said that the water was terribly cold, much colder than the night before, he thought. It probably was just about the same, but he had had no food and very little sleep. Very soon he was swimming mechanically and numbly, his mind dazed and far away from Brittany.

"It was half-moon," he said. "It got me all muddled because Half Moon Bay, that was the beach Junie 'n me used to go swimming at Sundays. We used to swim a long way those times—'most as far as I was trying to swim that night. But that was in the day-time and all sunny, 'n much warmer, too."

Half-moon, Half Moon Bay, and swimming with Junie. The thoughts rolled slowly round in his numbed brain as he ploughed on, hampered by the clothes that he dared not abandon, held up by his Mae West, borne forward by the tide. He kept the moon over his right shoulder in the endless, mechanical cycle of his motions. And presently the California sunshine was more real to him than the dark water he was swimming in, and Junie swimming by his side was more to him than just a memory.

"She used to tan a sort of goldeny brown, like her hair," he said, and his hands moved restlessly upon the sheet as he lay in the iron cot. And then he said unexpectedly: "If I'd ha' died that time, swimming across, I don't think I'd ha' minded much."

But he didn't die. He swam right across the entrance to the Rade de Brest, and he got to the other side.

He landed on the north coast at a point about due north of Toulinguet. He landed on a point of rocks and clambered slowly along it to the shore, stumbling and falling on the sea-weed in the darkness. He was so numb that he could hardly stand; he fell, over and over again, before he got to firmer ground. He was so cold that his mind worked very slowly.

He came to a little beach beneath an earthy cliff after a time and rested there. The weather had deteriorated during the night; the wind was now from the south-east and it was beginning to cloud over. He sat resting for some time in a stupor that was half sleep; then he grew so cold that he had to get up and move about, infinitely weary.

The coast that he had landed on was lower and more easily scaled than the cliffs that he had left. The earth cliff he was resting up against was barely thirty feet high; above that the fields began. He knew what that would mean; barbed wire and land-mines, and a greater intensity of German sentries. He got up presently and began to make his way westwards along the rocks and beaches underneath the cliff.

After a time he came to a larger beach where a cart-track ran down from inshore. It seemed to him that the cart-track, the low fields beside it, would make a focus for defence; there would be a pill-box somewhere near-by manned by a picket of Germans. In the low fields there would be land-mines and barbed wire. He turned and went back for a quarter of a mile to a point where the cliff was thirty or forty feet in height, banking upon a paucity of defence in the more difficult locality.

He scrambled up the cliff without great difficulty and wormed his way forward over the grass. There was barbed wire ahead of him, but only a few strands of it on low, triangular supports. He lay watching for ten minutes and then negotiated it without great difficulty, and crawled on inland. Presently he came to a stone wall and began to walk upright, finding his way from field to field, heading about north-west.

Dawn came, and found him three or four miles inland from Le Conquet. Under a grey cold sky he saw a country of small fields surrounded by stone walls, with a few scattered cottages and farms built of grey stone. It was a country just like Cornwall over the sea a hundred and ten miles to the north, Cornwall, where he longed to be.

He was desperately cold and weary, and tormented with hunger and thirst. He found a little stagnant pool and had a long drink in the growing light. Then he found a field of sugar-beet and grubbed up three or four of them. Carrying them in his arms he skinned one with his knife and began to eat it, wandering on from field to field seeking for a place where he could lie hidden.

In that windswept country, cover was very scarce. He found a clump of blackberry bushes growing up against one of the stone walls; fearing immediate detection if he went on, he pressed himself feet first into concealment under this beside the wall. The thorns tore his skin and his clothes, but he dug further into it till he was well concealed. And all the time he went on munching at his beets.

Presently, cold and numb and tired, he fell asleep.

When he awoke it must have been about the middle of the forenoon. He stirred and rolled around, tearing himself again among the brambles. And immediately he did that, all Bedlam was let loose. A dog began to bark and clamour at his bush. He lay dead-still, but the row continued. It ran round barking and snuffling at various points of the bush till presently it found where he had gone in. There it stayed barking at him, just out of his reach. It was a mongrel, black and white, he said; about the size of a collie.

There was nothing he could do about it, short of coming out and pelting it with stones. He lay there and it went on barking. And then he heard a footstep, and a voice, a woman's voice, calling off the dog.

"Qui est?" she cried sharply. *"Qui est là-dedans?"*

There was nothing for it; slowly he dragged himself from his concealment and looked up at her. She was a peasant woman of thirty-five or forty, roughly dressed and dirty; from the look of her hands, covered in soil, she had been pulling beets. She stood there looking down at him, sarcastic. *"Et à qui les betteraves?"* she said.

He spoke a moderate Quebec French, but he did not understand her accent. He lay there on the ground looking up at her, puzzled. And then she looked at him again and took in his sodden clothes, his draggled hair and his torn hands. She said quickly:

"Vous êtes un échappé?"

He understood that one. *"Suis officier anglais,"* he said, and his old charm came back to him. *"Il y avait un naufrage."*

She caught her breath. "Ah . . ." And then she said in her Breton dialect: "Where do you want to go?"

He said simply: "To England, madame." He smiled up at her. "I have important business to attend to there."

"Business?" she said. "What do you mean?"

He said: "I have to get another ship and come back here again to kill more Germans."

She stared at him, and he smiled back at her. "There was firing and a battle down in the Iroise the night before last," she said. "Were you in that?"

He nodded.

"What do you want me to do?" she asked uncertainly.

There was no uncertainty in his reply. "I want to eat a very large hot meal," he said, "and to drink beer. And after that I want to find a boat. Any sort of boat will do, so long as I can steal it and escape."

She stared at him with wonder in her eyes. "You are a strange man," she said at last. "Stay there and I will tell my husband. Do not come out at all; get right inside again. There is a German post within a kilometre of us here."

She went away, and he crept back into the bush, wondering what was going to happen. He had not long to wait. Within an hour she was back again, this time without the dog. She bent down to his hole beneath the bush and thrust in a large, blackened tin dixie. It was hot to his touch.

"There is food, Englishman," she said urgently. "There is no beer. Now listen to me. Stay here till it is quite, quite dark; do not come out at all. Then, when it is very dark, you can come out, but leave the can under the bush; I will get it to-morrow. Follow the wall to the west till you come to the lane. Two fields down the lane, to the north, there is our farm on the right. Knock three times on the door quietly and we will let you in."

He repeated her instructions.

She said: "If you have bad luck and the Germans take you, do not betray us." Then, before he could answer, she was gone.

He lifted the lid off the dixie. There was about half a gallon of a thick fish soup in it, stiffened with potatoes and vegetables, and with a wooden spoon floating on the top. Lying in the bramble bush he got down every drop of this; no food had ever seemed to him to be so good. And then, warm again, he fell asleep once more.

It was very nearly dark when he woke up. He lay and watched the last of the daylight fade, and presently he scrambled from the bush and made his way along the wall. At about seven o'clock in the evening he was knocking at the door of the farm.

It opened to him, and he went through a black-out curtain into the farm kitchen. The woman was there, and there was a man about fifty years of age, in shirt-sleeves and unshaven. They were a decent enough pair.

The man said: "Did you meet anybody in the lane?"

Colvin said: "Nobody at all." He paused, and then he said: "Thank you for the food; I left the dixie under the bush. I had eaten nothing for a day and a half."

The man approached, and laid a hand upon his arm. "She said that you were wet," he remarked. "Are you dry now?"

"Aye," said Colvin. "I don't want any clothes." All this was carried on in halting French, Breton on their side and Quebec on his.

The man said next: "She says that you are looking for a boat to steal. That is now very difficult, because of the Germans. They put a guard on boats with motors, and even upon boats with sails. You will not be able to steal a boat, in these parts."

"I don't want a big one," Colvin said.

"You cannot cross La Manche to England, rowing."

He said: "I can that."

"You must be mad."

"Sure I'm mad," he said. "So would you be, in my place."

There was a momentary pause.

"Is there a rowing-boat that I can take?" he asked.

The man said slowly: "At Le Conquet, when the fishing-boats are out at night, they leave a boat upon the mooring—a very small, old boat, you understand, that they can get to shore in when they have moored the fishing-boat. But since the Germans came the boats, even the little ones, are padlocked to the mooring chain, and the oars are taken away. Each night the German soldiers go to see that all the boats are properly secured."

By his side the woman said suddenly: "There are oars here in the loft, but they are not a pair."

Colvin said: "That don't matter. Let me have a look at them?"

The man said: "Would you swim out to the boat, in the black night?"

Colvin showed them his Mae West, which he still wore beneath his jacket, and they fingered it with interest. "Such thick rubber!" said the man, "in time of war!"

The woman turned away to the fire, lifted a pot and poured out a great bowl of the same fish soup. She set it on the table with a length of bread. "Eat this," she said. "I will fetch the oars."

He sat down gratefully to the meal, and she went out. The man followed her, but returned after a minute. In his hand he carried a small, rusty hacksaw. He laid it on the table in silence.

Colvin took it up, smiling. "Say . . . " he said. He felt the serrations with his thumb; they were well worn, but it was sharp enough. "You got everything."

The woman came back with the oars. They were worn half

through by the thole-pin and one was a foot longer than the other. "They'll do," he said. "Now, how do I find this boat?"

"Finish your meal," the man said. "I will guide you there."

Colvin ate every morsel that he could; he ate on steadily for half an hour. Then he leaned back and pulled out a wet, stained pocket-book and searched in it. He found two sodden one-pound notes.

He got to his feet and laid the notes upon the table. "You folks been pretty nice to me," he said in halting French. "Oars and a hacksaw, they cost money, and not easy to get. And then there's the food, and that. I'm real sorry that it's only English money I've got, but maybe you'll get change for it one day."

The man shook his head, and pushed the notes back towards him. And then he did what seemed to Colvin a queer thing. He stood straight up, as straight and serious as a priest at the altar, and he made the V sign with two fingers.

Colvin stared at him. He had seen the V sign in England chalked on walls by little boys, *ad nauseam*. He had seen it in the newspapers, in advertisements for motor-cars, salad cream, and tooth-paste. He had seen a red-nosed comedian in a London theatre chalk it on the backside of a young woman who happened to be bending over. Never before had he seen it used by people who believed in it.

After a moment's hesitation, he stood up straight himself and repeated it self-consciously. Then he turned to the woman.

"Madame," he said, "the British Admiralty will repay me this money, and you have children to think of. There are children, are there not?" A little enamel pot standing in the corner had not escaped his notice.

She said: "I took them to my mother to-day, in case they should talk."

He said: "When next you go to Brest, buy them a present from the British Admiralty. Perhaps a ship would be most suitable."

They both laughed at that, and she took the money and stuffed it in the pocket of her dress.

Ten minutes later he was standing in the darkness with the man, the oars over his shoulder and the thole-pins in his pocket. Wrapped round the oars there was a sheet of canvas that had covered a leaky pigsty roof, and once had been a portion of a sail. It was all the fabric that they had to give him. He stood with the man while their eyes grew accustomed to the darkness, the echoes of the woman's *'Bonne chance!'* ringing in his ears.

"I will go first, and noisily," the farmer whispered. "Follow me at a hundred metres, and as quietly as you can. If I meet Germans I will make sufficient noise that you will know."

The wind was still south-east, but it had strengthened; the sky was mostly obscured by cloud, though here and there patches of starlight showed. It was about half-past eight when they left the farm. The man led Colvin by roads and lanes for nearly two hours, strolling ahead, singing or muttering to himself.

They met one German picket. Colvin heard the challenge, and a long incoherent argument commence, and he got over the hedge into the field. He made a detour round the argument, and when he heard the man proceeding on the road he followed on beside him in the field. Presently they were going on upon the road as before.

They walked for about two hours in that way through the night. Then the lane that they were following petered out into a grass pasture, and here the man was waiting for Colvin.

"This is the place," he whispered. "You must go very quietly now. Upon the other side of this field is the sea, the north side of the little bay that is Le Conquet. The village is on the other side, the south. Over there," he pointed to the west, "is Kermorvan. I do not think that there are any Germans here, but there are land-mines in places. In those places there is one strand of barbed wire, on posts."

They went on towards the water over the field. They found a patch of land-mines and followed the wire along until it ended; then they came to a formidable hedge of wire. They threw the piece of sail on this and negotiated it without great difficulty; then they were on the shore with water lapping on the rocks at their feet.

The man pointed over the water at a dim mass, seen very faintly in the thin starlight when you put your head down very near the surface. "There is one boat," he said. "There may be others, but I cannot see."

He stood up. "There you are," he said. "This is all that I can do for you. You have boat and oars now; may the good God be with you."

Colvin said: "One day, when peace comes, if I am still living, I will come back here and we will talk of this."

He went back to the wire and the farmer recrossed it on the sail; Colvin regained the sail with some difficulty and went back to the shore. It struck him then that he had never learned the farmer's name.

Ten minutes later he was in the water again, swimming to the dimly seen boat, towing the oars behind him by a cord around his shoulders. It was not a long swim, not much more than a hundred yards, and that now to him was nothing, helped by his Mae West. Before he reached the boat he saw another one, a little to the west.

He climbed into the boat and examined it. It was about twelve feet long and heavily built; it was fouled with sea-gull manure and seemed very old. There was a little water in the bottom of it and there was a cigarette tin at the stern, evidently used for bailing. A stout chain over the bows, with a padlock, held it to the mooring.

He dropped into the water again and swam over to the other one, but that was in a worse condition than the first, and he swam back again.

It was not much of a boat to cross the Channel in, but it would have to do. He pulled himself into it and then, cold in the wind, he set to sawing through the mooring chain. The wind was still in the south-east, and freshening.

Presently the chain parted quietly in his hand. He made it fast with a bit of cod-line, and then considered his position. He had oars and thole-pins, and a piece of canvas that he hoped would make a sail. He had no food or water; he had not attempted to bring any since he had to swim out to the boat. He was wet to the skin, and his boat was very old. Probably she would leak like a sieve.

"I pretty near chucked it up," he said to me from the bed. "But then I thought that if the Jerries got me I'd be shot, as like as not, 'n if that was to happen I'd be better off at sea. And so I went."

What he did was this: The wind was very nearly fair to carry the boat out to sea into the Four Channel. He dropped into the water again with very little buoyancy in his Mae West, and, swimming, tried to push the boat towards the south. The wind took her and he worked on her, ready to duck round to the other side of her if any firing started up. But no fire was opened on him, and no light came. He slid past the rocks of Kermorvan, fifty yards clear, and the wind carried him out into the rocky channel.

The tide was running very strongly to the southwards round the land, and the wind was southerly. The boat spun round and round in a heavy tide rip; he had great difficulty in getting into her. When he was in her the motion was so violent that he had difficulty in rowing, and in an hour he was carried south nearly to Pointe St.-Mathieu. But by that time he was about two miles off the land.

Then, with the moonrise, the tide turned and the wind veered more to the south, and began to blow quite hard. Rowing north before it he was carried up to Le Four at a great speed; he could not judge exactly where he was, but he was probably off Le Four at about three in the morning.

There were still three or four hours of darkness before him. He had stopped once or twice to bale out with the cigarette tin, but the leaks were not too bad. He now stopped rowing, and bent about half the area of canvas that he had to one of the oars as a sail, and stepped the oar at the bow thwart, and sailed on northwards, steering with the other oar over the stern.

"It was just dandy, that," he said. "I went on a couple of hours that way, 'n if it hadn't been for the weather I'd have felt like a million dollars."

But the weather was against him. In the dark night he went rushing in his crazy little boat down the steep slopes of sea, with the water tumbling and crashing all around him and a high crest raised behind him overhead that threatened to fall down upon him and engulf him. Then, at the bottom of the trough, his clumsy vessel would broach to and need the whole of his strength and skill upon the steering oar to get her straight again. While he was heaving and labouring she would rise sluggishly as the swell passed beneath her, and then forward once again in her mad rush.

"I was a durned fool," he said weakly. "But I wanted to get right clear of the coast before the day. And then I broke the oar."

Struggling to get her straight after one of those rushes, he put too much weight upon his steering oar, and it broke off at the worn part by the thole-pin. He grabbed for the blade and missed it as it floated from him; then she had broached to and in the dim light a wave crest towered above him and crashed down.

"Lucky she didn't turn clean over," he observed. "Durned lucky."

He did the only thing; he threw himself down in the water on her flooded bottom boards. A swamped boat with the weight well down in her seldom turns over, and in a minute or two he got the oar down that had served him as a mast. And sitting so, up to his neck in water as she rode over each swell, he set to work to get her free of water, first by rocking her and then by scooping out the water with his folded canvas. Time after time she filled again just as he thought to get a little freeboard showing, but in the end he won. The first light of dawn found him sitting on the bottom boards of the lightened boat, bailing down the water that he sat in with the cigarette tin.

"It was blowing pretty near a gale by that time, from about south-west," he said. "I reckoned that I'd better stay down, lying in the bilge, 'n let her go."

In that weather it was all that he could do, and the safest course, but there was another side to it. He was still very near to the French coast. An open boat with a man rowing or sailing it northwards would be an obvious target for machine-gun fire from any German aeroplane. But a boat drifting in a rough sea with a body lying motionless in the bottom of it was a common sort of sight; the German gunner might well think of the labour of cleaning his guns when he got home again before he fired on a thing like that.

He stayed down like that all day, numb and soaked and bailing every now and then with his tin. Towards evening he got up on the thwart, thinking to try to sail again, but the motion when he raised the oar was so sluggish and alarming that he quickly struck his mast again, and slipped down on the bottom boards. "She went easily that way," he said. "With any weight up top, she wasn't so good."

The wind in the Channel was about Force 7 that night, south-west, and the temperature about 38 to 40 degrees Fahrenheit. The wind kept up all the next day and the following night, but it grew gradually colder.

"I thought I was done for," he said simply. "Days 'n days, and each day worse and colder than the last."

All of us may one day have to face that sort of thing. It had never come to me, nor has done yet, but I was curious to know what the threshold of death looks like. "Did you think about things much?" I asked. "Or was it kind—of numb?"

"I didn't seem to have no control," he said. "Half the time I was blubbering like a kid."

"Because you knew that you were for it?" I said gently.

"Oh shucks, if wasn't that. It was Junie's watch. She bought it with her own money 'n give it me, back in San Diego. It was the only thing I had of hers, and it was stopped and spoilt, with the water all in it."

The sick-bay steward came in for the second time, and I got

240

up to go. "Don't worry about that," I said. "I'll have it cleaned for you."

I travelled back to London that afternoon, and went straight to my office. There was a note there asking me to ring McNeil as soon as I came in; I picked up the telephone and spoke to him at once.

"Is that Martin?" he said. "I've got a bit of news for you from the other side. Two messages."

"I've got a bit for you," I said. "I've seen Colvin. He's in Haslar Hospital." I told him very shortly how he had been picked up.

"That's fine," he said. "Look, would you like me to come round to you?"

"No, I'll come to you," I said. "I've got to go out anyway. I'll be with you in half an hour."

I rang off, and then rang up N.O.I.C. Dartmouth. "Commander Martin speaking," I said. "Admiralty. Look, sir, you remember that Wren who used to drive the truck for my party?"

"Leading Wren Wright?" he said.

"That's the one. She was engaged to one of the officers, Lieutenant Rhodes."

"Was she? I didn't know."

"I can't get any news of Rhodes," I said. "But one of the other officers, Lieutenant Colvin, has turned up. He's in Haslar. Would you tell her that? As a matter of fact, it would be quite a good thing, if you could spare her for a day or so, if she went to Haslar to see Colvin. They were all in it together, and he has no relatives in this country. I think we might give her a railway warrant for that, if she wants to go."

"All right," he said. "I'll see to that. I'd like to know as soon as you hear anything further."

"I'll keep you informed," I said.

I went out then, and took a taxi to the London Chronometer Company in the Minories. I asked to see the manager, and when he came I remembered him and he remembered me. "I came to see you about five years ago with the recording chronographs we had in *Foxhound*," I said.

He nodded. "I remember, sir. How are you keeping?"

"Not so bad." I gave him Colvin's watch. "It's had sea water in it for a week," I said. "I want a really good job made of it, and I want it done quickly."

"You don't want much, do you?" he said dryly.

"Look, do the best you can," I said. I told him a little of the story. "It's a case we're interested in at Admiralty."

"What if I find it needs a new movement altogether?"

"Give it one," I said. "But get it looking like it was before."

I left it with him, and took a taxi back to McNeil's office in Pall Mall. He passed me two messages across the table, both of them marked across the top in red MOST SECRET, as was usual.

The first said:

RENNES. The 145th regiment of infantry, part of the 64th Division, has arrived in Rennes. This division has been on the Russian front in the Rostov sector, and has now been transferred to Brittany because of the increasing unrest in this district. Units of the division are to be quartered at Morlaix, Carhaix, Douarnenez, and Quimper. The division is much under strength and is now not more than 5,000 men. The clothing and equipment of the men is in bad condition. Ends.

I glanced at McNeil. "This is very good news," I said quietly. "This is what you have been working for."

"Anything that takes pressure off the Russians is good news," he said. "Look at the other one." He said that in a tone I didn't like.

I picked up the second message. It read:

DOUARNENEZ. A proclamation issued by the Commandant announces that thirty hostages have been arrested, comprising ten men past working age, ten women, and ten children. It is stated that the town is harbouring an English officer who is believed to be a survivor from a British ship sunk in the Iroise and to have been concerned in setting fire to German vessels. The hostages are to be shot on November 15th unless this officer is given up. Ends.

I stared at this thing, not knowing what to say. "It's probably Simon," I said at last. "He must have got ashore."

The brigadier said: "Simon is the least likely of the lot. Simon can pass anywhere as a Frenchman; he'd have no need to go into hiding. No, it may be Boden or it may be Rhodes. One of them, at least, is still alive."

"Just," I said bitterly.

There was absolutely nothing we could do, and nothing much to be said. It was one of those things it's really better not to think about too much.

"How's Colvin?" McNeil asked at last.

I told him the story briefly. "He'll be all right," I said in the end. "I suppose he'll be about a month in hospital. He must have been in that boat for five days and nights, and that's not funny in this weather."

"No," he said, "it's not."

I left him soon after that, and went back to my office. It was November the 9th, and there were six more days to go before November the 15th. I turned to the arrears of my ordinary work as anodyne, but I could not tire myself sufficiently to sleep.

I went down to Newhaven to see the admiral next day, to report to him how the matter stood. It was a winding-up report, of course; as an operation of war the *Geneviève* incident was over and done with. All that remained to do was the final clearing of the paper work, dockets to Casualties Section, and that sort of thing, and in that the admiral was not much interested.

"Will you want to see Lieutenant Colvin, sir?" I asked.

"I don't think so, Martin," he replied. "Not unless he particularly wants to see me. See the Second Sea Lord's office when the time comes about his posting. See that he gets a job that will suit him."

"Very good, sir," I said.

It was a relief to turn to other work.

I went back to London and the days dragged on. They were grey, windy days, raining most of the time. I heard indirectly that Barbara Wright had been to Haslar to see Colvin and had gone back to Dartmouth next day, but I did not get in touch with either of them. I had nothing good to say.

No further messages came from the other side.

My two years at Admiralty expired about that time, and I raised the matter with V.A.C.O. one day when he was in the office. "My two years is up at the end of this month, sir," I said. "I'd like to get to sea again, if possible."

He nodded. "I knew it was about this time." And then he said, rather unexpectedly: "I shall miss you, Martin. You've been a great help to me."

I said awkwardly: "That's decent, sir. Would you—do you want me specially to stay on?"

He smiled. "I suppose you hate it here. You'd rather go to sea."

I said: "Well—quite frankly, yes. I'd rather be at sea. But if you want me, sir, I'm quite willing to stay."

He shook his head. "I wouldn't stand in your way."

That was that, and I went on in the office in a better frame of mind. And the next day I had a telephone call from Plymouth, from the Chief of Staff.

He said: "Martin, is an R.N.V.R. officer called Rhodes anything to do with that party of yours? Operation Blanket?"

"Yes, sir," I said. "He was the—er—the special gunner."

He said: "Well, he's back. He came back wounded, with a boatful of French fishermen. They came into Falmouth this morning."

A sort of sick wave of relief passed over me. "I'm glad to hear it, sir," I said. "Is he much hurt?"

"Chest and lungs, I think," he said. "He's in the naval hospital there."

I said in wonder: "It's nearly a fortnight old, that operation, sir. He must have been ashore—on the other side."

"I think he has."

I glanced at my watch. "I think I'd better slip down to Falmouth myself, right away."

He said: "Well, I think you might. There are one or two rather curious features that I can't very well tell you over the telephone."

I said: "I'll go down there to-day."

"You'll find our Intelligence Officer down there," he said. "I'll ring through to him and tell him that you're coming."

I rang up McNeil to tell him, but he was out of London. So I caught the afternoon train to Cornwall alone, and sat all day wondering and speculating about what had happened on the other side. The train was late and we did not get in till nearly midnight; I turned into the hotel and slept uneasily.

I was down at the Naval Centre early next morning, and met the Intelligence Officer, a retired lieutenant-commander. He was most interested in checking up on the *bona fides* of the fishermen and he was taking them all off to London on the morning train. "I haven't seen this officer, Rhodes," he said. "He wasn't very well yesterday." He paused and then he said cautiously: "If what I've heard is true its a very queer story."

"What's queer about it?" I enquired.

He shrank back into the maddening caution of the Intelligence. "I'd really rather not discuss the matter at the moment," he said. "It's all got to be sifted."

244

I said: "I'm down here to see Rhodes and to find out what happened to my party. The fishermen aren't my concern. Suppose I stay down here and see my officer, and then meet you back in London? What I learn from him may pad out what you get from them."

He agreed to that, and I went up to the hospital. I was beginning to know the smell of hospitals quite well on this infernal job. I saw the surgeon-commander first, in his little white painted office.

"You're Commander Martin?" he enquired. "I'm glad you've come. This young chap Rhodes has been asking for you ever since he came in."

"How is he?" I asked.

"Not too grand. He's got a wound in the left shoulder and chest that touched the lung. The trouble is that it's a fortnight old. It's had attention of some sort during that time, but it's in a pretty nasty state."

I said: "Can I see him this morning?"

The surgeon said: "Oh yes. He won't settle down till he's had a talk to you. Make it as short as you can, but he's got a lot he wants to tell you."

He paused. "Before you go in there, there's one thing I should like you to see," he said. "It's puzzled us a good bit."

He rang the bell and a steward appeared at the door. "Get that uniform," he said. The man went out and the surgeon turned to me. "I won't keep you a moment."

The steward came back with a bundle of clothes tied up with string. They unrolled it on the floor. It was a German petty officer's uniform with short pea jacket of thick navy blue cloth bearing the eagle's wing and swastika, a cap with the same emblem, a blue jumper with a blue naval collar, and trousers to match.

"These are the clothes he was wearing when he was admitted into hospital," the surgeon said. "It's a German naval uniform."

I turned the clothes over. "So I see. What were the men with him wearing? The fishermen?"

"They were wearing ordinary Breton rig—black floppy tam-o'-shanters and those rusty-coloured sail-cloth ponchos that they wear. They weren't in any uniform."

I was handling the jumper, and my fingers struck a sticky mess. There was a four-inch rent in the back of it; I looked at the cloth, at my fingers, and then up at the surgeon.

"Yes," he said. "That's blood. The wearer of these clothes was stabbed in the back." He picked up the pea jacket. "He had his coat on. Look, here's the corresponding hole."

I laid the clothes down, wondering at the morbid imagination that had made him show them to me. "I'll get along and see him, if I may," I said.

He stared at me. "I'm not sure if you understand," he said. "Lieutenant Rhodes wasn't stabbed. His wound is in the shoulder, and from the front." He paused. "There's no mark on his back at all."

I said impulsively: "But the blood's still sticky! Do you mean that somebody else was wearing this rig, and was stuck in the back?"

"I can't see it any other way." He paused. "I was very puzzled. I thought you ought to see the clothes before you went in to see him."

I nodded. "It's probably as well."

He took me in to Rhodes. The young man was in a ward with about fifteen other patients in it. He was lying raised a bit with pillows. He was much thinner in the face than I remembered him; his black hair had been cropped close to his head, making him look very different. His left shoulder was a mass of bandages. There was a nurse with him.

" 'Morning. Rhodes," I said cheerfully. "How are you feeling?"

He said in a thin voice: "I'm all right, sir. I've got a lot I want to tell you."

The surgeon spoke to the nurse, and she began arranging screens around the bed. "You'll be able to talk quietly in there," he said. "Don't be any longer than is necessary."

I said: "Rhodes, we've got to be as short as possible, so that you can get some rest. I'm going to do the talking first of all, and tell you what I know. In the first place, Colvin's back in England. He's in Haslar Hospital, and going on all right."

His face lit up. "Oh, good," he breathed. "How did he get away?"

I told him briefly what had happened. Then I told him what we had learned from the M.G.B. lads, and from the secret messages that had come over from the other side. It took about ten minutes. "Now, look," I said. "I'm going to ask you questions, and you answer them. It'll be easier for you, that way. First of all, what happened to Simon?"

He said: "He's still in Douarnenez. We've been there

246

together. When *Geneviève* was sunk, the shell hit the stem. I was just getting out of the flame-thrower seat, and I got this in my shoulder. And then I was in the sea, and Simon was helping me, sir, in the water. And he pulled me along, and we got to one of the fishing-boats."

"I see," I said. "What happened to Boden?"

Rhodes said: "Oh, he was killed."

"Did you see him killed?"

"No, sir."

"Was he the officer who was on the keel of the boat, firing with a Tommy-gun?"

"Yes, sir. They were all talking about it in Douarnenez. He put out the searchlight. Jules was the other man with him, sir."

"How do you know he was killed, if you didn't see it?"

There was a pause. "He wanted to be killed," Rhodes said.

I left that, and turned back to the main story. "Just tell me now, as shortly as you can, what happened when you got into the fishing-boat."

I have put together what he told me with what we learned from the fishermen and from another source upon the other side. This is what happened:

When Rhodes was thrown into the water he bobbed up again at once, because his Mae West was blown up. He said that there were several men in the water with him. He knew that something had happened to his shoulder and he kept coughing, and each time he coughed, he said, funny things seemed to happen in his chest. He was in no great pain.

Presently he saw Simon, and Simon saw him, and swam towards him, and began to help him. Simon was unhurt. He called Rollot, the *maître*, and between them they took Rhodes in tow and began to swim with him towards the fishing-boats, seen dimly in the background. Those were the boats that had been with them in the Anse des Blancs Sablons.

While they were covering two or three hundred yards to the nearest of the boats the M.G.B.s roared past, dropping their charges, the duel between Boden and the destroyer went on, and the searchlight was put out. There was still a fire raging on the bridge of the destroyer which gave some light, and the moon was bright. The fishing-boats, as soon as they saw survivors swimming to them, steamed in to pick them up. Rhodes, Simon, and Rollot were taken on board one boat. He thought that about five or six, out of their crew of twelve Free Frenchmen, were taken on board another. He did not know their names, for a very good reason. As soon as they reached Douarnenez all these Frenchmen, most of whom were Breton lads, merged with the crowd and vanished quietly away. There was no reason for them to do otherwise. It was the best thing they could do.

There was some urgency for the boat that had picked them up to get back to Douarnenez without delay, because each of the rescuing boats had on board ten Tommy-guns and ammunition. They were counting upon the events of the night and the scattering of the fleet to relax the normal supervision of the boats in harbour, and this actually happened. They steamed straight to Douarnenez at full speed, and entered harbour at about four in the morning, still in bright moonlight.

Rhodes, Simon, and Rollot came into harbour down in the fish-hold of their boat covered over with a pile of nets. They had contrived a pad and bandage for Rhodes's wound, but they could provide no dry clothes. With the cold and wet, and with the stiffening of his wound, Rhodes was becoming feverish, and from that time onwards he saw everything opaquely, blurred by a high temperature.

The master of their boat, a man called Corondot, went on shore as soon as they picked up the mooring. He went to the little harbour-master's office on the quay, which was also the office of the German fish control. Here, in a state of anger, he reported that he had brought his boat back, having spent a few hours dodging about the Iroise being chased by British gunboats. Where was the protection of the Reich? he asked. For himself, he was fed up. The last thing he had seen was another battle in the distance, with flame and firing and God knows what. For himself, he proposed to stay in harbour till the seas were made safe for honest fishermen.

There were five other skippers making similar complaint, each talking at the top of his voice. Besides those, most of the old German petty officers were there, each telling his own tale and adding to the din. The telephone upon the little desk rang every half-minute and had to be answered, the old harbour-master had one rating to assist him, who spoke only German. It was a fine, confused party, all concentrated in the harbour-master's office. Nobody paid any attention to what was going on down at the quay.

The ten Tommy-guns and ammunition were landed quite easily, put on a hand-cart, and pushed unconcernedly up into the town. Simon and Rhodes with the Free Frenchmen landed at the quay. The latter melted quietly away into the darkness of the streets.

Rhodes landed at the steps, feeling sick and faint, with a stiff throbbing in his chest. It was moonlight still; he looked over to the main jetty and he could see great blackened patches near the end of it, the aftermath of the fire that they had made a month before. It was a quiet, still night, and rather cold. It was incredible to him that he should be standing there, listening while Simon spoke volubly in French in a low tone, discussing with their rescuers a plan of action.

In a few minutes they made up their minds, and Simon turned to Rhodes. "Stick it," he said in English, in a whisper. "There is a hide-out for us here, till we can get away. It is about five hundred metres to walk. Can you manage to walk so far?"

The boy said: "I'm all right, sir."

Simon said: "Try to walk naturally and easily, like a fisherman going home. I will be near you. We will get a doctor for you very soon."

They set off, walking up-hill through narrow alleys, up stepped, cobbled slits between the houses. The town was black and still. They came out into wider streets, with shops; at one point they passed a German sentry. There were six or seven of them walking in a bunch together; the leader checked his pace, and said in slow French that the boats had come back early.

The man nodded in his steel helmet. "What happened?" he enquired. "We heard firing."

Their leader said sourly: "The *sale* English made a raid. Here we are back again, and without one fish—not one. If you Germans cannot keep the English off, you'll get no fish. I don't care, either way."

The man stepped back, motioning them on. They went on and left him standing at the corner of the street, his rifle slung over one shoulder.

They were taken to a net-store, a tarred shed behind a sail-maker's loft. Rhodes was very, very tired by the time they got there. He collapsed wearily upon a bolt of sail-cloth, and sat holding a candle to light Simon and another man as they pulled nets about to make a bed, and spread a blanket over all. Then the other man fetched a bucket of water with some disinfectant in it, and they removed the blood-stained, soaked pad from his shoulder, and replaced it with another.

It was dawn by then, and in the grey light that filtered in around the eaves they laid him down upon the bed that they had made, and Simon covered him with another blanket. "Try to get some sleep," he said in a low tone. "A doctor will come presently to see your shoulder. In the meantime, we will get our friends here to bring some food, some soup for you, perhaps. Would you like that?"

Rhodes said: "I'm all right, sir. I don't want anything to eat. What's the next thing? Can we get away?"

"Lie there, and rest, and try to get some sleep. I think we may be all right to stay here till you are better. While you are resting I will talk to our friends, and we will make a plan."

Rhodes lay back on the nets, and presently he fell into a feverish sleep, the first of many that he was to endure in that shed. He dreamed that he was in *Geneviève* firing the flame-thrower, but the gun was filled with carbolic solution and when he fired it at the destroyer it would not light, but sprayed the decks with disinfectant. And Brigadier McNeil was there, smart in his khaki tunic, his red tabs, and his brilliantly polished buttons and Sam Browne, and he said: "Time they had a wash-down, anyway." And Rhodes said to himself: "What a fool I am, of course, carbolic's no good in this thing. I must try it on Worcester Sauce." And he turned the three-way cock with the brass handle to the other tank, and fired again. And the gun lit and the flame hit the destroyer, and her side flared up and burned away like tinsel, and instead of men inside her there was only his black Labrador dog Ernest, and his buck rabbit Geoffrey, perishing in the flame that he had turned on them. And he burst into floods of tears, and in his misery Barbara was there. In her quiet voice she was saying: "It's all right, Michael, it's quite all right. It's only a dream. Look, you can wake up."

Then he was awake, tears pouring down his face, hot and stiff, and with a raging thirst. That was the first of many such dreams that he had.

On the evening of that first day, the doctor came.

He was a short, plump, white-faced man called Dottin; he had a grey moustache and he was very correctly dressed in a black suit. The old fisherman, Bozallec, brought him to them and stood aside with Simon in the darkness of the shed while he examined Rhodes.

"He is a safe man," said the fisherman. "You may talk freely to that one."

Presently the doctor called for warm water and for his bag, and began to put a dressing on the wound. When that was over he laid Rhodes down upon the blanket, wiped his hands, and walked across the shed to Simon. Together they walked out of hearing of the bed.

"You are his friend?" the doctor said. "I have not seen you before."

"I am an Englishman," said Simon bluntly. "I was with him in the vessel that was sunk."

The man stared at him in amazement. "I would never have believed it. He"—he jerked his head towards the bed—"he is clearly English. But you, monsieur, you speak French to perfection. You have lived long in a department in the Paris region, or perhaps in the north-east?"

"I have lived most of my life in France," Simon said.

"So. Well, your friend should be in hospital. He has a high temperature, and while the wound now is still clean, it may not remain so. That is my advice to you, monsieur."

"Is it possible to take him into hospital without the Germans knowing?"

The man shook his head. "That is not possible now. Once it was, but not now, not since the shooting in the streets on the night of the great fire at the quay. The Germans insist on seeing every person in the wards each day."

There was a pause. "Can we keep him here and see how he gets on?" Simon said at last.

The doctor shrugged his shoulders. "Certainly. But you may have to choose in the end, monsieur, between captivity for him and death."

Simon nodded. "That is understood. But while there remains any chance of getting him to England, I will not give in. He has experience and knowledge locked up in his head, most valuable to the Allies. It will be of benefit to France, no less than England, that he should get away. I tell you this, monsieur, from my certain knowledge—I, Charles Simon." He spoke with true French vehemence.

Dottin glanced at him keenly. "I have heard of Charles Simon." He paused. "This knowledge that you speak of," he said carefully. "Would that have to do with—fire?"

Simon nodded. "He is the operator of the flame-gun," he said simply. "He designed much of the apparatus himself. Now, monsieur, you understand that it is necessary for him to return to England at whatever cost."

The doctor said: "I understand that it is very necessary to get him out of Douarnenez."

Simon glanced sharply at him in enquiry.

"You do not understand the situation here, perhaps," the doctor said. "One month ago, to the day, the English made a raid upon the port, with fire, and they destroyed two *Raumboote* at the quayside and two guns upon the jetty. Was that his ship that made the raid?"

Simon nodded without speaking.

"That night, fifty-three casualties, German soldiers and sailors all of them, were taken into the Municipal Hospital, monsieur, with burns. Some of the burns were not extremely bad, but all of them got worse, in every case. It has been most puzzling. The Germans have brought specialists from Leyden with a new treatment, using Cilzamene, and they have done no good, no more than we. Of the fifty-three men admitted, seventeen have died and thirty-six are still alive, all of them very much worse than in the first few days. I have never heard of burns like these. They are beyond experience, monsieur."

Simon nodded. "That may be."

The man said: "If the Germans were to take a prisoner from that ship they would make him talk, to tell what oil was used that burns like that. They would stop at nothing to make him talk."

"They would use torture?"

"Most assuredly."

Simon smiled. "They would get nothing out of me," he said. "I do not know the secret. But you see now, more than ever, monsieur, that that one"—he nodded to the bed—"must get away."

The doctor turned, and looked back to the bed. "He is not fit to travel," he said. "I have heard it said that men can get away from France in spite of the Germans, if they have courage and determination, and great strength. Two young men left this town about six months ago to walk to Spain, to try to get to England to de Gaulle. I do not know how they got on. But that one could not do a trip like that."

He turned away. "I will come again to-morrow, in the evening," he said.

Simon did not go out, but spent that evening and the whole of the next day in trying to work out a plan, and in discussion with Bozallec. Rhodes was no better; he spent much of the time sunk in a hot sleep. The doctor came again at dusk to change the dressing, and that day ended with no plan made, and no vestige of a plan in sight.

Next morning Bozallec came with a long face. "I have had news," he said bluntly. "The Germans know that there are English hiding in the town. There is a proclamation of the *Oberstleutnant Commandant* that is stuck up at headquarters on the wall, and at the Mairie, and in the market."

"What does it say?"

"It says that there are English hiding in the town, survivors from a ship sunk in the Iroise. It says that they are to be surrendered to the commandant to-day, or else the town will suffer severe penalties."

"How did they find out?" Simon asked.

The old man said: "I, too, wanted to know that. In this town, soon after the Armistice, there were a few informers, but they had bad luck with their health during the winter. I do not think there are any informers now living in Douarnenez. I wanted to know how the Germans came to know this thing, because it seemed to me that an informer might have done it. But it was not that."

"How was it?"

"It was the men in the destroyer. They were too busy with their fires to note the boats carefully, but they saw several boats from the fleet picking up survivors from the water. And when they got to Brest they remembered this. That is how the Germans know that there are English in the town."

There was a short silence. "What will the people do?" asked Simon. "Will they give us up?"

The old man said angrily: "This place is not a Vichy rabble. This is a town of seamen, a man's town."

There was a silence. "Lie low," the old man said at last. "Do not, on any account, be seen outside this place, even for one minute. It may be necessary that you stay here for some days, or even weeks. I do not think the Germans dare do anything against the town. They have not got sufficient troops to face a rising here."

Three days later they were still there, with Rhodes in much the same condition, though rather weaker. Bozallec's summary of the situation seemed to be justified; the time for the surrender of the fugitives had expired and two days had followed, in which the Germans had done nothing. Bozallec came to visit them each day, more confident with every visit. "It is blowing over," he said. "It will be necessary for you to wait here for some time to come, but then we will be able to contrive something."

On the morning of the next day he came later than usual, and at first sight of him Simon knew that there was something wrong. "Bad news, I think," he said quietly.

"Aye," said the fisherman, "bad news it is. They have arrested thirty people to hold for your surrender. Ten of them are children. Jeanne Louise is one, my own great-niece." He spat.

"They did not fear a rising of the town," said Simon, bitterly.

The old man said: "They did indeed. They waited for three days till they were reinforced before they did this thing. Soldiers have come from Russia to police Brittany, monsieur—thousands and thousands of them. There are fifteen hundred new ones here to-day, a ragged, scruffy lot, but with plenty of machine-guns. Now they have courage to arrest women and old men and little girls of seven years. Good German courage!" He spat again.

Simon asked: "What will they do with them?"

"They will be shot upon November the 15th," the old man said, "unless you are surrendered to them first."

11

IN the dark shed, stuffy with the fumes of tanning, there was silence for a minute. Then Bozallec said angrily: "They cannot do that to us now. It is not last year now. Last year they shot thirty people in one day, in August, in the market-place, but then we had no guns. Now we have Tommy-guns to use: it is different altogether."

Simon said: "You have seventy Tommy-guns, no more. Last week you might perhaps have done something, but not now. Seventy men with Tommy-guns cannot fight fifteen hundred with machine-guns."

He glanced at the fisherman. "You will have to give us up," he said quietly. "It is the only thing that you can do."

The man shook his head. "I cannot speak for the others," he said. "They must decide. But I have lived in this place fifty years, monsieur, and I do not think they will do that. If you were ordinary fugitives, or British agents, they might take that course. But you are different, you two."

"Why are we different?" Charles Simon asked.

The fisherman said: "Before you came and started hurling

fire upon the Germans, things were very bad here in Douarnenez, monsieur. The war went on and on, and we were impotent. The Germans were on top of us, and they had everything their own way. We could not see an end, nor any hope, nor anything before us but the life of slaves. Slaves! We Breton folk!"

He paused. "I want you to understand," he said. "The first *Raumboot* that you set on fire, we did not fully comprehend. There were queer stories that the English had done it, but no one knew. All we knew for certain was that the Germans in it had died miserably in torment, and we thanked God that some small part of all the misery that they had caused had come to them."

He went on: "Then you came, monsieur, and told us that the English had done it, and that they would do it again. And that same night you did do it again, right in our own port here in Douarnenez. We saw the fire and saw the Germans in the flames—and we saw your vessel, too, monsieur. One of our sardine-boats, Jules Rostin's *Geneviève*, that his son had escaped in at the Armistice. It was even one of our own ships that did this thing. Thirty Germans were burned to death that night, Monsieur Simon, and over fifty taken off to hospital. And they are dying still . . .

"I cannot tell you what that meant to us," he said. "That there were free men near us, fighting these foul oafs that had grabbed our city, fighting them, burning them, and making them afraid. There was a mutiny in Brest, monsieur, a naval mutiny. The *Raumboote* crews would not come here to Douarnenez after that night; they had to shoot a lot of them. This town regained its courage from that day. Each time we passed a German in the street we used to light a match, just to remind them of the way that their companions died. We got them grey and nervous in a week or two, so that they started and jumped round at a step behind them. And their commandant appealed for reinforcements, saying that he could not hold the town unless he had more men. That is true."

"I know," said Simon. "We heard that in England."

The fisherman went on: "And then you brought us guns, little machine-guns that could be hidden away. A man with a sub-machine-gun has something tangible to pin his courage to, monsieur; when things are very bad he can go to it and caress it, and polish it and oil it, and think what he will do with it one day. It gives a purpose to his life."

There was a short silence. "I do not think that you need

fear to be surrendered to the Germans, Monsieur Simon."

Simon said: "I think the next move lies with us; we must do something now. But now I tell you this, Bozallec, and you must repeat this to your friends. There is to be no fighting with those guns until the English give the word. United with the English you can fight the Germans and defeat them, but if you fight alone you will be wiped out and the town destroyed. Understand that. Tell your friends this. Charles Simon says that they are not to use the guns until word comes from England."

He paused. "And another thing," he said. "Tell your friends this: once before Charles Simon told them what was going to happen, and he spoke the truth. And now, Charles Simon says that they need have no fear for their relations, for the thirty hostages, men, women, and little children. Charles Simon says that all of them will be released, unhurt. Tell them that."

He stood for a moment in silence, thinking hard. "Is Father Augustine of the Church of Ste.-Hélène still in Douarnenez?" he asked.

"He is still here."

"I should like to talk to him," said Simon. "Can you bring him to me, in this place?"

"Assuredly," the old man said. "I will bring him to-night." He paused, and then said curiously: "Does he know you, monsieur?"

Simon said: "We met and talked together once, in February last. I do not think that he will know my name."

Bozallec went away, and Simon moved to the back of the store where Rhodes was lying on his bed, awake. "What's the news now?" the young man asked. "How's it all going, sir?"

Simon said: "Not too bad. I think I can begin to see my way out of this place."

"Back to England?"

"Yes, back to England."

"How, sir?"

Simon said: "I will not tell you now. Lie still and rest, and think of quiet things. When I am certain not to disappoint you I will tell my plan and what your part in it will be. Till then, be patient."

Rhodes turned restlessly upon the blanket. "Give me a drink of water, would you? It's so bloody hot."

In the middle of the afternoon there were steps upon the stair that led up to their store. Bozallec came in, and he was followed by a priest in black canonicals. Simon went forward to meet them.

"Good evening, father," he said quietly in French. "We have met before."

In the dim light the priest peered forward at him. "You are Charles Simon?" he enquired. "I have heard of you, but have we ever met?"

Bozallec turned to leave them and clumped down the stairs. Simon said: "I am the man you talked to in the night, on the platform of the station at Quimper, in February last."

The priest drew in his breath sharply. "So!" he said. "You were the man at Quimper; I have often thought of you. And you are now Charles Simon."

Simon motioned to a bale of net cord. "Will you sit down, father?" he said. "I have much to say to you."

The priest sat down, and waited for him to begin.

"Father," said Simon at last. "Do you remember what we talked about that night?"

"I remember very well, my son. We spoke about the Power of God, and of fire."

"Yes," said Simon, "that is what we spoke about. I was a spy then, father, in France on a mission for the English, to learn German secrets."

The priest glanced at him curiously. "Who are you?" he asked. "You are a Frenchman, from the East?"

Charles shook his head. "I am an Englishman," he said, "though I have lived in France for half my life. I am a British officer."

The priest nodded. "I have heard of others such as you."

There was a momentary silence. "There are others like me," Simon said at last. "We are lonely people, father, without homes or wives or families—not quite like other men. It may be that we see more clearly to the end, than men who live more normally. I know that when you spoke to me that night about fire, the temporal weapon of Holy Church, you set me thinking, searching, and devising on the basis of your words. In England, by sheer chance I came upon men learning the use of fire. So that in the end, father, we brought fire to the Germans here, and your words were fulfilled."

"There is no chance in these affairs, my son," the priest said gently. "Only the hand of God."

Simon inclined his head. "There is a young man with me

here," he said, "wounded, and in no good condition. He cannot travel far; he should be in a hospital. He is a British officer, like me, father, but he speaks only English. He is the gunner of the flame-gun that we used."

He paused. The priest said nothing.

Simon went on: "When we were talking together in the night, at Quimper, you said that God from time to time reveals the secret of the temporal weapon to mankind, that they may fight the Powers of Evil in the world, and beat them down. I am a sinful man, father, weak in the faith. I do not know if what you say is true. But if it is, then I say this to you: This young man with me, this young Englishman, has been touched by the hand of God for the benefit of all mankind. All that we have done has been made possible by his great knowledge of the principles of fire. He is a chemist in times of peace. Much of the gun itself was made to his design, and he designed the oil we hurl upon the Germans. There is knowledge and experience locked up in his head which is possessed by no one else. If he should die, or else be given to the Germans, knowledge that has been revealed to him by God goes back to God, and we are as we were. It may be that it is destined to be so."

Father Augustine said: "All things are in the hands of God, my son. But that does not mean that we are to lie supine, or refuse to use the wit and strength that God has given us, to work His will."

Simon nodded. "So I think. Father, we must get this young man back to England, that the work may go on."

There was a pause. "You have done great things in Douarnenez," the priest said slowly, "by the Grace of God. It was to the English that the temporal weapon was revealed before; again it is the English who are His instruments. I do not understand why this is so, why not the French. But that is by the way. Through that Grace and the power of flame this region has regained its courage. Men now go about our streets with their heads up, spitting towards the Germans, who three months ago were sullen and impotent, sinking into slavery. I have no need to hesitate, my son. I will give you what help lies within my power."

He glanced at Simon. "There are only two of you to be helped out of France?"

Simon said: "Only one." He nodded to the bed. "The others, they were all Bretons. They have found safety, each in his own way."

"What will you do, yourself?"

Simon said: "I speak French well enough to pass in the crowd, father. We need only think of him, of getting him to England."

The priest said keenly: "They are saying in the town, Charles Simon says no harm will come to the hostages."

Simon coloured awkwardly, and said nothing.

"Is that correct, my son?"

"We have one thing to do, father, and one thing only. That is to see that this young man gets back to England. Let us talk of that."

"As you will."

They sat in earnest conversation for an hour. Then the priest went away; he came back late that night, to meet the doctor and Bozallec in the net shed with Simon. They sat in earnest conference far into the night before breaking up, the priest to walk boldly through the moonlit streets, the others to slink furtively in the shadows back to the open windows of their homes.

On November the 12th, in the forenoon, they roused Rhodes from a semi-coma, and made him get out of bed. The doctor gave him an injection in the unwounded arm; he began to feel stronger, and much clearer in the head. They made him walk about a little in the loft, to ease his legs. Then they told him what he had to do.

"It is only three hundred yards," Charles Simon said. "Whatever happens you must walk that naturally. You will be quite alone, but we shall be not twenty yards behind you. You must pay no attention to the hand grenades. Walk straight down to the quay, and to the boat."

Rhodes said: "What will you do, sir?"

Simon said: "Don't worry about me. I shall be close behind you as you walk, to signal for the hand grenades to be let off, if it is necessary. If all is very quiet and safe, then I will come with you in the boat. But you are not to wait for me. If there is trouble I shall merge in with the crowd and I shall come back to England by the way I know, the way I went before, in February. In that case I shall be in London before you."

They brought water then and shaved Rhodes, and washed his face and cut his hair to a close, stubbly crop. And then they led him downstairs from the loft, into the sail-maker's yard. There was a light rain falling; the cold air blew fresh into his face, making him dizzy and light-headed. The injection that he had been given had cleared his head, but he still had a high temperature; he felt his way uncertainly, as if he were walking upon marbles.

Bozallec turned to Simon and the doctor. "He is very weak, that one," he said. "He will never walk like a German."

Dottin eyed Rhodes critically. "I have another dose for him," he said. "He will be better than this."

Simon said: "I will talk to him. He has great nervous strength to draw upon, and it is only three hundred metres."

There was a hand-cart in the yard, a two-wheeled affair with a long handle. Bozallec lifted up this handle to the horizontal, and Simon and the doctor helped Rhodes to get up on to the platform. They laid him down upon it, making him as comfortable as possible with a sail as a cover and a pillow; then they covered him over with a heap of fine blue sardine nets.

In that way they wheeled him boldly out into the street and half a mile through the town, past ragged German soldiers staring into shops, past German soldiers in brand-new uniforms walking uncomfortably in new boots, past German sentries upon guard at the street corners. They wheeled him into a small covered yard through double doors, which they closed behind them. There they uncovered him, and helped him into the house, and sat him down in a cane rocking-chair in the shabby little back room of a shop.

Dottin bent over him. "Cognac," he said quietly in French. "Just a little, with water, in a glass."

He felt better after that. An old man, whom he did not know, poured him a bowl of soup from a great pot that stood upon the hearth; Simon crouched down beside his chair and fed it to him with a spoon. "There is still an hour to go," he said. "Stay quiet here, and rest."

Rhodes drowsed a little, hot and tired. From time to time he opened his eyes; nothing was changed. He could see through the open door of the back room into the shop; it appeared to be a small general shop, with a few groceries, vegetables, and households goods upon the shelves. The old man was pottering about behind the counter.

Presently there were more people in the back room, and in the shop. There was a priest, Rhodes said, in a black soutane, as well as Simon and the doctor and the old fisherman who had brought him there. The doctor and the priest came into the back room and stood behind the door, screened from the shop.

Simon and Bozallec stood smoking in the shop, chatting to the old man behind the counter.

In a few minutes the bell at the shop door jangled, and the door opened and closed. A man came forward to the counter. He was a German petty officer in uniform; over his jumper he wore a short pea jacket, with a blue muffler round his throat. There was an automatic pistol in a holster at his belt. He moved forward, and said something to the man behind the counter. From the back room Rhodes watched, tense and suddenly awake.

The old man stooped beneath the counter. "It is a special favour," he said in Breton French. "I would not do this for every one. One hundred and fifty francs." And furtively he showed a duck, plucked and dressed and ready for the oven.

The German said: "It is too much," and leaned across the counter to pinch the breast. Rhodes saw Bozallec lift his right arm quickly and strike it down into the middle of the German's back. There was a thumping, rending sound and the man spun round, fumbling at his holster. Then they were all on him and bore him down on to the floor. There was one stifled cry, and then nothing but the heavy breathing of men struggling upon the ground. And presently that ceased, and Simon and Bozallec got up, dusting their clothes. The German lay motionless upon the floor, face down, his scarf bound tightly round his face. It was only then Rhodes saw the handle of the knife.

The old man said: "Quickly. Into the back room, before he bleeds."

They carried the body in and laid it down at Rhodes's feet; he saw the old man with a bucket and swab cleaning the floor of the shop. Then the door was shut, and they began to strip the pea jacket and uniform from the German.

Simon said: "Come on, lad. Up you get, and get your things off."

Presently Rhodes had German trousers on and German boots; the jumper, roughly wiped, was ready for him. Dottin, the doctor, opened his little case, filled his hypodermic carefully against the light, and gave him the injection. He wiped the puncture with a pad of wool. "So," he said in heavily accented English. "Now you will be able to walk well."

They wiped his face over with a cold wet towel, several times, and wiped his hands and his ears. Then, very carefully and gently, they inserted his wounded arm into the jumper, and arranged the light blue, striped collar on his shoulders. And then they helped him into the pea jacket.

Dottin said: "I will go down and warn them to be ready for him with the boat." He left the room.

Rhodes stared around him, seeing everything with a new clarity. There was a dead man at his feet, whose clothes he now was wearing. Simon was adjusting the scarf at his neck; his arm was throbbing painfully. He glanced down at the body. "What will you do with—that?" he asked.

Simon said: "Bozallec is going to look after him. I think he will stuff him down a sewer, probably."

With every minute Rhodes could think more clearly. "I don't like it," he said uneasily. "These people here are running a most frightful risk for us. Everybody seems to be. If the Germans get to know of this they'll all be in an awful jam."

Simon stood before him, face to face. "Rhodes, pay attention to me now," he said earnestly. "It all depends on you. These people, they have taken a great risk for you; you must not let them down. If you are caught and found to be an Englishman the Germans will make a search, and they will find this body, and these people will be shot and all their wives and little children will be shot also. That is what the Germans do, in a case like this. That is what these men have risked, so that you may go free."

Rhodes drew a deep breath. "That passes the buck to me," he said.

Simon nodded. "How are you feeling now?"

"I'm feeling pretty well all right."

"Can you walk straight and steadily now, stepping out like a German?"

"I think I can. Tell me the way again."

Simon said: "It is barely three hundred yards. When you go out of this door turn to the right, *that* way, and go straight down the street, down-hill towards the harbour. Remember that you are a German, that you walk stiff and erect. You must not stop, you must look around you; you are a German sailor upon duty. When you come out on the quay you will see steps immediately ahead of you, down to the water. Walk straight to them and down into the boat that will be waiting there. Sit down in the stern exactly in the middle, and sit up very straight and motionless as they row you off."

"Very good, sir."

Simon said: "If there is any trouble for you, we will make

explosions as I said. Pay no attention to them; walk straight on. A German upon duty is like that."

The priest stepped forward from the background and spoke in French to Simon. Simon turned to Rhodes. "He wants to bless you," he said quietly. "You must kneel down." He took Rhodes by his arm and helped him down on to the floor.

The scene stayed etched deep in Rhodes's memory. The dingy little room, the murdered German on the floor by him stripped and squalid in his underclothes, the Bretons standing by with inclined heads, the low words of Latin passing over him. The priest followed with a few sentences in French that Rhodes did not understand. Then Simon helped him to his feet.

Simon said in a low tone: "He said this. He asked that you should be taken safe to England through the dangers of the sea and the dangers of battle and the danger from the air, so that fire might come again, through you, against the Germans in France."

Rhodes turned to the father. "Fire will come again," he said, "whether I get back or I don't. In England there are other chaps like me. But if I get back safely to my country I shall remember what you people have done for us, all my life."

Simon translated; Father Augustine nodded, smiling gently at Rhodes. Then they led him out into the shop, now as neat and tidy as before. At the door into the street they paused and peered out through the lace curtain covering the half-window. "All is clear," said Simon. "Turn to the right immediately you get out, and straight down to the quay. We shall meet in London."

Rhodes opened the door, and stepped out into the market-place. A fair number of civilians were passing, and there were a number of German soldiers strolling about, newcomers to the town. He turned to the right, and began to walk down the narrow, cobbled street towards the harbour.

He went dizzily, desperately trying to control the movements of his limbs. Each step must be confident and firm—so. He must not look at the ground at his feet, but well ahead of him. He must hold himself straight—it was only three hundred yards. Only about two hundred and fifty now. Here was a raised kerb coming that he must step over without stumbling—that was a good one. Two hundred yards only, now. He was feeling sick. God, he must not be sick. He must walk straight, he must keep upright, he . . . must . . . not . . . be . . . sick.

Simon and Bozallec followed down the lane behind him, about

twenty yards behind. Now and again they saw him make a false step and sway a little; each time he pulled himself together and went on firmly. At half the distance Bozallec said: "He is doing well, that one. I did not think that he would do so well."

Simon said: "I think he will succeed."

They followed on behind, watching him as he went. There were eyes on him all down the narrow street, eyes that watched him from behind lace curtains, through the chinks of doors, from behind and from in front. Rhodes did not know it, but there were nearly fifty people watching each step that he made, praying for him each time he stumbled, cheered when he walked straight ahead down to the quay.

Simon and Bozallec, following behind, watchful, saw a German officer turn from the quay ahead and enter the lane, walking up to meet Rhodes. Barely fifty yards separated them. Bozallec said quickly: "That officer is clever. He will see."

Simon drew a red bandana handkerchief from the trouser pocket of his blue serge trousers and flourished it before blowing his nose. Inimediately from an alley by their side there was a sharp, cracking detonation. The officer ahead shot into a doorway, grasping the Luger at his belt. Another explosion followed a little way away, and then a third.

Simon and Bozallec broke into a run, dashed forward past Rhodes stumbling forward in a dream, and checked themselves in confusion opposite the officer. They turned, looking backwards up the street. Bozallec said to the officer, panting and excited: "An explosion, *Monsieur le Capitaine*. Truly, that was a bomb."

Behind their backs, screening him from the German, Rhodes stumbled forward to the quay. "I know that, fool," snarled the officer. "I know what a bomb sounds like. This is your treachery again; this town will pay for it."

Rhodes was clear; they turned and ran ahead of him again down to the quay. A fourth explosion sounded up the street. They came out on to the quay, and met a crowd of French and Germans flocking to the entrance of the alley. Simon turned and pointed up the lane. "Up there," he shouted. "Somebody has let bombs off, up there. The officer wants help!"

All eyes were on him; in the confusion Rhodes passed out of the lane on to the quay. The steps lay before him. He passed through the crowd unnoticed, walking steadily with a desperate concentration. He went straight down the steps. There was a boat waiting at the bottom with men ready at the oars.

A hand steadied him as he got into the boat, as he sat down at the stern. "Sit stiff and upright—so," a voice whispered. "That is the way they sit in boats, those swine."

They pushed off, and rowed out into the harbour to the black sardine-boat lying at the mooring.

On the quay the tumult soon died down. Bozallec stood with Simon leaning on the rail, looking out over the harbour. One by one the fishing-boats were slipping their moorings, backing and turning, moving out into the bay towards the shepherding *Raumboot.* It was already evening.

Bozallec said presently: "That is the one. That one going astern behind the tunnyman." He looked round at the weather. "Rain to-night," he said. "It will be easy for them to work out to the north. To-morrow morning he will be in Falmouth."

He turned to Simon with something like reverence. "What will you do, monsieur?"

Simon stirred. "I shall go up to the hotel," he said. "The Hôtel du Commerce. I want to sleep in a bed for to-night."

He was still in the fisherman's clothes that they had all worn upon *Geneviève.* He had a few hundred francs in French money; he went up to the market-place and bought himself a suit of clothes, a new shirt, and a collar and tie. He bought a very cheap fibre suitcase to put the other clothes in, and carrying that he walked along to the hotel.

He spent the evening in the hotel, as he had spent so many other evenings of his life in France, sitting in the café reading a paper, smoking, drinking Pernod, and watching a couple at the next table play a game of draughts. The proprietor was not there that evening, and no one noticed him. He dined well, with as good a bottle of Burgundy as the house could produce, and went up early to his bed.

He slept late, and it was after nine when he came down to the café in the morning. He called through the kitchen door for a cup of coffee and a *brioche*; the proprietor brought it to him himself. He stared at Simon when he saw him.

"Monsieur has stayed with us before?" he enquired. "Your face is familiar."

Simon said: "I was here in February last, on business. You told me then about Father Zacharias, and the little boy, Jules."

"I remember," said the innkeeper. "You were travelling in cement."

He left Simon to his coffee, but presently he came back again, carrying a big black book. He opened this and laid it on the table, with a pen and a bottle of ink. Monsieur did not register last night," he said. "If he would be so good. Name, Christian name, occupation, and address."

Simon took the pen and put down "Simon Charles". Then he glanced up at the innkeeper. "My occupation is that I am an officer in the British Army." he said, "and my address is in London. Shall I put that down?"

The man stared at him. "Charles Simon," he breathed. "Are you crazy? I remember now—that was your name before."

"It is still my name. I have never had another."

"You do not understand. The Germans come each day to see this book." He stared at the entry. "There are only three names above. I will take the page out, and three separate people can write the names again."

"What time do the Germans come?" asked Simon.

"After *déjeuner*, always at the same time."

Simon got to his feet. "It will not matter to me if they see it then," he said. "Do as you like about the book."

The man said: "Where are you going to? Stay here, indoors, and I will arrange something. There are people in Douarnenez who will help you, monsieur."

Simon said: "The people here are in trouble enough over me. I am going first to the presbytery."

He went out; the innkeeper followed him to the door and stood watching him as he went down the street. The morning was bright and sunny after the rain, the streets swept by a fresh, keen wind from the Atlantic. Half-way to the presbytery a man stopped him, asking for a light for his cigarette.

Simon passed him a box of matches; the man stooped by him to shield the flame. "They got away," he said. "One of the boats was missing when dawn came. The fleet has just come into harbour. The Germans are very angry about it."

He straightened up. A German sailor passed by them in the street going towards the harbour. The man lit another match and flipped it at him scornfully. The German scowled angrily at them. The man spat on the pavement at his feet, and gave the box of matches back to Simon.

Simon said: "That is good news for Douarnenez, and for all France. One day the English will come back, and bring their fire again." He smiled gently. "Charles Simon says so."

He went on down the main street past the great church to the small house beside it, and knocked at the door of the presbytery. It was opened to him by Father Augustine himself; when he saw who it was he pulled Simon inside quickly and shut the door. They stood together in the narrow passage.

Simon said: "Father, all has gone as we had planned. By now my friend will be in England and in hospital in his own country. There is an officer at the British Admiralty who will be looking after him. His little friend, his fiancée, will be with him and he will be happy. All this is due to you, and I want to thank you for it."

The priest said: "We are all instruments of Almighty God. Give your thanks to Him."

Simon inclined his head.

"And you, my son?"

"My time is getting short. I want to cleanse my soul, father."

The priest said gently: "You could have escaped with your friend quite easily. Why did you not go with him?"

There was a little pause. Then Simon said: "I am practically a Frenchman, father, though I have British nationality. But all my life I have thought of myself as English. I wanted to be English, as my father was. Now, for eight months, I have been an officer in the British Army. A proper British officer would not go away and leave these hostages. I do not want women and little girls of seven to be killed so that I may go free."

He left the presbytery half an hour later, and walked down to the harbour. All his life the sight of boats had fascinated him, the smell of tanned sails and salt water, the lap and shimmer of the waves. He spent an hour down at the waterside in peace, storing up memories. He walked out on the jetty, still black from the fire, and wondered what had happened to his own four-ton yacht at St. Malo. Then he went back into the Café de la République and drank a glass of Pernod.

Presently he left the café and walked up the hill, towards the German headquarters.

Under the great swastika flag he turned in at the door between the sentries, stiff and erect with rifles and steel helmets. There was a desk in the front room; behind it was an *Unterfeldwebel* of the German Army, and a private.

"I have come about the thirty hostages," Simon said in French. "You can let them go. I am a British officer, the only one who landed in Douarnenez."

12

IT took Rhodes about three-quarters of an hour to tell me what he knew, and he was very weary by the time we had finished. Towards the end the nurse kept looking in every two or three minutes, mutely begging me to pack up and go. I made it as short as I could, and got to my feet.

"You'd better rest now, Rhodes," I said. I hesitated, and then said: "I shall be in touch with Dartmouth. Would you like to see Miss Wright?"

He said: "She's just had leave, sir. They wouldn't let her come down here, would they?"

I laughed. "I'll certify it as a service journey. You'd like to see her, wouldn't you?"

He flushed. "I don't know if you know. We got engaged—just before this show."

"She told me," I said. I picked up my cap. "I'll see about that, Rhodes. Come and see me in London when you're on your feet again, and we'll talk about what you are to do next."

I left the ward, and went back to the surgeon's office. There I scribbled a message for him to get telephoned to Dartmouth, and left in a hurry for the station. I got the London train by the skin of my teeth, and sat all morning as it wandered on through Cornwall.

The train drew into Newton Abbott station early in the afternoon; Leading Wren Wright was on the platform there to meet me. It was my fate to tell her things on Newton Abbott platform, in the clamour of the trucks and milk-cans, the hissing of steam heat from the carriages, and the bustle of the crowd. I got out quickly and went up to her.

"Look, Miss Wright," I said. "You got my message?"

She stammered: "He—he's all right, is he, sir?"

I said: "He's not a bit all right. He isn't going to die, but he's got a very nasty and neglected wound in his left shoulder. He's in Falmouth Hospital, and he'd very much like to see you down there."

She said "Would I be able to get leave?"

I had written a note in the train, and now I gave it to her. "Take this to the commander," I said. "Give him my compliments and tell him that I'm sorry I haven't been able to telephone him. I've asked if he can spare you for a week to be

268

with Rhodes, in this letter. But it rests with him entirely, you know. I can't give you leave."

She said ingenuously: "I'll get it if you've said you want me to have it, sir. He thinks an awful lot of you. They all do."

"I've done nothing in this show," I said. "Nothing but sit on my backside in an office and watch other people do the work."

There was a short pause. "Do you know what happened to Captain Simon and Lieutenant Boden, sir?" she asked.

I said: "Simon got on shore all right"—I dropped my voice —"but he's still over on the other side. Keep your mouth shut about that. I'm afraid it's very nearly certain that Lieutenant Boden was killed."

She nodded; she had evidently expected that. "I was sure it must have been him," she said. "He was the man with the Tommy-gun, when she was floating upside down?"

"I think he was," I said.

She raised her head. "It was the best thing," she said. "He'd never have settled down, after the war."

I did not agree with her. "People get over things."

She shook her head. "Not Boden. He was hurt too much."

It was not a matter one could argue, especially on Newton Abbot platform; besides which, she was more his age and knew Boden better than I did. Behind me a porter was shouting out for passengers to take their seats, and slamming doors as he passed down the train. I moved towards my compartment. "Look after yourself and see that doesn't happen to Rhodes," I said.

She said: "It might be the other way about."

Down at the end of the train the guard blew his whistle, waving his green flag. I got into my compartment and leaned out of the window for a few last words to her. "Don't worry about that," I said. "He'll never go to sea again—he never should have gone this time. Rhodes is a Special Branch officer— green stripe. He'll be on shore for the remainder of the war."

She said: "He'll hate that, sir."

The train began to move. I grinned at her. "I know he will," I said. "But you won't."

She laughed at that; it was the first time that I had seen her laugh for weeks. The last thing I saw of her was that she was still laughing on the platform, waving to me with the letter in her hand that was to give her leave. I'm not sure that it's correct for a Leading Wren to wave like that at a commander.

I saw McNeil that evening in his office in Pall Mall, and told him what I had been doing, and what I had learned from Rhodes. It took about half an hour to tell the story as I then knew it. In the end I said: "Simon is still in France, apparently. We might hear from him before so very long."

He shook his head. "I don't think so. There was a message in to-day about him." He unlocked a drawer and passed me one of his MOST SECRET flimsies that I was beginning to dislike. It read:

DOUARNENEZ. The thirty hostages which were to be executed on November 15th were all released on November 14th. A British officer named Charles Simon is said to have surrendered to the Germans on that day. This man is said to have been a survivor from a British ship sunk in the Iroise, and to have been concerned in some way with the recent fires in minor German war vessels. Ends.

I passed it back to him in silence. "That's the end of that," I said heavily at last. "We shan't see him again till after the war."

"No," said the brigadier. He said no more than that. It seemed to me that there was nothing more to say.

I left him and went back to my normal work. Nothing happened after that for the best part of a fortnight; indeed, there was nothing more to happen. That party was all cleaned up, or so I thought. Colvin came out of hospital about the end of November and came up to see me at the Admiralty one afternoon. I made him sit down and smoke, and we chatted for a short time about this and that.

Presently I said: "What's your position now, Colvin? They're giving you a decent spell of leave?"

"I wanted to see you about that, sir," he said. "The surgeon-commander down at Haslar, he's being mighty particular. I get a month's leave now. Well, that's okay, although I don't know what in heck you do with a month's leave in this country in December. But after that, he says I'll be for light duty on shore for six months at least, 'n possibly for longer. That don't seem reasonable to me."

"How do you feel yourself?" I asked.

"I must say I get mighty tired with little things," he confessed. "Walking upstairs, 'n that. And shaving, I keep cutting myself. But that'll all go off, after a month."

"How old are you, Colvin?"

"I'm forty-eight." He hesitated. "I did knock off five years, but the commander at Haslar, he got hold of all my papers when I was in hospital."

"Bad luck," I said.

"You see the way it is, sir," he explained. "I don't want to get stuck down in one of them places like the Clyde or Liverpool, not knowing anybody in this country, 'n nothing to do but get into trouble. I'd be better off at sea."

I bent down and opened one of the drawers of my desk. I pulled out a little box. "By the way," I said. "I got your watch back. I think it's all right now."

He was very pleased. He took the box and opened it. The London Chronometer Company had done a good job on it; they had given it a complete new movement and polished it up till it looked like new. They had even sent it back in a little wash-leather bag.

"Say," he said, "that's dandy." He put it to his ear and listened to it ticking. And then, unable to resist, he turned it over and read the inscription that he must have known by heart: "Jack Colvin from Junie, September 17th, 1935."

"I certainly am grateful, sir," he said. "How much do I owe you?"

"Nothing," I said. "I got the admiral's secretary to take it on his petty cash account."

He said: "That's mighty nice of the admiral." He paused. "It worried me more 'n anything else," he said, "the way I'd used this watch. But now it's better 'n it ever was before."

I turned back to the job in hand; I had other things to do that afternoon besides settling up Colvin. "Look," I said. "There's a shore job that I think might suit you. It's the armouring of merchant ships—wheel-houses, gun zarebas, and all that. It wants somebody who knows merchant ships, to go on board each ship and say in each case what has to be done—and then to see the work is done right. It's not difficult work, but it wants a chap like you to do it. It means rowing in with each skipper, talking it over with him, and then modifying the standard scheme to suit the particular conditions in each ship."

I paused. "Could you tackle that?"

"I guess so. It sounds the sort of thing I used to do when I was Marine Superintendent over on the coast."

I nodded. "That's what I had in mind. And more than that, it seemed to me you might have local contacts that would help you." He looked up, puzzled. "These are the Lease-Lend ships I'm talking about," I said. "This job would be on the west coast of America. Your headquarters would be in San Francisco."

There was a momentary silence. "Have I got this right?" he asked. "You mean you want me to go out to 'Frisco for this job?"

"If you want to go," I said. "It's an opportunity I thought perhaps you might like."

"Would I like it!" he breathed. "Say . . ." And then he stopped and said: "Who put you up to this one, sir? Who told you that I wanted to get back to 'Frisco? Was it young Boden?"

"He said something about it. I was very glad to know."

He stared down at his finger-nails. "He was a mighty fine kid, that," he said. "They don't make them any better."

He raised his head and looked at me. "I do want to get back to 'Frisco," he said quietly. "I got a personal reason, sir— nothing to do with the Navy." He was still holding the watch in his hand, "I said I wasn't married when you asked me, first of all," he said. "That's right enough, if you go by the law. I couldn't have drawn marriage allowance—at least, I reckon not. It wasn't regular, you see."

"I understand," I said. "This is Junie, is it?"

"Aye," he said, "it's Junie. Seems to me some folks get married and it takes right off, and they don't get no more trouble. Young Boden, he was one o' them, I guess. But others never seem to hit it right."

I could not comment upon that.

"I been married a lot of times," he said simply, "and each time it finished up in trouble, up till the time when I paired up with Junie. We got married by a minister as if it was all regular, but it wasn't regular at all, on account of all the other times." He paused. "Later on, and when this war came, I'd have give my eyes if it could have been made a proper marriage. But that's what you can't do."

"You lived together for four years, didn't you?" I asked.

"More like five," he said. "Close on five, it was. I don't want any better time than that."

"Do you think she'll be there still?" I asked. "Two years is a fair time." I meant, a fair time to expect a girl to hang around without a letter and without marriage lines, but I didn't say so much.

"Aye," he said, "it's a long, dreary time. I think I'll find her hanging on for me in 'Frisco still. If not, well, that'll be too bad. But any way it breaks, I'm real grateful that you've given us the chance to set up house again."

"If I were you," I said, "I should think up a cablegram and send it off to her. You'll have a month to do on this side, getting hold of the job. I should think you'd be in San Francisco some time in February."

He left me soon after that, and I went on with my work. I saw him again a few days later, when he looked in to show me the answer to his cablegram. He was as pleased as a dog with two tails, and insisted on me reading it. It said:

Got your cable but where you been all this time Billy died last autumn guess colic George and Mary send love will we live Oakland some dandy new apartments fifteenth street since you left oceans of love stop now no more dough—Junie.

"Billy was her cat," he explained. "I'm real sorry about Billy. He was a good, tough kind of cat, 'n a match for any dog."

I handed him back the cable. "I should send her some dough to be going on with, if you've got any," I remarked. "I've been finding out about your marriage allowance. They cater for a case like yours. You can draw it, but you've got to make a declaration. Look, this is what you've got to do."

I went through the Admiralty Fleet Order with him and explained it to him in detail. "I did hear something about this," he said at last.

Thinking of the girl in Oakland, I was a little short with him. "You might have done something about it," I said.

He looked abashed. "Guess I never had a commander that I'd care to talk it over with before," he said.

I told him he was a fool, and sent him away to make out his declaration.

About a fortnight later McNeil rang me up. "You might look in some time," he said. "I've got a couple more flimsies in about *Geneviève*."

I went round to his office after lunch. He took them from a drawer and passed them to me. "Not very good news, I'm afraid," he said.

The first one read:

Rennes. A British officer named Charles Simon was

273

executed at the rifle range to-day. This man was convicted
of an act of espionage at Lorient last spring, at which time
his status was that of a civilian. It is believed that the severe
damage caused to the U-boat base was due to information
passed by this man to the British. Ends.

I looked up at the brigadier. "I'm very sorry about this,"
I said.

He nodded. "So am I." He paused. "I was very much
afraid that this would happen," he said quietly. "It would
have been a miracle if they hadn't spotted him."

"You think some German recognised him, and remembered?"

He shrugged his shoulders. "Something of the sort. I don't
suppose we'll ever hear the details now."

"He must have known what he was doing," I said slowly.
"When he gave himself up, he must have known the risk."

McNeil said: "He was probably thinking of the hostages."

"Of course." I sat there staring at the message in my hand,
and the slow anger rose in me. "We've been a couple of bloody
fools over this," I said at last. "We should have managed
better."

"What do you mean?" he asked.

"I mean just this," I said. "Simon was the best officer for
working on the other side this country ever had, or is ever likely
to get. And now he's dead. We should have thought more
deeply before risking him again in Douarnenez."

"It's not so easy to rope in these chaps," McNeil said heavily.
"The better they are, the more difficult they are to manage.
You know that." I did, and I was silent. "He was a damn
good man," he said. "But there are others just as good."

"You can't have so many Simons as all that," I replied.
"We've gone and wasted one of them."

"Wasted . . ." he said thoughtfully. "I'm not sure that
you're right." He glanced at me. "Did you read the other
one?"

I turned to the other flimsy. This one said:

Brest. The civil population have devised a means of
harassing the Germans which is proving very effective. The
name Charles Simon is written upon walls or chalked on pave-
ments. This device is spreading rapidly, and it has been
observed as far away as St. Brieuc. In every case the
Germans have reacted angrily, and show concern at the

spread of the movement. A man of this name was executed recently at Rennes. Ends.

I stood there reading this again, and as I did so I could feel the hate swelling and seething on the other side. I put down the flimsies, sick of the whole miserable business.

"In any case," I said, "this winds up *Geneviève*. Simon was the last of them to be accounted for, and now that's over."

The brigadier nodded. "It's all finished now. I'll let you know if anything else turns up."

"I shan't be here," I said. "I'm going back to sea." It was a relief to talk of cleaner things. "They're giving me one of the Tribal class destroyers."

"Glad to go?"

I said: "Yes. Somebody has to do this Admiralty work, of course, but I'd rather be at sea with a definite job to do. Here you work all day in the office, and nothing ever seems to be achieved."

He stared at me. "I don't know what you want," he said. "The operations that we did with *Geneviève* have been a most successful show."

"We lost the ship and all her crew," I said bitterly.

"We lost a fishing vessel and two officers," he retorted. "Against that we destroyed three *Raumboote* and damaged a destroyer. We killed not less than ninety Germans. We landed seventy machine-guns, and put fresh heart into a town that needed it. And not the least part, we drew off a division from the Russian front."

"A pretty scruffy sort of a division," I remarked.

"I grant you that," he said. "It was a very tired division. But it was a division, none the less, taken from the Russian. front at Rostov."

He turned to me. "Who knows what that may mean?"

*This book
designed by William B. Taylor
is a production of
Heron Books, London*

*Printed in England by
Hazell Watson and Viney Limited
Aylesbury, Bucks*